...or the Work of
...dria Bellefleur

"[*Count Your Lucky Stars* is] a warm hug of a queer contemporary romance with sparkling prose, heartfelt dialogue, and delicious dirty talk."

—*Library Journal* (starred review)

"With perfectly woven vulnerability and playfulness, *Written in the Stars* is a riotous and heartfelt read. I was hooked from the very first page!"

—Christina Lauren, *New York Times* bestselling author

"*Written in the Stars* is everything I want from a rom-com: fun, whimsical, sexy. This modern *Pride and Prejudice* glitters with romance."

—Talia Hibbert, *New York Times* bestselling author

"Alexandria Bellefleur is an author to watch. Her writing is joyful and heartfelt, and her voice sparkles with a delightful mix of wit, humor, and good-natured sarcasm. I can't wait to see how she wows us next!"

—Mia Sosa, *USA Today* bestselling author

"Bellefleur has a droll, distinct voice, and her one-liners zing off the page, striking both the heart and funny bone. She has a gift for comedy, possessing more style and panache than a debut writer has any right to. . . . There's a sparkling quality here, one that mirrors the starry title. Bellefleur writes as if she's captured fairy lights in a mason jar, twinkly and lovely within something solid yet fragile."

—*Entertainment Weekly*

"This book is a delight."

—*New York Times Book Review* on *Written in the Stars*

"A delightful rom-com that once again gives us the beloved fake relationship trope—and the fuzzies you didn't know you needed."

—Shondaland on *Written in the Stars*

"[A] distinctly modern frolic, charming and effervescent and entirely itself."

—*Washington Post* on *Written in the Stars*

"Something fresh and totally queer."

—*O, The Oprah Magazine* (Best LGBTQ
Books of 2020) on *Written in the Stars*

Count Your Lucky Stars

By Alexandria Bellefleur

Written in the Stars
Hang the Moon
Count Your Lucky Stars

Count Your Lucky Stars

A NOVEL

ALEXANDRIA BELLEFLEUR

AVON
An Imprint of HarperCollinsPublishers

HarperCollins books may be purchased for educational, business, or sales pro-motional use. For information, please email the Special Markets Department at SPsales@harpercollins.com.

FIRST EDITION

Designed by Diahann Sturge

Title page image © Khaneeros / Shutterstock, Inc.
Emojis throughout © FOS_ICON / Shutterstock, Inc.
Male face palm emoji on page 53 © Cosmic_Design

Library of Congress Cataloging-in-Publication Data has been applied for.

ISBN 978-0-06-300088-9

22 23 24 25 26   CPI   10 9

Printed and bound by CPI Group (UK) Ltd, Croydon, CR0 4YY

Count Your Lucky Stars

Chapter One

In the seven months Olivia Grant had worked at Emerald City Events as an assistant event coordinator, she had encountered her fair share of odd demands. But the Roberts' stipulation that their wedding menu be lacto-ovo-pescatarian-vegetarian and Keto-friendly was a new one.

"OTP? What the hell is that?"

"The dating app? One True Pairing? What rock have you been living under?"

Olivia drained the dregs of her tea, which had long gone cold, and tried to tune out her coworkers' chitchat.

"Uh, I've been *married* for twenty-five years?" Naomi said.

"That's no excuse. Their ads are everywhere. Come on. I bet even Olivia knows what I'm talking about."

"Hmm?" Olivia finished skimming the email from the caterer for the Roberts' wedding—which mostly amounted to confusion and consternation about what the hell he was supposed to serve—before lowering the screen of her laptop. She'd commiserate with him later. "Sorry, even I know what?"

Kira, marketing director at Emerald City Events, leaned her chin on her hand. "OTP. Please tell me you've heard of it."

Olivia shrugged. "Sure. Hasn't everyone?"

Kira shot Naomi a pointed look and smirked. "See?"

"And like I said"—Naomi wiggled her left hand, the platinum wedding band gleaming against her deep brown skin—"married."

"So was Liv."

The tan line on Olivia's ring finger had faded months ago, unlike the habit she had of running her thumb along the space where her wedding ring had once rested. She tucked her hand under her thigh and smiled. "I thought you were seeing that barista. What's her name? Blake?"

"Oh, totally. Strictly secondhand knowledge of the app on my part. I've got a cousin who met their boyfriend on the app, but that's it." Kira grinned at Naomi. "But at least I know about it."

"OOC, OTP, AO3, PWP, you kids and your abbreviations." Naomi tutted. "You wanna know the only three-letter acronym I give a damn about?" She tapped the pin on her lapel and grinned. "COO, thank you very much."

Kira crowed in delight. "*PWP?* Naomi, you naughty girl, what have *you* been reading?"

Olivia hid her smile behind her fingers.

Utterly unabashed, Naomi shrugged one shoulder. "I like what I like."

"I've got another three-letter acronym for you." Kira swiveled her chair from side to side, in time with each letter she listed. "VIP."

She waited for the punch line, for Kira or Naomi to expound on what those three letters meant in the context of their conversation. "Who's a VIP?"

Emerald City Events, Seattle's premier events management company, catered to a variety of clientele, from street festivals to nonprofits to Fortune 500 tech companies. Olivia had yet to help with an event for any of their higher-profile clients, but she knew they existed.

"Brendon Lowell," Kira said. "Owner and creator of OTP."

That explained why Kira and Naomi were discussing the dating app.

"Does he want to hire us for an event?"

"Mm-hmm. His wedding." Kira leaned her elbows on her desk. "Lori's upstairs having kittens."

Olivia frowned. "Shouldn't Lori be thrilled?"

"She would be," Naomi said. "If he hadn't called her last-minute."

Oh. "Shotgun wedding?" She wrinkled her nose. "Do people still call them that? I mean, do people even *care*?"

"You're the one who grew up in BFE, Liv. You tell me." Kira snickered, sobering quickly. "Sorry, it's really not funny. Brendon Lowell had plans to get married over on the Olympic Peninsula. The venue was all-inclusive—event planner, catering, DJ, decorations, cake, the whole shebang offered in-house. Sounds great, right?"

Call it a hunch, but Olivia was going to go with *no*.

"Apparently there was a fire at the venue yesterday. Extensive damage to the rental house and ceremony space. They've canceled all events through the end of the year." Kira grimaced. "Lowell got a full refund on his deposit, obviously, but they're starting from scratch with three weeks until the big day. Guests have already booked flights, so they're pretty adamant about not changing the date."

Three weeks was less than ideal, but it was doable. With the right budget, Olivia could probably plan a wedding in half that time. Money talked, and it opened doors. Facts of life. "Lori could pull it off."

"Lori could pull it off *if* she weren't already booked that day," Naomi said, brows rising. "Hell, she'll *still* pull it off, even if it kills her. She's upstairs, trying to figure out how to break it to her other client that she's going to miss their big day."

"Lori's had me step in before."

Kira's lips drew to the side. "Yeah, except the other client? It's her *daughter*."

Olivia's jaw dropped. "Lori's going to skip her own daughter's wedding?"

"Mm-hmm." Naomi pursed her lips. "VIP."

"The *Seattle Times* is covering the Lowell wedding for the Vows section," Kira explained. "It could be huge for ECE. Lori doesn't want to miss out on that."

And she didn't have to.

"I can do it."

Kira and Naomi stared.

"What? I *can*." Olivia stood and smoothed down the front of her skirt. "I'm going to go talk to Lori."

This was her chance to prove herself, the break she had been waiting for, *hoping* for since she'd packed up her Subaru and left Enumclaw eight months ago.

A look passed between Kira and Naomi before Naomi dropped her eyes. "Good luck."

Despite her blustering, Olivia had a feeling she was going to need all the luck she could get.

Emerald City Events was located out of a charming two-story Craftsman in the Ballard neighborhood of Seattle. Lori's office encompassed most of the sprawling upstairs, the whole place extensively renovated and open concept.

Lori's desk was visible from the top of the stairs, but she wasn't seated behind it. Instead, she stood in front of the window, forehead pressed to the rain-splattered glass, shoulders hunched. Usually, Lori was the pinnacle of calm, cool collectedness, unflappable under pressure. For her, this was practically a breakdown.

Olivia rapped her knuckles against the wall. "Knock, knock. I, uh, heard there's a bit of a scheduling fiasco?"

Lori's spine straightened as she lifted her head, stepping away from the window. She turned and smiled, all teeth and faux brightness, her eyes hardly creasing at the corners. "No fiasco. I trust you completely."

Olivia's heart tripped over the next beat.

"Sasha will be in great hands on the day of her wedding."

Sasha. Lori's *daughter*, Sasha. Olivia wasn't sure whether to take that as the world's highest compliment or greatest insult, Lori entrusting Olivia with her daughter's wedding when there was another solution, *right* there, staring her straight in the face.

Olivia clasped her hands together loosely and crossed the room, stopping beside Lori. "Or."

Lori's expression barely budged, save for the gentle rise of her left brow. "Or?"

Olivia took a deep breath. "*Or* you could go to your daughter's wedding and let *me* plan the Lowell wedding."

Lori dropped her eyes and sighed. "Olivia—"

"I'm *good* at this, Lori."

"Of course you are." Lori crossed her arms and sniffed. "I hired you, after all."

Olivia held her breath.

"But I feel like the Lowell wedding might be a tad ambitious for your first solo gig."

Every event since Olivia had started working at ECE had been *a tad ambitious* according to Lori.

Olivia deflated. "Oh."

Lori turned, staring out the window, where outside, a fine mist fell from the gray sky. She drummed her fingers against her arm and sighed sharply through her nose. "I've worked with Brendon Lowell on several events in the past—company parties, corporate retreats, that sort of thing. He's easy to work with, knows what he likes, and he's local to the area. Best part of all, he *loves* weddings."

"Sounds like a dream," Olivia murmured, trying to tuck away her disappointment.

"If not for the poor timing, I'd have been over the moon,

having a wedding like this land in my lap." Lori's scowl reflected in the glass. "It's the sort of wedding that practically plans itself. With a budget like his, how could it not?"

Olivia frowned. If Lori was trying to make her feel better, it wasn't working. "I'm sorry?"

Lori clicked her tongue against the back of her teeth. "And the *Seattle Times* coverage? That has the propensity to be *huge* for business. Granted, the wedding would have to go off without a hitch . . ." Lori looked at her askance. "What I'm saying is, don't fuck this up."

Her jaw dropped. "Wait. What? Are you—*Lori*."

Olivia's eyes stung from all of this emotional whiplash.

The thin gold bangles on Lori's wrist jangled when she batted at the air. "I beg you, please don't get mushy on me. My nerves are shot. If you start to cry, *I'll* cry, and I *loathe* crying."

Olivia pressed her lips together, stifling a laugh.

Lori rolled her head to the side and smiled. "You're right. You *are* good at this. Which is why I'm going to give you the Lowell wedding."

Lips still pressed tight together, her squeal escaped as a high-pitched *meep*. "Thank you, thank you, thank you—"

Lori lifted a hand, cutting off Olivia's effusive thanks. "You pull this off, and consider the word *assistant* scratched from your position, okay?" Lori rounded her desk and reached for her glasses, sliding them up the bridge of her nose. "We can discuss a raise in your salary later." Lori lifted her head and smiled. "Sound good?"

It sounded freaking *fantastic.* "Perfect."

"Great." Lori tore a sheet of paper from her notebook and held it out for Olivia to take. "Monday. Six p.m. sharp. Brendon and his fiancée, Annie, would like to tour The Ruins. Fabulous hidden gem in Queen Anne? You remember it, right? We had an event there a few months ago. It was for—"

"The Martins' golden anniversary." Olivia nodded. "I remember."

Lori arched a single brow, one corner of her mouth rising simultaneously, looking pleased. Olivia warmed faintly at the unspoken praise. She had a sharp memory, necessary in a profession like this.

"Good." Lori pointed at the paper in Olivia's hand. "Brendon's and Annie's cells are listed at the top. Backup numbers for the Maid of Honor and Best Woman are below those. Just in case."

Listed on the paper beneath B. Lowell and A. Kyriakos was D. Lowell and M. Cooper.

M. Cooper.

Olivia traced the inked name with the tip of her finger. In a city of nearly four million people, what were the chances of *this* M. Cooper being the same M. Cooper Olivia knew from high school? Her face warmed; the rest of her, too. Slim. The chances were slim.

"I'll forward you his email with details on budget and guest list. Lucky for us, we already have a head count."

Lucky was right.

"Well, go on." Lori shooed Olivia out of the office. "You've got a lot work ahead of you."

"I'm just saying, maybe it's time to put some feelers out, start the hunt for a new roommate. It's been six months since the last one moved out."

As if Margot Cooper needed the reminder of how long it had been. It was the longest she'd lived alone, a fact of which she was painfully aware. "I *know*, Elle."

"Doesn't the quiet bother you?" Margot's best friend frowned and leaned her shoulder against the crosswalk pole. "It would bother me."

Elle didn't have to worry about coming home to an empty apartment. A little over a year ago, she'd moved out of the place she and Margot had shared and in with her girlfriend, Darcy, at the same time Annie—Darcy's best friend—had moved in with Margot. *That* arrangement had lasted a brief two months before Annie had moved in with her now-fiancé, Brendon, Darcy's brother.

None of it would've happened had Margot and Elle, the voices behind the astronomically successful social media–based astrology business Oh My Stars, not partnered with Brendon's dating app, One True Pairing, to incorporate astrological compatibility to the app's matching algorithm two years ago. Not only had it been a smart career move, beneficial for both OTP and Oh My Stars, but Margot had also lucked out, finding a close friend in Brendon. And thanks to Brendon, Elle had met Darcy. Wins all around.

Except for the part where Margot was down a roommate

and now came home to an empty apartment, ate dinner alone more nights than not, and had started saying good night to her plants. An admission she could kick herself over confessing to Elle, the reason behind this whole conversation.

"Maybe I'll get a cat," she mused, stepping out into the street when the light turned green.

Elle snorted. "Except for the part where you hate cats."

"I do *not* hate cats." She sniffed. "I have a . . . healthy respect for anything that could rip my face off."

It was common sense. Self-preservation. Survival skills.

Elle bumped Margot with her hip. "Healthy *fear*, more like."

"Call it what you want." Margot shrugged. "I'm strongly considering adopting a cat."

Elle whipped out her phone, eyes flitting between the screen and the building up ahead. "And I think you should strongly consider getting a *human* roommate. You know, someone you can actually talk to."

Margot opened her mouth.

"Someone who can actually talk *back*." Elle nibbled on her bottom lip, footsteps slowing to a stop in front of the entrance to the venue. "I know you're a little gun-shy after your last roommate."

More like last *string* of roommates.

Margot snorted at Elle's tact. "I'm not gun-shy. I'm being selective, and for good reason. I've already put feelers out, Elle. I've got my ear to the ground. I *know* I need a new roommate." She huffed. "Preferably one who doesn't have a habit of taking Ambien, sleepwalking into my closet, and popping a squat over my shoes at three in the morning."

Elle cringed.

That wasn't even taking into consideration the roommate who'd stolen Margot's credit card or the one who'd owned an ant farm. An ant farm Margot had known *nothing* about until she'd woken up to the floor *moving* on one memorable Sunday morning.

Margot's recent luck with roommates wasn't just bad, it was abysmal.

Elle stared, eyes wide and full of sympathy, and it made Margot's skin itch. The perks and pitfalls of having a best friend who knew her so well that she could hear what Margot *wasn't* saying.

"Look, can we just . . . put a pin in it and circle back around?" Margot flipped her wrist over, checking the time on her Fitbit. Five 'til. Now wasn't the time or the place for Margot to throw herself a pity party. "It's almost six."

Elle stole another peek at her phone and smiled. "Darcy texted. They're already inside."

Stepping through the door, Elle led the way down a winding hall lined with doors on each side, the sound of Brendon's boisterous laugh growing louder as they approached. Margot ducked her head inside an open door and cringed at the decor. Between the heart-shaped, glitter-filled balloons floating aimlessly along the perimeter of the room and the pink confetti littering the floor, it looked like Cupid had jizzed all over the reception space.

At the end of the hall, Elle drew to an abrupt stop and gasped. *"Wow."*

Margot hurried to catch up before following Elle's gaze up to the ceiling. "Holy shit."

The ceiling of the ballroom was stunning, painted in shades of lilac and lavender, bleeding down into periwinkle and pink, all the softest shades of dusk, when twilight descended into night and the stars came out to play. Little pinpricks of silver and champagne dotted the ceiling, and the glow of the chandeliers made everything ethereal and dreamy. *Perfect* for Brendon and Annie.

Across the room, Brendon beamed. "It's great, isn't it?"

Tucked into his side, Annie smiled up at him. "I like what I see."

Elle greeted Darcy with a quick kiss before lacing their fingers together. "It's like something straight out of a fairy tale. If you guys don't get married here, *I* will."

Darcy stared at Elle as if she were the source of all the light in the room.

A bittersweet pang struck Margot in the chest, stealing her breath.

She didn't always feel like a fifth wheel—her friends were good about keeping the PDA to a minimum, and even then, a little PDA didn't bother her—but it was happening more often lately.

A wedding was a party, marriage a piece of paper and permission to file your taxes jointly; Brendon and Annie, Darcy and Elle, they were already coupled up, wholly committed, and madly in love. It was silly to let an event that was, more than anything, symbolic mess with her head, but Margot couldn't help but feel like her friends were all forming a club and she wasn't invited.

Not unless she brought a plus-one.

"Elle's right," Margot said, trying to echo her enthusiasm. "I think this place might be it."

Brendon laughed. "You're just saying that so you don't have to tour another venue."

Is *that* what he thought? Jesus. "I know I'm not always sunshine and rainbows, but that doesn't mean I don't care."

Of *course* she cared. Flowers and first-dance songs weren't her favorite topics, but Brendon and Annie cared about it all, so *she* cared about it. She was the Best Woman. Caring about Brendon was pretty much what the role dictated. But even if she weren't the Best Woman, she'd have still cared because he was her friend. He was stuck with her.

"Trust me," he said, eyes still crinkled with laughter. "No one expects *you* to be sunshine and rainbows."

Her brows knit. What was *that* supposed to mean?

"It's not an indictment," Brendon tacked on, eyes widening in alarm as if he'd realized he'd said the wrong thing. "We like you exactly as you are."

Annie nodded briskly in agreement, but Margot couldn't help but feel like maybe it wasn't true. That maybe her friends would like her better if she *were* a little more sunshine and rainbows.

Margot dug inside her bag for her lip balm. She'd just have to try harder, lay it on thicker. "Who are we waiting on?"

Brendon fished around inside his pocket. "The facility manager had to step out to make a call, and the wedding planner texted a couple minutes ago and said she's trying to find a place to park. She should be here—"

"I'm so sorry I'm late." Breathless laughter came from behind their group. "Parking was a pain."

The lid to Margot's ChapStick slipped out of her fingers and bounced against the floor before rolling a foot away. Great. She crouched, shuffling forward to snag it from beside Darcy's foot.

Brendon grinned. "No worries. Olivia, right? I'm Brendon."

"It's so nice to meet you."

"Likewise. This is my fiancée, Annie; my sister, Darcy; her girlfriend, Elle."

"Hi," Elle chirped.

Margot stood, dusting off her knees.

"This is my friend and Best Woman—"

"Margot?"

All the air left Margot's lungs in a punched-out exhale as soon as she locked eyes with the statuesque blond across the room.

Olivia Grant. Holy shit.

Olivia's pouty, lush lips parted, mirroring Margot's shock. An abundance of tawny hair spilled out from beneath her dark red beanie, tumbling down her back in soft waves, longer than Margot remembered. For a moment, Margot was too tongue-tied to speak.

Elle's forehead furrowed, and Margot coughed.

"Olivia." Her voice actually cracked. Kill her now. "Right. I thought you looked . . . familiar." *Familiar.* Ha. *Familiar* was for acquaintances. Not whatever the hell they once were. "It's, um, Olivia Taylor now, right?

Not that Margot had looked Olivia up online or anything. Not that she'd specifically *not* looked, either. *Maybe* she'd taken a peek at her Facebook profile, but only because it had popped up under *suggested friends*. Margot hadn't sent her a friend request or anything like that. They weren't friends. Not anymore. Olivia whatever-her-last-name-was was just someone Margot used to know.

Someone Margot had once spent the better part of a week with naked, tangled up in the sheets of Olivia's childhood bed, wringing multiple orgasms out of, until Margot's jaw had ached and Olivia's voice had grown hoarse. Five days that were, arguably, the best of Margot's life, full of toe-curling sex and laughter that made her stomach hurt. The start of *something*, a new chapter between them, one where Margot didn't have to spend another second secretly pining for her best friend because all her feelings were returned.

Or so she'd thought.

"It was." Olivia coughed and clasped her hands in front of her for a brief moment before dropping them back to her sides where they dangled loosely, like she didn't know what to do with them. "It's Grant again."

Margot's eyes dropped to Olivia's left hand, her ring finger bare.

Huh.

Interesting.

"Wait." Brendon pointed between the both of them, looking confused. "You two know each other?"

Color rose in Olivia's cheeks, and Margot remembered tracing the southward spread of that blush with her fingertips, tasting it with her tongue, Olivia's skin soft as satin and hot beneath Margot's lips. For a split second, Margot went dizzy, blood rising to the surface of her skin, mimicking Olivia's flush.

Know each other. Margot swallowed hard. You could say that.

"Olivia and I go *way* back." Back to Girl Scouts and slumber parties and double-dog dares and pinky promises made beneath the stars. Promises that had been long since forgotten, broken. "It's been, what, eleven years?"

Olivia's hazel eyes rounded as she met Margot's stare across the room. "Give or take. We, um, we went to school together," she said, words rushing out of her in a jumble. "In Enumclaw."

"Damn." Brendon's eyes darted between them. "Talk about serendipity, right?"

Margot forced out a chuckle.

The universe was playing a cosmic joke on her, that was for sure.

Chapter Two

*C*ontract signed and deposit placed, Olivia quickly updated the Google Sheet itemizing Annie and Brendon's wedding budget—*hello*—filling in the field beside *venue*. The rest of the column auto-adjusted, doing the math for her. Olivia saved then toggled over to her calendar, blocking out a time slot for a cake tasting with a local bakery ECE and Lori had worked with many times and who was willing to accommodate the tighter timeline. Immediate tasks accomplished, Olivia cast a quick glance around the venue's courtyard. Annie and Brendon had wandered off a few minutes ago, hand in hand, stating their desire to *get the lay of the land for the photos*. Across the courtyard, Brendon's sister blushed when her girlfriend whispered in her ear, both of them lost in their own little world. Olivia made another sweep, craning her neck to peer past the fountain and through the glass-paned door. She frowned.

Margot was missing.

Margot Cooper.

Olivia fought the urge to shiver, fingers curling into fists at her sides as a flush inched its way up her jaw without her permission.

She'd call this *fate*, if she weren't unsure whether she still believed in that sort of thing. Four million people in this city and *M. Cooper* and her Margot turned out to be one and the same. Olivia swallowed hard. Not *her* Margot. Not anymore.

Olivia puffed out her cheeks, her exhale measured. Now was not the time to lose herself in the past, in old hurts that should've healed. She had a wedding to plan. Lori was counting on her to pull this off. Olivia's future was riding on the success of this wedding, on her ability to put her skills to task and pull this off. Screwing up was not an option.

Flipping the cover over the screen of her tablet, Olivia tucked it away inside her purse and left the courtyard in search of Brendon and Annie.

They weren't in the dining room or the ballroom, either. Olivia hiked her purse higher on her shoulder and made a left down the winding hall, which more closely resembled a maze, what with the sheer number of intersections and doors to choose from. It was a place she could easily get lost in if she wasn't careful, her memory of the exact layout a little hazy from the anniversary party she'd assisted Lori with months ago.

From the outside, the venue was unassuming, plain brick like any other warehouse in the area, not a place anyone would look at twice. Stepping inside was like falling through a looking glass, like entering a whole new world, a wonderland of glitzy chandeliers, ornate murals, creeping vines, and old-world exposed brick. It was achingly romantic, like something out of a fairy tale, the sort of place where Olivia had dreamed of getting married when she was little.

Olivia's thumb brushed the bare skin beneath the knuckle of her third finger as she ducked her head through an open door. She drew up short, heart rate ratcheting, and cleared her throat. "Hi."

Margot spun toward her, dark eyes wide behind the lenses of her cat-eye glasses. "There's an elephant in this room."

A laugh bubbled up inside Olivia's throat. "You *think*?"

Margot's face turned red, matching the color of the plaid shirt she wore unbuttoned over a black crop top so tight it might as well have been a second skin. The bare strip of her stomach was pale and flat, and Olivia's own skin pebbled with goose bumps.

"Funny." Margot gestured toward the life-sized and lifelike elephant, wrinkly and gray with huge ivory tusks, stationed in the corner of the room. "Who the fuck puts a fake elephant in a dining room?"

Olivia stepped inside the room, leaving a healthy distance between her and Margot as she lifted a hand, curling her fingers around the elephant's right tusk. "It was built in 1931 for the Paris Colonial Exhibition."

Margot's eyes followed her, watching her like a hawk. "Since when did you become a fount of obscure knowledge?"

"Eleven years is a long time," Olivia said, hating how that was meant to come out like a joke but her voice cracked halfway through, earnestness seeping out like blood from a wound.

Olivia regretted leaving her coat in the car. What she wouldn't have done for one more layer, another defense against Margot's unflinching stare that managed to strip Olivia down and leave her feeling naked despite her sweater. She glanced down and winced. Her sweater that was covered in cat hair. *Cute.*

"The, um, facility manager, Chris, mentioned it at the beginning of the tour," Olivia explained, trying to surreptitiously brush away the cat hair. "I guess you weren't paying attention."

Margot's throat jerked. "Maybe I was distracted."

Olivia ducked her chin, fighting a losing battle against the upward twitch of her lips. *Distracted.* That was . . . *something.* "You cut your hair. It looks great."

Margot ran her fingers through her lob, causing her plaid shirt to open further and reveal more of her bare stomach. "Thanks."

She'd dyed it darker, too, black instead of brown. It barely brushed her collar when she moved her head.

Olivia uncurled her fingers from the elephant's tusk and dropped her hand, crossing her arms under her chest. "How've you been?"

Margot shrugged. "You know." No, not really. "Fine? And you? How are you? How've you been?"

"How much time do you have?" Olivia joked.

Margot braced her shoulder against the wall. "So you and Brad, huh?"

Leave it to Margot to dive directly into the deep end. Never afraid of charging in headfirst. "Divorced. Last spring."

"My condolences." Margot's brows rose over the black rim of her glasses. "Or congratulations? I'm never really sure what's appropriate."

Olivia was over the split, but talking about it usually didn't make her laugh, not like it did now. Divorce wasn't funny. Most people treated it like something to be ashamed of, like *she* should be ashamed of herself. "We, uh, we just wanted different things."

She could say more. Start at the beginning instead of the end. She could tell Margot all about dropping out of college when Brad had suffered a football-career-ending injury. About how she'd followed him back home to Enumclaw and how they'd gotten married because he'd asked and that's what she'd always wanted . . . right? About years spent giving and giving and giving, handing over pieces of herself until Brad had asked her for the one thing she wouldn't give him.

But she'd rather not say all that. There was no point.

Margot was just someone Olivia used to know, and now Olivia was planning her friend's wedding. It would be in both their best interests to keep things strictly professional.

As professional as possible when she knew exactly how to touch Margot to make her babble and beg.

"How'd you meet the groom? Brendon," Olivia asked before Margot could pry harder.

"Elle and I, we created Oh My Stars."

"I follow you guys on Twitter." And Instagram, too. She'd been following Oh My Stars since its inception years ago, back when Margot had still been at UW and Olivia had only just become Mrs. Brad Taylor. "You were always interested in astrology."

The skin between Olivia's shoulder blades itched, a memory of Margot tracing constellations into the bare skin of Olivia's back surfacing.

Margot nodded. "We partnered with his app, OTP, a couple years ago to add astrological compatibility to their matchmaking algorithm. Brendon introduced Elle to his sister, Darcy, and he and I became friends."

"That sounds really great, Margot." Olivia smiled. "It sounds like everything worked out the way you wanted."

Like all her dreams had come true. Good for her.

Margot dropped her gaze, tracing the mosaic tile floor with the toe of her boot, expression giving nothing away. Margot had always been too good at that, locking everything up, impossible to read. Olivia had tried, *God*, had she tried, but every time she thought she'd figured Margot out, Margot would do something to make her second-guess everything she thought she knew. Everything she believed to be certain.

"How long have you been in Seattle?" Margot asked, changing the subject.

"Since last summer."

Not even a year.

"There you are." Brendon poked his head inside the room and grinned. "We were wondering where you two wandered off to."

He stepped further into the room, Annie by his side. Elle and Darcy followed.

Margot pushed off the wall, tucking her thumbs inside her front pockets. Her black denim rode lower in the front, revealing another inch of smooth, pale skin and the barest hint of black ink curving around her hip. Olivia's mouth ran dry. That was new. "You all set?"

"Sure are. We were thinking dinner. Maybe that Indian

place we like since we're not far from Darcy and Elle's," Brendon said. "Olivia, you should join us."

Olivia blinked, long and slow, forcefully tearing her eyes from that bare expanse of skin, gaze lifting and landing on Margot's face. A knowing smirk played at the edges of Margot's mouth. Heat rose in Olivia's cheeks, creeping up to her hairline, her skin likely matching the color of her burgundy beanie. She swallowed hard and smiled apologetically. "I wish I could, but I should really be going. I need to email the florist and—"

"It's nearly seven," Annie said, looping her arm through Brendon's. "What are the chances the florist is going to email you back?"

"Annie's right." Brendon smiled. "Come on. I'm sure you and Margot have plenty of catching up to do."

She met Margot's eyes. One of Margot's brows rose as if daring Olivia to . . . what? Say yes? No? Olivia bit her lip. Margot was more of a mystery than ever.

Dinner. Brendon and Annie would be there, too, at the very least, as a buffer, and at the end of the day, all of this was about the two of them. Their wedding. As long as she kept that in mind, she should be fine.

"All right." Olivia slipped the strap of her purse down her shoulder, where it caught against the crook of her elbow. She reached inside for her phone, wanting to, at the very least, set a reminder for herself to email the florist first thing in the morning. "Let me just . . ."

She'd missed a call, having set her phone to silent during the tour. Mrs. Miyata, her landlady, who lived three doors down, had left a voicemail.

Olivia bit back a sigh. Considering the time, Cat was probably kicking up a fuss. If she didn't get her dinner by seven, she'd start yowling as if she were dying, little drama queen. Luckily, Mrs. Miyata had the spare key, so she could pop open a can of Friskies to keep the monster at bay. She'd done it before and hopefully wouldn't mind doing it again.

"Let me just make a quick call."

Olivia was barely out the door when Brendon zeroed in on Margot, sporting a shit-eating grin. *"So."*

"So what?"

Brendon shook his head slowly, eyes narrowing minutely, studying her with intent. As if she were a puzzle he planned to solve. "Olivia seems nice."

Great. Margot should've seen this coming: her friends— lovable bunch of nosy assholes that they were—giving her the third degree. Except, no. Call it kismet or fate, serendipity or just a damn coincidence, but Olivia had appeared without warning. Nothing could've prepared Margot for *this.*

"She is." Margot crossed her arms, fighting against the urge to shift her weight from one foot to the other. "Or she was, I guess. I don't know. A lot can change in eleven years."

Clearly, it had. Olivia had married Brad and divorced him in that time. *We just wanted different things.* What a pat answer that told her *nothing.* It was like when celebs split over irreconcilable differences and it later turned out to because someone had cheated or their finances were fucked. Who pulled the plug? Olivia? Did it even matter?

"You know, I don't think I've ever heard you talk about high school," Brendon said. "Not once."

Elle nodded. "You hardly even talked about it when we were in college."

"Because it was high school," Margot said. "High school in *Enumclaw*. Not exactly riveting stuff. There's really nothing to tell."

Nothing she wanted to or had any intention of telling, at least.

"You know"—Brendon's lips quirked—"when someone says there's nothing to tell, there usually is."

Brendon was perceptive. Sometimes a little *too* perceptive. His tendency to stick his nose where it didn't belong made for a dangerous combination.

"We were friends." Margot shrugged, throwing Brendon the smallest, least likely to bite her in the ass, of bones. "We drifted apart after high school. Plenty of people do. I went to UW and she went to WSU. End of story."

Brendon stared, scratching his chin.

"Leave her alone, Brendon," Darcy said, cutting in, saving Margot the hassle of having to do it herself. "If Margot doesn't want to talk about it, she doesn't have to."

Margot sighed. Finally someone who saw reason.

"Besides, have you *met* Margot? When have you ever known her to do something she doesn't want to?"

Margot frowned. "I mean—"

"She's locked up tighter than Fort Knox." Darcy ignored her. "If Margot doesn't want to talk about something, good luck wheedling it out of her."

"Me?" Margot jabbed her thumb at her chest. "When have you *ever* known me to shy away from speaking my mind?"

And that was rich, coming from Darcy, considering how tight-lipped she'd been about her feelings for Elle at the beginning of their relationship.

Darcy turned to Brendon. "See, stubborn."

Annie snickered and Elle's lips twitched, like she was trying not to laugh. The effort, while quite clearly in vain, was noted and appreciated.

"Wow," Margot intoned. "Really feeling the love here, guys."

Brendon opened his mouth.

"Margot's right." Elle met Margot's eye and smiled. "If she says there's nothing to tell, there's nothing to tell, and that's all there is to it."

Margot's shoulders relaxed, the tightness in her chest replaced with warmth. Elle got it. Margot mouthed a quick *thanks*, and Elle winked.

Three weeks. As the Best Woman, how often would her path cross with Olivia's, really? Margot had to get through tonight, and then there'd be . . . what, the rehearsal and the wedding itself? They both had a vested interest in making sure this wedding went off without a hitch. They could set aside their past for one month. One month and Margot could forget all about Olivia Grant. Out of sight, out of mind.

Olivia was probably out in the hall, thinking the same thing. *Speak of the devil.* Olivia returned, looking pale-faced and wan, her phone clutched tightly in her right hand. She stopped just inside the room and cleared her throat. "Hi. I'm really sorry, but I'm going to have to bail on dinner. Something came up, and I have to go take care of it."

Margot frowned at the way Olivia's voice quivered. She opened her mouth to ask if Olivia was okay, but stopped before she could voice the question. It wasn't her business.

Brendon didn't have the same reservations. "Is everything all right?"

Olivia started to nod before the move morphed slowly into a shake, her head swerving. "I just got off the phone with my landlady. Apparently there was a—a problem with the plumbing in the unit directly above mine that caused the bathroom to flood. My ceiling is . . . The damage was pretty extensive, I guess, and they're going to have to bring in fans so mold won't set in, and after, they'll have to replace the joists and the . . . I guess the drywall or plaster or . . ." Olivia shut her eyes. "I'm not even really sure. It was a lot to take in."

"Jesus," Margot muttered. That sounded like a nightmare.

"I'm imagining you'll have to find somewhere else to stay," Darcy said, face pinched with concern.

Olivia nodded. "I guess the integrity of the ceiling is questionable. It's leaking and . . ." She laughed, frazzled. "It's a mess."

Annie pressed her fingers to her lips. "Oh, shit."

Brendon raked his fingers through his hair. "Did they say how long the repairs are going to take?"

"No. My lease is month-to-month." Olivia's bottom lip started to tremble, and she quickly pursed her mouth, a dozen little dimples forming in her chin. "I have a feeling I won't be moving back in any time soon."

A sharp twinge of sympathy shot through Margot's chest.

"I'm sorry," Olivia blurted, batting at the air. "Geez, you don't want to hear about this. This is—this is *not* your problem. I'm, um, I'm just going to go—"

"Do you have somewhere you can stay?" Brendon's eyes flitted to Margot, then back to Olivia. "A friend's place, maybe?"

What.

No.

Shit.

Olivia's eyes went glossy, welling with tears. "I'll figure something out."

Margot's stomach dropped.

Fuck.

Brendon turned, his brows rising pointedly, managing to communicate plenty without him having to open his mouth to say a thing. *I'll figure something out* wasn't an answer. Or, it was, just not the one Margot had been hoping to hear.

Clearly, whether Olivia was willing to admit it or not, she was in need of a place to stay and Margot . . . *fuck her life* . . . Margot had a spare room. All her friends *knew* she had a spare room. And as far as they also knew, she had no reason *not* to offer it up to Olivia . . . the girl she knew from high school.

An old friend.

Nothing to tell was swiftly coming back to bite her in the ass.

Margot swallowed a groan because, *fuck*, she was probably— no, *definitely*—going to regret this. It was a catastrophe waiting to happen, but she couldn't *not* offer, not when Olivia was standing there, close to tears but refusing to let them fall, putting on a brave face instead.

It was so typical of her, of the girl Margot once knew. Olivia was so quick to blot everyone else's tears, to serve as a shoulder to cry on, but never to let anyone see *her* fall apart.

The ache in Margot's chest grew sharper, harder to ignore. She wouldn't be able to sleep at night if she didn't at least extend the invitation.

"Hey." She crossed her arms, standing straighter even though Olivia still towered several inches over her. "If you need a place to stay, you can crash at mine. If you want."

Olivia's lips parted, hazel eyes rounding. "That's kind of you to offer, but I wouldn't want to impose."

Annie tugged on Brendon's arm, leading him across the room. Elle and Darcy followed, giving Margot and Olivia some semblance of privacy. Except for the part where they were conspicuously quiet, eyes averted but clearly listening in.

Margot focused on Olivia and tried to tune out her well-meaning-but-nosy-as-fuck friends. "You wouldn't be. Imposing, I mean. I've got two bedrooms and no roommates, which I've been meaning to do something about."

Margot hadn't anticipated the universe giving her a big ole kick in the pants, but hey. *Unexpected.*

Olivia stared at Margot with big, unblinking eyes.

"*Roommate?*" she asked, sounding unsure.

"I'm not suggesting it has to be permanent. Not that I'm *not* suggesting . . ." Damn it. Why was this so difficult? With anyone else, Margot had no problem saying exactly what she meant. "It could be on a trial basis. Or if you just need a place to crash for however long it takes you to find somewhere else, that's chill, too." Margot's throat narrowed, more words creeping up without her consent. "It's not like you're a stranger. We—we know each other. I mean, I think my parents honestly tried to claim you as a dependent on their taxes one year."

A smile played at the edges of Olivia's mouth, and Margot . . . was staring at Olivia's lips. Margot didn't know where to look. She crossed her arms, but that felt defensive, so she dropped them to her sides, where they hung, aimless. Margot had no idea what she was doing.

Olivia's eyes darted to where Margot's friends stood, and Margot followed her gaze. Brendon whipped around and stared up at the ceiling, honest to God starting to *whistle*. Olivia huffed out a quiet laugh and dropped her voice, whispering, "Are they always like that? Your friends?"

Margot arched a brow. "Are they always . . . what? Nosy?"

"No." Olivia's lips quirked. "Well, yeah. That, too. Are they always so bad at hiding it?"

She smiled fondly. "The trick is to let them think they're stealthy. That way they never try to improve."

"Clever," Olivia praised. Her throat jerked, and her smile waned. "Look, I didn't mean to imply that I didn't want to—to take you up on your offer." A faint blush rose in Olivia's cheeks. "I'm surprised you're offering. That's all."

Margot frowned. She had zero desire to rehash their past, not ever, but certainly not here, where her friends were listening.

"It's ancient history, Liv," she murmured, scratching her nose so Brendon—snoop that he was—wouldn't try to read her lips. "How about we leave the past in the past?"

So what if they'd had a week-long fling while Olivia and Brad were broken up over spring break senior year? Brad had returned from Mexico, skin tanned and hair bleached from the sun, and when he'd begged Olivia to take him back, she'd said yes.

Sure, Margot had thought their week together had *meant* something, but clearly it hadn't, and now it was nothing but a chapter in Margot's past. No, a *footnote*. Time healed all wounds, yada yada *whatever*. Margot wasn't carrying a grudge, she wasn't carrying a torch, and she didn't need to talk about it.

Olivia tugged her beanie down over the tops of her ears and gave a short, sharp nod. "Right. I can do that."

Of course she could. *She* wasn't the one who'd had *feelings*.

"Cool." Margot cleared her throat. "So?"

"Are—are you sure about this?"

No, not one bit. But she wasn't about to back out. Not after offering, not with her friends standing by. Not when Olivia wasn't just someone Margot used to know, but Brendon and Annie's wedding planner.

She'd show Brendon sunshine and rainbows.

"I wouldn't have offered if I weren't."

Olivia's lips curved upward in a tentative smile. "Thanks."

Margot shoved her hands inside her pockets and jerked her chin at the door. "We should probably head out and grab your stuff before it gets too late."

"Packing. *Joy.*" Olivia heaved a sigh. "I swear I feel like I only just got settled."

"Packing?" Brendon rocked back on his heels. "Did I hear you say *packing*? Because we can help with that. I'll order pizza."

Olivia's eyes sparkled with mirth, her teeth sinking into her bottom lip. She shot Margot a look, nothing more than a brief flicker of her eyes, but it put a weird lump in Margot's throat because it was the start of something new, even if it was only a shared understanding that Brendon wouldn't know subtlety if it bit him on the ass.

Margot rolled her eyes and took a step in the direction of the door. Olivia reached out, cool fingers brushing the back of Margot's hand. Despite being a whisper of a touch, it made Margot's pulse roar inside her ears.

A soft pink blush crept up Olivia's jaw as she dropped her hand to her side and smiled sheepishly. "You're not allergic to cats, are you?"

Chapter Three

Olivia hovered in Margot's foyer, Cat mewling softly from the carrier at her feet. Poor thing was probably confused, not understanding why she'd been shoved inside a carrier, put in a car, and driven across the city. Olivia crouched down, slipping her fingers through the plastic grate. Cat leaned in, sniffing her fingers before rubbing her face against them. "I know. It's been a long day."

And it was nowhere close to being over.

Margot stepped out into the hall, Elle trailing after her. She jerked her thumb over her shoulder. "I didn't know where the best place was to put to the litter box. The bathroom's too small, so I set it in your room."

Olivia's room. Her room in the apartment she now shared with Margot, for the foreseeable future. Somebody pinch her.

Olivia stood, earning an aggrieved-sounding meow from Cat, who was probably sick of being cooped up in her crate, roomy though it was. "Thanks. I've got a mat that goes under it so she won't track litter."

Elle ducked low, peeking inside the carrier. It was difficult to see inside, with Cat tucked up in a tight little ball of dark, fluffy fur and glinting green eyes. "What's her name?"

Olivia blushed. "Cat."

Elle cocked her head, clearly confused. "How long have you had her?"

"Um." She did the math. "Almost eight months."

Elle frowned. "So . . . it's not just a placeholder? *Cat?*"

Margot huffed out a quiet laugh and Olivia's stomach somersaulted at the sound. "It's from *Breakfast at Tiffany's*. Holly Golightly names her—well, it isn't *hers*, that's the whole point. She names the cat *Cat*." Margot's lips twitched. "I'm assuming that's where you got the name."

It was Olivia's favorite movie. No matter how many times she watched it, that kiss in the rain still made her shiver and Paul Varjak's speech about belonging putting an ache in her chest that persisted long after the credits rolled. It was the same ache she'd felt when she thought about Margot over the last decade.

Olivia wasn't surprised Margot caught the reference. She'd forced her to watch the movie a dozen times, easy.

"I found her by the trash outside my apartment the week after I moved here." They were both alone in the big city, and Olivia had figured they could be alone together. "It seemed fitting."

Margot's lips quirked. "You can let her out of the cage, if you want."

Olivia cast a glance at the open door that led out into the main hall. Brendon, Annie, and Darcy had made one final trip out to the parking lot, offering to grab the last of Olivia's boxes, most already stacked in her new bedroom.

"Here." Margot flattened her palm against the door, shutting it with a soft *snick*. "No chance of her making a run for it."

"Thanks." Despite her squat little legs, Cat was wily. She had a tendency to explore, no space off-limits as long as she could fit. But even that was open to interpretation because Olivia had once found her wedged between the refrigerator and the wall. Cat was better at getting herself into trouble than out of it. Olivia could relate.

She dropped to her knees and unlatched the door to the carrier. Cat unfurled herself and crept closer. She stuck her nose in the air and sniffed, then sneezed. The smell of patchouli was faint, a stick of ashed incense poking up from a ceramic holder shaped like a lotus. Cat took a tentative step into the living room, appraising her new surroundings.

"This is where we live now." Olivia stroked the fur between Cat's ears. "You like it?"

Cat mewed softly and circled Margot's ankles before slinking deeper into the apartment. She leaped onto the sofa and batted at a bright blue beaded accent pillow.

"I hope that's okay," Olivia offered belatedly, cringing slightly. "It's hard to keep her off the furniture."

More like impossible. Cat did what Cat wanted to do. Olivia could fuss, but Cat had no keeper.

Margot shrugged. "It's fine with me."

The front door swung open and Brendon stepped inside, cardboard boxes stacked two high in his hands. Annie followed, carrying Olivia's vase of flowers. Olivia had drained the water, but the purple variegated carnations were fresh, purchased just yesterday. It had seemed a shame to throw them away. Annie set them atop the breakfast nook and smiled. "That's the last of it."

"Thank you so much." Olivia tucked her hair behind her ears. "I—I really appreciate you all helping. You didn't have to."

"You're helping make the wedding of our dreams happen, and in under a month." Brendon shook his head. "Hauling a few boxes a couple of blocks is the least we can do."

"I mean, that's my *job*." She laughed. They were paying her to help. Well, they were paying *Lori*, and Lori was paying her, but same difference.

"Still." Brendon rocked back on his heels. "Any friend of Margot's is a friend of ours."

Margot averted her eyes.

Friends. So that's the story Margot was going with. All right. Nice to know.

"Well, thank you." She drummed her fingers against the outsides of her thighs. "Really."

Brendon smiled, eyes crinkling. He turned to Margot. "We should probably get out of your hair. Let you settle in."

"It's been a long day," Annie said, nose wrinkling softly in sympathy.

"You have lots of catching up to do," Elle added. "Even more so now, considering . . ."

They were roommates.

Funny how years ago—before they'd grown apart and *long* before they'd fallen into bed—they'd talked about what it would be like, living together. It had been the plan. Graduate and move to the city, together. Margot had painted a pretty picture with her words. Late nights and libraries and watching the sunrise from rooftops, of all-night diners and coffee shops, parties that offered more than beer and Everclear. A city where all their dreams could come true. Olivia still had a corkboard hidden away in her closet back home, covered in purple-and-gold UW paraphernalia.

Olivia had never dreamed they'd live together under circumstances like these. It would've required her, at fifteen, sixteen, seventeen, to have imagined a future where she didn't get that scholarship she needed, where she went to WSU instead so as to not burden Dad financially, where she and Margot stopped speaking, where she married Brad and spent a decade stuck in neutral, spinning her wheels before divorcing him, moving back home—a million bad decisions she tried not to beat herself up over because the past was the past.

Everyone slowly migrated in the direction of the door.

"See you for the cake tasting," Brendon said.

Olivia nodded. "Looking forward to it."

Elle waved as they disappeared down the hall. Margot shut the door, fingers lingering on the lock, her back to Olivia. Reality set in, and along with it, an oppressive shroud of silence. For the first time in eleven years, she and Margot were alone together. Really, truly alone. No one to barge in, no interruptions.

Olivia cleared her throat. "Thanks for letting me stay here."

"No big." Margot slipped past her, arms brushing. "You want something to drink?"

She could use a margarita the size of her head right about

now, but she wasn't about to make requests. Hard alcohol was probably a bad idea. It might've taken the edge off, but the last thing Olivia needed was to feel more unsteady than she naturally did around Margot. "Sure."

Olivia hovered in the doorway of the kitchen while Margot ducked inside the fridge. Margot shut the door with her elbow, a beer held in each hand. "Here."

Olivia stared at the bottle of proffered beer, its neck dangling from between Margot's fingertips, her nails short and neat, painted a shade of red so dark Olivia had first thought they were black. If her hand shook when she reached out to take the bottle, it was only because it had been a long day and the adrenaline was wearing off. "Thanks."

Margot lifted her own beer to her mouth, tipping it back, throat jerking when she swallowed. She lowered her bottle, tongue darting out against her bottom lip. A smudge of ruby lipstick lingered on the mouth of the brown glass.

Margot jerked her head to the right, hair swishing against her jaw as she disappeared around the corner into the living room. Olivia followed, stumbling on the tangled fringe of a threadbare rug that bore a single singe mark near one corner. She clutched the sweating bottle between her palms and made a sweep of the apartment, taking in the details she hadn't noticed when she first walked in.

Like the embroidery hoop on the sliver of a wall by the kitchen that contained a cross-stitched phrase she had to squint to read. *Behold! The field in which I grow my fucks. Lay thine eyes upon it and see that it is barren.* Funny. She chuckled under her breath and turned on her heel, cocking her head, studying the framed paintings hanging from the exposed brick wall. Her jaw dropped.

Wow. Georgia O'Keeffe's flowers looked downright subtle by comparison. These drawings were . . . realistic and—Olivia squinted harder, face flaming. She considered herself pretty darn flexible, but her body didn't bend *that* way. Olivia perched on the couch beside Cat and pressed a hand to her cheek, trying to cool it off, her fingers damp with condensation from her beer bottle.

Margot's brows ticked upward, the corners of her mouth twitching as she watched Olivia.

"Your art . . . it's really . . ."

Margot smirked.

Olivia flushed, floundering for the right word. *"Erotic?"*

That was it. Erotic. Broad black brushstrokes kept the art from veering into vulgar territory.

"They're a relatively new addition. I bought them to make Brendon uncomfortable after Elle moved out and Annie moved in." She shrugged. "You stop noticing them after a while."

How much sex did someone have to have to become desensitized to paintings of *other* people having it? More sex than Olivia was having, clearly. She ducked her chin, trying to will her blush away, her cheeks so hot she could've sworn there was steam coming off of her. Olivia stole a surreptitious peek at Margot from the corner of her eye, watching as she tilted her head to the side, considering the series of sketches on the wall. Margot's slender fingers skimmed the front of her throat,

lingering on the hollow between her collarbones, dark nail polish and the sharp cut of her hair stark contrasts against her pale
skin, making her look a little like one of those canvases come
to life.

Margot turned, catching her staring, and Olivia's heart
tripped over the next beat, speeding, sending another wave of
blood rushing to the surface of her skin.

"So." She wheezed out a laugh. "This is awkward."

The proverbial elephant in the room had tripled in size.

"Don't see why it has to be." Margot set her beer on the table,
sans coaster, and kicked her feet up beside it, ankles crossing,
the picture of chill. Everything Olivia wasn't. "Like I said. It's
ancient history, Liv. I'm over it."

Over it. Olivia frowned. What was *that* supposed to mean?
Over *what*? What did Margot have to get over in the first place?
Olivia was the one who'd had her hopes dashed and her heart
broken by Margot, not the other way around.

Or maybe it *was* her fault. After all, she'd been the one to
kiss Margot.

Olivia couldn't say with any degree of certainty when exactly her feelings for Margot had changed. It wasn't like she'd
woken up one morning and suddenly found herself wanting
her best friend. There was no grand movie moment where their
eyes locked and Olivia's breath caught and a lightbulb went
off inside her head. It had been gradual, so slow that her own
feelings had crept up on her. Little touches had started to make
her blush and then Margot's gaze had gained a new dimension.
It wasn't something Olivia could touch but she could certainly
feel it traveling along her skin, tickling the space between her

shoulder blades, raising the hair on the back of her neck, narrowing her throat and damming up words that before had always come so easy. *Awareness.* Followed by confusion and uncertainty, not only that it was Margot but that, *wow*, Olivia was significantly less straight than she'd previously thought. She'd driven herself crazy questioning whether the way Margot's hand lingered on her leg was intentional, reading into every look, every touch, every text. Wondering if just maybe what she felt was mutual.

But Margot—who'd been openly bi since ninth grade, two years later clarifying that if she had to stick a label on herself, *pansexual* was a better fit—had never said anything, and Olivia had been too afraid to say something, to risk ruining their friendship.

Until spring break senior year.

Brad had broken up with her before he left for Cancún—one of the many offs in their on-again, off-again relationship—and Margot had come over with junk food and a bottle of vodka she'd swiped from her parents' liquor cabinet. They'd had the house to themselves, Dad out of town on a fishing trip. Emboldened by a few too many sips of liquid courage and the way Margot's eyes lingered on her lips, Olivia threw caution to the wind and kissed her and—Margot had kissed her back. One kiss led to another led to their clothes coming off led to sex. Great sex and laughter, and for the first time Olivia hadn't had to stop herself from doing all the small things she'd ached to do, like tangling their fingers together or brushing her lips against the ball of Margot's shoulder. She could stare at Margot openly, happily, *hungrily*, without fear of what would happen if she got caught. If there was such a thing as a perfect week, that had been it.

But reality had come crashing down on her the following Monday. Brad wanted to act like their breakup hadn't happened, that it was more of a *pause* than a full-stop split. When she didn't immediately fall into his arms, he'd had the audacity to seem confused. She'd texted Margot. *Can you believe it? What should I tell him?*

Olivia had expected Margot to tell her that Brad could go fuck himself. That he was delusional. She'd wanted Margot to tell her Brad couldn't have her.

Don't worry about me saying anything to anyone. What happens on spring break, stays on spring break, right? ☺ Margot had texted instead.

After that, they didn't talk about it, what happened between them that week, but Margot always had an excuse when Olivia asked to hang out, usually that she was too busy studying for finals. Brad hadn't let up, blowing up Olivia's phone with a constant barrage of texts, begging her to take him back. Two weeks later, she did, and a week after that, she received a letter from the financial aid department at UW notifying her that her scholarship application had been rejected. Graduation came and went, Margot moved to Seattle, and the rest was history.

In the end, it was Olivia's fault for assuming their week together had meant something. Regardless, Margot was right. That was then and this was now, and rehashing old hurts wouldn't help. It would only make her feel sorrier for herself.

"Right. You're totally right. We should leave the past in the past. Let sleeping dogs lie." She tucked her hair behind her ear and laughed. "We had sex. Big deal."

As soon the words were out, Olivia cringed, heat wrapping around her neck and spreading up her jaw. Okay, so maybe there was such a thing as being *too* candid. At least she hadn't tacked on the bit about it being the best sex of her life, true as it would've been.

"No big." A muscle in Margot's jaw ticked when she smiled. *"Trust me."*

Olivia's whole body burned. Okay, ouch. "Right."

Margot lifted her beer by the neck and tipped it back, draining it in one swallow. She stood, perfectly steady, and stretched, her pants riding indecently low, and Olivia was treated to another hint of that ink creeping up Margot's hip. She backed up a step before turning and heading in the direction of the kitchen. The sound of rummaging and then a drawer sliding shut followed. Margot returned, brandishing two shiny keys. She set them on the coffee table, side by side. "Silver one's for the door to the building, and the brass key is for the apartment."

Olivia reached forward and ran her finger along the teeth of the closest key. Something about having her own key made this real. "Thanks."

"No problem." Margot tucked her thumbs in her pockets and cast a sweeping glance around the apartment. "I'm going to head to bed, but we should find a time and . . . I don't know, talk about . . . Jesus, I don't know. *Logistics.*"

Right. Logistics. If they couldn't keep this strictly professional, it would at least be best to refrain from bringing their past into play. To limit their interactions to their shared interests—Brendon and Annie's wedding—and communal space. Boundaries. No more bringing up their week together, Olivia's feelings. Keep it polite and distant.

Distance was absolutely paramount.

Olivia bobbed her head. "Sounds good. Tomorrow?"

Margot nodded. "Sure. I've got a meeting in the afternoon, but I should be back in the early evening." She cast a glance in the direction of the kitchen. "Feel free to raid the fridge, if you want. We—Elle and me, and Annie, too—were pretty easygoing about sharing food and splitting the grocery bill, but if you have a problem with that . . ."

"No." She shook her head. "All good with me."

Margot cracked her knuckles. "The shower's kind of finicky. You have to pull the knob before you turn the water on if you want to take a shower. If you try to do it the other way around, the knob sticks."

"Good to know, thanks."

All she wanted right now was to fall face-first into bed. She'd only gotten a brief look at her room, but the mattress was a clear step up from the pullout she'd been ruining her back on for the last eight months. Her old apartment, while nearer to ECE's office, offered little in terms of space. Her living room tripled as a bedroom *and* personal office. Margot's apartment—hers now, too—was downright roomy by comparison.

"Tomorrow, then." Margot backed slowly toward the hall.

Olivia waved and immediately wished she hadn't. How utterly dorky. "Good night."

Margot's lips twitched upward in a barely-there smile before she turned and disappeared down the hall. Her door shut, and Olivia slumped back against the couch.

What a day.

Not that it had been all bad. It certainly could've been worse. She and Cat could've been sleeping in a hotel or a sleeping bag on her coworker Kira's floor. Even her car. She would've only been able to swing any of those options for a few days while diligently hunting for a new apartment. Had that not panned out . . .

She probably needed to let Dad know that she was living somewhere new. Not that he was likely to mail her anything, but he might. Stranger things had happened.

"Livvy, hey," he answered on the first ring.

"Hi, Dad." She picked at the label of her beer. It was soggy, easy to peel at the corners. "Now's not a bad time, is it?"

Dad huffed. "Never."

A pleasant ache radiated behind her breastbone. In the background, she could hear what sounded like the television. Football, probably. "So. Do you remember Margot?"

"Margot?" He hummed quietly. "Used to eat all our food?"

"Dad." She laughed.

He chuckled. "What about her?"

She nudged her beer bottle further from the edge of the table and leaned back against the couch, tucking her feet under her. "I'm kind of living with her now?"

"How do you *kind of* live with someone?"

She rubbed her eyes. "It's a . . . It's new. I was just calling to let you know I have a new address. I'll text it to you, okay?"

"Is everything okay, Liv?"

Her throat chose the worst possible moment to grow impossibly tight. "Mm-hmm. I'm fine. Everything's fine."

Dad went quiet. "Are you okay on money, because I don't have much, but I can send you—"

"No. I'm good. It's just been a long day. There was a plumbing problem at my old apartment; that's why I moved. I'm— I'm really fine. I promise."

Dad *hmm*ed over the line. "You sure?"

"Yes, I'm sure." She forced a laugh. "I'm actually doing really well, otherwise. Lori's letting me take point on a wedding, and it's—it's a really big deal, Dad."

"Good for you, Liv. I'm sure you're going to be great."

Cat hopped off the other end of the couch and stretched, letting out a sweet, contented-sounding meow. At least one of them was feeling right at home.

"Enough about me. How are you? When's your next doctor's appointment?"

"Next Tuesday, I think. Or Wednesday, maybe? I've got it written down somewhere."

Written down somewhere. All she could do was shake her head. "Speaking of writing things down, how's your food diary going? You are still keeping up with it, right?"

Dad grunted. "Mm-hmm."

Yeah, that sounded promising. "Dad."

"I am. Honest."

"And you're filling it out *properly*?"

Left to his own devices, Dad would subsist on a diet of pork rinds and TV dinners laden with enough sodium to float a brick.

Dad chuckled. "It amazes me how you manage to hover from a hundred miles away. It's a talent, really."

"You're exaggerating." She smiled. "It's only fifty miles."

"I'm fine. I'm doing everything the doctor asked me to. And I'm even working fewer hours, okay? You worry too much."

She worried the right amount. A heart attack was nothing to joke about, even a mild one.

"I'm glad you're working less. That's a relief. Stress isn't good for you."

Dad gave a soft grunt. "Why don't you leave the worrying to me, okay? That's *my* job. I should be worrying about you."

"And like I said, you don't need to worry about me. This wedding could be huge. If I pull this off, Lori's going to promote me. That means a raise and more events and—this is what I came here for."

Event planning. Turning other people's dreams into a reality, bringing them to life. *That* was what Olivia wanted.

"How's everything else going up there?" He coughed. "You, uh, meet anyone?"

"*Dad.*"

"I just want you to be happy, Livvy."

She could be—she *was*. She was doing just fine on her own. Just fine. "I'm good."

"Must be nice at least, having a familiar face around now," Dad said. "Margot."

Nice wasn't quite the word she'd pick. Dizzying, maybe. Definitely surreal.

"Mm-hmm." She pulled her phone from her ear and checked the time. "Look, I should I let you go. I'm pretty beat."

"All right. Love you, kid."

"Love you, too, Dad. Talk soon."

Chapter Four

What Cocktail Should You Order Based on Your Zodiac Sign?

Aries—Dirty Vodka Martini
Taurus—French 75
Gemini—Long Island Iced Tea
Cancer—Old Fashioned
Leo—Espresso Martini
Virgo—Gin and Tonic
Libra—Cosmopolitan
Scorpio—Manhattan
Sagittarius—Negroni
Capricorn—Vesper
Aquarius—White Russian
Pisces—Mojito

$\mathcal{B}$ell and Blanchard Brewing Company, a small, locally owned and operated brewery, was the latest—and largest, save for OTP—partner Oh My Stars had teamed up with to date. In the past, Elle and Margot had diversified OMS's revenue stream by accepting sponsorships and paid advertisements from zodiac-centric brands they themselves liked enough to rep—perfume, astro-themed activewear—but this was a step above. Oh My Stars would be collaborating with the brewery to launch a series of astrology-inspired beers, one for each sign, to be released during the corresponding season, beginning with Aries and ending with Pisces.

Margot was jazzed about the partnership. She was firmly in the *beer good* camp. What she was *less* jazzed about was spearheading the partnership sans Elle.

Not that Elle wasn't involved—this was an Oh My Stars venture after all, and Oh My Stars was and would forever be run fifty-fifty by them both—but as their business had grown, *boomed*, so had the need to delegate. They'd done some variation of delegation since day one; Elle handled the majority of the chart readings they offered by phone or Zoom, in part because clients responded better to Elle's outgoing, bubbly personality, and also because Elle genuinely enjoyed the one-on-one interaction more than Margot did. Margot preferred the behind-the-scenes work infinitely more—website maintenance, content creation for their social media channels, research, and now beer test tasting.

Margot was living the dream.

She just, you know, wished that she got to do it with Elle.

These days, as busy as they both were, Margot was lucky if she got to see Elle outside of their weekly OMS planning chat . . . once? Twice? More often if the whole group was getting together at Elle and Darcy's for game night, like they would be soon. So while Margot was meeting with brewers and discussing hops and yeast and IBU, sampling Bell and Blanchard's current brews while distilling each zodiac sign into traits that could be represented in beer, Elle was handling back-to-back sessions with clients.

Things were changing, and it wasn't *bad*, but it was taking some time for her to get used to it.

Margot juggled a complimentary six-pack of beer from the tasting she'd just attended—the first of many promised to her by the brewery—and flipped through the mail as she stepped inside her apartment. Credit card statement, phone bill, junk, junk, *more* junk, coupon to Sephora for her birthday next month. She tossed the stack on the entry table along with her keys, set the beer on the floor, then reached down to unlace her boots and—

"Jesus." Margot jumped back and gasped. Cat sat in the middle of the foyer, head cocked to the side, staring up at her with those peridot-green eyes.

That was *also* going to take some getting used to.

She cleared her throat. "Hi, Cat."

The cat blinked at her.

Wait. Shit. Eye contact was a no-no. Then again, this was *Margot's* apartment. Did she really want to demonstrate deference inside her own domain?

Cat opened her mouth and yawned out a meow that showed

off her many pointy teeth and—Margot quickly averted her eyes. *That* answered that question.

She shuffled past, boots still on, and booked it down the hall to her bedroom, shutting the door once she was inside. Everything she'd told Elle about maybe adopting a cat? Total bullshit. Cats had terrified Margot ever since her great-aunt Marlena's fluffy white Persian had fallen through the canopy of Margot's bed, waking Margot up from a dead sleep by landing on her . . . claws out and yowling. They'd both been fine, but the scars—mostly only emotional, thank *God*—had lingered.

Maybe living in close quarters with a cat could be good for her. A form of . . . exposure therapy, desensitizing her over time. Either that, or Cat would claw her to death in her sleep. She couldn't help but see it as an analogy for her and Olivia. Living together would either benefit them both or explode in Margot's face. One or the other. Margot had never been very good at operating on anything but a scale of either/or, all or nothing, particularly when it came to Olivia.

Margot grabbed her phone and fired off a quick text to her oldest brother, Cameron.

MARGOT (5:14 P.M.): Cats—what do I need to know about them?

As a veterinarian, Cameron had to possess some wisdom worth her while. Tips, tricks, warnings, *anything*.

ANDREW (5:16 P.M.): why are you asking
ANDREW (5:16 P.M.): you hate cats

She screwed up her face. *Great.* She'd clicked on the wrong message thread, texting the family group chat instead.

MARGOT (5:17 P.M.): Sorry, I meant to just text Cam.

MARGOT (5:17 P.M.): And I don't HATE cats, I have a healthy respect for them.

ANDREW (5:18 P.M.): "respect"

MARGOT (5:19 P.M.): 🖐 😏

CAMERON (5:20 P.M.): What kind of cat are we talking about?

Margot frowned.

MARGOT (5:21 P.M.): The kind with black fur, a smushy face, and squat little legs? You're the expert.

CAMERON (5:22 P.M.): 🙎

CAMERON (5:22 P.M.): Sounds like a Scottish fold.

CAMERON (5:23 P.M.): Male or female? Spayed/neutered? Age? Indoor or outdoor? Is it a stray? Feral?

Margot's head spun. Another message appeared before she could type out a response.

ANDREW (5:24 P.M.): you still never answered why you're asking

MARGOT (5:25 P.M.): I'm sorry, did you ask a question? I didn't see a question mark

She answered Cameron's questions one by one.

MARGOT (5:26 P.M.): Female, idk, idk, indoor now, not anymore, and I sincerely hope not.

CAMERON (5:27 P.M.): 🙎 🙎 🙎

CAMERON (5:28 P.M.): I'm with Andrew on this. Why the sudden interest in cats?

MARGOT (5:30 P.M.): I'm thinking about getting one?

ANDREW (5:31 P.M.): was that a question????

Jesus. *Brothers.*

MARGOT (5:32 P.M.): My roommate has a cat.

"No, no, *no.*" Margot cringed, wishing there was an *unsend* button she could press. It was too late. The knowledge was out there for her entire immediate family to see.

ANDREW (5:33 P.M.): roommate

ANDREW (5:33 P.M.): ?!

MOM (5:33 P.M.): I didn't know you had a new roommate, honey.

Margot palmed her face.

MARGOT (5:34 P.M.): Can we please focus on the cat?

CAMERON (5:35 P.M.): What's their name?

Margot didn't see why *that* mattered, but okay.

MARGOT (5:36 P.M.): Cat.

CAMERON (5:37 P.M.): No, the roommate.

ANDREW (5:38 P.M.): or the cat
CAMERON (5:38 P.M.): 🧑
ANDREW (5:39 P.M.): what
ANDREW (5:39 P.M.): excuse me if i want to know the cat's name too dude

Margot sighed. This conversation was quickly devolving into *who's on first* territory.

MARGOT (5:40 P.M.): No, the cat's name IS Cat.

She chewed on her lip.

MARGOT (5:40 P.M.): The roommate's name is Olivia.
ANDREW (5:41 P.M.): who names their cat CAT
CAMERON (5:42 P.M.): Olivia, clearly. Keep up, Andrew.

Margot stared up at her ceiling, regretting her whole life.

CAMERON (5:43 P.M.): Where'd you meet her?
ANDREW (5:44 P.M.): i'm guessing cam means the roommate not the cat 😂
MARGOT (5:45 P.M.): You know, nvm. All I wanted was to know how to avoid being eaten in my sleep but it's fine. I'll be fine. If you don't hear from me, just assume I died and went on to become dinner.
ANDREW (5:46 P.M.): circle of life ✌️
MOM (5:47 P.M.): That reminds me: do you ever hear from Olivia Grant?

Margot swallowed hard. No one, not even her family, knew the specifics of her relationship—or *non*relationship—with Olivia. Mom *maybe* knew about her crush, but as far everyone else was concerned, she and Olivia had only ever been friends. Best friends. Margot had never seen the point in telling them otherwise. There wasn't anything worth telling.

MARGOT (5:49 P.M.): Funny story actually. My new roommate IS Olivia Grant.

MARGOT (5:49 P.M.): Small world, huh?

ANDREW (5:50 P.M.): whoa weird

CAMERON (5:51 P.M.): I thought she was married to Brad Taylor?

DAD (5:52 P.M.): No, they split up last year.

Margot shut her eyes. Okay, that was enough family time.

MARGOT (5:53 P.M.): Sorry got to go! I have plans. Talk soon. 🖤

ANDREW (5:54 P.M.): "plans"

CAMERON (5:54 P.M.): Avoid petting her stomach and hind area.

ANDREW (5:55 P.M.): what the fuck

ANDREW (5:55 P.M.): boundaries bro

MOM (5:57 P.M.): I think Cameron was talking about the cat, honey.

Margot threw her phone down on the bed and pressed the heels of her hands into her eyes until a kaleidoscope of bright colors and funky shapes danced behind her lids. *Avoid petting her stomach and hind area.*

And *awesome*, now Margot was thinking about touching Olivia, how Olivia liked to be touched, *where* Olivia liked to be touched.

This was wrong. Olivia was right next door. Margot had no business thinking about how impossibly soft Olivia's skin was or how her blush spread all the way to her belly button when Margot undressed her. It was wrong to think about the way Olivia's bottom lip trembled when she whispered the word *please* or how her breath had stuttered when Margot had put her mouth at the crease of her thigh. How her fingers had tangled in Margot's hair, not afraid to pull, and how her voice had cracked on Margot's name when she came. How she bruised so easily, imprints of Margot's mouth left behind on the soft curve of Olivia's stomach and hips and the sides of her breasts and how Margot had wondered if, days after, Olivia had gotten herself off, one hand pressed against those marks and the other buried between her thighs.

Down the hall, the bathroom door shut. Margot dropped her hands, blinking into the brightness of her room.

Fuck.

So much for not thinking about it.

Margot pressed her thighs together, heat rising in her face, a miracle her glasses hadn't fogged. The throbbing between her legs was persistent and hard to ignore, harder because she wasn't entirely sure she wanted to ignore it.

Things were awkward enough between them without having

to look Olivia in the eye over a bowl of breakfast cereal with the knowledge that she'd rubbed one out to thoughts of her. Not years ago, but *now*.

There was a line and that was certain to cross it.

Even if Margot didn't care, if she threw caution to the wind and said *fuck it*, that thoughts were thoughts and they didn't mean anything unless she allowed them to, the walls were paper-thin.

She glanced at her phone. She could do what she'd done in the past and put on music to drown out the sound of her vibrator or—

The bathroom door opened, the sound of some Taylor Swift song carrying down the hall before shutting off. A second later, Olivia's bedroom door closed.

Margot drummed her fingers against her bedspread. *Or* she could kill two birds with one stone and take care of herself in the shower, where the water would muffle her noises. That sounded like a much better plan.

Reaching into her nightstand, Margot dug around, searching for—no, not that vibrator, she wanted . . . that one. No bells or whistles, just a tried-and-true, waterproof bullet vibe.

Margot carried it over to her dresser, quickly shuffling through her drawers for a pair of sweats, a tee, and some underwear. Margot bundled the vibrator inside her fresh clothes and made it halfway across the room before doubling back, snagging her phone and swiping open her Spotify app. Clothes cradled to her chest, Margot opened the door and stepped out into the hall—

"*Oof.*"

She and Olivia collided with enough force to knock her off balance, causing her to drop everything in her hands as she steadied herself against the wall. Her glasses slipped, and Margot quickly slid them up the bridge of her nose.

Olivia was barefoot, her toenails painted a pale lavender, her big toes a deeper shade of purple. Her long legs were bare, too, her towel barely covering the tops of her thighs, the edge of the towel straining against her breasts. Margot's gut clenched, her mouth going dry at the unexpected sight of Olivia standing in the middle of the hall, mostly naked.

"Sorry." Olivia blushed, hugging her arms around her body. "I left my, um, my clothes in . . ." Her eyes, already averted, widened to the size of saucers. "In my bedroom . . ."

Margot frowned and followed Olivia's gaze to the floor where her own bundle of clothing had fallen, and beside it, her bright blue vibrator.

"Um." Margot puffed out her cheeks, a wicked flush winding its way up her jaw.

Words failed her. There was no mistaking the vibrator for anything other than exactly what it was and—she wasn't *ashamed*. She masturbated, big fucking deal. Margot was the friend her other friends came to for sex toy recommendations. She was *happy* to talk about sex, solo or otherwise. But there was a distinct difference between telling Elle that buying a vibe with suction-magic technology would be a life changer, and Olivia—*Olivia*—knowing Margot had concrete plans to get off, not at some indistinct point in the future but *right here right now* in the shower they now shared.

Shit. If she couldn't speak, she should at least *move.* Pick it up. Do *something* other than stand there staring at her vibrator like it was going to sprout legs and hightail it back into her bedroom. Huh. That *would* be a nifty feature.

Right. *Moving.* Margot cleared her throat and stepped away from the wall she'd plastered herself against. Olivia's eyes darted further down the hall, before widening even more.

"Cat, no!"

Margot followed Olivia's gaze just in time to witness Cat crouch low, her butt wiggling from side to side, once, twice before she propelled herself through the air, pouncing on Margot's vibrator.

A low buzz filled the hall as the bullet whirred to life. Cat hissed, as if surprised, before wrapping her front legs around the vibe, contorting herself into a tight little ball, bunny-kicking her prey.

Olivia clapped her hands together briskly. "Cat, stop it. *Stop.*" She clutched her towel to her chest and approached Cat with caution. "Let it go. *Bad kitty.*"

Cat froze, curled up in her ball, pointy teeth pressed against the silicone.

"Go." Olivia made a shooing gesture. *"Go."*

Cat let out an indignant meow before sprinting down the hall at breakneck speed, fleeing the scene of the crime. Margot's bullet vibe skittered atop the hardwood floor, buzzing louder, yet somehow not as loud as the blood roaring inside her skull.

"Um." Olivia bent down, hand faltering in the air for a

split second before she scooped Margot's vibrator off the floor. She turned it over, biting her lip as she studied the base, making a soft "*Aha*" as she found the *power* button and pressed it. She cleared her throat and held the now-silent toy out for Margot to take. "You, uh"—she winced—"might want to wash that?"

Margot was pretty sure her soul had left her body. There was a strange lightness to her limbs as she reached out, taking her vibrator, clutching it awkwardly. Wash it. Right. There was black fur stuck to the silicone, not to mention cat spit.

She stared at Olivia, words continuing to fail her.

Olivia stared back, face flushed neon, her lips twitching. She jerked her chin at the vibrator. "I guess it's safe to say that's . . . pussy approved."

Olivia snorted, and that was just—Margot crunched forward, convulsing with laughter.

She couldn't quit. Each time it felt like she could stop if she could just get a breath in, she'd glance at Olivia, red-faced and shaking, and it would start all over again, the laughter building and building and building on itself. She wasn't even sure *why* she was laughing, only that she was, wheezing and sputtering and gagging on her own spit, and it felt like she couldn't breathe.

"I—I can't believe you *said that*," Margot sputtered. "That was so bad."

Everything ached from the soreness in the back of her throat to the burn in her stomach muscles, but it wasn't *bad*. Once she could breathe again, her chest unknotted and it was almost refreshing. Cleansing.

Olivia slumped against the wall, wiping tears from the corners of her eyes. "*I* can't believe my cat tried to kill your vibrator."

The chances of Margot ever being able to use this vibrator without thinking of this moment were slim. Besides, there were tiny teeth marks in the silicone. The toy was pretty much done for.

But she didn't say that. She didn't say much of anything, words dying in her throat when Olivia shifted, towel parting, revealing the bare curve of her hip, silvery pink stretch marks on display. Margot had never wanted to trace someone's skin with her tongue so terribly in her life while simultaneously wanting to melt through the floor, residual mortification leaving her dizzy.

Olivia's laughter petered off, her face pink and her eyes bright. Her tongue darted out to wet her bottom lip, chest rising and falling a little faster as she met Margot's stare.

"Well." Margot averted her eyes and rolled her lips together. "I'm going to go and . . . I don't know . . . crawl inside a hole."

Olivia ducked her chin, doing a shitty job of smothering her smirk. "I don't know." She shrugged and looked up through her spun-gold lashes. "You've got to admit, this was one hell of a way to break the ice."

Margot scoffed out a laugh. "Fair enough."

"If you aren't busy"—Olivia's eyes dipped to the vibrator, and another wave of heat crashed over Margot—"did you want to have that talk?"

"Talk?" Margot echoed.

Olivia's brows rose. "You know. Logistics."

Right. *Logistics.* She nodded briskly. "Sure. Meet you in the living room?"

Olivia smiled. "Let me get dressed and I'll be right there."

Chapter Five

Olivia took a seat on the free cushion beside Margot, tucking her legs under her. On the television, an old episode of *Three's Company* cut to commercial.

Margot held her laptop steady atop her knees as she leaned forward, grabbing the remote off the coffee table and muting the television. "One sec. Let me tweet this . . . and done."

"If you're busy, that's fine," Olivia said. "We can talk later."

"It's all good. See?" She swiveled her laptop so Olivia could see the screen. Her browser was open to Twitter.

Olivia took a closer look.

What TV Show Should You Watch with Your Roommate Based on Their Zodiac Sign?

Aries—*2 Broke Girls*
Taurus—*Broad City*
Gemini—*Two and a Half Men*
Cancer—*New Girl*

Leo—*Friends*
Virgo—*The Odd Couple*
Libra—*The Golden Girls*
Scorpio—*Don't Trust the B— in Apartment 23*
Sagittarius—*The Big Bang Theory*
Capricorn—*Will & Grace*
Aquarius—*Mork & Mindy*
Pisces—*Three's Company*

"Content creation for Oh My Stars," Margot explained.

"I always kind of wondered how you came up with these."

"It's basically distilling whatever the list items are to their main properties. So, with television shows, it would be the theme or the relationship between the characters or . . . vibe." Margot cracked a smile. "It's not an exact science."

Olivia grinned.

"Then I match them to the zodiac signs based on their most significant traits. I'm not saying if you're a Gemini your favorite TV show featuring a roommate relationship is *The Odd Couple*, I'm just positing that it's the show that most closely captures the traits of that sign." Margot shrugged. "And if it doesn't feel like a good fit, you should check your rising sign. Same goes for horoscopes. You're actually better off checking your rising sign since that's what determines the houses in your chart. Your horoscope for the day or week or month or whatever time frame takes into consideration the transits of the planets and how they move through the different areas of your chart. Your rising sign gives you a more complete picture."

She scanned the list, stopping at Libra. "*The Golden Girls.* Fair enough."

For some reason, Margot laughed. "Sorry. That's just, um, a very Libra reaction. *Fair enough.*"

She'd missed Margot's laugh, how it started in her chest and seemed to burst from her lips, throaty and smoky. "Question— I've always wondered, how does compatibility work? With astrology?"

Hopefully that was much smoother than *what's your sign?* Besides, she already knew Margot was an Aries.

Margot's brows rose. "Synastry? That's . . . Well, there are a few aspects you can look at. Aspects are the angles between planets and other celestial bodies and points of interest in a chart. There are hard aspects, which can pose a challenge, and easier aspects, which are . . . harmonious, I guess is the right word. With synastry, you can overlay the charts or there's software that does it, and you can see how person A's planets aspect person B's and what houses of the chart they activate and vice versa."

Olivia kept her eyes on the screen. It felt like her heart was going to punch through her rib cage, but hopefully her voice wouldn't warble. "So, say, Aries and Libra? What kind of aspect do they make? Are they, um, compatible?"

Margot shrugged. *Shrugged.* Olivia bit off her sigh before it could escape her.

It wasn't so much that she cared about their astrological compatibility but that she'd hoped the question might serve as a stepping-stone of sorts. That Margot's reaction might give Olivia a hint at what was going on inside Margot's head, not just now, but years before. Why everything between them had been so good, brimming with possibility, a whole future ahead of them, until Margot had pushed her away.

All Olivia wanted was a little clarity. She'd call it closure, but something about that word put a terrible taste in her mouth.

"They're directly opposite to one another, which can bring balance to a relationship since each sign possesses qualities the other lacks. But it's a bit more complicated than that. Everyone thinks of sun-sun compatibility, but that's a tiny, *tiny* piece of the puzzle. There's sun-moon, moon-moon, Venus-Mars, moon-Venus—it all depends on what you're looking for. Good communication, similar values, interests. The seventh house is where we tend to look for information on partnerships like marriage, but the fifth house is about passion—not just sex, but that, too—and the eighth house rules sex as well, but in a transformational, even transactional sense? There's a lot to look at." Margot pursed her lips. "But compatibility isn't my area of expertise." She cringed. "*Astrological* compatibility isn't my area of expertise."

Olivia crept even closer to the edge of the couch until her knee gently butted up against Margot's right arm. "You explained it really well."

Margot turned her head, and, without makeup on, Olivia could make out the tiny spray of freckles on the bridge of her nose. The left corner of her mouth rose in a half-hearted smile. "Thanks." She lowered the screen on her laptop before setting it on the coffee table. "All right. Roommate logistics."

"Right." Olivia nodded. "I made a list."

Margot's brows rose. "You made a list?"

"Just to organize my thoughts. I didn't want to forget anything." Olivia smoothed the edges of the paper against her bare thigh. "I haven't had a roommate since freshman year of college—I lived with Brad, but that was different—so this is all kind of new."

Margot folded her arms atop her knees. "Feel free to tell me to fuck off, but can I ask you a personal question?"

Something about the way she'd phrased that, straddling the line between bluntness and propriety, made Olivia laugh. It was so perfectly Margot. "I think we passed *personal* a while ago, don't you?"

It was only after the words were out that she realized how Margot might take them. Olivia had only meant with the whole *plucking Margot's vibrator up off the floor after her cat had tried to maul it* thing. Not *I know what face you make when you come* personal. But that, too.

Margot's tongue swept against her bottom lip. "You and Brad wanted different things. What does that mean?"

Olivia dragged her eyes from Margot's mouth before she got caught staring. "It's kind of a long story."

Margot's expression shuttered. "If you don't want to talk about it—"

"No, that's not it." She didn't relish talking about it, no, but more than that she didn't know where to start. It was a mess. A drama-filled mess. "Long story short, Brad wanted a baby and I didn't."

Children had never been and would never be what she wanted, and she'd told Brad that from day one, but then she'd turned twenty-six and he'd started dropping hints. He'd called them jokes at first, and she'd rolled her eyes and laughed—her mistake. But it kept happening. And then one day Brad had asked her point-blank when they were going to start a family. The saddest part was that all along, she'd been under the impression they already were a family.

Margot frowned. "You never wanted kids."

"He thought I would change my mind, I guess."

Olivia had budged on practically everything else; Brad had assumed this—a baby—would be the same.

"Brad thought you would change your mind." Margot's eyes narrowed. "Or he thought he could change it for you?"

Olivia forced a laugh past the lump in her throat. "Am I really that transparent?"

She'd always admired Margot's quiet confidence, how Margot knew what she wanted and she didn't let anyone stop her from going after it. How easily she could tune out other people's opinions of her or her dreams. Olivia wasn't built that way, wasn't brave like Margot was, didn't know how to live by *do what you love and fuck the rest*. It took Olivia forever to make decisions, and she cared too much about what people thought. It wasn't anything for her to be proud of, but she'd never felt quite so ashamed of it as she did now, Margot looking at her like she felt sorry for her.

"I guess I just know you." Margot rested her head against the back of the couch. "Or I did."

Did. Olivia hated that, that the entirety of their friendship existed in the past tense. Back when they were in school, she never would have imagined the possibility that a *week* would go by without her speaking to Margot, let alone *years*. But of course she wouldn't have. No one ever dreams of their problems when they think about the future.

"Anyway, Brad wanted a baby and I didn't, and when I made it crystal clear he seemed to accept it. Or I thought he did." For a split second, her chest constricted, making it difficult to breathe. "I hadn't told my dad the specifics, but he knew things between Brad and I weren't great and I wasn't happy. He suggested we go to couples counseling, which we did, *once*. It didn't do much because Brad was different there . . . more open, but less honest? If that makes sense."

Margot nibbled on her lip, listening intently.

"After that didn't work, Dad finally told me if I wasn't happy, I should . . . consider my options. Which was surprising, because Dad always got along with Brad. I mean, they still get along, which is good. I'm glad Dad has someone in town who he could call if he needed something. Anyway, I didn't want to. Consider my options. I made a commitment. I figured every couple has a rough patch." Olivia picked at her nails. How was this *still* difficult to talk about? "Then Emmy Caldwell—you remember her from school, right?—showed up at my front door to tell me she and Brad had been sleeping together for the past six months and she was pretty sure she was pregnant with his baby."

"Jesus, Liv," Margot murmured. "That's . . . *shit*."

Olivia sniffled then laughed, even though it wasn't funny. It was either laugh or cry and she'd cried enough over Brad to last a lifetime. "It was pretty awful. I was shocked? I don't—maybe I shouldn't have been. There were probably signs, and the fact that I'd missed them speaks to how bad things between Brad and me had become. Anyway, I moved back in with my dad and I filed for divorce and we didn't have many assets—we were renting the house from his parents—and he didn't contest the filing, so it all moved pretty quickly. Within six weeks, we were divorced."

"Damn, Liv. I don't really know what to say." Margot reached out and squeezed Olivia's shoulder.

Olivia didn't mean to, but she swayed into Margot's touch, into the warmth of her hand seeping through the thin cotton of Olivia's T-shirt.

She'd received plenty of warnings and advice before moving to Seattle, from Dad and from the internet. No one had ever warned her of the very specific loneliness that came with living in a city where you knew no one, how easy it was to become touch-starved. *Of course* she leaned into Margot's touch. She was honestly surprised she didn't climb into Margot's lap and *purr*.

"There's nothing *to* say, really. It was a mess." She snorted. "Want to know the real kicker?"

Margot dropped her hand and cringed. "Do I?"

"Turns out, Emmy wasn't even pregnant. Total false alarm. She found out and didn't say anything to Brad because she was worried he'd . . . I don't know, change his mind or something." Which he had. He'd called and left voicemails and finally knocked on Olivia's front door, begging her to come back, alternating between issuing apologies and being irate when she didn't swoon. It was too late for that. "Long story short, I married the wrong guy. Wrong person."

Her heart stuttered when all Margot did was stare.

"Anyway, enough about me." Olivia curled her fingers around the edge of the list of roommate logistics she'd compiled, leaving damp fingerprints behind that turned the paper translucent. "I'll just start at the top here. Laundry."

"It might help if I told you where that was, huh?" Margot rolled her eyes at herself. "It's in the basement, which is significantly less creepy than it sounds. Promise. You've got to use your key—the one for the outside door—to get inside, so it's pretty secure. The lighting's a fluorescent nightmare, but they put in new washers and dryers last year. Everything's high-efficiency, so you don't have to worry about wasting umpteen quarters to make sure your shit's dry."

She was just happy there was laundry on-site. "I think I might run a load of darks before bed. I can throw yours in with mine, if you want."

For some inexplicable reason, the tips of Margot's ears went pink. "It's fine."

"Are you sure? Because I don't mind." Laundry was one of those tasks she actually enjoyed, unlike washing dishes, which she did, but not without massive amounts of internal grumbling.

Margot nibbled on her lip for a moment before laughing under her breath. "You know what? Sure. You handled my vibrator, like, ten minutes ago. I guess touching my underwear is pretty tame by comparison."

Handled wasn't quite the word Olivia would have used. In a perfect world, her ideal scenario of how she might handle Margot's vibrator would've included far less clothing.

"All right." She forced herself to focus back on the list instead of the fantasy playing out inside her head. "Let's see. I, uh, kind of googled a list of crucial conversations to have with a new roommate, but some of these sound silly since . . ." Her tongue darted out, wetting her bottom lip. "Like you said, we know each other. Unless you developed any allergies I don't know about . . ."

"It would be news to me."

Olivia smiled. "I guess we don't really need to talk about pets, since you're already *well* aware I have a cat."

Margot snorted. "I don't know. I asked Cameron what I needed to know about cats. He didn't give me much to work off, but something tells me *nothing* could've prepared me for what happened in the hall."

At least she was able to laugh about it. This would've been painfully awkward had Margot been pissed.

"How are your brothers, by the way?" she asked. "Cameron's working as a vet, right?"

If Margot's earlier statement hadn't been a clue, Olivia was pretty sure she'd seen his name added to the sign outside the animal clinic a few years back.

"Mm-hmm." A soft smile crossed Margot's face. "He is. And Andrew's down in San Diego, working on his master's in marine biology. They're both good. My parents, too."

Even if they'd spent more time at Olivia's house growing up, Olivia had always liked Margot's family. They were loud and expressive and had always made Olivia feel welcome. "I'm happy to hear that."

"My mom actually asked if I'd heard from you. I told her you were living here now."

Not for the first time, Olivia wondered whether Margot had told her family, *anyone*, what had happened between them. Even leaving out the specifics, just that *something* had happened. It was unlikely. "Bet that took her by surprise."

Margot shrugged. "Kind of? I think she thought you were still married. I know Cam thought you were. Dad knew." Margot's nose wrinkled. "He's such a damned gossip."

Olivia chuckled. "Is he still teaching?"

"Nah. He retired . . . two years ago? Being home all the time is driving him nuts, so says my mom, at least. So what does he decide to do? He joins the HOA and this local book club full of grannies. I swear, you can't sneeze in that town without my dad knowing about it."

Olivia clapped a hand over her mouth. "I think I know the book club you're talking about. Brad's grandmother—the one who actually liked me—is a member."

She was pretty sure they didn't even *read* the books they selected, they just got together to drink and dish the dirt.

"And *that* would explain how he knew about you and Brad." Margot shut her eyes and laughed softly. "Leave it to my dad." She opened her eyes, hair sweeping against the sharp curve of her jaw when she tilted her head to the side. "How's your dad doing, by the way?"

"He's good." Olivia swallowed hard. "I mean, he's doing better now. He, um, he had a heart attack at the same time I was going through the divorce. So, almost a year ago?"

"Jesus, Liv." Margot's brow puckered. "I'm really sorry to hear that."

Talking about this put a lump in her throat she hadn't expected, but maybe she should've. Margot was the first person she'd told, the first person she'd talked about this with outside of doctors and nurses and hospital staff and Brad. Her friends from school had all moved away, and the ones who had moved back or never left had all acted like divorce was contagious. They'd all been polite, but that was it. An act.

Margot had never been like that. With Margot, what you saw was what you got, and Olivia had *always* been a fan of what she'd seen.

"Thanks." Olivia tucked her hair behind her ears and scratched the side of her neck. "It was mild. As mild as a heart attack *can* be, I guess. I had planned on moving to Seattle right after the divorce was finalized, but then *that* happened, so I stuck around for a few more months until Dad practically pushed me out the front door. Told me I was hovering and driving him nuts." She picked at her cuticles. "I wouldn't have dreamed of leaving town had his bloodwork been anything less than stellar."

Even then, a tiny voice in the back of her mind that sounded suspiciously like Brad still whispered that she was selfish for leaving, for putting herself first, even though Dad was fine.

"I'm glad he's okay," Margot said.

"Me too." They shared a smile before Olivia dropped her eyes, scanning the list again. "Communal spaces. How do you want to handle the vacuuming and that sort of thing?"

"I try to vacuum and Swiffer at least once a week. Same with cleaning the bathroom." Margot ran her hand down the front of her shin, tugging the fabric of her leggings smooth. "We could trade off?"

"I'll clean the bathroom this week and you can do the floors and then next week we'll switch. Does that work?"

"Sure. Sounds good to me." Margot drummed her fingers against her legs. "Also, I'm sure you already saw, but there's a whiteboard on the side of the fridge in case we're out of something. Milk or whatever. I mean, we can text, obviously, but sometimes it's nice to have a reminder right there in the kitchen."

"Perfect." Olivia snagged a pen off the coffee table and jotted down a quick note. "Whiteboard for notes. Got it. Okay, let's see . . . trash. Is there a chute or do we need to haul it down to the dumpster?"

"There's a chute. Down the hall, to the left." Margot rested her chin on her knee.

Olivia dropped her gaze back to the list. "Do you have any pet peeves I should know about?"

"That you don't already know?" Margot huffed out a laugh. "I don't know. None come to mind."

"Nothing? Nothing at all?"

Margot shrugged. "I work from home—well, sometimes I'll go to Elle's, but usually I'm here—and I'm not very easily distracted. I don't need complete silence to focus or anything. I do occasionally record for our video series and sometimes I'll hop on Instagram Live for Q&As, but I do that in my room, so as long as you don't crank your music ridiculously loud, it's fine."

"No blaring music, got it."

"How about you? Any pet peeves I should know about?"

Olivia smirked. "Somehow I don't foresee you leaving the toilet seat up, so not really."

Margot cringed. "I feel like there's a story behind that."

Unfortunately. "Brad was constantly forgetting to put the seat down. I got up to pee in the middle of the night and fell in. I'm talking legs up in the air, ass all the way down in the bowl."

"Oh, shit."

"It was awful. I had one of those Ty-D-Bol cleaner tablets in the tank, you know, the ones that turn the water blue? It stained my skin. I walked around looking like a Smurf from the waist down for two days before I got to the store and bought a better loofah."

Margot clapped a hand over her mouth, muffling her chuckle. "It's not funny. It's just . . . the visual."

"It's a little funny," Olivia conceded.

"Not that I picture it being a problem, but note to self, never leave the lid up. Anything else?"

Olivia folded her list in half and ran her nail down the seam, forming a sharp crease. "Should we talk about bringing people home?"

Margot fumbled her phone. "What?"

"If I wanted to have a couple friends over." She didn't have many close friends, not anymore, but she'd had Kira over for drinks once or twice, and Margot obviously had a tight-knit circle of friends.

"Friends." Margot nodded quickly. "Oh yeah. That's—that's totally fine."

"Cool. I would text you first, if you weren't home. You know, so you wouldn't walk in and wonder who these strange people were in your apartment."

"Same." Margot blew out a breath that ruffled her bangs, the flush along her cheeks not quite fading. "I'd, um, do the same. If I have my friends over."

She kept underscoring that. *Friends* as opposed to some alternative—

Wow. Okay, Olivia could see where her initial question might've been open to interpretation. Not that she planned on having dates over. Olivia had done *casual* exactly once, and look how well that had turned out for her. Not that she'd known it was casual at the time. Not that it mattered. The point was moot.

She wasn't going to be bringing anyone home unless they were friends, and what Margot did was her business. Olivia didn't need to know, and she wasn't about to ask.

Chapter Six

"*I*t's open!"

Margot let herself inside Darcy and Elle's apartment for game night, leaving her boots at the door. *No shoes inside* was Darcy's rule, not Elle's, but one Margot was happy to follow. As much as she enjoyed *playfully* ruffling Darcy's feathers, Margot had zero desire to discover what Darcy would do if she were to track dirt on the impeccable—if not impractical—cream-colored carpet.

Sitting on the floor with her back to the door, Elle didn't so much as lift her head when Margot entered the living room. "There's wine in the kitchen. Don't worry, it's the good stuff."

By *good stuff*, Elle meant *of the boxed variety*, as opposed to Darcy's favorite wine, the price as difficult to stomach as the name was to pronounce. *Good* was a bit of an overstatement in Margot's book, but she'd take Franzia any day over a glass of wine so expensive she'd feel guilty drinking it.

"You do realize I could be anybody, right?" Margot veered to the right, careful not to slip as she stepped from carpet onto the kitchen tile, her socks offering no grip. "I could've been a murderer for all you knew, and you invited me in."

"Murderers don't knock, Margot," Elle said from the other room.

"You don't know that." Margot searched the cabinet for something sturdier than Darcy's thin-stemmed wineglasses. Game night called for durability, not delicacy. "I'm sure that's what they want you to think. Lull you into a false sense of security all while hiding in plain sight."

"You've been watching too much true crime again, haven't you?" Elle sounded amused.

"It was a true-crime podcast, actually." Margot grabbed a stemless glass from the back of the cabinet and filled it with rosé before returning to the living room.

"I thought I heard voices." Darcy stepped out from the hall. "Brendon and Annie still aren't here?"

Elle shook her head. "Not yet. They had to stop by the nursery, remember?"

"Excuse me?" Margot must've misheard her. "Did you just say *nursery*?"

Darcy snickered. "I'm going to finish this report. If I'm not out by the time they get here, come get me."

"Um, hello, can we please address what you just said about Brendon and Annie stopping by a *nursery*?"

"A *plant* nursery, Mar." Elle giggled. "Oh my God. If you could see your face."

"Okay, color me confused. It's game night. What do we need plants for?"

Elle gestured to the coffee table, and for the first time, Margot actually examined everything Elle had laid out, beyond the gel pens and Sharpies. A spool of twine rested beside a pair of scissors, two differently sized hole punches, and a stack of cobalt-colored card stock. Two boxes of flat-bottomed glass globes had been shoved beneath the coffee table beside a folded plastic tarp.

This didn't look like game night. This looked like Margot was about to get suckered into her three least favorite letters—DIY.

Margot groaned. "But it's game night."

And she'd been looking forward to this for weeks. Letting loose with a little wine and trouncing her friends at board games. It was supposed to be the highlight of her week.

"We'll totally have time for charades after," Elle promised. "Annie's swamped with work, and she asked if we could help her with the wedding favors."

"They couldn't, I don't know, hand out mini bottles of booze instead?"

Elle gestured to the spread atop the coffee table. "They're buying mini succulents so every guest can have their own little love fern."

It was a bit of an inside joke between Brendon and Annie, a play on the love fern in *How to Lose a Guy in 10 Days*. Brendon had gifted Annie with a miniature succulent, dubbing it their love fern, hard to kill.

"Cheesy, yet adorable," Margot conceded.

Elle leaned back, resting her weight on her hands. "A little *cheese* never hurt anyone." She wrinkled her nose. "Unless you're lactose intolerant like Darcy, but that's only if you're being literal."

Margot snorted. "True."

"Come on, Mar." Elle snagged a handful of markers and spread them out like a fan. "It's arts and crafts! What's not to love?"

"What's not to love?" She set her wine on the table atop one of Darcy's fancy marble coasters and lifted her left wrist. "I'm pretty sure I got carpal tunnel from addressing wedding invites, because I couldn't climb for over a week." She schooled her expression in an attempt to unequivocally express how serious this was. "I couldn't masturbate without my elbow twinging, Elle."

"Oh, boo-hoo."

Margot took back every good thing she'd ever said about Elle, who was not actually a ray of sunshine but instead a heartless monster. "Excuse me, Miss *I have a girlfriend who will make me come whenever I damn well please.*"

"You know, you, too, could have a girlfriend who gives you orgasms whenever you want, if you'd ever actually—"

"No." Margot held up a hand. "Thanks."

Margot liked her life the way it was. *Exactly* the way it was. Uncomplicated. She had her friends, her business with Elle was solid, and if she needed to scratch an itch she could either do it herself or find someone to do it for her, no strings attached. Nothing needed to change.

"Okay. Backing off." Elle frowned. "Do you really not want to help with the wedding favors? Because the four of us could probably get together another time if you'd rather skip it."

Margot puffed out her cheeks, shoulders slumping. No, she

didn't want that, to be left out. "No, of course I want to help. You know me. I just have to bitch about it first. Get it out of my system, you know? I promise I will be nothing but sunshine and rainbows when Brendon and Annie get here."

"*No one* expects that of you, Margot." Elle stuck out a socked foot—they were toe socks, fuzzy and bright blue—and nudged Margot's leg. "We like you exactly as you are."

"Brazen and bitchy?" Margot chuckled under her breath, only halfway joking.

Elle smiled. "Bold and no bullshit."

Margot ducked her chin. "Shucks, Elle. You're going to make me blush."

Someone knocked on the front door.

"Come in!" Elle shouted.

Annie stepped into the living room, Brendon close behind, each carrying a small pallet containing easily four dozen succulents.

"Hey." Annie beamed. "Can I set these down somewhere?"

As if summoned by the mere idea of dirt winding up on her carpets, Darcy appeared. "There's a tarp under the coffee table."

Elle snagged it and shook it out, laying it flat atop the floor so Annie and Brendon could set the plants down.

After making two more trips out to the car to retrieve yet *more* succulents, Brendon clapped his hands together and, with a zeal that Margot usually reserved for happy hour and BOGO shoe sales, said, "Let's get this party started."

Tongue poking out from between his lips, Brendon finished tying off a twine bow with a quiet little *ha* of delight. He wiped his hands on his knees and reached across the table, making a grab for Margot's Reese's Pieces.

She smacked his hand aside. "Excuse you."

Brendon laughed. "You're so weird about sharing food."

"You try growing up with two brothers and talk to me about sharing food." Margot popped a Reese's Piece in her mouth. "I swear if it wasn't glued down, they'd tried to eat it. It's a dog-eat-dog world." She grinned. "Every man for himself."

Elle snickered. "There's more in the kitchen, Brendon."

Brendon stood and saluted Elle before disappearing around the corner.

"So, Margot," Annie said. "How's the roommate situation working out? You and Olivia getting along?"

Did an immense amount of—what she was pretty sure was mutual—sexual tension count as *getting along*?

Work seemed to keep Olivia busy. Whether that was a regular thing for her or Brendon and Annie's last-minute wedding required overtime, Margot wasn't sure. Either way, Olivia had been out of the apartment all day yesterday, coming home after Margot had already crawled into bed. Margot had only seen her briefly this morning. Olivia had smiled sleepily, dashing out the door with a travel mug of coffee in hand, offering a soft *have a nice day* over her shoulder.

Margot had wandered into the kitchen for her own cup of coffee, drawing up short at the sight of a smiley face scribbled on the refrigerator whiteboard and fresh flowers in a vase—an actual one made of glass, not the plastic pitcher that pulled double duty on the rare occasions Margot got flowers—on the breakfast bar.

It was taking a little time for her to get used to coming out of her bedroom to find Olivia curled up on the couch, Cat purring away innocently from the windowsill, but it wasn't *bad*. A little stiff and stilted still, but getting better. Margot actually liked it.

"She hasn't stolen my credit card, let her ant farm loose, or gone on a hallucinogenic bender and peed in my closet, if that's what you're wondering." Margot fixed the bow on her last globe. No matter what she did, it came out crooked, hanging sad and lopsided, nothing at all like Darcy's impeccable bows, with their pristine symmetrical loops. Oh well. Done was better than perfect. "Her cat did try to kill my vibrator, though. So that was fun."

Silence followed for a beat, two beats—

"Is that a . . . metaphor?" Darcy asked.

Annie bent forward laughing, slapping her knee. "Her pussy killed your vibrator. Holy hell, what's it made of?"

Darcy snickered. "Her vagina or the sex toy?"

"Either!" Annie wiped her eyes. "Wait, better question— what's her kegel routine? I am *impressed*."

"Is no one going to address the question of *why* Margot's sharing sex toys with her new roommate?" Elle frowned. "Not judging, but I think there are more appropriate ways to make someone feel welcome."

Annie waggled her brows.

"Filthy minds, all of you." Margot huffed, sidestepping her history with Olivia. "I meant her actual cat. *Cat*. She pounced on it. Tore up the silicone. I had to toss it."

"This isn't awkward at all," Brendon muttered.

"Oh, please, I've seen your bare, freckled ass doing unspeakable things to Annie in the middle of my kitchen, unspeakable things that required me to metaphorically bleach my brain so that I could continue to look you in the eye," Margot said.

He smiled sheepishly. "Fair point."

"So yeah, aside from my vibrator's premature death, things are good."

"You should've invited her," Brendon said. "Tonight. That would've been fun."

Everyone nodded.

Margot let herself imagine what it would be like if she were to bring Olivia along to a game night. They might have even numbers for a change. Margot's eyes swept the room, lingering on Annie's head propped against Brendon's shoulder and Darcy's hand resting on Elle's thigh, the way they seemed to naturally gravitate toward one another without even thinking about it.

She sucked in a shaky breath. Even numbers might be nice.

"Maybe next time."

Margot shifted, crossing her legs the other way, frowning when something poked her in the hip. She leaned back, wiggled her hand inside the pocket of her jeans, the tips of her fingers brushing up against—what was that? Folded paper? Odd. She didn't remember leaving anything in her pockets, and she'd just washed these jeans yesterday.

The paper gave, slipping free. In Margot's hand was a folded rectangle of notebook paper, the kind torn free from a composition notebook, blue lines bisecting the page. It had been folded meticulously, with care, the creases clean, the flap tucked just so, a perfect miniature envelope. Margot flipped it over. A heart, drawn in pink gel pen, adorned the front. There was no name, not that it needed one. There was no doubt who it was from.

Careful not to rip the paper, Margot unfolded the tiny origami envelope by pulling on the tucked flap. The paper gave easily, opening in her hand.

Have a great day ☺

The way her lips curved in a replica of the smiley doodled on the paper was completely involuntary.

Margot hadn't done laundry yesterday. *Olivia* had, and she'd left Margot a note, the exact kind they'd stealthily passed each other during class.

Suddenly warm, Margot folded the paper back up, returning it to her pocket the way she'd found it. When she lifted her head, Elle was staring at her, head cocked to the side curiously. Margot shook her head and mouthed, *"nothing,"* even though it felt like something. Something she didn't understand. Something she didn't want to try to explain.

She turned her attention to the TV. The movie they'd had playing in the background had ended, the Netflix home screen auto-playing a preview of a movie she hadn't seen.

"What do you guys want to put on next?"

Annie yawned. "I think I've got to call it a night, guys."

Margot double-checked the time. "It's not even eleven."

And they hadn't ever gotten to charades like Elle had promised.

Darcy stood, stretching her arms over her head. "Annie's right. I'm beat and we've got to wake up early."

Elle groaned. "Five a.m."

"What in God's name do you have to get up at five for?" Margot asked.

She was pretty sure, in all their years of friendship, that she'd never seen Elle awake at seven, not unless she'd pulled an all-nighter.

"Yoga class," Annie said, gathering the glasses from the table.

"Oh." Margot nodded slowly. "You guys are taking a yoga class. Together."

Without her.

Elle frowned. "We'd have invited you, but you hate yoga."

"I never said I *hated* yoga."

"You said the class I took you to *wasn't for you*," Darcy said.

True. Darcy had dragged Margot to a Slow Flow yoga class, and the instructor had gone on and on about *focusing on her flow* and *quieting her mind*, and all Margot had been able to think about was how she wasn't supposed to be thinking, chastising herself for thinking *about* thinking, wash, rise, repeat.

"Well, okay. Maybe I said that." Margot stood. "But you still could've asked."

One of Darcy's brows rose. "Even though you'd have said no?"

Margot crossed her arms. "Okay, when you put it like that, it sounds stupid."

She just wanted to be included. If she was going to opt out, she wanted it to be on her terms. Was that really so much to ask?

Elle smiled softly. "We'll definitely invite you next time."

"Thank you." Margot turned and nudged Brendon with her elbow. "Want to go climbing tomorrow?"

Brendon ran his fingers through his hair and winced. "Uh, I would, but see—"

"It's a couples' yoga class," Annie said, biting her lip.

Oh.

Margot dug her toes into the carpet. "You could've just said."

Preferably before she'd made a fool of herself, but whatever.

"Sorry," Elle blurted, blue eyes wide and apologetic. "We just thought—"

"It's fine." Margot waved her off with a breezy smile. "Like you said. I hate yoga anyway." Not as much as she hated being left out, granted.

Elle frowned. "You could still come."

"To *couples' yoga*?" Darcy arched a brow.

"Sometimes people show up without partners," Elle argued. "It's like on roller coasters when they put two single riders together. Or a single rider with two people. We could trade off poses like we do teams on game night." Elle smiled brightly. "Or the instructor could partner with you."

Margot would rather die. "Really. It's fine."

Elle's lips twisted to the side. "If you say so."

Margot quickly changed the subject. "We're still on for cake tasting, though, right? Saturday?"

Everyone nodded, slowly migrating in the direction of the

door. Margot trailed behind Brendon and Annie, letting them go on ahead.

Elle leaned against the open door. "Are you sure everything's good with you and Olivia?"

"Why wouldn't it be?"

"I don't know." Elle shrugged. "Just, you never mentioned her, and I was . . . wondering if there was a reason for that."

Not one that Margot wanted to discuss.

Rather than fib, Margot sidestepped Elle's question altogether. "We're fine, Elle. If something happens and that changes, I promise you'll be the first person I tell."

Chapter Seven

Incoming call: Brad

$\mathcal{A}$ pit formed in Olivia's stomach, somehow hollow and heavy at the same time.

Her thumb hovered over the screen. It would be so easy to swipe the call away, send Brad to voicemail. But knowing Brad, he'd just keep calling, even though it was after ten p.m.

Almost a year after their divorce had been finalized, and Brad still called her when he'd had too much to drink, and other times when he couldn't remember the name of the electrician they used or which company to call to service the heater. These were all things he should've known or been able to find out on his own, but he came to her instead, acting as if they were merely on a break, one more *off* patch in the history of their on-again, off-again relationship.

She took a deep, bracing breath and lifted the phone to her ear. "Brad."

For a second, there was nothing but heavy breathing and then, "Livvy? Hey."

She cringed at his co-opting of Dad's nickname for her. "What are you calling for, Brad?"

More heavy breathing. "I miss you."

Six months ago, Olivia might have felt a pang of . . . *something.* Bittersweetness. Nostalgia for what they'd had, a remembrance of early days, when Brad had still acted like he cared and she had believed they would grow old and gray together.

Now she was just annoyed. Not as annoyed as Brad would be when he woke up, hungover, but still pretty damn annoyed.

Brad wasn't happy when he'd had her, and now he wanted what he couldn't have.

"How much have you had to drink?"

"Not that much, Livvy," he slurred.

She rubbed her eyes. "You can't keep calling me like this. Drink some water and go to bed."

"I miss you, though. I just—I need someone to talk to. You're the only one I can talk to."

A spike of irritation ratcheted her pulse. She should just block Brad. Block his number and spare herself this frustration. But she couldn't. Not when there was always the chance that Brad would be calling because something had happened to Dad. Because Brad was a lot of things, selfish and arrogant and moody and not the person for her, but he'd always liked Dad, always gotten along with him. And he'd promised. Promised to let her know if anything happened. Olivia was obviously Dad's emergency contact, but he was so tight-lipped, so reluctant to make her worry. He'd driven himself to the damn hospital when he'd started having chest pains at work, and she'd only found out when she had because a nurse had called her.

Despite thinking Brad was a piece of work for what he'd put her through at the end of their marriage, Dad was still friendly with Brad's parents, was still polite when he ran into Brad around town. If something happened . . . Dad might not come right out and tell Brad, but maybe he'd let it slip. Or maybe Brad would hear something through the grapevine. He was Olivia's best connection—last and only connection, save for Dad—to the town.

"You've got to find someone else you can talk to, Brad. Call your mom or something. I'm sure she'd love a call from you."

"I don't wanna," Brad groaned petulantly.

The knob on the front door jiggled, and Olivia saw an out, an escape from this cluster of a conversation, a reason to end the call that wouldn't weigh on her conscience. "Look, I'm sorry, but I have to go. Drink some water and go to bed."

Olivia ended the call as the door swung open. Margot pitched her keys into the bowl on the entry table and shut the door, slumping against it, eyes closed.

Olivia set her phone down on the coffee table beside the shoe-box full of keepsakes she was sorting through, screen side down. She cleared her throat. "Hey."

Margot jumped, elbow slamming into the door. She hissed through her teeth, cradling her arm, and Olivia cringed in sympathy. That had to have hurt.

"Hey." Margot stepped into the room and gave a self-effacing chuckle, massaging her elbow. "It's going to take me a second to get used to that, living with someone again."

Olivia smiled. "You're home early."

Margot had left a note on the whiteboard that read *game night*, and Olivia had assumed she'd be home late, midnight at the earliest. It wasn't even a quarter past ten.

"Everyone has an early morning, apparently. Everyone *except* me." Margot pressed the heel of her hand into her eye and sighed. "Sorry. Ignore me. Didn't mean to rope you into joining my pity party." Margot dropped her chin and laughed softly, staring at the floor. "Probably not the sort of party planning you had in mind, huh?"

Margot didn't need to apologize, not to Olivia and certainly not for having feelings.

"Do you . . . want to talk about it?"

For a split second, it seemed like Margot might take Olivia up on her offer. She opened her mouth, then sighed and shook her head. "Nah. It's nothing."

"You sure?" Olivia prodded. "I'm happy to listen."

Margot raked her fingers through her hair and offered Olivia a tired smile. "I'm sure. I'll just sleep it off." She squinted. "What's that?"

"What's what?" Olivia followed Margot's bleary gaze to the coffee table. "Oh. I was just going through my boxes. Finally."

Margot stepped closer, surveying the explosion of photos smudged with fingerprints, lucky pennies, and ticket stubs. Olivia's corsage from junior prom, dried and brittle, rested atop a stack of notes scribbled in gel pen, once passed between her and Margot during class. The tassel to her graduation cap was knotted, tangled up with a macramé friendship bracelet. Margot's hand hovered over the stack of folded notes before she shifted, lifting a picture from the table with a smile. "I didn't know you kept all this stuff."

"Of course I did." The idea of the alternative, getting rid of any of it, had never even crossed Olivia's mind. She nodded at the bookshelves against the wall. "I noticed you had some spare shelf space out here, so I put a few of my books on the bottom shelf. I hope you don't mind."

She mostly read on her phone these days, but she had amassed a collection of paperbacks she couldn't bring herself to part with, novels she loved so much she reread them, new releases from her favorite authors, and well-loved classics with cracked spines and yellowed pages that had come loose from their glue.

"'Course not." Margot crossed the room and kneeled in front of the shelf, tilting her head and studying Olivia's contribution. She brushed the spines with her fingers in a sort of delicate reverence that reminded Olivia of how Margot had once touched her. "That's what they're there for."

"Brad didn't like the books I read," Olivia confessed, chewing on the edge of her thumbnail while Margot plucked a book off the shelf, skimming the back blurb before replacing it, repeating the process with another and another. "So I kept them under the bed."

For years, she'd kept them stacked neatly out of sight because Brad hadn't wanted them on the living room shelves, visible to visitors. He had made fun of them, deriding the covers, scoffing and calling them shallow, predictable, poorly written. On several, memorable occasions, he'd cracked them open, folding the covers back roughly, reading from them aloud, making her blush. He would hunt for the sex scenes and laugh while he read, and too many times she'd laughed along with him, shrugging when he called them trashy, downplaying her interest. Brad had accused them of giving women unrealistic expectations. Eventually she'd gotten tired of his jokes that weren't funny, of him glaring at her while she read, all his pointed huffs and none-too-subtle sighs. She'd tucked most under the bed, the rest split between the attic and her childhood bedroom, only reading them when he wasn't around and sticking mostly to e-books so he couldn't see what she was reading when he was.

Margot hugged the book she was holding to her chest and scowled. "Are you serious?"

Olivia drew her knees up and ducked her chin, feigning interest in the purple polish on her toes so Margot wouldn't see her blush. "Unfortunately."

She knew how it sounded, how it made *her* sound—pathetic. That this was Margot she was talking to only magnified her shame. Margot had always been so self-assured, so confident, so *what you see is what you get, and if you don't like it, tough*. Olivia had wished she were like that, that she cared less about what people thought of her. She was trying, but it wasn't easy, and with Brad, she'd never stood a chance, their relationship broken for so long there'd been no fixing it.

Giving in had been easier than pushing back, less exhausting than arguing. When she was in it, too close to see the forest for the trees, it was easy to convince herself that *giving* was natural, that it was what made a marriage work, last. It took Brad asking for the one thing she wouldn't give for her to realize her concessions didn't count as compromises, not when she was the only one ever giving. Brad never met her in the middle, never even came close.

Margot's cheeks were flushed, her eyes bright, and her scowl furious. Her jaw ticked, her nostrils flaring delicately. "He didn't deserve you, Liv."

Olivia's tongue felt thick in her mouth. Maybe not, maybe Brad hadn't deserved her, but he'd wanted her for longer than a week, which was more than Olivia could say for Margot. "I don't know if it's about *deserving*, but thank you."

Margot turned the book over in her hands, scowl softening as she read the back. "Mind if I borrow this one?"

Olivia's mouth popped open. "No. No, go for it. Help yourself."

"Thanks." Margot traced the swooping letters that made up the title. "I saw someone talking about it online. I guess it's getting adapted?"

The tension knotting her shoulders loosened. "I heard that, too."

She should've known Margot wasn't going to judge her for what she liked or ask her to tuck away parts of herself like Brad had. Just like she should've known Margot wouldn't call her weak for putting up with Brad and his bullshit for too long.

She should've known she was safe with Margot.

Margot crawled across the carpet on her knees and set her borrowed book down on the edge of the coffee table before dragging one of Olivia's half-unpacked boxes closer, two fingers tucked around the edge of the cardboard. She peeked inside. "You've got more books in here."

Olivia's heart crept inside her throat. "Those aren't—"

Too late. Margot had already reached inside, plucking one of the books from the depths of the box, brows inching their way toward her hairline as she scanned the cover. "*Hole-Hearted to Whole-Hearted: Moving On and Starting Over.*"

Heat licked at the sides of Olivia's face. "That's not mine."

Margot stared.

"Okay, it's mine," Olivia amended, squirming under Margot's curious stare. "But I didn't buy it." She coughed. "My, uh, my dad bought it. For me. He thought it would be helpful or something. He's supported all my decisions, but he only understands not being married anymore from the standpoint of . . . grief. And there is that, but for me it's all tangled up with relief, too."

Margot flipped the book over, skimming the back, just like she had Olivia's romance novels. "Was it?"

"Was it what?"

Margot looked up. "Helpful."

"Oh." She tucked her hair behind her left ear and shrugged. "I guess? It talks about setting boundaries and looking to the future instead of wasting time playing the blame game. That just because your ex wasn't the right person for you doesn't mean that person isn't out there." She smiled. "Nothing I didn't already know."

Whether she believed it was a different story. Or if they were out there, what were the chances she would be the right person for them, too? Life was far from fair; it would be just her luck that her perfect person would find her wanting.

Margot set the book back into the box before she reached out and plucked her old friendship bracelet off the table, rolling it between her fingers. The knotted ends were frayed, the black letters on the pastel rainbow beads faded from wear. Her lips quirked at the corners. "Watch out using that phrase around Brendon." She huffed gently. *"Right person."*

Brendon had created a dating app, sure, and the way he looked at Annie with total moon eyes certainly supported his reputation as a hopeless romantic. But Margot made it sound as if there was more to it than that. "Why do I get the feeling there's a story there?"

"Brendon, Brendon, Brendon." Margot laughed and shook her head, managing to look both fond and exasperated. "He loves his job. He takes it *very* seriously. Very *personally*." Margot rolled her eyes. "He thinks it's his mission in life, his *calling* practically, to help everyone around him find love." Her nose scrunched on the last word. "The fact that he successfully set up Darcy with Elle only made him more dogged about it, more . . . confident that he's meant to be this—this match-maker."

He sounded well-meaning, but she could see where that could get old fast. Joining a dating app and searching for love was one thing; having potential love matches foisted on you when you weren't interested was something else altogether. "I'm going to go out on a limb and guess that you've been the . . . victim? Of one of his matchmaking schemes?"

Margot's face did something complicated, scrunching as if she'd sucked on a lemon, before her brows rose and she sighed, shoulders slumping. "He's tried. I'm usually pretty good at putting him in his place, gently yet firmly, but I've been known to cave on occasion. I've never let him set me up with someone, but I go through the motions if we're out somewhere and he introduces me to a friend of his. When Brendon inevitably wanders off to give us time to chat, I make it clear if I'm not actually interested."

Not actually interested in the friends Brendon tried to set her up with, or not interested in dating, *period*? "So you aren't seeing anyone?"

Olivia held her breath. That was probably something she should've asked before, when they were having their roommate chat. She'd had the perfect opening when she'd asked about having people over, but she'd flustered too easily. *Margot* made her fluster too easily.

"No." Margot's tongue darted out, wetting her bottom lip. "I'm not."

Do you want to be? sounded like a cringe pickup line even if that wasn't how Olivia meant it. But when Margot didn't tack on a helpful adjoiner, she had to ask *something*. She wouldn't be able to sleep otherwise, her curiosity niggling at her. "Are you interested in finding someone?"

Had it been a question of *wrong time, wrong place* when they were younger, or was Olivia just the wrong person?

Margot slipped her fingers beneath her glasses and rubbed her eyes. "I'm not *not* interested. I just don't feel like I *need* someone. Like I'm lacking without my *special other half.*" Margot scoffed softly, brow knitting harshly, her scowl returning. "I'm a whole person. And the idea of needing to find someone to make you complete seems like bullshit to me. The right person shouldn't *complete* you, they should love you the way you are. And it's cool if they make you want to be better, but they should never make you feel like you're too much or not enough exactly as you are." Margot took a deep breath and released it slowly. "Sorry." She chuckled. "Soapbox. I have a lot of feelings, I guess."

"I like your feelings," Olivia blurted, face heating. "I mean, your feelings are valid."

Margot blushed, the tops of her ears turning a darker shade than her cheeks. She laughed under her breath. "Thanks. As much as I love my friends, sometimes I feel like they don't get it. They're all in relationships and so happy and I'm happy *for* them, but based on how they talk sometimes I get the feeling they wish I were in a relationship because it would be easier for *them*. Like it would tie our friend group up into a nice little six-way bow. No loose strings."

"I'm sorry you feel that way. No one should ever take your friendship for granted."

Not any friendship, but certainly not Margot's. Margot had been the most loyal friend Olivia had ever had, and she knew from experience what it was like losing that, missing it, wanting it back.

It was funny. Well, perhaps *funny* wasn't the right word. Ironic, maybe—Olivia always used that word wrong—how she hadn't regretted sleeping with Margot, but she'd absolutely regretted the aftermath. How, without meaning to, it had complicated everything, something she'd *thought* had brought them together instead adding distance between them.

Margot wrapped the ends of her friendship bracelet around

her narrow wrist and shrugged. "I'm not saying they're taking me for granted, but it just sucks to think that they potentially rank our friendship lower than their relationships when they aren't comparable, you know? Love isn't supposed to be quantifiable, relationships held up against one another, *pitted* against one another. That's a shitty thing to try to do, like asking someone to compare their love for their mother to their love for their partner or their best friend."

When Margot frowned at her wrist, unable to knot the ends of the bracelet together with one hand, Olivia reached out to do it for her.

"It's like, I don't care about you less because I don't want in your pants, you know?" Margot paused and lifted her eyes, a low creak escaping her parted lips. "General *you*. Not you specifically. Not that I'm *not* saying . . ." She turned her head to the side and chuckled. "Wow, I'm going to shut up."

Olivia bit her lip, smothering her smile at how flustered Margot sounded. Whether Margot had wanted in Olivia's pants had never been the question. Or it had been, but only until it had been answered. It wasn't the prevailing question now. "I know what you were trying to say."

"Do you?" Margot laughed, a flush creeping down her neck and disappearing where her slouchy crewneck sweater draped beneath her collarbones. "Because I think I got lost somewhere in there."

Olivia finished tying the bracelet, but let her fingers linger, adjusting the way the braided rope and beads sat. Olivia's thumb grazed the fragile skin over the inside of Margot's wrist, making her shiver, and Olivia could've sworn she felt Margot's pulse skip. "You value your friendships. It's—it was always one of my favorite things about you."

Margot's throat jerked. "Yeah?"

Olivia nodded and went for broke. "I feel like a dork, but no one really teaches you how to make friends as an adult. Would you . . . maybe want to be friends? Again?" She laughed. "God, I feel like I should write this down on a piece of paper. *Check yes or no.*"

Margot rolled her lips together. "I don't know."

Olivia's heart stalled, then sank.

"It's not like we aren't living together. I mean, hell, you've gotten acquainted with my, uh, my sex toy collection. I have some friends who can't say the same." Margot's lips quirked and, *whew*, okay, *joking*. Relief flooded Olivia's veins.

She pressed the heel of her hand to her forehead and laughed. "This is true. Although"—her lips twitched—"*acquainted* is kind of an overstatement."

And if they were going to discuss qualifiers of intimacy, there was the fact they'd slept together.

Margot's teeth scraped against the swell of her bottom lip, her brows rising. Her flush had yet to fade. If anything, it had deepened, turning her dark pink from her hairline all the way down to where her soft-looking sweater met equally soft-looking skin. "Fair. I guess *collection* might be a bit of an overstatement, too." The front of her throat jerked when she swallowed. "You've only seen one."

God. Okay. It wasn't like that was an invitation. Even if Olivia wished it were—*no*. She had no business going there, down that path. She'd been down it before, and look where it had gotten her. She'd literally *just* thought about how she'd regretted the complicated aftermath of their coupling, the consequences. "True."

Margot smiled, all dark eyes and flushed cheeks, and Olivia tried to ignore the throb between her thighs, how everything south of her navel was suddenly hot and ached.

"So." Olivia blinked hard and pasted on a cheery smile. "Friends?"

"Sure." The left corner of Margot's mouth tipped up in a smirk, erasing Olivia's efforts at ignoring the ache between her legs. "Friends."

Chapter Eight

What Wedding Cake Flavor Are You Based on Your Zodiac Sign?

Aries—Peanut Butter Cup
Taurus—Dulce de Leche
Gemini—Marble
Cancer—Lemon Poppyseed
Leo—Red Velvet
Virgo—French Vanilla Bean
Libra—Pink Champagne
Scorpio—Coffee Cream
Sagittarius—Tiramisu
Capricorn—Carrot Cake
Aquarius—Coconut
Pisces—Funfetti

The Sweet Spot, a perfectly innocent bakery with a very naughty name—or maybe Margot just had a dirty mind—

usually closed at six, but had been willing to accommodate Brendon and Annie's schedules, staying open late for their cake tasting.

A sampling of petit fours had been presented on pedestal stands, five of each of the six flavors Brendon and Annie had selected for tasting, flavors ranging from a traditional vanilla to lavender honey. Margot picked at the ultra-thick, sugary-sweet fondant covering a coconut—*gag*—mini cake and stared surreptitiously across the table while Olivia went to town on her pink champagne petit four.

A fleck of edible gold leaf clung to the center of Olivia's bottom lip. Her tongue darted out, only managing to nudge the shiny fleck closer to the corner of her mouth. Olivia either thought it was gone or hadn't realized it was there in the first place, because she scooped up another forkful of cake, bringing it to her lips. Her mouth closed around the fork, and her lashes fluttered softly against the smooth skin beneath her eyes. The tines of her fork made a gradual reappearance and a soft hum of contentment slipped from her lips as she chewed slowly, savoring the bite. Eyes open but lids low, Olivia lifted the fork back to her lips, lapping at the frosting that clung to the space between the tines.

A breathy groan filled the air, more desperate than satisfied.

Four curious sets of eyes locked on her.

Motherfucker, *she* had made that noise, all pleading and pornographic and—*ugh*. The tips of Margot's ears burned so badly she feared they would pop right off like little turkey timers signaling she was well past done. She coughed, as if doing that could *possibly* pass that groan off as . . . congestion and not a desire to get up close and reacquainted with Olivia's tongue.

She shivered. Nope. Bad Margot.

"Mar?" The corners of Brendon's eyes crinkled with concern. "You feeling all right?"

"Mm, yep." She reached out, knuckles knocking into her glass of ice water, skin slipping against the condensation. A drop of water slipped down the back of her hand and circled her wrist as she took a long drink, studiously avoiding looking anywhere near Olivia. "I'm fine."

"Are you sure?" Annie frowned. "You're looking kind of flushed."

Christ on a cracker, couldn't a girl be horny in peace?

"It *is* a little warm in here," Darcy said, earning herself top billing on Margot's list of favorite people. "I think they've got the heat set a touch too high."

Darcy's eyes darted from Margot to Olivia and back to Margot, a dimple forming at the corner of her mouth when she smirked. That was, without a doubt, a look to file away for closer inspection later.

"So." Brendon set his napkin beside his plate, eyes focused on her. "What do you think, or do you not care?"

"I care," Margot blurted. "I totally care."

Brendon's face twisted, half frown, half smile, one hundred percent amused. "Okay . . . so, thoughts?"

Margot winced. Shit. "Um, what was the question?"

Everyone chuckled, Olivia included, her laughter ringing out like a bell, pretty and sharp. Margot's heart stuttered then sped. It was difficult to get up in arms about being made fun of when Olivia's smile made her eyes brighten.

"You care, but you don't know what it is you care about?" Darcy's brows rose.

"I personally think it's a testament to my boundless capacity for caring, that it's not even a prerequisite knowing what it is I care about."

Darcy grinned. "And I personally think it's a testament to your ability to bullshit that you were able to say that sentence with a straight face."

Across the table, Olivia pressed her fingertips to her mouth, stifling her smile.

"Fine, you caught me. I spaced out for a second."

Margot tossed her napkin down beside her plate and slouched back in her chair, ankle accidentally brushing against Olivia's beneath the table. Olivia's whole body twitched at the contact, her eyes flitting up, gaze locking on Margot's. *Whoops.* Margot slid her foot away and Olivia broke eye contact, dropping her eyes to the table. A few seconds later, Olivia's foot bumped up against Margot's and didn't move.

Margot swallowed hard. Okay. She was officially Victorian-era-level horny if a—potentially?—accidental game of footsie was making her sweat.

None the wiser, Brendon smiled. "Cake flavors, Mar. You got a preference?"

"They were all pretty tasty," she hedged, not wanting to put her foot in her mouth and perform a repeat of the time she'd told Brendon—gently—that "At Last" by Etta James wasn't, in her opinion, the right choice for his and Annie's first dance.

That was the song you dance to when you're . . . you're fifty or on your second marriage. Brendon was younger than Margot, only by a year, but still. At last his love had come along? Sure, he'd crushed on Annie *long* before they got together, but come on. He hadn't waited *that long*.

They'd selected a different song, a song that was a much better fit for them in the end, but Brendon had been bummed. The last thing Margot needed was to inadvertently insult his or Annie's favorite flavor in the name of being honest.

Margot shrugged. "Can't go wrong with any of them."

Unless they picked lavender honey or coconut or—*ew*—pistachio. Cake was supposed to taste like cake, not like the ingredients in a DIY face mask or potpourri. But, hey, it wasn't her wedding, and the last thing she wanted was for someone to accuse her of being anything but supportive. She'd force down a whole slice of lavender-pistachio-coconut grossness with a smile on her face if it kept her friends happy.

Across the table, Olivia stared at Margot dubiously.

Brendon shrugged. "Huh. Okay." He turned and looked at Annie. "Um—"

"Margot likes the peanut butter chocolate," Olivia said, smiling. "She's always been a sucker for that combo." Her eyes dropped to Margot's empty plate, the one where the peanut butter–chocolate petit four had been before Margot had devoured every last crumb, almost licking the plate before ultimately deciding that would've been rude. "I guess some things don't change."

Her body didn't know what to make of that; her chest went pleasantly warm, touched by the sentiment, but a tendril of heat slithered down, pooling low beneath her belly button, affected by the way Olivia's voice had lilted, almost flirtatious.

"Yeah?" Brendon sat up straighter. "You liked that one?"

Margot nibbled on the edge of her lip. She had . . . but not as much as she'd liked watching Olivia enjoy the pink champagne cake.

"Maybe you should stick with something less likely to pose an allergy risk," Margot said. "I liked the pink champagne cake, too."

"That's a good point," Annie said. "About possible allergies. I wasn't even thinking that, but you're completely right."

"You could do extra cupcakes," Olivia suggested. "One layer cake, so you have something to cut for photos and so you can save the top tier for your anniversary, if that's a tradition you want to follow. Or, instead of cupcakes you could have a separate groom's cake."

Brendon cringed. "No groom's cake. It makes me think of the red velvet armadillo cake in *Steel Magnolias*."

Margot shivered. "Please, no."

"No red velvet, either," Darcy said, wrinkling her nose. "It's pretentious chocolate."

"And you *don't* like it?" Margot teased. "Color me surprised."

Darcy's eyes narrowed, lips twitching at the corners. "Cute."

"I try." Margot flipped the ends of her hair.

Olivia grinned, eyes flitting around the table. "No groom's cake. And no red velvet. This is good. We're narrowing our options down."

"Cupcakes do sound nice," Annie mused. "We could have more flavors that way, too. Make picking a little easier."

"So, peanut butter chocolate for some of the cupcakes," Olivia said. "And—"

"Pink champagne," Margot blurted, the image of Olivia tonguing her fork baked into her brain.

Annie nodded. "I liked that one." She picked up her fork. "I think I'm going to need to taste a few of these again."

Darcy snorted. *"Make picking a little easier."*

"Shut up." Annie laughed and elbowed Darcy.

Brendon leaned his elbows on the table. "So, Olivia."

She still hadn't moved her foot from where it was pressed snug against Margot's. "Mm-hmm?"

"I forgot to ask this the last time I saw you—*first* time I saw you." Brendon's smile went lopsided. "What made you want to go into event planning?"

Margot could answer that. Growing up, Olivia had wanted to be a professional mermaid, an ice dancer, a paleontologist, and an event planner, in that order. All but the last had been phases, short-lived. Event planning had stood the test of time, Olivia the first to volunteer to plan sleepovers and camping trips, later joining the student council and spearheading everything from spirit week to bake sales to prom. Olivia had an eye for detail, a hard-on for checklists, and the patience to bring her exact vision to life. Margot couldn't imagine a more perfect job for her.

"I can't really remember a time when I *didn't* want to be a party planner," Olivia said. "I've always enjoyed planning events. Birthday parties for myself when I was little, school dances when I was older." She smiled and shrugged. "I guess I just really love the idea of bringing a vision to life and maybe making someone's day, or, when it comes to weddings, making someone's dreams come true."

Predictably, Brendon looked completely sold, his smile bright and his eyes huge. "I love that. That's why I started OTP." He laughed. "Not the first part, but making someone's dreams come true."

Margot smothered her smile with a sip of ice water. She hadn't ever thought about it until now, but she had a habit of surrounding herself with altruistic optimists. First Olivia, then Elle, then Brendon.

"I've heard only wonderful things about OTP," Olivia said, shuffling her plates to the side, clearing room to rest her hands on the table. She nudged her chocolate–peanut butter petit four toward Margot with a quick wink.

Margot flashed her a smile and slid the plate closer, reaching for her fork. She mouthed a quick *thanks* before digging in, swallowing a bite of cake and, with it, a moan. Shit, that was good stuff.

Brendon shrugged, somehow striking the balance between casual confidence and humility. There wasn't a disingenuous bone in Brendon's body, which helped keep his words from toeing into humblebrag territory. "I like to think we're doing a good thing." His brow furrowed softly, eyes narrowing as he chewed on his bottom lip. "Say, Olivia, are you seeing anyone?"

"No, no." Margot set her fork down, shaking her head brusquely. "Do not answer that question, Liv." She turned to Brendon, leveling him with a hard stare. "We do not ask strangers if they're single. It's invasive."

Brendon held up his hands, face the picture of innocence, all wide *who me?* eyes and lips parted, ready to spout an excuse. "Olivia's not a stranger. She's our wedding planner, and she's *your* friend."

"It's not your business, Brendon," Margot said, jaw clenching. "Butt out."

"It's fine." The shiny gold hoops in Olivia's ears danced against the sides of her neck when she shook her head. "I'm not currently seeing anyone, no."

Brendon smiled. "Would you like to be?"

"Jesus," Margot muttered.

Annie bumped Brendon's shoulder. "Babe, maybe ease off?"

Brendon's lower lip jutted out.

"You're giving off *we saw you across the bar and really like your vibe,* energy," Annie said.

He frowned. "We *do* like her vibe."

Annie whispered something in Brendon's ear that made him blush.

"For the record, that was not a proposition," Brendon clarified, scratching his jaw. "It was a general question."

Olivia tucked her hair behind her ears. Her face had turned a soft shade of pink, her neck slightly darker, her flush working its way north. "I—"

"You do not have to answer. Plead the fifth," Margot said, rolling her eyes. "Brendon, as much as we adore him, hasn't quite grasped the concept of boundaries."

"I think he understands boundaries perfectly well," Darcy said. "I think he simply chooses to ignore them."

Brendon clutched his chest, expression wounded. "I came here to have a good time, and I'm honestly feeling so attacked right now."

"2014 called and they would like that joke back." Margot softened the jibe with a smile.

"Olivia." Brendon turned to her, still clutching his chest. "Do you see what I go through? These people call themselves my friends."

"I'm your sister," Darcy said, tapping away at her phone, probably texting Elle, who hadn't been able to make it to the cake tasting, having agreed to babysit last minute for her older sister. "I'm stuck with you."

He turned his puppy-dog stare on Annie. She patted him on the cheek. "You know how I feel about you."

Margot grinned and gestured at her plate. "I'm just here for the food."

Olivia chuckled. "It's fine, Brendon. If I didn't feel comfortable answering, I'd tell you precisely where you could stick your question." Her smile went impish. "Politely, of course."

Brendon, Annie, and Darcy burst out laughing, Olivia's frankness clearly taking them by surprise. Margot grinned, well aware of how clever Olivia could be. It was nice to see her opening up, shaking off the stiffness Margot wasn't used to, relaxing and settling into her skin the way Margot had remembered. She'd missed Olivia's easy smiles and raunchy jokes and—she'd missed Olivia.

Missed her, full stop.

"Good to know," Brendon said. "So . . . ?"

Olivia clasped her hands together atop the table. "I just got divorced last year. And while I'm not heartbroken—I'm over it—I *was* married for almost ten years, so I've been enjoying having some time to myself. Getting my career off the ground has been my number one priority."

Brendon nodded along. "All good points."

Margot narrowed her eyes, waiting for the other shoe to drop.

"But if the right person were to come along, would you be open to dating?" Brendon asked.

"I mean . . . I guess?" Olivia shrugged. "If it was the right person at the right time, I wouldn't say no to, um . . ." She rolled her lips together as if searching for the right word. "Seeing what could happen?"

Brendon grinned. "What would you say your type is if, on the off chance this person were to come along, so, you know, I could send them your way?"

Margot rolled her eyes and shoved her chair away from the table. "Bathroom," she explained when everyone looked up at her.

It wasn't so much that she needed to pee as she wasn't in the mood to hear Olivia describe her *perfect person*. Some clone of Brad, only better, without the douchebag personality. Not Margot. Margot was good for a week, for a rebound fling, nothing more.

She shut herself in the single-stall bathroom in the back of the bakery and locked the door. Jesus, did she sound bitter. She closed her eyes. Eleven years later, and she should've been over this. She *was* over this—at least, last week she was—and then Olivia had tumbled back into her life and there were all these *feelings* she could've sworn she'd worked through rising to the surface.

Maybe Margot hadn't worked through her feelings about what happened in high school as much as she'd buried them, pushing them away via repression and self-recrimination. Not the healthiest of coping methods, admittedly, but Margot was nothing if not a work in progress.

So, maybe she wasn't as *over it* as she'd claimed to be. Thinking about how she and Olivia had ended, grown apart, *whatever* put a bitter lump in her throat and an ache in her chest, and Margot didn't know what to do with this, this *feeling*.

Only that she needed to do *something* because her friends weren't stupid and neither was Olivia and sooner rather than later someone was going to pick up on the fact that Margot was less fine than she was letting on.

The timing was shit, that was for sure. She couldn't exactly hole up in her room with a wedding to plan, a wedding to *attend*, and Olivia living right down the hall. Margot would laugh if she weren't so entirely screwed by circumstance.

She set her glasses beside the sink and splashed cold water on her face, avoiding her eyes, her liner actually even on each side for once. An odd twist. Her life went belly-side up, and she managed a perfect cat eye. Go figure.

Having stalled for long enough, she slipped out the bathroom, footsteps slowing to a crawl as Brendon's voice carried down the hall.

". . . Margot like in high school?"

Margot tiptoed closer, wanting to hear what Olivia said

when she wasn't around. When Olivia didn't know Margot could hear her. Maybe it wasn't the most virtuous thing to do, listening in, but hey, *work in progress.*

"What she was like in high school?" Olivia laughed. "Gosh, Margot was . . . pretty quiet, actually."

"*Margot?*" Annie sounded incredulous. "Are you sure we're talking about the same person?"

Everyone laughed, and Margot rolled her eyes, creeping a little closer and stopping just at the inside of the hall, tucking herself behind a ginormous rubber fig.

"She wasn't a wallflower or anything like that. Margot was just always really comfortable in her own skin. She had this quiet confidence I always admired, and I guess she never felt like she *needed* to be the loudest voice in the room in order to be taken seriously," Olivia explained.

Margot's face warmed.

"And she was always intensely loyal. You should ask her where she got the scar on the backs of her knuckles from." Olivia laughed and Margot ducked her chin, smiling at the floor.

Brendon chuckled. "Sounds like Margot."

"She was—she was my best friend," Olivia said softly.

Margot swallowed hard and pressed the heel of her hand into her sternum as if she could massage away the ache inside.

"I'm sure you're happy that your paths crossed," Brendon said.

"I am," Olivia agreed. "I count my lucky stars, that's for sure."

Margot dropped her face into her hands. *Damn.*

"Margot?"

Margot jumped, clapping a hand over her chest. Beneath her palm, her heart thundered. "Darcy. Fuck. You scared me."

"What are you doing hiding back here?"

"Hiding? Psh. I'm not hiding."

Darcy's lips quirked. "You're crouched behind a potted plant."

Margot crossed her arms. "I will have you know that I was . . . was . . ."

One of Darcy's brows arched.

"I was about to . . . to . . ."

Darcy's left eyebrow rose, joining the right. "Don't hurt yourself."

Margot's cheeks burned. "Shut up. Did you come back here for a reason or just to call me on my shit?"

"I *did* want to talk to you. If you have a minute."

Margot made a show of tilting her head from side to side in mock consideration. "I'm in high demand, but I guess for you, I could spare at least that."

Darcy braced her shoulder against the wall. "I wanted to talk to you about Elle, actually."

Margot waited.

"I'm going to ask her to marry me."

Margot sputtered, choking on air. Darcy frowned.

"I'm fine. Just swallowed my spit funny." She flapped her hand in front of her, waving off Darcy's concern. "I could've sworn you just said you were going to ask Elle to marry you."

"I did." Darcy laced her fingers, wringing her hands. "What? Do you think it's too soon?"

"Um." Margot scrambled for a slightly more diplomatic answer than her gut response of *fuck yes*. "I mean." God, she was drawing a blank. "You're hardly U-Hauling it."

Darcy nibbled on her bottom lip, looking less than reassured.

"If you're worried whether she's going to say yes, don't." Margot nudged Darcy with her elbow. "Elle will absolutely say yes."

Darcy smiled, small and wobbly but a smile nonetheless. "You think?"

"I'm sure of it." Margot scratched the side of her neck. Did this bakery sell alcohol? "Have you thought about how you plan to ask? I know Elle's partial to Ring Pops. *Or*, hear me out. Prize in the bottom of her cereal box. She'd love that."

"I was thinking I'd take her up to the observatory at UW. It's where we had our first *real* date, under the stars. I thought it was fitting."

Margot didn't know what to say because *damn*. Darcy had put *thought* into this. This wasn't a hypothetical. She had plans. Hell, knowing Darcy, there were probably checklists and spreadsheets and risk assessments involved. She was serious. *This* was serious.

Margot shifted on her feet, feeling out of her depth and underprepared. This was like one of those stress dreams she still had about college. Nightmares where she'd realize she'd signed up for a class, completely blanked, and never attended or turned in any of the assignments, and her entire GPA hinged on acing a final on organic chemistry or astrophysics, something so advanced she had zero chance of bullshitting her way through. "That's . . . *Wow*. When do you think you're going to pop the question?"

"I *was* thinking after Brendon and Annie get back from their honeymoon."

Next month. Holy shit.

"But then I decided I don't want to wait and, besides— Brendon would probably consider me getting engaged to be a wedding present to *him*, considering he's the one to thank for introducing me to Elle in the first place." Darcy wrung her hands together and smiled. "I want to do it before we head up to Snoqualmie for the bachelor-bachelorette party."

They were leaving in four days. *Four. Days.*

"It—*wow*. It sounds like you've got it all figured out, Darce."

Like she didn't need anything from Margot at all.

Darcy shrugged. "I wanted to make sure I wasn't completely deluding myself, hoping that she'll say yes."

"Trust me. I'd be the first person to tell you if you were delusional."

"That's what I was counting on."

Margot cleared her throat. "Well, I think it's great. I'm—I'm really happy for you. You and Elle . . . I couldn't hope for a better person to have fallen in love with my best friend."

Darcy ducked her chin, her smile small and achingly fond. "Thanks, Margot. That means a lot to me." She coughed lightly and blinked fast before tilting her head to the side, brown eyes scrutinizing as they danced over Margot's face. "So. You and Olivia."

Margot's throat went dry. "Me and Olivia what?"

Darcy stared at her like she could see all the little cracks beneath Margot's skin. "Margot."

Fuck. Margot palmed her forehead, a frazzled laugh slipping out, too loud in the narrow hallway. "Am I that obvious?"

Darcy bobbed her head from side to side. "Obvious? No, not really. Can I tell there's something you aren't saying? Yes."

Margot puffed out her cheeks. That wasn't quite so bad. At least she didn't have her feelings stamped across her forehead for everyone to see. "I'm, uh, working through some . . . *things*. Feelings and shit."

Darcy's lips twitched. "Feelings and shit?"

If only Darcy knew what Margot was dealing with, she wouldn't give her grief over her ineloquence. "Shut up."

"No, no, now I'm curious." Darcy grinned. "Are these *pants* feelings or *chest* feelings?"

Margot was in hell. "Elle is seriously rubbing off on you if you're using the words *pants feelings* unironically." She sighed. "And yes, I realize I just said *rubbing off*. My life is ripe with innuendo."

"It is, isn't it?" Darcy agreed. "Cats and vibrators and rubbing off. It's a gold mine."

"I'm dealing with a blast from my past and all the many, varied emotions that have reared their head thanks to it. Cut me some slack if I'm not on top of my game." She raked her fingers through her hair, tugging at her ends until her scalp stung.

Darcy sobered. "Look, if you don't want to talk about it, that's fine. Unlike my brother, I won't push."

Margot nodded, shoulders lowering from where she'd had them hiked defensively by her ears.

"But if you *do* decide you want to talk about it, you know

where to find me," Darcy said. "Or Elle. You know she'd listen."

Elle would probably tell Margot all of this was fate and that
everything would fall into place if Margot just followed her
heart. Only, following her heart had fucked everything up
once; Margot would be damned if she let that happen again.

"Thanks, Darcy," Margot whispered. "I appreciate the offer.
I'm not . . . there yet, but maybe I'll take you up on it some
other time. But only if there's wine involved."

Darcy batted at the air and scoffed. "Obviously."

"Good." She narrowed her eyes. "Until then—"

"My lips are sealed. I heard nothing." Darcy mimed locking
her lips and throwing away the key.

"Good." Margot nodded decisively. "Because if you do go
and blab—"

"You'll what? Break into my apartment and move everything
three inches to the left and fuck with my flow?" Darcy laughed,
reciting a threat Margot had made when Elle and Darcy had
first started dating. "Your bark is a whole lot worse than your
bite, you know that?"

"Yeah, yeah," Margot grumbled. "Not that this heart-to-
heart hasn't left me feeling all warm and fuzzy inside, but we
should probably head back out there."

Margot shoved away from the wall and made it two steps
down the hall.

"Word to the wise, Margot?" Darcy called out quietly. "If you
don't reckon with your feelings, sooner or later your feelings are
going to reckon with you. Just something to keep in mind."

Chapter Nine

$\mathcal{M}$argot tossed her keys on the entry table and made a beeline for the couch, where she threw herself down and stared up at the ceiling.

Married.

Elle was getting married.

On a logical level, Margot knew she wasn't losing Elle. She wasn't losing any of her friends. But Elle was going to be someone's *wife*. Even if Margot wasn't technically losing anyone, it was still the end of an era, the beginning of a new chapter.

All her friends were settling down, and Margot? She had yet to find a brand of shampoo she liked well enough to commit to, let alone a whole person.

Olivia wandered into the living room, barefoot and soft-looking in her chunky cashmere cardigan and pink pleated skirt that barely brushed the tops of her knees. She nudged Margot's feet aside and took a graceful seat, fingers skimming the skin of her thighs as she smoothed her skirt down with a brush of her hands. The pleats splayed open, the hem of her skirt rising several inches.

Margot tore her eyes away before Olivia could catch her staring.

"Are you all right?"

Margot lifted her head. "Why wouldn't I be?"

"I don't know." Olivia frowned. "You've been quiet since we left the bakery."

"Oh." Margot let her head fall back against the arm of the couch. "No, I'm fine."

Olivia nibbled on her lip. "If you say so."

A beat of silence passed, then another, and another.

If you don't reckon with your feelings, sooner or later your feelings are going to reckon with you.

Margot sighed. "Darcy cornered me coming out of the bathroom. She's planning to propose to Elle."

A bright smile graced Olivia's face. "Really? That's fantastic. Did she tell you when she . . ." Her words trailed off, smile faltering. "Wait. Is it *not* fantastic?"

Margot groaned and slipped her glasses off, setting them down on her stomach. She rubbed her eyes, pressing hard until colors burst behind her lids. "No, God no. That's not—of course it's fantastic." She exhaled harshly and lowered hands, blinking into the brightness of the living room. Her vision blurred softly at the edges until she slipped her glasses back on. "I'm happy for Elle—and Darcy—but it's just . . ." She swallowed twice, throat aching. "It's nothing. Forget I said anything."

Margot's eye burned, her lids itchy, like the skin was too tight. *Fuck.*

Olivia's fingers curled around Margot's ankle, thumb brushing the bare skin along the inside of her foot. "It doesn't sound like nothing."

"I'll sound like a bitch." Margot choked out a laugh. "Scratch that, I *am* a bitch."

A good friend would be doing a fucking happy dance when their best friend got engaged, and here Margot was, sinuses burning, signaling the impending rush of tears.

Olivia made a soft sound of dissent. "You aren't a bitch, Margot."

She took a deep, pained breath and pinched the bridge of her nose, eyes scrunching. "I'm happy for Elle. I *am*. But— fuck." Her stupid chin quivered. "There shouldn't be a *but*. I should be happy, full stop, no qualifier. Just over-the-moon thrilled that my best friend is going to be marrying the love of her life."

"You're allowed to feel more than one emotion at a time," Olivia said, squeezing Margot's ankle gently. The sweep of her thumb back and forth was soothing, soft without tickling. "It doesn't make you a bitch."

"I feel like it makes me a bad friend," Margot confessed.

"You'd be a bad friend if you decided to take your feelings out on Elle or Darcy, if you let your feelings change your friendship with them."

"I don't want to do that," she agreed. "That's the last thing I want."

For Elle to think Margot was harboring anger or resentment about her good news. To let her feelings get in the way of their friendship, to push Elle away.

"I guess that's the thing," Margot whispered. "I *don't* want my friendships to change."

"And you're worried they will?"

"I don't see how they won't." Margot sniffed. "Elle's going to be someone's wife, *Darcy's* wife. And that's—I *am* happy. They're perfect for each other. Darcy's everything Elle ever talked about wanting."

Despite being total opposites, neither ever asked the other to change, to be someone other than exactly who they were. They loved each other, flaws and all.

"I'm just so used to being Elle's go-to, you know? The person she calls when she needs someone to talk to, a shoulder to cry on, her best friend, and now . . ."

"You're worried you won't be that person anymore."

"I don't want to lose her," she confessed.

Margot didn't want to lose *any* of her friends.

"You're right," Olivia said. "Elle's going to be Darcy's wife, but you're still going to be her best friend. It's apples and oranges. No one else can bring to the table what you do." Olivia's lashes swept against her cheeks when she lowered her face, smiling softly. "No one can replace you, Margot. You're one of a kind."

"One of a kind, huh?" Margot's voice shook, heart rising into her throat. "Like one of those imperfect pieces of produce in that subscription box?"

Olivia's bright bark of laughter made Margot's heart swell further. She shook her head, earrings dancing against the sides of her neck. "What are you talking about?"

"You know." Margot scooted back until she was sitting,

propped against the arm. She wedged her toes under Olivia's thigh. "The ugly produce no one wants but there's nothing wrong with it, so they created a subscription box to reduce food waste. Watermelons with weird scars and funky-shaped squash and curly carrots. Bell peppers with extra little offshoots, appendages that look awfully phallic." She shrugged. "You said apples and oranges and my brain kind of ran with it."

"You are *definitely* one of a kind," Olivia teased, smile as soft as the fingers now tracing the tops of Margot's feet. "I mean it. You're irreplaceable, and I can promise you that your friends don't want to lose you anymore than you want to lose them." Olivia's eyes locked on Margot's, the intensity of her gaze sending a shiver skittering down Margot's spine. Olivia's shoulders rose and fell, her full lips parting as she exhaled, and for a split second Margot could've sworn a tiny fleck of gold foil still clung to her bottom lip. "Trust me. I'd know."

Fuck. Margot's chest throbbed like at any second she might bust open like a piñata, feelings pouring out of her like candy. "I missed you, too, Liv."

Olivia's lower lip wobbled, her teeth trapping it. Light from the corner lamp caught on—sure enough, a small piece of shiny foil.

"You have gold foil on your mouth," Margot said, swallowing thickly when Olivia's teeth scraped against the swell of her lip, leaving it plump and dark. "It's from the cake, I think."

Olivia ran her fingers along her lip line. The foil didn't so much as budge. She looked at her hand and frowned. "Is it gone?"

"No, just—come here." Margot leaned forward, hand shaking as she reached out, dragging the pad of her thumb along the satin swell of Olivia's bottom lip. Lips still parted, Olivia's warm breath tickled Margot's knuckles and made her insides clench, heat pooling between her thighs.

The foil flecked off, transferring to Margot's skin, and she quickly dropped her hand.

"All gone," Margot panted.

Olivia's throat jerked, the high crests of her cheeks flushed crimson. "Thanks."

Margot's pulse pounded in her head, at the base of her throat, between her thighs.

"Popcorn," she blurted.

Olivia frowned. "Popcorn?"

Margot hopped off the couch, stomach swooping when she tripped on the fringed edge of the rug. She righted herself and wiped her clammy palms on her thighs. "Do you want some? Because I'm going to make some."

Olivia worried her bottom lip between her teeth. "Sure. I guess." She stretched forward for the remote. "I'll find something on TV."

Margot escaped to the kitchen and braced her hands against the counter. Fuck, fuck, *fuck*. She needed to pull it together. Get a grip. Her feelings for Olivia had fucked everything up for her once; she refused to let that happen again, no matter how badly she ached to press Olivia down onto the couch and feel Olivia tremble beneath her fingers, *around* her fingers. *Fuck.*

Margot clenched her eyes shut, but all that did was superimpose a hundred fantasies on the back of her lids. A running reel of memories. Her fingers curled around the kitchen counter until her knuckles turned white.

Olivia had always been tactile and a little bit of a flirt. It didn't *mean* anything. Just because she'd wanted Margot once, for that one week eleven years ago, didn't mean she wanted Margot again, wanted her *now*.

Friends. Margot sucked in a deep breath, air shuddering between her lips. She held it until her lungs ached and her heart kicked at the wall of her chest, then let it out slowly, shoulders dropping and heart rate slowing to something approaching normal. Friends. Margot could totally do friends. She was *great* at doing friends. Oh, Jesus. Great at *being* friends.

Reaching inside the cabinet beside the stove, Margot pulled out a bag of extra-buttery movie-theater-style popcorn. She ripped off the plastic, unfolded the bag, and popped it in the microwave, adding an extra thirty seconds because there was nothing she hated more than anemic popcorn, pale and with the kernel unpopped, the center hard enough to break a tooth.

When the microwave beeped, Margot divided the popcorn into two bowls, one for her, one for Olivia, no chance of buttery fingers brushing when they both reached in at the same time.

A little less hot beneath the collar, Margot wandered back into the living room, a bowl in each hand. "Find something? We can always look on Netflix."

Olivia took her bowl with a smile, gesturing to the TV with the remote. "TMC's running a Shirley MacLaine marathon."

Margot curled up on the opposite cushion. Right now, the channel was on a commercial. "What's on?"

Olivia finished chewing before answering, "*The Apartment*."

"That's a good one." Margot sifted through the bowl, picking out the darkest pieces, little kernels burnt to perfection.

"You remember when you had mono?"

"Oof. Don't remind me. I thought I was going to die that summer." Margot cringed.

Olivia bumped her shoulder and when Margot turned, her eyes brightened. "It wasn't *all* bad. We stayed in bed, remember? That part was nice."

"You practically moved in with me." Margot's chest squeezed, hot and tight. "You even skipped cheer camp."

Olivia had surrendered her spot on the varsity squad sophomore year just so she could spend the summer marathoning Turner Classic Movies from Margot's bed. In between spells of feverish fatigue and moments of feeling like run-over shit, Margot was pretty sure she'd thanked Olivia. Now she wasn't sure.

"Worth it." Olivia grinned and slipped a fingerful of popcorn in her mouth, her lips already glossy with butter. Margot swallowed a pitiful mewl. She'd never wanted to suck on something so badly in her life.

The commercial ended with a jingle, and Margot faced the screen, heartbeat drowning out the sound of Shirley MacLaine bantering with Jack Lemmon.

Not even five minutes later, Olivia nudged her arm. "Here."

Margot blinked. Olivia held out her bowl of popcorn. She'd scavenged for the extra-dark pieces, burned and black, pushing them to one side and leaving the pale, golden kernels on the other.

"I know you like the burnt pieces best." Olivia swayed close, bumping their shoulders together. "Or, you did."

Something fluttered in her chest, quickly followed by an *ache*, like pressing on a tender bruise. It hurt, but she couldn't leave it alone.

"I do." Margot swallowed hard. "I—not much about my taste has changed."

Olivia stared, gaze flickering between Margot's eyes and her mouth.

"Same," she breathed.

Margot's heart thundered inside her head, drowning out the sound of the television until it was nothing but static, senseless white noise. She clutched the bowl of popcorn to her chest, the plastic rim pressing into her sternum. "Is there something on my face?"

Olivia's eyes dipped, her lids lowering and her lashes casting a shadow against the skin beneath her eyes. The perfume of her hair, honeysuckle sweet, clouded Margot's senses as she leaned in and—since when had Olivia gotten so close? Close enough to make out the blue veins on her eyelids, and admire the slightly crooked line of her nose, the finely formed bow of her lush lips, and the dimple in her chin.

Margot held impossibly still, arms all but vibrating, shaking around the bowl of popcorn in her lap. She couldn't make herself move; it was the closest to an out-of-body experience she'd ever had, watching as Olivia crept closer, the distance between their faces dwindling.

Olivia exhaled, breath blowing buttery and sweet against Margot's mouth, a prelude to the press of her lips. Goose bumps broke out along Margot's skin as Olivia's lips pillowed against hers, soft and so brief. Before Margot could even shut her eyes, Liv had drawn away, lashes fluttering open, looking into Margot's eyes, gaze dreamy and—

"Fuck."

Olivia laughed, and something about that sound cracked Margot wide open. Before she knew what she was doing she had one hand wrapped around the back of Olivia's neck, her bowl of popcorn toppling to the floor. She drew Olivia close and kept her there, sealing her mouth over Olivia's, swallowing the little gasp that escaped her lips.

This was a bad idea, but Margot was—fuck, she was weak and she wanted. Wanted Olivia's hands in her hair and Olivia's mouth on her neck and Olivia's body pressed snug against hers. She wanted and she craved and fuck it, maybe she was greedy, too.

But it was hard to remember all the reasons why wanting was wrong when Olivia's mouth opened under hers, tongue sneaking out and dragging against the seam of Margot's lips in the slowest, sweetest torture, offering herself up for the taking.

Chapter Ten

*M*argot's hand slipped under Olivia's sweater, thumbs skimming the skin of Olivia's waist then brushing the very bottom of her rib cage, making her shiver. A muffled moan escaped her parted lips because, God, it had been *years* since a kiss had made Olivia feel this way, this hot, this achy, this desperate and out of control like she had to have more. Not a want but a need, up there with breathing.

Palms dragging against Olivia's skin, Margot squeezed her hips and pulled her closer until their knees bumped, and Olivia was forced to clutch at Margot's shoulders for balance. Margot tore her mouth from Olivia's, lips skimming over her chin, her jaw, trailing kisses to the sensitive patch of skin right beneath her ear, making Olivia shiver and squirm atop the couch, her nails biting into Margot's sweater.

Olivia swallowed hard, breath coming in fast, shallow pants. "Should we—should we talk about this?"

"You want to talk?" Margot nipped the lobe of Olivia's ear, and she whimpered. "Right now?"

Margot pressed a kiss to the hinge of Olivia's jaw, tongue darting out to taste her skin.

"I don't—um." Olivia's breath shuddered from between her lips. "Maybe?"

This felt like something they should address. Something they should talk about. Make sure they were both on the same page. But it was so hard to think with Margot touching her, Margot's mouth on her neck, fingers grazing the skin of her stomach, thumbs flirting with the underwire of her bra before dragging down, down, down, and slipping beneath the waist of her skirt, teasing as they dipped under the lace band of her panties. *Close.*

"I can talk," Margot whispered against her skin, nose sliding along Olivia's jaw. "I can tell you about how last night, I got myself off thinking about spreading your thighs and taking you apart with my tongue. How wet I got remembering how you taste and how when I slipped my fingers inside myself I pretended they were yours." Margot's right hand slid out from under Olivia's cardigan and ghosted over Olivia's wrist, where her pulse stuttered and sped, tangling their fingers together. Margot's thumb brushed the back of Olivia's hand, a gentle sweep along the back of her knuckles. Olivia's breath caught in the back of her throat. "I can tell you about how hard I came, clenching around my fingers, thinking about how I made you soak your sheets."

"Fuck," Olivia whimpered, pulse throbbing between her legs, heavy and insistent.

Margot's lips curved, a hot puff of air escaping, damp against Olivia's neck. "Want me to keep talking?"

This was so far from the talking Olivia had meant, but she couldn't bring herself to mind. Not when Margot was whispering hot and dirty in her ear.

"Please," Olivia murmured.

Margot hummed, fingers of the hand still beneath Olivia's cardigan sliding higher, curving around the side of Olivia's body, over her ribs, brushing the bottom of her breast. Margot's thumb grazed Olivia's nipple through the thin lace of her bra. Her teeth nipped at Olivia's ear at the same time as she pinched her nipple, making Olivia gasp, her thighs clenching together. "Is this okay?"

She pinched harder and Olivia whined, squirming. Olivia lifted a trembling hand from Margot's shoulder and tangled it in her hair.

"*God*, yes." She panted. "Please. Don't stop. Keep talking."

"You're so soft, Liv," Margot whispered, hand still cupping Olivia's breast. "And you're wearing too many clothes."

"Yeah?"

Both Margot's brows rose as she leaned back, fingers drawing teasing circles over Olivia's lace-covered skin, causing Olivia to openly shiver. The corners of Margot's mouth curled in obvious delight. "Yeah." Her tongue darted, wetting her bottom lip, and her dark eyes swept over Olivia's face, a flash of something that looked like insecurity flickering within them. "Do you want to go to my room?"

Olivia's tongue was thick, stuck to the roof of her mouth. "Yeah. Yes."

One hundred percent, absolutely, unequivocally *yes*.

A shy smile tugged at the corners of Margot's mouth, her

face flushed pink. "I had my annual appointment last month. Everything came back negative, and I haven't been with anyone since."

Olivia's heart thudded hard against her sternum. "Um, same. I mean, not last month. I got tested after . . . you know." She didn't want to talk about Brad right now. "And I haven't been with anyone since, either."

If Margot thought it was strange that she hadn't slept with anyone since Brad, she didn't say. Fingers still laced with Olivia's, Margot helped her off the couch, letting go to steady her when she swayed softly, legs wobbly and knees weak. Margot's hands slipped under Olivia's cardigan, fingers curling around her hips, pressing close, walking Olivia backward.

"Keep talking," Olivia whispered.

Margot crowded Olivia, pressing her back against the hallway wall. Margot's breath puffed against her mouth, a prelude to the tender brush of her lips.

"You want to know what I want to do to you?" Margot whispered against Olivia's mouth, one hand sliding out from Olivia's sweater to cradle the side of her neck, Margot's thumb brushing against Olivia's chin, skimming the front of her throat.

Olivia's whole body prickled with heat. "Mm-hmm."

Margot crowded closer, brushing her lips along Olivia's jaw, tracing the path her fingers had just made, only with her lips. Margot's tongue darted out, licking the hollow above Olivia's collarbone, teeth gently scraping her skin, making her shudder. Olivia's head fell to the side as she bared her neck.

"God, Liv." The hand on Olivia's hip inched lower, sliding beneath the waist of her skirt and between Olivia's thighs, cupping her over the damp lace of her underwear. "You have no idea how badly I want to put my mouth on you. *No idea.*" Margot nuzzled at the side of Olivia's throat, whimpering softly. "Jesus, just the thought of you riding my tongue has me fucking soaked, Liv."

"Please." Hips canting into Margot's hand, Olivia sought friction, *something*. "Touch me."

Margot's hand slid higher, fingers slipping beneath the lace of Olivia's underwear and lower, sliding over Olivia's trimmed curls, fingertips circling her clit, making the muscles in Olivia's stomach jump. "Like this?"

Olivia clutched at Margot's upper arms and arched into her touch, hips dancing, back bowing away from the wall.

"More," she rasped.

Lips dragging up Olivia's throat, Margot slid her fingers down Olivia's slit. A hiss escaped Margot's mouth. "Fuck, you're dripping."

Two fingers sank inside her with ease, and Olivia clenched around them, heat unspooling slowly inside her belly when Margot crooked them forward. What started as a slow drag quickly stole the air from Olivia's lungs as Margot's fingers sped, pressing hard and fast.

Olivia's thighs trembled, her hands sliding down Margot's arms to curl around her elbows, clutching hard, feeling shaky, like she was going to fly apart, like she wasn't quite sure where she'd land. *"Fuck."*

Margot laughed, breath damp and hot against the side of Olivia's neck. "You're so pretty like this. Shaking and desperate." Her teeth nipped at the sensitive skin of Olivia's earlobe, drawing a high whine from the back of Olivia's throat. "And *so* wet. You're dripping down the back of my hand, Liv."

Her face burned, heat rising to the surface of her skin at the slick sounds coming from between her thighs each time Margot curled her fingers. *"Please."*

Margot pressed a kiss to the side of Olivia's jaw, sucking at her skin. She ground the heel of her hand against Olivia's clit and—Olivia's knees buckled, unable to support her weight, the pleasure too sharp, too good, her legs too weak to withstand it and hold her upright.

Margot caught her around the waist and laughed. "You're so sensitive. I forgot."

Olivia dropped her head forward, burying her face and muffling her whimper against Margot's neck. "I was so close."

"Shh." One hand stroked the back of her head, fingers tangling in her hair, Margot's short nails raking gently against her scalp. "I'll get you there."

Of that, Olivia had no doubt.

Other than Margot, Olivia had only been with Brad, and he had never asked what she wanted, had never seemed to care. Sex with Brad hadn't been *bad*, sometimes it had actually been *good* or something close enough, but what she wanted, her pleasure, had never been his primary concern. It had definitely never been the objective, and she wasn't stupid—she knew that was wrong and not fair and sure as hell problematic, but there were only so many times she could move his hand, literally place his fingers where she needed them, before she gave up, trying more trouble than it was worth.

Talking about it hadn't worked; all Brad had done was look

bruised before snapping that there was nothing wrong with the way he fucked her, that it had worked just fine for other girls, implying that there was something wrong with her. It had probably never even crossed his mind that *just fine* was a sad, sad bar.

Sex with Margot was different. Margot had actually cared if Olivia got off, cared about what she liked, gave her what she wanted. Getting off hadn't seemed to be Margot's primary concern. Getting Olivia off—several times—seemed to have been what Margot cared about most.

There wasn't a doubt in Olivia's mind that Margot would get her there, probably more than once.

Margot tugged on Olivia's hair gently, drawing her head back until they were face-to-face. Margot's cheeks were flushed pink, the tips of her ears a fiery shade of red, undoubtedly hot to the touch. Eyes bright, Margot trapped her lower lip between her teeth and smiled. "Bed?"

Yes. Olivia bobbed her head. "Bed."

Hands biting into the curve of Olivia's waist, Margot herded her further down the hall, reaching around her for the doorknob, nudging her into Margot's bedroom, where it was dark. Margot flipped the light switch, bathing the room in an amber glow. Her hands returned, ushering Olivia deeper into the room until the backs of her knees hit the mattress and she tumbled down, bouncing softly. Margot followed her, bracketing her with a hand on either side of her head, caging her in with her body as her mouth descended, crashing down on Olivia's, making her head spin.

Just when Olivia's lungs started to burn, needing air but not wanting this to end, Margot drew back, leaving a trail of kisses down the front of Olivia's throat. Like she couldn't get enough.

Margot smiled against Olivia's skin and tugged at the hem of her sweater. "Help me get you naked."

Shoulders pressed to the mattress, Olivia arched her back. Hands neither coordinated nor graceful, they managed to rid her of her sweater. Margot's lips twitched, one finger flicking the tiny decorative gold bell between the floral lace cups of her bra. "Nice."

Olivia laughed. "Shut up."

Hands pressed against Olivia's shoulders, Margot urged her to lie back. She followed Olivia down, mouth fastened to her neck, sucking a mark against the side of Olivia's throat.

"I didn't say I don't like it." Margot kissed away the sting and smiled. "It's pretty. I just think I'd like it better on my floor."

Margot moved lower, lips scraping the surprisingly sensitive patch of skin drawn taut over Olivia's collarbone, and lower still, skimming the swell of her breasts. One of her hands slid up Olivia's back, short nails dragging along her spine on the way to the clasp of her bra, nimble fingers separating the hooks and eyes expertly.

Margot's fingertips tickled the backs of her arms as she dragged the straps downward, tossing Olivia's bra across the room. The air inside the apartment was warm, and her blood must've been about a million degrees, but something about having Margot's eyes on her made her skin prickle.

Margot's hair trailed across Olivia's flushed skin as she ducked her head, lips fastening to the peak of Olivia's right breast. A keen escaped Olivia's lips as she threw her head back against the pillow, eyes scrunching shut as Margot's tongue laved her skin.

Olivia's hands scrambled against Margot's back, squeezing, slipping beneath the hem of her sweater and dragging it upward, nails digging into the skin beneath her bra strap when Margot's teeth scraped against her nipple. Her hands shook and her back bowed, hips bucking as Margot walked her fingers down the center of Olivia's stomach, finding the zipper at the side of her skirt. The sound of the zipper's teeth was loud as Margot lowered it, fabric falling apart, air cool against the side of Olivia's hip and upper thigh.

She lifted her hips so Margot could slip the skirt down her legs and over her feet before dropping it to the floor. A ragged whimper escaped her lips. "Please."

Margot's lips were red and wet, and her cheeks were full of color, her eyes dark and bright. "Please *what*?"

She tugged at the hem of Margot's sweater. "Touch me."

Margot's fingers skimmed Olivia's sides. "I am."

Olivia bucked her hips. *"Margot."*

Margot surged forward, mouth covering Olivia's as she ran her hands up the inside of Olivia's legs, stopping at the crease of her thighs, fingers making maddening little swirls against the edge of her underwear. Teasing. Jesus. Olivia buried her hands in Margot's hair, nails scraping her scalp as she rolled her hips.

Margot's fingers hooked around the crotch of her panties, tugging them to the side, and *God*, Olivia was going to faint, she knew she was. It was going to happen, an inevitability, the tension too much, the lace of her underwear biting against the crease of her thigh, the air cool against her where she was hot and aching, riding the edge of desperation, her body still strung tight from almost coming in the hall.

All of it was too much, and yet somehow, not enough. It was maddening, the way Margot's other hand stroked a circuit from her knee to her hip. Finally, *finally* Margot took mercy on her, fingers brushing her clit and sliding through her folds, making her whole body jolt, just as sensitive as Margot had said.

"Fuck," Margot muttered, and Olivia was pretty sure that was *her* line, because *Jesus*.

She exhaled harshly and stared up at the ceiling where a faint crack shot through the plaster.

"What do you want, Liv?" Margot pressed a wet kiss just above her hip bone.

Articulating her desires was kind of beyond the realm of possibility at this point. She moaned instead.

"Just tell me what you want." Margot kissed her again, a little lower. "Tell me and I—whatever you need, Liv, just tell me and I'll give it to you." She sounded wrecked. "I want to give it to you."

"You."

Margot nuzzled the crease where her leg met her body, her hands wrapping around Olivia's thighs as she settled between her spread legs. "You want my mouth?"

Olivia opened her mouth to answer in an affirmative, but her simple *yeah* died a sudden death in the back of her throat as Margot ran the flat of her tongue up Olivia's center.

Good was an understatement. Her back bowed, nearly jack-knifing off the mattress. A shudder wracked her body, her fingers curling, and her nails biting into the bedspread beneath her when the tip of Margot's tongue flicked against her clit.

A jumble of nonsense sounds spilled from her lips as Margot made her thighs quake and her body tremble like a plucked string, two fingers crooking up inside her, that brilliant tongue lapping at her gently.

Close. She just needed a little *more.* She scrunched her eyes shut and slid her hand down her belly, fingers making fast and firm circles over her clit the way she liked best.

Wet heat engulfed her fingertips as Margot's tongue ran between her fingers, sucking them between her lips. Olivia pried her eyes open, breath catching in her throat as she glanced down. Even though Olivia was the one shaking and a breath away from falling apart, Margot's pupils were blown wide, only a thin ring of dark brown iris remaining. Her tongue, shiny and pink, was wrapped around two of Olivia's fingers.

Margot's teeth nipped at Olivia's fingertips before she nudged her hand aside.

Desperation drew a groan from her lips. "I'm so close."

"You want to come?" Margot continued to fuck Olivia with her fingers.

Olivia nodded, breath escaping her in shallow pants. "Uh-huh."

Margot curled her fingers hard and Olivia's muscles went taut. "Beg me for it."

Heat pooled between her thighs, her body burning, face on fire as the sound of Margot's fingers sliding into her grew louder, bordering on obscene. *"Please."*

"I know you can do better than that, Liv." Margot chuckled, tongue darting out, giving a quick kitten lick to her clit.

Olivia whimpered. "*Please.* Fuck. Margot. Please don't stop. *Please, please, please*—"

Margot's lips wrapped around her clit and sucked, tongue flicking hard and fast against the bundle of nerves.

It hit Olivia like a lightning strike down her spine, ripples of pleasure curling her toes and snatching the air from her lungs, the pleasure so sharp, so good it hurt. Her back bowed against the bed, her eyes snapping shut as she shook, coming apart at the seams.

Margot didn't let up. If anything, she doubled down, fingers curling a little faster, a little firmer, pressing against the spot inside her that she could never seem to reach by herself.

Olivia crunched forward, legs drawing up reflexively, fingers tangling in Margot's hair. "I—I can't—"

Before Olivia could finish telling Margot that it was too much, too good, that there was no way, she *couldn't*, Margot nudged her over the edge for a second time.

Her first inhale almost hurt, chest stinging as everything between her thighs continued to pulse in time with her heartbeat. Margot gentled, fingers no longer curling and thrusting, instead giving Olivia something to clench around as she came back to Earth. Tiny aftershocks made her tremble, and Margot's kisses turned into soft little licks as opposed to precise swipes.

The spots behind her lids disappeared as Olivia's breath evened out, her heart rate returning to normal, no longer frenzied like it was trying to escape through the wall of her chest.

Slowly, she pried her eyes open, blinking as the room came into view, reminding her that while it might have felt like Margot had sent her to outer space, she hadn't. Not literally, at least.

Margot had her chin resting on the soft swell beneath Olivia's belly button, her fingers tracing idle abstract shapes on the skin of her stomach and hips, little circles and lines that made Olivia shiver and—those weren't abstract shapes, they were letters. An *O*, an *M*, a heart. Margot drew their initials, re-creating the doodles she'd once drawn in the margins of the notes they used to pass in class.

Olivia's heart squeezed.

Margot was watching her, eyes so dark they almost appeared black, her smile a dizzying combination of fond and smug, and it made Olivia's core clench even though she was the dictionary definition of spent. She reached down and with shaking fingers tucked an errant strand of hair behind Margot's ear.

"Good?" Margot asked, turning her head, lips skimming the inside of Olivia's wrist.

A laugh escaped her. "Understatement."

Margot dropped her hand and sat up on her knees, reaching for the hem of her sweater and dragging it up and over her head.

Olivia rested her weight on her elbows. "Come here."

Margot balled her sweater up and tossed it on the floor before crawling closer, knees bracketing Olivia's hips as she dipped her head, kissing Olivia softly. Tempted by the new skin available to her, Olivia gripped Margot's waist. She was hot and felt like silk under Olivia's fingertips.

Olivia dropped her hands to the button of Margot's jeans,

then lowered the zipper. Margot broke the kiss, smile going crooked, almost shy as she leaned back, shimmying both her tight jeans and underwear down her thighs, leaving them in a heap beside the bed.

And Margot had called *her* pretty.

She was all smooth, pale skin and dark hair, black ink winding up the side of her hip, accentuating her curves and—Olivia's breath caught in her throat. Wrapped around Margot's wrist was her faded, frayed friendship bracelet, the one Olivia had held on to for the years, the one Margot had plucked from Olivia's keepsake box. She was still wearing it, and now, not much else.

A pretty pink flush crept up Margot's chest when she wrapped her fingers around Olivia's left wrist, sliding it down her stomach, guiding Olivia's hand between her legs. The curls between her thighs were dark and glistening with arousal, her inner thighs damp. Margot dragged Olivia's fingers through her wetness, a tiny gasp escaping her lips as their fingers brushed her swollen clit.

For a moment, Margot was all soft sighs and circling hips, bitten-off whimpers and throaty moans, her eyes slipping shut as she rocked against Olivia's hand. Despite having come twice, want prickled low in Olivia's belly. The sight of Margot with her head thrown back, undulating over Olivia's hips, her wetness coating Olivia's fingers, was enough to make her want more.

"Come here," Olivia repeated, tugging Margot closer, one hand on her hip.

Margot leaned forward, hair spilling around her face.

"No." Olivia wrapped both hands around Margot's thighs and wiggled a little further down the bed until she was completely flat, save for the pillow beneath her head. She licked her lips and craned her neck slightly, raising up and meeting Margot's eyes. Olivia arched both brows. "Up here."

Margot's jaw fell open. "You want me to . . ."

Olivia nodded, heart hammering in her throat. "Mm-hmm."

That endearing shade of red crept higher now, up Margot's throat and along her jaw. Even the tips of her ears turned neon. "Oh. Fuck." Her tongue darted out, wetting her lips. "Okay. Just . . . gimme a sec."

Careful of her where her limbs were, Margot crawled higher up the bed, higher up Olivia's body, until her knees bracketed Olivia's head. Margot curled her fingers around the headboard, holding herself up, and straddled Olivia's face.

Olivia wrapped her hands around the backs of Margot's thighs and drew her closer, lower, breathing her in, before turning her head and pressing a kiss to the inside of Margot's trembling thigh.

Margot's breath stuttered from between her lips. "Pinch me if you need to breathe or—*fuck*."

Olivia ran her tongue up the center of Margot's slit all the way up to her clit, moaning softly at her taste. Margot's body jerked, hips pressing down, rocking against Olivia's mouth.

"Fuck." Margot panted.

Olivia smiled at the stuttered, labored breaths escaping Margot. She lapped at Margot's clit, long strokes with the flat of her tongue, before gaining speed, flicking faster with the tip.

Margot's arms trembled as she clutched at the headboard. "Inside."

Fingers squeezing Margot's ass, Olivia dragged her tongue down to Margot's entrance, slipping inside, but just barely.

Sliding a hand between Margot's thighs, Olivia ran her fingers down Margot's slit, pushing two inside with ease, her own core clenching when Margot fluttered around her, a choked-off whimper falling from her lips.

A mottled flush crept up Margot's neck as she panted into the quiet of the room. Her thighs trembled as she rode Olivia's face, head flung back and spine arched. Her breasts swayed, dark hair swishing against her neck as she bit her bottom lip, turning it red. Margot's flush spread down her chest, even her stomach and the skin of her inner thighs turning a peachy shade of pink.

Sweat dampened the space between her breasts, and the air was thick with the scent of her arousal. All Olivia could smell was sex, sweet and musky and so perfect. She worked her fingers a little faster and wrapped her lips around Margot's clit, sucking hard. Margot keened, body shaking, clenching hard around Olivia's fingers as she fractured.

Margot slumped over, falling against the bed face-first with a frazzled laugh, their limbs jumbled, one of Margot's legs draped across Olivia's torso, Olivia's arm wedged beneath Margot's body.

Margot's skin was tacky, damp with sweat, her hair halfway in her face as she lay spent. Olivia's heart stuttered. *She'd* done that. Turned Margot into a soft and messy thing, loose-limbed and satisfied. Undone and all the more beautiful for it.

Margot's breathing slowed, and she lifted her head, her eyes opening a fraction. "Hi."

Olivia smiled, heart floating up like a helium balloon, rising into her throat. "Hey."

Margot rose up onto her hands and flipped over, staring up at the ceiling. A ghost of a smile graced her lips. "That was . . ." Her brows rose. "Wow."

"Wow," Olivia echoed in agreement, laughing softly. Sweat began to cool on her skin and she sat forward, looking for a blanket, a sheet, something to cover up with.

On the other side of the bed, Margot stood and stretched, arms rising over her head, back popping. She bent down and swiped her sweater off the floor, slipping it over her head, flipping the ends of her hair free from the collar.

Olivia frowned. Margot didn't so much as look her way once as she gathered the rest of her clothing off the floor. She slipped her underwear up her legs and tossed her jeans into the laundry basket beside her closet before crossing her arms, wobbling as she scratched the back of her calf with her opposite foot, still avoiding Olivia's eyes.

"So." Margot cleared her throat. "This was fun."

Olivia nodded. "Yeah."

"We should, um, do it again sometime." Margot gave a sharp, decisive nod, her eyes flickering over to Olivia's before she looked away. "If you want."

Olivia held her breath, waiting for her to say something else. Something . . . *more.* Anything, really. Proof that this meant as much to Margot as it did to her. That it wasn't just scratching an itch, sating the absurd sexual tension that had simmered between them since she'd moved in.

Silence stretched between them and the back of her throat ached.

God, Olivia was so *stupid*. Getting her hopes up . . . over what? Sex? She should've learned her lesson the first time. That sex didn't mean everything, didn't necessarily mean *anything*. Eleven years later and she was none the wiser, repeating history.

Margot didn't *want* her, not all of her. And Olivia couldn't even be angry. Margot hadn't promised her anything. Olivia had just assumed. And she couldn't say anything. Margot was her roommate, they lived together, and Olivia was planning her best friend's wedding. All complications that should've kept her out of Margot's bed, but Olivia had wanted her so desperately she'd thrown herself at Margot, thinking—

Wrong. She'd thought wrong, and now she had to suck it up.

She *needed* this wedding to pan out. She *needed* this apartment. She—*God* . . . she wanted Margot.

She knew what it was like, not having Margot in her life. She'd lived that and—she didn't want to go back, didn't want to go through that again. Olivia refused to erase the progress they'd made, sacrifice their friendship all because what? Because she couldn't have everything she wanted?

Everything she wanted. Olivia swallowed hard. Now *that* was a fairy tale. No one ever got everything they wanted, certainly not her, at least not in her experience.

She couldn't have everything, but maybe she could still have *this*. Margot as a friend, maybe something more, and maybe *one day*—

No, Olivia wouldn't indulge that desire. If she let it blossom, bloom, she'd get her hopes up and . . . this was *good*. This could be enough. She could be happy.

Something with Margot would always be better than nothing.

Chapter Eleven

ELLE (9:57 P.M.): MARGOT

ELLE (9:58 P.M.): !!!!

ELLE (9:58 P.M.): 😳 😭 😳

MARGOT (9:59 P.M.): Are you okay?!

ELLE (10:00 P.M.): <image attachment>

*O*h.

Oh, *wow.*

Margot's breath caught as stared at a slightly blurry selfie of Elle and Darcy beaming at the camera. In it, Elle had her hand held up in front of her, displaying a dazzling round-cut diamond that gleamed brightly from her ring finger.

Margot's phone rang, and she took a deep breath, smiling when she answered because she'd read somewhere that people could pick up on that sort of thing in your voice. "Hey—"

A piercing screech made Margot wince and tug the phone away from her ear.

"Did you see? Did you see it?" Elle demanded. "*Margot!* I'm engaged!"

A genuine laugh escaped her. "I saw it, Elle. Congratulations!"

Elle let loose a softer, slightly more subdued but equally as joyful squeal. "Darcy took me up to the observatory and it was—*God*, Mar. It was perfect. And this ring! Oh sweet Saturn. Darcy said she wanted to get me my birthstone, but apparently amethyst isn't very durable. Something abouts a Mohs' scale? I don't even know. But then she found this! The halo's shaped like a *star*, and get this—the band is inlaid with actual meteorite. From fucking *space*."

Margot chuckled at Elle's out-of-control enthusiasm. "It sounds perfect, Elle."

"It is, it *really* is." Elle gave a happy-sounding sigh. "Darcy's on the phone with Brendon right now, and I know I should've probably called my parents but . . . you're the first person I wanted to tell."

A knot formed in Margot's throat, the backs of her eyelids stinging. "I'm glad you called." She swallowed before her voice could crack. "I'm—like I said, I'm so happy for you." She laughed. "*Fuck.* I mean, *damn*, Elle. You're engaged."

Engaged to be married. Holy shit.

Margot's bedroom door inched open and Cat peeked inside. She inspected her surroundings with curious sniffs as she wandered further into the room, detouring to Margot's closed closet door and smacking it with her paw. When it didn't budge, Cat headed over to Margot's bed. Margot tucked her feet up under her and frowned when Cat let out a demanding little trill.

"Margot?"

"Sorry." She cringed. "I, um, got distracted. You were saying?"

"I asked if you'll be my Maid of Honor, silly." Elle laughed. "Darcy's making faces at me—hold on." The line went muffled, Elle's voice distant. "Sorry, Darcy says I should've asked you in a note or a gift box or something."

"Oh!" She pressed the heel of her hand into her chest as if she could massage away the ache inside. "I, uh, don't need a gift box."

"I could buy you a box of wine?"

Margot laughed. "I won't say no to wine."

"*So?*" Elle asked, sounding impatient but mostly just eager.

"So of course." Warmth bloomed between her ribs. "I'd be honored." Her lips quirked. *"Ba-dum-tss."*

Just like she'd hoped, Elle chuckled. "I'm glad. Oh, this is going to be so great. It's March, and obviously nothing's set in stone, but Darcy and I were thinking about a winter wedding, so that would mean . . ."

Cat crouched low and leaped onto Margot's bed, landing gracefully on all fours, the duvet barely depressing beneath her weight, which was made of mostly fur and sass. She stomped around, pawing at Margot's pillows before stopping directly in front of Margot.

And staring.

"Mar? Are you still there?"

Margot sighed. "Yeah, I'm so sorry. I am. I'm just—this cat keeps staring at me and I don't know if it's a friendly stare or an *I want to eat your face* look." Margot had woken up at four in the morning to the unsettling feeling of being watched. She'd rolled over, and sure enough, *somehow* Cat had found her way into Margot's room, Margot's *closed* room, hopped up onto Margot's bed, lain down, and proceeded to purr like an engine. Whether that meant Cat was warming up to her or simply studying her, lying in wait for the right moment to attack, Margot had no fucking clue. "But I'm totally listening."

Elle went quiet before clearing her throat. "Are you sure you're okay? You sound a little . . . off."

Off. Fuck. Margot dropped her head into her hand and swallowed a sigh. The last thing she wanted was for her—her *weirdness* and messy, all-over-the-place feelings to get out. She was dealing, working through them. Talking to Olivia had helped, but Margot wasn't going to magically feel less like her friends were leaving her behind, and it definitely wasn't going to happen overnight. It was going to take time and, honestly, seeing proof that just because everyone was getting married didn't mean everything would change.

For Elle's sake, for the sake of their friendship, Margot needed to pull her head out of her ass, *stat.* "You want to know the truth?"

Elle sucked in a sharp breath. "Hit me with it."

"Darcy already told me she was planning to propose. She pulled me aside and told me after the cake tasting, so—so that's why I sound off. I was trying to act surprised, and you know me, I can't act for shit."

Elle laughed, obviously relieved. "You had me worried for a second. Geez. Okay, I can see that happening. So you've known since Saturday?"

"Mm-hmm." Margot scratched her jaw, eyes flitting to Cat and away. Cat kept staring, little head cocked slightly to the side, her small body forming a squat triangle as she sat. Her front paw reached out, patting the bed in front of Margot's knee, and she meowed. Margot frowned. "Look, I absolutely want to chat more about this, okay? Maybe when we're up at the lodge tomorrow for the bachelor-bachelorette trip, yeah? We can sip spiked cider and you can tell me all about it. Right now, I've got to figure out what this cat wants."

"Good luck." Elle snickered, then gasped. "Wait! Do you think Olivia could help with our wedding?"

Cat meowed louder, stomping closer, getting all up in Margot's space, stepping on Margot's socked feet with her front paws.

"Um, I don't see why not. You should definitely ask her."

"Okay, you go take care of your *cat*astrophe." Elle chuckled at her own joke. "I'll talk to you later, 'kay?"

"Later." Margot ended the call and tossed her phone down beside her with a groan. She looked at Cat and frowned. "How do you think I sounded? Pretty convincing?"

Cat sneezed.

Huh.

"Okay, whatever that's supposed to mean." Margot sighed. "I *am* happy for Elle, you know? I'm just . . . conflicted. Which is normal, I guess. I just need to—to get a grip. Pull it together. Because that's what good friends do."

Cat cocked her head, whiskers twitching. She patted at Margot's leg—claws mercifully retracted—and meowed.

If only she knew what the cat was saying—*oh, wait*. She'd downloaded an app, the one that apparently translated cat-speak into English. It sounded suspect, the science behind it pretty much nonexistent, but there was no harm in trying.

Margot opened up the app and hit the *record* button.

Cat stared at her, silent.

"Meow?" Margot tried.

If she wasn't mistaken, she could've sworn Cat's eyes narrowed, judging her.

"Come on. *Now* you want to be quiet?"

She closed the app with a sigh.

Almost immediately, Cat gave a soft, kittenish-sounding mewl.

"You're kind of an asshole, you know that?" Margot smiled. "It's okay. I can be a little bit of an asshole sometimes, too."

Cat's tail swished from side to side. She stood, stretched, then hopped off Margot's bed, sauntering across the room. She stopped just shy of the door and looked back over her shoulder, giving a sharp, insistent meow that made it clear she wanted *something*.

Margot sighed and stood. "What is it? Did Timmy fall down the well?"

Cat's eyes narrowed into green slits.

Yeesh. Tough crowd. "Okay, to be fair, I'll admit that a dog joke might've been in poor taste. But most of my cat jokes are in *equally* poor taste, so it was kind of a lose-lose."

With a swish of her tail, Cat left the room, looking back once, as if making sure Margot followed.

Instead of turning left toward the living room, Cat went right, turning the corner into Olivia's room. Margot's footsteps faltered.

Because of Cat, Olivia kept her door open at all times, even when she wasn't home. Like now. Olivia was downstairs in the basement, doing a load of laundry.

Cat gave another sharp screech, looking at Margot as if wondering what was taking her so long. *Assuming* that's what that cat wanted. Margot didn't know. It was all a guessing game.

"You need to wait until your . . ." She trailed off. Cat mom? Handler? *Human?* Hell if she knew. "You've got to wait 'til Liv comes back, you little monster."

Margot couldn't just waltz inside Olivia's bedroom, even if the door was open. There were boundaries. Having sex didn't automatically negate their need for their own space. *Privacy.* They'd never said bedrooms were off-limits, but wasn't it implied? Margot couldn't just—

Cat wailed like a banshee, hitting a pitch that shouldn't have been possible. Margot cringed and—fuck it. If ever there was a time to throw caution to the wind, it was now, her eardrums practically bleeding as Cat freaking caterwauled. It wasn't like she'd be snooping through Olivia's belongings. All she wanted was to figure out what the hell was wrong with this cat and make her stop screaming. Olivia would understand.

Margot stepped inside the room and flipped the lights. She cast a glance around the room, gaze stutter-stopping at the corner near Olivia's closet. Cat sat beside her litter box with a subtle yet discernible frown on her already scrunchy face. Her ears were down and flat, and she wailed once more.

Margot held her breath and stepped closer and—

"Are you *shitting* me right now?"

Cat blinked, utterly unrepentant.

Margot pulled her shirt up over her nose. Cat hadn't bothered to cover her business. Just left it there, bold as could be, in the center of the litter box.

"I'm not cleaning that," Margot muttered. "You can wait until Olivia comes back."

Cat looked up, doing her best damn impression of Puss in Boots, all wide, innocent eyes. A sad little mew escaped her. Margot shook her head, turned on her heel, and—

Another one of those banshee-like screams filled the air.

Margot shut her eyes.

This was her life now. Being led around by a cat, a cat who had destroyed her favorite vibrator, and now demanded she clean up her poop. Oh, how the mighty had fallen.

Margot huffed and spun on her heel. "Okay, fine. Just this once. This is not going to become a habit, you hear me?"

Cat stared.

Pooper scooper . . . pooper scooper . . . where would Olivia keep a scooper? Margot checked beside the litter box, finding a stash of lightly floral-scented bags for depositing Cat's business in. But no scooper. She crouched low and checked under Olivia's desk. Squat. Beside the door. Nope. Unless it was right in front of Margot's eyes and she'd missed it, the pooper scooper was nowhere to be seen.

Cat let loose another aggrieved-sounding meow as if this was taking too long.

Margot took a deep, bracing breath and shook open one of the pastel pink bags. A sweet lavender scent filled the air, masking the odor coming from the litter box. Margot shoved her hand inside the bag and crouched in front of the box.

"I can't believe I'm actually doing this," she muttered.

Cat stood and circled the box, taking a seat directly beside Margot, watching. Inspecting. *Judging.*

Hand encased in a thin layer of plastic, Margot carefully reached inside the litter box, fishing out the piece of poo.

"This is degrading," she muttered under her breath. "And demoralizing." She glanced at Cat, who had her little head cocked up at Margot, eyes wide, whiskers twitching. "Wipe that self-satisfied smile off your face." Cat leaned in and bumped Margot's arm with her head, starting up a low, rumbling purr. Margot's insides melted. "Oh, Jesus, you're too cute. You played me like a fiddle, didn't you? Ugh. I bet you're laughing inside, aren't you? *Ha, humans have thumbs, but look at you, shoveling my shit. Who's the smarter species now?*"

"Margot?"

Oh, shit.

Margot shuffled on her knees, pivoting to face the door. Olivia stood, laundry basket propped against her hip, a frown furrowing her brows.

"Um." Margot lifted a hand, the one protected by a thin layer of plastic, holding Cat's poo. "This isn't what it looks like?"

Olivia pressed her lips together, looking like she was trying not to laugh. "Honestly? I don't even *know* what this looks like."

Margot dropped her chin and chuckled. "Okay. Your cat kept whining and she—she pulled a Lassie and led me in here and there was"—she waved her hand and, okay gross, that was a bad idea—"*this*. I couldn't find your litter scooper, so I . . . improvised?"

"You improvised." Olivia's shoulders shook with silent laughter.

"People pick up their dogs' droppings with little plastic bags all the time. This isn't any different."

Except for the mortification. That was exciting and new.

Olivia set her laundry basket down and crossed the room. She stepped on the foot pedal of the trash can against the wall and pointed at a handy-dandy compartment tucked inside the lid, where the pooper scooper was hidden out of sight. "It keeps everything nice and odor-free."

"Right." Margot's face warmed as she stared at her hand full of cat poo. "This isn't awkward at all."

Olivia laughed. "I, um, appreciate the effort."

Carefully, Margot slipped the plastic down her arm and over her wrist, turning the bag inside out. She tied it off and tossed it in the open can, Olivia's foot still depressing the pedal for her.

"I'm going to go scrub my hands," she mumbled, slipping out into the hall and into the bathroom.

Olivia followed a few seconds later, Cat cradled in her arms like an overgrown furry baby. She leaned against the doorjamb, watching as Margot pumped hand soap into her palms, coating them in a liberal lather.

"I really do appreciate it," Olivia said, hiking Cat a little higher. "You could've waited until I came back."

Not really, with Cat practically howling her displeasure.

Margot shrugged and turned off the tap, flicking excess water from her fingers before reaching for the hand towel. "It's fine. I hope you don't mind I went into your room."

"Why would I mind?" Olivia bent down and set Cat on the floor when she started to wiggle.

Margot turned and leaned her hip against the sink. "I don't know. I guess I didn't want you to think I was invading your . . . I don't know, privacy or something. I wasn't in there snooping. Strictly shoveling poo."

Olivia stepped closer, stopping when their toes bumped, both wearing socks. Olivia's were white with a pink stripe across the toes, Margot's basic black. Olivia smiled. "It's not like I have anything to hide. And besides"—she rested a hand on either side of the sink by Margot's hips, boxing her in—"I trust you."

Margot's heart bungeed into her throat. "Cool. That's . . ."

Olivia's lips twitched, eyes roving over Margot's face.

She swallowed hard. "I trust you, too."

A broad smile lit up Olivia's face. The hands on either side of Margot closed in, sliding over the sink, settling against Margot's hips and squeezing softly. Olivia's fingers skimmed the highest point of Margot's ass, and then she leaned in, head tilting to the side, the tip of her nose brushing Margot's, breath wafting warm and sweet against Margot's mouth.

It was almost embarrassing how weak her knees went from such a chaste kiss. A sigh escaped her as she gripped Olivia's arms, losing herself in the softness of Olivia's mouth and the sweet, subtle perfume of her skin.

Olivia drew back, ending the kiss before Margot was ready, a tiny wrinkle between her eyes. "Was that okay?"

"Yes? I mean, a little brief for my taste, but—"

Olivia ducked her head and laughed. "No, I meant kissing you. Is it okay if I do?"

Color her confused. "Why *wouldn't* it be okay?"

"We didn't really talk about it."

No, no, they hadn't.

As soon as the sweat had started to cool against her skin and her heart rate was no longer racing, Margot had—in what wasn't one of her finest moments—panicked.

The *one* thing she wasn't supposed to do, a line she wasn't supposed to cross, and what had she done? She'd taken a running leap and hurled herself over it, headfirst.

But then again, it wasn't sex that had complicated everything between them the first time. It was that Margot had had *feelings*.

The only reasonable solution was to take *feelings* completely off the table. Prevent them from forming in the first place. To keep things between them casual.

"I don't want to overstep or do anything that makes you uncomfortable," Olivia added.

Short of pushing Margot away or leaving, there was nothing Margot could imagine Olivia doing that would make her uncomfortable.

"You won't," Margot said.

"So, I can kiss you?"

Margot nodded. "You can kiss me whenever you want."

Olivia's lips curved. "Careful. I might get greedy."

Please do.

Margot laughed. "Somehow, I don't see myself complaining."

"Good." Olivia leaned in, pecking Margot quickly.

"You have plans tonight?" Margot bit her lip and snuck her

hands under the back of Olivia's tee, trailing a finger up her spine and biting back a smile when Olivia shivered.

Olivia's hips jerked forward, a soft, sweet laugh escaping her lips. "Other than folding laundry?"

"Screw laundry." Margot reversed the course of her hands, tucking them under the waist of Olivia's jeans. Her thumbs traced circles along the dimples at the base of Olivia's spine, touching sensitive skin that made her press even closer. Olivia's grip on Margot's hips tightened, fingers biting into Margot's ass, making her grin at how easy it was to elicit a reaction from Olivia.

Or maybe Margot was just that good at it. Yeah, she liked that option much better.

"Mmm. Aren't you supposed to say something like *why do laundry when you can do me instead?*"

"You know me so well." She leaned in, pressing her lips to the velvety-soft skin just beneath Olivia's ear.

Leaning her head to the side, Olivia bared her neck, giving Margot more room to work with, more skin to worship. A soft hum escaped her throat before the hands grasping Margot's hips squeezed and Olivia stepped back, her hum of content morphing into a regretful groan that Margot couldn't help but echo. "Before I forget. Brendon texted me."

"Okay?"

"He invited me up to Snoqualmie for his and Annie's joint bachelor-bachelorette trip," Olivia explained, thumbs inching under the hem of Margot's shirt. "Is that okay?"

Olivia's fingers made maddening little circles against Margot's sides. Goose bumps erupted across her skin, and for a split second her brain went fuzzy, lost in the sensation. "Um. Why wouldn't it be?"

Olivia shrugged. "They're your friends." And Margot was ninety-nine percent sure Brendon was trying to adopt Olivia into the fold. "I don't want it to be weird."

"Zero weirdness," Margot said. "At least not for me?"

Olivia drew her lip between her teeth. "Have you, um, told them . . . ?"

About what? Saturday? Or years before?

Margot shook her head. She was going to assume Olivia meant the former, otherwise she probably would've brought it up before now. "It hasn't really come up. With the wedding and everything."

"Right." Olivia nodded quickly. "Makes sense."

Plus, there was that whole thing where Margot didn't know how to begin explaining this to her friends. The past, the now, none of it. Knowing Brendon, he'd probably get it in his head that *casual* was a pit stop on the way to falling in love. He'd take it upon himself to play Cupid, to make their relationship into *more*.

He'd hassle her, his heart in the right place, but the road to hell was paved with good intentions. *This*, her and Olivia, felt precarious enough without added meddling. Even if it was well-meaning.

"This is kind of a weird ask, but . . . do you think we could keep this quiet?" Margot winced. "That sounds terrible. Jesus. It's just, you've met Brendon. You've seen how he can be, and that's only in the handful of interactions you've had."

Olivia nibbled on her bottom lip, staring over Margot's

shoulder into the mirror. "They're *your* friends, Mar. You can tell them or not tell them whatever you want." She flashed Margot a smile and shrugged. "I'm just their wedding planner."

And the wedding was in under a week. Olivia would no longer be *just* their wedding planner. Hell, she was already more than that. Margot's roommate, Margot's friend, Margot's—*something*.

"It doesn't have to be forever," Margot said, her stupid voice cracking on the last word. Forever. Wow, way to imply that this thing between them had longevity. Fuck. Margot's stomach knotted. Something else to talk about.

"I guess it wouldn't hurt to, um, keep things under wraps until after the wedding," Olivia said. "Keep things focused on Brendon and Annie."

"Right." Margot nodded quickly. "And, um, we can decide to tell them or not after."

"Sure." Olivia smiled and resumed tracing shapes into Margot's skin. "The grocery store down the street is open twenty-four hours, right?"

"No. Only until midnight. Do you need something?" Something that couldn't wait?

"Cat's out of food. I thought I had another can in the pantry, but I don't." Olivia's lips twisted to the side. "That, and I know Annie and Brendon said no gifts at the bachelor-bachelorette party, but I don't want to show up empty-handed. I was thinking I'd bake cookies, and you have no sugar."

Typical Liv, needing to bring a hostess gift. Margot smiled. "You know, most people bring alcohol or . . . I don't know, a dip."

Olivia's brows rose. "A dip?"

"Yeah. You know, sour cream or hummus or—I don't know. *Dip.*"

Brendon was the first of her friends to get married. The whole of her knowledge of bachelor and bachelorette parties came from movies like *The Hangover* and *Bridesmaids*.

Olivia smiled. "I guess I'm not most people, then."

"No," Margot agreed, warmth spreading through her chest. "You aren't."

Olivia ducked her head, but there was no mistaking the way her smile began to curl. "If I'm baking cookies, I need sugar. A few other odds and ends, too."

"We've got break-and-bake dough in the fridge," Margot said, erring on the side of simplicity. That, and it was hard, though not impossible, to fuck up premade dough.

Olivia wrinkled her nose. "I want to make *real* cookies. My grandma's cookies."

Oh, shit. "You mean the chocolate cookies with—"

"White chocolate chunks?" Olivia nodded. "Yup. My grandma's tar cookies."

Margot's mouth watered. She stepped away from the counter and fished her phone out of her pocket. "It's only after ten."

Olivia cocked her head. "Want to go with me? Keep me company?"

Margot shrugged. She wasn't doing anything. "Sure. Let me grab my jacket."

Three minutes later, they were out on the rain-splattered sidewalk. Margot tugged her hood over her head and crossed her arms against the chill, setting off down the street in the direction of the QFC.

A blast of heat blew her hood back as soon as they stepped through the automatic doors and into the grocery store. Bypassing the carts, Margot paused in front of the bank of registers. "I'm going to head to the freezer section. Meet you by the self-check?"

Olivia nodded, already shuffling in the direction of the aisle marked *pet care*. "Sounds good."

Margot meandered toward the ice cream, stopping to snag a bag of Reese's off the endcap of an aisle, grabbing a box of Sour Patch Kids, too, because Olivia had an affinity for things that were sour and sweet and—*huh*. A snort escaped her, earning her a sideways look from a woman wearing a fur coat pushing a cart full of mayonnaise. Thirteen jars of Kraft mayonnaise and not a single other item in her cart, though it looked like she was seriously considering the bag of Pop Rocks in her hand.

Capitol Hill after dark was an interesting place, that was for sure. Margot loved it here.

Ooh, Ben & Jerry's had a new flavor featuring peanut butter cups *and* peanut butter swirls. Margot cracked open the freezer, a chilly blast of air nipping at her face as she bypassed the closest pint and grabbed the second out of habit. She was still bitter that they'd discontinued her favorite flavor, sending it to the flavor graveyard, because apparently *some* people had no taste and couldn't appreciate a good thing. *This* was a small concession, one she was eager to try.

"Hey." Olivia ducked her head around the aisle, arms laden with sugar, cocoa powder, chocolate chips, and several cans of Friskies cat food in delightful flavors like—Margot squinted—*chicken griller* and *cheesy ocean feast*. Yikes. Margot would stick with peanut butter swirl, thanks. She smiled ruefully. "I forgot a basket." A smile played at the edges of Olivia's mouth when she spotted the Sour Patch Kids in Margot's other hand. "Are those for me?"

"These?" She wrinkled her nose. "Oh, I was about to put these back on the—"

"Shut up." Olivia laughed and stepped closer, crowding Margot up against the glass door of the freezer, earning a glare from the woman with the cart full of mayo and, now, Pop Rocks, who was perusing the Magic Shell fudge sauce at the end of the aisle.

Margot pressed her lips together, muffling a snicker. She dropped her voice to a whisper. "Look at her cart. Think she has big plans for tonight?"

Olivia's eyes darted to the left, doing a double take at the contents of the cart. "Holy—okay, I don't want to yuck anyone's yum, but some things aren't okay."

"Right?" Margot muffled another laugh when the woman grabbed every single jar of fudge sauce, easily six, off the shelf and added them to her cart.

"I mean, *Kraft*?" Olivia tutted. "Hellmann's or bust."

Laughter bubbled up Margot's throat and past her lips. *"Liv."*

Olivia beamed at her, hazel eyes crinkling. She leaned closer, breath warm against Margot's mouth. The very tip of her nose brushed Margot's once, twice, three times before she pressed a kiss to the corner of Margot's mouth.

"Tease," Margot muttered, breathless, practically vibrating from holding still, letting Olivia come to her.

"Not if I follow . . ." Olivia frowned. "I'm buzzing."

Margot chuckled. "You give me tingles, too, Liv."

Olivia burst out laughing. "No. I mean, *yes*, but I meant my butt's buzzing." She stepped back and turned, looking at Margot over her shoulder. "Could you grab my phone? My hands are full."

Oh. Margot wiggled her fingers into the tight back pocket of Olivia's jeans, prying her phone free. The name on the screen caught her eye. "Why the hell is Brad calling you?"

Saying his name put a funny taste in Margot's mouth, bitter like she'd drunk coffee that had gone cold and stale. Admittedly, she'd never been Brad's biggest fan, and not only because he'd dated Olivia. When he hadn't ignored Margot, he'd called her *Cargo*, a childish taunt that had butchered her name and implied she was Olivia's sidekick, her *baggage*, all in one fell swoop. Of course, he'd only called her that when Olivia wasn't around because he was also a coward of the highest order, but *whatever*. The past was the past, and that was the whole point.

Olivia's eyes widened. "Um. I don't know." She juggled the cans in her arms, dropping one. It clattered against the floor, rolling down the aisle and under the freezer. Olivia frowned at it. "He just . . . does sometimes."

Margot goggled at her. "As in, he does this on what? A regular basis?"

Olivia's throat jerked. "Define *regular*."

"Jesus," Margot murmured. Olivia's phone continued to vibrate against her palm. "You answer?"

Olivia cradled the remaining cans, eyes flitting between Margot's face and that lost can. "I . . ." She cringed sharply and gestured to the phone with her elbow. "Could you just . . ."

"Are you serious?" Margot stared at her. "You want me to answer it?"

Olivia cringed. "I'll be so quick. Just . . . hold it up to my ear?" She stared at Margot with wide eyes and—*ugh*, Margot couldn't believe she was doing this. A testament to how little she wouldn't do for Olivia.

She swiped at the screen and held the phone against Olivia's ear.

"Brad?" Olivia rolled her lips together and shifted her weight from one foot to the other, looking as uncomfortable as Margot felt. "Now isn't a good time."

Margot bit down hard on the inside of her cheek.

Olivia shut her eyes. "No. It's in the junk drawer." She sighed, forehead creasing in irritation. "The junk drawer, Brad. The catch-all drawer in the kitchen. The one below the coffee maker. The one that sticks when you—yes, that one. It's in there. Check in the back." Olivia's shoulders slumped, and Margot was tempted to hang up the phone for her. "No, Brad. I have to go. Good n—"

Margot ended the call with a little more gusto than strictly necessary, jamming her finger against the screen. She reached around Olivia and slid the phone back into her pocket, then stepped back, crossing her arms. "How often does Brad call you, Liv?"

One of Olivia's shoulders rose and fell, too jerky to be casual. "Sometimes. I don't . . . It's not like I'm keeping track. It's enough to be a nuisance, but not enough to be a problem."

A nuisance *was* a problem. Anything that put a frown that

severe on Olivia's face was a problem, and she shouldn't have to put up with it.

"What's he even calling you about at"—Margot dug inside her pocket for her own phone—"eleven at night, anyway?"

Olivia rolled her eyes. "He was looking for the spare garage door opener."

"And he called *you*?"

A can of cat food teetered, stacked precariously atop the rest. Margot snatched it just as it fell, holding on to it for Olivia.

Olivia nibbled on her lip and nodded. "It's—it's always stupid little things, Mar. I just shrug it off. It's not worth getting up in arms about. Trust me."

"Why haven't you told him to fuck off?" Or, better yet . . . "Why do you even take his calls? Just block his number."

"I asked him to stop."

"You *asked* him." Margot's tongue bulged against the side of her cheek.

Olivia blew the hair out of her face with a weary sigh. "It's not that simple."

Margot bit her tongue against the urge to blurt out that it sure sounded simple to her. Cut-and-dried. *Fuck off.* Two little words, but . . . she wasn't in Olivia's shoes. "Help me understand what makes it complicated, then."

Olivia stared at her for a second, eyes flitting over Margot's face as if weighing the sincerity of Margot's request. After a moment, her gaze dropped to ground between them, her voice quiet but steady. "It's not like I *want* to take his calls, but I can't just block his number." Her jaw ticked, a muscle beneath her ear jumping. "I've asked him not to call me unless it's about something serious."

Margot was trying to understand, but it didn't make sense. Olivia and Brad had been divorced for a year, and from the sound of it, they didn't share close mutual friends. They didn't have pets or kids to shuffle from one house to another. And they hadn't exactly ended on the best of terms, what with Brad being a cheating ass. The longer she puzzled through this in her head, the less it made sense and the more frustrated she got on Olivia's behalf, her blood pressure rising. "Okay. What would possibly be serious enough for Brad to need to contact you?"

Olivia shrugged, sending another can tumbling. It rolled across the tile floor all the way to the end of the aisle, stopping against the wheel of the cart belonging to the woman with all the mayo. The woman nudged the can back toward them with a kick. It stalled out midway down the aisle, and Margot left it there. She'd pick it up later.

"I told you about my dad. About his heart attack last year," Olivia said, staring down the aisle at the can. "He's doing okay, but . . . I know he doesn't like me to worry. But it's not like I worry for no reason. Dad's not always the most forthcoming. He drove himself to the hospital when it happened. He only let the nurse call me when he found out he was going to be admitted overnight." Her voice cracked and she sniffed hard. "When he tells me he's fine, I can't help but worry that his definition of *fine* and mine aren't the same." Olivia gave another one of those bone-weary-sounding sighs that made Margot want to bundle her up and take her back home. It had only been a couple weeks, but already Margot's brain had made the transition to thinking of the apartment as *theirs* and not just *hers*. "So I asked Brad to let me know if he hears anything. Dad's still friendly with Brad's parents. He and Dad run into each other sometimes. They go to the same football watch parties. It's a small town. People hear things I don't from fifty miles away."

"Do they ever," Margot muttered under her breath. "My dad's the resident busybody, apparently, remember?"

Olivia cracked a smile, the first in too long.

Margot inhaled deeply and nodded slowly. "Okay. So you asked Brad to keep you posted if something happens to your dad." She couldn't say she agreed with that plan, but she could understand where Olivia was coming from. "But he calls you out of the blue. About garage door openers?"

"Stupid things," Olivia agreed, head bobbing. "Like I said, I've asked him to stop, but it's not worth getting upset over. I answer, I try to keep it brief. You heard. Then I let him go." Olivia's lips flattened. "It's irritating, but I can't block him. What if he calls and it's actually something important?"

A throat cleared. The woman wearing the fur coat with the cart full of mayo stood, brows raised impatiently as she stared at the freezer behind them. "You're blocking the frozen yogurt."

"Shoot, sorry." Olivia offered a smile and stepped out of the way. Rather than merely shuffling to the side, she nodded toward the front of the store. Margot followed after her, swiping the can off the floor on the way to the checkout.

"I'll get it." Margot waved Olivia off, paying for the cat food in addition to the ice cream, candy, and ingredients for cookies.

Olivia tucked her wallet away with a smile. "Thanks."

It wasn't until they were back out on the street that Margot circled back around, not ready to drop the subject. "It sounds to me like you've requested a boundary and Brad continues to ignore it. That's not okay, Liv. I know you care about your dad, I . . ." Margot swallowed, the next words out of her mouth almost *I love that about you.*

Margot's heart skipped a beat before crashing hard against the wall of her chest. All the blood in her head seemed to drain south, leaving her dizzy. Where the hell had *that* come from? She didn't *love* Olivia. No. If Margot loved anything, it was Olivia's endless capacity to care about people, strangers and friends and family and stray cats alike.

She sucked in a lungful of air. It wasn't anything worth freaking out over. Even if she did love Liv, Margot loved lots of things. Ice cream. Tequila. Her air fryer. Her friends. No big. Olivia cared, and so what if Margot loved that about her?

It wasn't like she was *in* love with her.

"It just pisses me off," Margot said, picking up as if she hadn't stopped midsentence and gone silent for a beat too long, too telling. "I am—I am *incensed* on your behalf because . . . damn it, Liv. You deserve better than Brad trying to con you into talking to him for whatever bullshit he calls you about. He is a grown-up. He can find a garage door opener without having to resort to calling his ex-wife. The ex-wife he took for granted. I guarantee you he *knows* why you answer, and he's counting on that. He's counting on you being kind. Counting on you wondering and worrying, and if on the off chance he *isn't*? If he's just selfish and oblivious? That's not any better.

That's not an excuse. Your boundaries and your feelings and what you want matter. You deserve better, Olivia."

By the time she'd finished speaking—*ranting*—she was practically panting on the street corner, her face flushed so severely that she was surprised the misty rain falling around them didn't turn to steam against her skin.

Olivia blinked, spun-gold lashes clumping together. Light from the streetlamp reflected off her eyes, bringing out the flecks of gold in her irises and turning the center ring of deep forest green that hugged her pupil into a brighter, brilliant shade of emerald.

The smooth column of Olivia's throat jerked as she stepped forward, resting her hands on Margot's waist. Margot held impossibly still as Olivia leaned in, pressing an achingly sweet kiss against Margot's bottom lip. Olivia drew back but didn't go far, staying close enough that Margot could make out the tiny drops of rain clinging to her lashes. "Thanks, Mar."

It took a second to make her muscles move, to nod. "No need to thank me. I was just being honest."

"What did you think I was thanking you for?" Olivia's lips tipped up at the corners, and Margot's heart stuttered. "What you said—all of it . . . that means a lot to me. That you feel that way."

Swallowing took effort as did her shrug. "Just—think about what I said."

"I will."

Chapter Twelve

Olivia dropped the grocery bags on the kitchen floor and began unpacking them, setting the sugar and cocoa powder down on the counter.

Circling her feet, Cat mewled, ignoring the bowl of dry kibble beside the fridge, demanding wet food instead.

"I'll get it." Margot slid behind Olivia and swiped a can of Friskies off the counter. She cracked open the metal pull-top lid and dumped the pâté on a plate. "Come on, you little monster. Time for food."

Olivia laughed. "Little monster?"

"She *is*," Margot said, snagging her Ben & Jerry's and carrying it over to the freezer. "The cat screams like a banshee. I swear, half the time she doesn't meow, she *howls*."

Margot wasn't wrong. Cat could reach a screeching pitch Olivia had never heard prior to adopting her. "She is a little bit of a hellion, isn't she?"

Cat's green eyes flicked up, ears twitching as if she knew she was being talked about. Her tail swished, and she lowered her gaze to the plate, focus returning to her food.

Margot laughed and shut the freezer. "Understatement."

Cat sneezed in Margot's direction. Olivia laughed before setting her hands on her hips, running through the recipe in her head.

Butter, sugar, eggs . . . shoot. Before leaving for the store, she'd grabbed the butter out to soften, but had forgotten about the eggs. "Could you grab two eggs for me?"

Margot nodded and ducked her head inside the fridge.

Vanilla extract, flour, cocoa powder, white chocolate chunks, salt, baking soda . . . Olivia gathered the ingredients one by one, placing them on the counter, separated into wet and dry. Margot set the eggs down on the counter, using the sticks as a barricade so the eggs wouldn't roll.

All she needed now was a bowl, a rubber spatula, and— "Where do you keep your mixer?"

Margot stared. "My what?"

"You know?" Olivia spun her finger in a circle. "Your hand mixer."

"Oh, right." Margot scratched her jaw. "Um. Let's see . . ." She crouched down and rifled through the cabinet beside the stove. Something fell, clattering loudly, metal on metal. Margot grunted and fell back on her butt against the kitchen floor, wearing a triumphant grin. Cradled against her stomach was a KitchenAid stand mixer, scuffed from age. Likely a hand-me-down, but still, absolutely a step up from a hand mixer. "Will this do?"

"Thanks. You want to cream the butter and sugar for me?"

Margot looked at Olivia like she'd lost her mind. "Me? You're trusting *me* in the kitchen? Me, who almost burned down your kitchen boiling water?"

Olivia flushed at the memory of Margot leaving a pot of pasta water boiling on the stove that memorable spring break. How she'd forgotten about it, how they'd both gotten distracted. How the pot had boiled dry and the smoke detector had beeped shrilly, the caustic smell of the burning plastic pot handle drifting up the stairs to Olivia's room, sending them both scurrying into the kitchen half-dressed. "I'm sure your culinary skills have undergone *some* amount of improvement over the last eleven years."

"Don't be so sure, Liv. I think you're underestimating my ability to survive on packaged foods and takeout."

Olivia tucked her hair behind her ears and shrugged. "It's butter and sugar. What's the worst that could happen?"

Margot shrugged and reached for the KitchenAid's power cord. "Famous last words."

Olivia reached inside the cabinet for a bowl and began measuring out the dry ingredients from memory. Margot, struggling with the wrapper on the butter, noticed. "You don't follow a recipe?"

Olivia shook her head, leveling off a cup of sifted flour with the back of a butter knife. "They're my go-to cookie. I could probably make them in my sleep."

"Brad's an idiot," Margot grumbled, frowning at the KitchenAid in concentration, studying the buttons. As soon as she flipped the on switch, butter spewed at high speed, splattering the kitchen backsplash. She shut it off and frowned. "Huh."

Olivia laughed. "Speed switch?"

Margot turned bright red.

This time, the mixer was much smoother, whipping the softened butter instead of obliterating it.

"You were saying." Olivia dumped the cup of flour into the bowl and grabbed the baking soda. "Something about Brad being an idiot?"

Margot's eyes flittered to Olivia's and back to the bowl where the KitchenAid was turning the butter and sugar into one homogeneous mixture. "What? Does the statement *Brad's an idiot* really require further explanation?"

Olivia pressed her lips together, trying in vain not to laugh. "Add this."

She nudged the bowl of dry ingredients toward Margot.

Margot reached for the bowl and tilted it, too much, too fast. A cloud of cocoa powder poofed in the air, making her cough.

"Margot."

"Sorry!" She reached for the speed switch and flicked it the wrong direction because the mixer made a loud whirring noise, whipping a violent splatter of chocolate dough around the room. A thick glob of it landed against Olivia's cheek and she shrieked, ducking for cover.

Margot swore loudly and powered the mixer off altogether.

Laughter bubbled up behind the tight press of Olivia's lips, bursting out in a sharp snicker.

Margot's face was dusted in a fine layer of pale brown powder, and there was a streak of gooey dough along her jawline.

She stood, frozen, staring at the KitchenAid as if it had gone rogue and personally wronged her. "What the . . ."

Olivia's stomach ached, her knees wobbling, finally folding under her as she slid down to the floor. The tile was cool under her thighs as she lied back, laughing up at the ceiling. The *ceiling*. Her eyes watered. There was batter on the ceiling, a starburst splatter of brown and yellow, the butter not quite mixed with the cocoa powder. An ominous stalactite of dough oozed down, not yet dripping.

Her head thunked back against the tile, her chest burning and her eyes streaming as she chortled.

She could barely make out the sound of Margot's approaching footsteps over her laughter.

"Rude."

Olivia cracked open an eye, laughing harder at the batter that dripped down Margot's forehead.

Margot crossed her arms. "You're just going to lie there and laugh?"

Olivia covered her face and nodded, struggling to breathe.

The batter fell from the ceiling, splattering wetly against the floor, startling Cat, whose fur fluffed up, standing on end. She darted out of the kitchen, abandoning what little remained of the food on her plate, and took cover under the living room coffee table. Probably not a bad idea to steer clear of the kitchen for the foreseeable future.

Margot surveyed what was left in the bowl with a frown. "Break-and-bakes?"

Olivia pressed her palms against the floor, heaving herself

up onto her knees before using the counter for leverage. "We'll just start over."

"Start over? Do you really think that's a—" A blob of batter splattered against the top of Margot's head, dripping down from that oozing stalactite as she reached for a rag. It ran down the center of her forehead, between her eyes, sliding down her nose. Her tongue darted out, swiping batter off her upper lip. "Sure. We'll start over. *What's the worst that could happen?*"

Olivia pressed her fingers to her mouth, stifling a laugh. "Second time's the charm?"

By the time Margot had scrubbed the ceiling and scraped what was left of the dough into a separate bowl and Olivia had finished wiping down the counters and floor, the new sticks of butter had reached room temp and were ready for creaming.

Olivia gestured to the KitchenAid. "Do you want me to—"

"No, no." Margot waved her off, glaring at the mixer through narrowed eyes. "I started this. I'm going to finish it."

This time, Margot managed to start the KitchenAid on a much more sedate speed setting, slowly creaming the butter and sugar together before adding in the eggs and vanilla. When it was time to add in the dry ingredients, Margot lowered the speed further, stirring everything together slowly and without splatter.

Olivia dusted her hands off over the sink and leaned her hip against the counter. Hands braced on her hips like she was ready for battle, Margot stared intently at the mixing bowl, narrowed eyes locked on the paddle attachment as it churned and whirled, incorporating the chocolate chunks into the batter. She was so focused, so—

Margot raised her head, eyes meeting Olivia's. One of her brows rose, a smudge of batter bisecting it. Olivia's lips twitched.

"What?" Margot demanded. "Is there something on my face?"

Her lips twitched as if even she couldn't keep a straight face at her own question.

Olivia laughed. "What would give you *that* idea?"

Margot reached up, wincing as she swiped a glob of batter from the shell of her ear. "Bets on how long I'll be finding batter in places it doesn't belong?"

"Hold still." Olivia reached out and thumbed the smudge of batter from Margot's forehead. "Look on the bright side. You're wearing clothes, which limits the exposure zone."

"Naked baking?" Margot frowned. "Don't get me wrong—I like to live dangerously, but that sounds like a recipe for disaster."

"*Ba-dum-tss.*" Olivia drummed her fingers against the counter. "Punny. At least it would be bak*ing* and not bac*on*."

Margot recoiled, hands rising to cover her chest. "I've never once, in all my life, been tempted to fry anything in the nude. Never."

Two cocoa powder handprints outlined Margot's breasts through her white shirt when she dropped her hands.

Olivia laughed and took a peek inside the mixing bowl. All done. She flipped the power switch and disengaged the locking mechanism on the bowl, pulling it free from the base. "Brad fried bacon shirtless once. Never did it again."

"Yuck." Margot stuck out her tongue. "Like I said, *idiot*."

That's right. She'd mentioned Brad before the batter had

splattered, distracting Olivia from finding out what Margot meant. "You said that earlier."

Margot hummed and pinched off a piece of cookie dough. She popped it in her mouth, eyes immediately falling shut, a moan escaping her mouth that made Olivia flush for reasons completely unrelated to the oven's preheat cycle. "Damn, that's just as good as I remember." Margot slumped against the counter, eyes fluttering open. "You're telling me Brad had you *and* regular access to these cookies and he *still* took you for granted?" Margot's lips curved upward. "Clearly, he didn't know how lucky he was."

Olivia's cheeks burned hotter. Heat spread down her jaw and the front of her throat, an ember of warmth flaring to life inside her chest.

Margot couldn't just say things like that. Not if she didn't want Olivia to get the wrong idea.

"Well." Olivia ducked her chin, staring at the kitchen floor, as if that might do something to disguise how Margot's words affected her. How *much* Margot's words affected her. Olivia's face was probably a neon-pink sign practically screaming *look what you do to me*. There was nothing casual about this feeling. "Now *you* get cookies."

Margot's socked feet entered Olivia's line of vision, her cotton-covered toes curling against the tile as she reached out, one hand with dark red–painted nails rising to settle against Olivia's waist. Her other hand rose, too, before sliding down, both hands tucking into the back pockets of Olivia's jeans. Warmth from Margot's palms seeped through the denim, causing Olivia to shiver as she stepped closer.

Olivia's heart thundered, her pulse pounding in her temples and at the base of her neck as Margot leaned in, lips grazing the corner of Olivia's mouth. One hand slipped free from Olivia's back pocket. Margot's fingers danced all the way up Olivia's spine, her palm cupping the back of Olivia's neck. Margot tilted her own head to the side, her lips pillowing Olivia's bottom lip in a tender kiss that caused Olivia's breath to catch in the back of her throat, her stomach suddenly full of butterflies.

Margot stepped back, dropping her hands, palms opening and closing like she didn't know what to do with them. The skin from her collarbone up to the crests of her cheeks was mottled with a pink flush, and the front of her throat jerked when she swallowed, her breath escaping in a shaky exhale, her smile even shakier. "Lucky me."

Chapter Thirteen

Rain splattered against the windshield, evergreens blurring past as Olivia drove down I-90, heading east to Snoqualmie.

Annie and Brendon's joint bachelor-bachelorette *extravaganza*—Brendon's word, not Olivia's (*extravaganza* made her think of the annual mattress sale at the furniture store off State Route 410)—was taking place at Salish Lodge & Spa, a resort getaway half an hour outside of Seattle, halfway between the city and the ski summit. They'd be spending two nights—Wednesday and Thursday—at the lodge, before heading back to the city in time for the rehearsal dinner on Friday night and the wedding the following day.

In the passenger seat of Olivia's Subaru Outback—it had all-wheel drive, unlike Margot's Toyota Camry—Margot stared at her phone, rattling off facts about the lodge where they'd be staying. "Ooh, get this. Every guest room has a gas fireplace—fancy—a shower with dual heads, and an oversized soaking tub. And there's an on-site herb garden and . . . *ooh*, there's an apiary that provides honey for both of the lodge's restaurants and the spa."

"Mm." Olivia sped up, passing a minivan going ten below the speed limit.

"Let's see . . . award-winning spa . . . steam room, sauna, soaking pools are available by appointment," Margot read from the site. "Fitness massage, tranquility massage, hot stone massage . . ."

That all sounded fantastic, but Olivia had too much to do to simply send the next two days relaxing in a spa. She needed to follow up with the vendors, make sure the final payments had been received by the suppliers, and deliver the final head count to the caterer for the rehearsal dinner and the reception. All of which she could do from the lodge, but she'd packed her laptop and double-checked the resort had reliable Wi-Fi for a reason.

"Hey." Margot waved her fingers, frowning softly. "Where'd you go?"

"Sorry." Olivia smiled and shook her head. "I'm just thinking about everything I still have to do with vendors and suppliers and . . . I don't know. I—maybe I shouldn't have agreed to come. There's just *so* much and—"

"Hey, whoa." Margot swiveled in her seat the best she could with the seat belt strapped across her body. "Brendon and Annie invited you."

"Right, and relaxing right now should be their number one priority," Olivia said, eyes flitting between the road and her rearview mirror as she changed lanes. "*My* priority is making sure their wedding goes off without a hitch."

"And you totally will," Margot said. "But I'm pretty sure you can squeeze in a massage, too."

Olivia hummed under her breath and rolled out her shoulders. "A massage *does* sound nice."

Margot looked over at her and smiled. "If you needed a massage, you could've just asked." Her brows wiggled. "I'm good with my hands."

Olivia's face heated at the memory of Margot using her hands to edge Olivia for what felt like an hour, driving her to the point of babbling and begging until finally Margot had wrung four orgasms from Olivia before relenting, leaving her a puddle of goo.

"That you are," Olivia agreed, voice a touch breathless.

Margot's smirked and turned her attention back to her screen.

Olivia reached for her bottle of water, suddenly parched. She flipped the rubbery straw up on her CamelBak and took a long drink, eyes flitting away from the road briefly to return the bottle to the cup holder.

On the center console, Margot's hand rested, slightly cupped, fingers curled toward her palm, facing up. Olivia had a sudden, jarring flashback to seventh grade, when she'd gone out on her first date to the movies with Michael Louis, a boy who'd had a sweet smile and an unfortunate floppy bowl cut that made him look like a cute mushroom, or Jim Halpert circa season one of *The Office*. They'd gone to see some cheesy action movie and sat dead center in the theater. He'd rested his hand on the armrest and stared, not at the screen, but at Olivia, until she'd gotten the hint and slipped her hand into his, his palm damp and warm and oddly sticky.

It wasn't a question that Margot was good with her hands or that she had clever, talented fingers that could drive Olivia to new heights of pleasure. It was a question of whether Olivia could hold Margot's hand.

Was that . . . something they did now? If Olivia slipped her hand inside Margot's, would she be pushing her luck?

Olivia held her breath, hand hovering above the cup holder, and—

A horn blared from the next lane over, the one Olivia had accidentally floated into. She gripped the wheel with both hands, careful not to overcorrect, and kept her eyes locked on the road, willing away her flush when Margot studied her from the passenger seat.

"They offer facials, too," Margot added.

Olivia bit the inside of her cheek. "That's nice."

A heavy electronic dance beat filled the car, and Margot groaned, chuckling at the same time.

Olivia only let go of the wheel for a brief second to crank up the volume until the bass thumped, shaking her seat. "Come on. You *know* you love this song."

"No." Margot shouted over the music. "I don't. And I still don't understand how you thought they were saying *like a cheese stick*."

"Excuse me for not knowing what a G6 was when I was seventeen."

"How does *cheese stick* make even a modicum of sense? I

think you need to get your ears checked." Margot turned the volume down until they could speak without shouting. "Maybe if you didn't listen to your music this loud, you wouldn't be constantly hearing the lyrics wrong."

"Constantly?" Olivia scoffed.

Margot spared her a quick glance, brows flicking upward. "You thought Madonna said *like a virgin, touched for the thirty-first time*." Margot snickered. "How the fuck does that even work?"

"Shut up." Olivia flicked her turn signal, taking the next exit. "I was nine when I thought that! I didn't even know what that song meant."

"Mm-hmm, *sure*."

"I mean it, I didn't—"

The song cut off abruptly and a soft chime came from the speakers, her phone connected to the speakers via Bluetooth.

Olivia glanced at the display screen. Dad was calling.

She glanced briefly over at Margot. "Do you mind if I take this? I'll be quick."

Ever since his heart attack, she made a point of answering when Dad called. Not that she hadn't before, but . . . she didn't want to risk sending him to voicemail if he needed her. Especially since she was usually the one reaching out, the one calling and checking in.

From the corner of Olivia's eye, Margot shrugged. "No worries. Don't rush on my account."

"Thanks." Olivia pressed her thumb into the button on the wheel to answer the call. "Hey, Dad. I hope that it's okay you're on speaker. I'm driving." Olivia licked her lips. "I'm in the car with Margot."

The line crackled for a second before Dad said, "Speaker's fine, Livvy. Hi, Margot."

Margot sat up straighter. "Hi, Mr. Grant. It's been a while. How are you doing?"

Her voice changed subtly, the pitch rising. Olivia's eyes flickered over briefly to discover Margot nibbling on her bottom lip, looking nervous.

"Hanging in there. Keeping busy."

"Hopefully not too busy," Olivia interjected.

Dad's sigh was exaggerated, heavily put upon. "Do you hear what I deal with, Margot? You don't hassle your folks like this, do you?"

Margot laughed. "They're usually the ones hassling me, sir."

Dad chuckled. "The way it's supposed to be. Livvy here worries too much."

Olivia rolled her eyes. "What's up, Dad?"

"Not much," Dad said. "Just hadn't heard from you in a few days."

A few days? That couldn't be possible. She'd last talked to Dad on . . . Oh God, it really had been a few days. At least four, whereas normally she tried to call every other day, if not daily, for at least a quick check-in.

"The wedding's been keeping me pretty busy, actually," she said. That and Margot, but Dad absolutely did *not* require details there. "The singer in the band we hired for the reception was rushed to the hospital yesterday with a ruptured appendix.

He's fine, but we're obviously out a band, so I had to make a few calls to find a suitable DJ—"

"Livvy," Dad interjected. "It's fine. I just thought I'd check in with you for once. Make sure Margot's not getting you into too much trouble."

Margot snickered. "Only the best kind of trouble, sir."

Dad barked out a laugh, and if Olivia weren't driving she'd have slumped down in her seat, mortified. She reached for the air vent, aiming it directly at her face.

"Good, good. That's what I like to hear," Dad said. "Livvy could use a little fun in her life."

"Oh, geez," she muttered under her breath, still loud enough for Dad to hear through the speakers, apparently, because he only laughed harder.

And Margot, traitor that she was, joined in, laughing brightly and chiming in with, "I couldn't agree more."

Margot slipped her hand off the center console and squeezed Olivia's thigh. She kept her hand there, casual as could be, like it was perfectly normal to rest her hand atop Olivia's leg while Olivia drove. Olivia still questioned her reality, that this was her life now, that Margot was in it and touching her. Maybe it was different for Margot, but Olivia had yet to build up a tolerance to Margot's touch. She wasn't certain she wanted to.

Olivia cleared her throat. "You had your appointment, right? With your cardiologist? How'd that go?"

"Everything's fine. My cholesterol, my blood pressure, all of it."

Fine. Her nose scrunched. "What does *fine* mean? And what about your triglycerides, those were still—"

Dad cut her off with a laugh. "Livvy, relax. The doctor says I'm healthy as a horse."

She pursed her lips. "Are we talking Seabiscuit, or the Red Pony?"

Margot clapped her free hand over her mouth, muffling her laughter.

"Jesus, kid." Dad huffed. "You are something. I'm *fine*. I would tell you if I weren't."

Olivia loosened her death grip on the steering wheel, working to swallow past the knot constricting her throat. "Promise?"

Margot's grip tightened, squeezing her thigh.

"Promise," Dad said, sounding sincere enough that Olivia was able to breathe again. "Look, I called to see how you were doing and also to let you know that a few of the guys from work and I are heading up to Nolan Creek in Forks to go fly-fishing. We're driving up on Friday, won't be back until Wednesday. I don't know how my reception's going to be, and I won't have my phone on me when I'm out on the water. Just wanted to let you know so you don't worry."

"Be safe," she said. "And have fun."

Dad chuckled. "Thanks. Good luck with the wedding. I'm sure it'll be fantastic."

"Thanks, Dad."

"Good talking to you, Margot. Make sure Livvy doesn't work too hard."

Margot grinned. "Will do, Mr. Grant. Have fun fishing!"

"Bye, Dad. I love you."

"Love you, too, kid. Talk soon."

Olivia ended the call with a press of her thumb against the wheel.

"It sounds like he's doing good," Margot said.

Olivia blew out her breath and nodded. "Mm-hmm."

Margot's thumb swept against the side seam of Olivia's jeans, warmth from her palm seeping through the denim. "I don't know, maybe it's just me or maybe it's the way you're driving fifteen over the speed limit, but I'm getting a vibe that you're not totally at ease."

"Shit." Olivia eased off the gas. "Sorry."

Margot shrugged. "You want to talk about it?"

Olivia puffed out her cheeks. "I just feel bad that I didn't check in. I normally do, but with everything going on, I spaced."

"It sounds like he's doing fine," Margot said. "He definitely didn't sound upset."

"No, but—"

"No *buts*. Your dad wouldn't want you to feel guilty for living your life, Liv." Margot plucked Olivia's phone out of the change holder. She shook it pointedly. "Pretty sure he specifically tasked me with making sure you have a good time. So that's what we're going to do. We're going to have a great time this week, celebrating Annie and Brendon, and *you* are going to relax. Okay?"

Olivia breathed deep and smiled. "I can try."

An hour later, Brendon met them in the lobby of the lodge with a warm smile. "You guys made it."

"We hit traffic a few exits back," Margot said. "Bumper-to-bumper."

"I think there might have been an accident," Olivia added, adjusting the strap of her duffel bag so it wouldn't cut off circulation to her arm. "We saw flashing lights."

"It's all this extra snow," Brendon said, gesturing for them to follow as he led the way through the lobby and down a long hall. "I'm glad Luke's got snow chains, otherwise I don't think they'd let us on Snoqualmie Pass."

"Luke? Who's Luke?" Margot frowned. "Do I even *know* a Luke?"

Brendon laughed. "My friend from college, Luke. I've mentioned him before."

Margot's nose wrinkled adorably, and she adjusted her grip on the case of beer she'd brought, her contribution for the weekend, courtesy of the brewery Oh My Stars was partnering with. "Hmm."

"I *know* I've mentioned him." Brendon's expression faltered. "Wait, didn't I?"

"The name sounds vaguely familiar . . ."

"We were roommates freshman year," Brendon tacked on. "I think I told you the story about the time he accidentally shrunk all his pants in the wash and went to class wearing a three-piece suit?"

A flicker of recognition passed over Margot's face, her eyes widening slightly behind her glasses. "Oh, *that* Luke. Okay, yeah, you've mentioned him."

At least Olivia wasn't going to be the only new addition on

this trip, the odd man out, everyone already closely acquainted with one another. "He's a groomsman, right?"

Margot did a double take. "Hold the phone. *Groomsman?* I thought it was just me and your coworker Jian?"

Brendon gripped the back of his neck, looking sheepish. "Shoot. Don't tell me I forgot to tell you."

Margot's hair swished against the sides of her neck when she gave a sharp shake of her head. "This is the first I'm hearing of there being another groomsman."

"I wasn't sure he was going to be able to make it to the wedding. *He* wasn't sure he was going to be able to make it. He's been in Minsk for the past few months treating patients with drug-resistant TB." He smiled over his shoulder. "Doctors Without Borders."

Olivia's brows rose. "Impressive."

"Right?" Brendon nodded, stopping in front of a bank of elevators. "Anyway, he managed to swing the time off and let me know a couple weeks ago. I guess with the fire at the first venue and having to make all of these new plans, it slipped my mind. Even then, he didn't think he was going to be able to fly in until Friday, but he found an earlier flight and managed to make it to town last night."

Margot gave a thoughtful hum. "How long is he in town for?"

"A week," Brendon said, thumbing the up button. "He's got to go back to Belarus for a couple weeks to finish up his rotation, then he flies back home for good. It'll be nice to have him back." His gaze flickered between the two of them, his smile broadening, lingering curiously on Olivia. "I think you'll really like him."

Wait. Olivia looked at Margot then back at Brendon, pointing at her chest. "Me?"

Brendon held his hand against the open elevator door, allowing the passengers departing to step out first before gesturing for her and Margot to step inside. "Yeah. He's great. Funny, caring, loyal." His smile went crooked. "Single."

Olivia's stomach lurched, and it had nothing to do with the elevator rising. She looked over at Margot for help, but Margot was staring at her phone, scrolling, expression giving not even a single clue as to what was going on inside her head. Olivia swallowed. "Um."

It was one thing to keep their relationship—she didn't know what else to call it; *arrangement* sounded sleazy and *friendship* didn't fully encompass the scope of what they were doing. A situationship, maybe? It was all a little fuzzy and undefined—under wraps. She didn't like it, wasn't a fan of having to pretend like she didn't want to kiss Margot or hold her hand, to curtail any of her impulses. But she could understand where Margot was coming from, not wanting her friends, Brendon in particular, butting in.

But here he was, doing it anyway . . . just not the way either of them had anticipated.

And Margot was no help. Did she even care that Brendon was trying to set Olivia up? Olivia clutched at the elevator's stainless steel handrail, head swimming, suddenly dizzy.

Was this situationship so casual that it wasn't even exclusive?

"No pressure," Brendon added, rocking back on his heels, hands tucked in the front pocket of his sweats, the picture of nonchalance. "I promise this isn't a setup. I just think you two might hit it off, that's all."

The elevator opened on the fifth floor. Margot was the first to step out, slipping through the doors as soon as she could fit through them. Olivia frowned and followed, itching to ask Margot what was going on inside her head.

But she couldn't. Now wasn't the right time, with Brendon beside them, footsteps slowing in front of the suite at the end of the hall.

He fished around inside his back pocket, pulling out the card to the room. The sensor on the door flashed green when he held the card to it, the lock making a soft whirring noise followed by a click.

"All our rooms are on the same floor, same hall, all adjoining," he said, opening the door and, with a wave of his hand, gestured them through into his and Annie's larger suite. They stopped inside a small entryway where several pairs of shoes lay heaped, as if kicked off and forgotten. Two coats hung in the closet, the sliding door left open. To the immediate right was a bathroom and to the left, another door left slightly cracked. Brendon nodded at the closed door and fished two more keys out of his pocket, glancing at each briefly before passing one to Margot and the other to Olivia. "Obviously feel free to keep your door closed, but for now we have them all open. Figured it would be convenient while we're all still up. Darcy and Elle are right through there, then Margot, Olivia, Luke, and last we've got Katie and Jian."

Margot blew the hair out of her face, lips remaining pursed even after her hair had settled. "Cool."

"Katie?" Olivia asked, not recognizing the name.

"She and Jian got married last year," Brendon explained. "They both work with me at OTP."

Olivia nodded, filing all away the names and relationships. "Got it."

Laughter carried from further in the suite. Brendon jerked his thumb over his shoulder. "Everyone's out on the patio. We've got the fireplace going and are about to roast marshmallows. Here, I can take those off your hands." He reached out, grabbing the case of beer from Margot, who gave him an appreciative smile. "We've got a bottle of champagne open, and Elle and Darcy brought wine, so this rounds our assortment of beverages out nicely."

"Please tell me there's food." Margot pressed her hand against her stomach. "Other than marshmallows."

"Oh, totally." Brendon backed away slowly. "We've got graham crackers and chocolate, too."

Margot frowned and Olivia felt her pain. Traffic had caused them to miss dinner. They'd done a number on the cookies they'd baked last night, but it wasn't *real* food.

"Kidding." Brendon grinned. "There's plenty of chips and finger foods, and if you guys want, you can always order room service." He nodded to their bags. "You guys can either drop your things here for now, if you want, or you can settle in first. We all got comfortable after dinner, but either way."

Brendon disappeared around the corner, leaving them alone in the entryway of the suite.

Olivia hiked the strap of her duffel higher on her shoulder and glanced down at what she was wearing. "I think I'm going to get out of these jeans."

Margot's lips twitched, and she cast a quick glance toward the hall before stepping closer, into Olivia's space, her body a line of heat against Olivia's side. "Need help?"

"Are you offering?" Olivia asked, heat wrapping around the sides of her jaw.

Margot hummed and hooked a finger under the waist of Olivia's jeans, right by the button, pulling the denim taut. It bit softly into Olivia's skin. Margot leaned in, lips brushing the shell of Olivia's ear, hot breath sending a shiver down Olivia's spine. "Maybe later."

Ugh. Olivia shut her eyes and groaned quietly. "You're so mean."

Margot pecked her cheek, lips lingering, dragging down to the hinge of Olivia's jaw. "Later," she promised, sliding her finger out of Olivia's pants.

Olivia opened her eyes and shook off the fog of lust that had made her head fuzzy in no time flat. She took a deep, cleansing breath and followed Margot through the door into the adjoining room, trying to ignore her sudden restless awareness of the space between her thighs.

Margot dropped her bag beside the queen-sized bed in her room and stretched, arms lifted over her head, the bottom of her sweater riding up, revealing a strip of her stomach. She smirked when she saw Olivia staring, then shamelessly grabbed the bottom of her top, drawing it over her head, leaving her in a sheer black bra that cupped her breasts and lifted them high, the lace pattern accentuating her curves and leaving little to the imagination.

Margot lifted her eyes, brows rising, a knowing little smirk curving her lips as she slid the straps of her bra down her shoulders before reaching back for the clasp. The fabric sagged in front of her body, her breasts falling subtly. There was a bruise in the shape of Olivia's mouth on Margot's left breast, right beside her nipple, put there last night.

Olivia almost swallowed her tongue. The noise that escaped her mouth was next-level mortifying, half gasp and half groan, one hundred percent reminiscent of a dying animal. Her eyes darted to the open door.

"Meet you in the other room?" Margot asked, digging through her duffel for a change of clothes.

Olivia tripped over her feet as she stepped backward. "You're terrible."

"The worst," Margot agreed with a smile. "Now go."

It wasn't until Olivia was in her room that she cursed softly. She'd had every intention of talking to Margot about Brendon's none too subtle attempt at matchmaking, but then she'd gotten distracted by Margot and her breasts and her flirting and her—everything.

Later, then. Unless there was nothing to talk about? She'd have to play it by ear.

Olivia dug out a change of clothes and set them aside while she wiggled out of her jeans. She tossed them on the bed and frowned. There was paper poking out of her back pocket. Paper. She couldn't for the life of her remember—

Wait. Olivia pressed her fingers to her lips and reached for the—yup, a folded envelope. It was small enough to fit in the palm of her hand with room to spare, a little crumpled from her having sat on it, but it was in the shape of a heart.

She turned it over before unfolding it. There was no note, nothing written on it, but Olivia was far from disappointed. The note didn't need to say anything. The very fact that Margot had played along, that she'd thought to tuck it inside Olivia's pocket, said enough.

Enough for now.

Olivia spared a final glance at herself in the mirror after changing quickly, shoving the sleeves of her oversized burgundy Henley up her arms. The sweater fell down to her thighs, a good thing because the leggings she'd packed were a little on the thin side, less opaque than she'd have preferred. Feeling like she'd struck the right balance of cozy and cute, she left the bathroom, padding out of her room and through the adjoining rooms on socked feet, following the sound of voices until she came to a sliding glass door someone had left open. She stepped out onto the patio, where the group of eight were gathered around the fire, one large U-shaped sectional eating up most of the patio.

"Olivia!"

All eyes turned to her. Okay, awkward. She smiled and waved. "Hey."

Brendon hopped off the couch and crossed the patio, stopping beside her. "Everyone, this is Olivia, Margot's friend and our wedding planner. Aka, the person responsible for keeping Annie and I from losing it over the last two weeks."

"Speak for yourself." Annie winked at him from her spot beside the fire. "I would've been fine with eloping."

Brendon groaned. "Annie, baby, we don't use that word."

She threw a marshmallow at his head, hitting him dead between the eyes, and laughed. "You're ridiculous."

"You wouldn't have me any other way." He reached down and snagged the marshmallow off the deck, tossing it back at her. Annie wrinkled her nose at the leaf stuck to it, ultimately tossing it in the fire. "Olivia, you've met most everyone." He pointed at a man and woman cuddled up on the far end of the sectional beside Annie. "That's Katie and Jian; they both work at OTP." They waved. "And this is my friend I was telling you about, Luke."

Brendon's friend stood. He was attractive in a clean-cut way, blue eyes and dark blond hair closely cropped on the sides of his head, slightly longer on top. He smiled, all blindingly white teeth, and offered her his hand. "It's nice to meet you. Brendon's told me you're quite the miracle worker."

She shook his hand, which was, thankfully, dry. There was nothing worse than a handshake that left you wondering why the other person's hand was mysteriously damp. "That's a bit excessive. I mean, God, you're a—a *doctor*. I plan parties and you save lives. If anyone's a miracle worker . . ."

Luke had yet to let go of her hand.

"You make dreams come true," Brendon said, with an air of gentle correction. "I'm pretty sure Annie and I owe you our firstborn for the magic you've pulled off, putting everything together last-minute."

"Firstborn?" *Yikes.* "Unless I read it wrong, that wasn't in our contract."

Across the patio, on one end of the sectional, Margot snorted.

"Point being, this wedding wouldn't be happening if it weren't for you," Brendon said.

Luke finally released her hand and dropped back into his seat with an easy smile.

"It's nothing. It's what I do." Olivia fiddled with the hem of her Henley. She'd far surpassed her quota of time spent in the spotlight for one day. "Speaking of, there *is* supposed to be in-room Wi-Fi, right?

"No working tonight," Margot said, brows rising. "Remember?"

Right. *Relaxing.*

"Margot's right. Absolutely no working." Brendon practically herded her toward the sectional.

"But I really need to make sure the new DJ has that list you—"

"You can check in the morning. For now, you sit right here"—he led her to the empty cushion beside Luke—"and I'll get you a drink."

Chapter Fourteen

Not a setup, her ass.

Margot picked at the peeling paper label of her beer as Luke stood and patted Brendon on the shoulder. "I've got it." Luke turned to Olivia and grinned. "What's your poison?"

Olivia tucked her hair behind her ear. "Oh, um, I'll just have a beer."

"Coming right up." Luke winked and headed straight for the snack table. He tilted the case of beer on its side, reading the label, chuckling softly. He looked over his shoulder at the group, eyes narrowing. "Okay, who's the hophead here?"

The *what*?

Brendon pointed at Margot with his marshmallow skewer. "Mar brought the beer."

Luke leaned back against the railing beside the table and crossed his ankles. He wagged his finger at Margot, tutting softly. "Ah, *you're* the hophead. Should've guessed."

What was *that* supposed to mean? "It's *beer*. Nothing to get all *Reefer Madness* about, Officer."

Luke threw his head back and laughed. "No, you misunderstand. It's IPA. *Hops*, therefore you're a hophead."

Short of being told she was wrong, there was little more that pissed her off than a line like that. *You misunderstand.* Maybe he wasn't clear. Margot smiled through clenched teeth. "Huh. Clever."

"Now, I've got to ask." Luke lifted a bottle from the case, holding it up to the moonlight as if that would do jack all. "Do you actually *like* IPAs, or is it just the first craft beer you tried and it stuck?"

Wait, did he just call her *boring*? Holy shit. Margot opened her mouth—

"We're partnering with that brewery," Elle said with a smile. "Margot and I. We're the voices behind Oh My Stars."

"Astrology, right?" Luke snapped his fingers in recognition, nodding quickly. "You know, I'd be interested in seeing a demographic analysis studying the correlation between people who prefer popular varieties of craft beer and those who buy into modern-day Western astrology."

Buy into. Margot's blood boiled. What a crock of condescending horseshit.

Elle's left eye twitched, and Brendon gave a preemptive wince. Margot took a deep breath. She would not rise to the bait, she would not rise to the bait, she would *not* rise to the bait no matter how much this dude was just asking to fuck around and find out.

"If only Elle and I weren't so busy," Margot said, and from the corner of her eye, Brendon's shoulders dropped in obvious relief that Margot hadn't snapped back.

Look at that. Margot smiled. *Growth.*

Luke frowned. "I don't think it would be that difficult. Two sets of a data and a simple t-test would tell you everything you need to know." He crossed his arms. "You know, the t-test—well, actually, it's the Student's t-test—was named after William Sealy Gosset, under the pseudonym *Student.* And interesting fact—Gosset worked for Guinness. He developed the t-test to prevent rival breweries from discovering the statistics Guinness used for brewing their beer. Ergo, it would be rather apt to use the t-test when analyzing your own data around beer."

"Speaking of beer." Olivia smiled pointedly at the bottle in Luke's hand.

"Right." He laughed and studied the bottle briefly before narrowing his eyes in obvious contemplation. "Are you partial to IPAs or would you be up for something a little different? A little less bitter, maybe?"

Margot frowned.

Olivia shifted slightly, then shrugged. "I—"

"Would probably like something to drink sometime this century," Margot muttered under her breath so only Elle could hear.

Elle pressed her lips together and elbowed Margot softly in the side, turning and staring at her with wide, laughing eyes.

"—don't really have a preference," Olivia said, shaking her head.

Luke set the bottle down. "I picked up a case of gose at Safeway. It's not as good as the stuff you actually get in Goslar, Germany, but it's close. Kind of a fruity, sour beer. You interested?"

"Um." Olivia laughed and threw her hands up. "Sure, I guess."

"Awesome." Luke grinned and headed for the door. "I'll be back in a jiffy."

As soon as Luke was out of earshot, Brendon turned to the group and laughed, albeit stiltedly, raking his hand through his hair. "I think he's nervous. Odd man out, you know?"

"We've all been there before," Annie said, and Olivia nodded.

Conversations splintered off, Brendon drawing Olivia into a conversation with Katie and Jian, Annie and Darcy speaking quietly with their heads together, each holding a glass of wine.

Elle cleared her throat quietly and tucked her hair behind her ear, fingers lingering on the side of her face, the rock on her finger twinkling when the moon hit it just so.

"Oh, Jesus." Margot slapped herself on the forehead. "Fuck, Elle, I'm sorry. Holy shit." She grasped Elle's hand, shifting it side to side and *ooh*ing when the light caught on the facets, reflecting a sparkling rainbow against Elle's sweatshirt. "Damn, go Darcy."

"Right?" Elle laughed and held her hand out, wiggling her fingers, and Margot kind of loved that Elle's nail polish was chipped, that she hadn't bothered fixing it just because she had a ring to show off. It was very Elle.

"I think you said something about a winter wedding?" Her eyes flitted to the patio door. Luke had a bottle of beer in each hand and was heading straight for Olivia. He handed her a bottle, leaned in and whispered something in her ear, then tapped the neck of his bottle against hers with a laugh that Olivia returned. "Did you and Darcy discuss . . . um . . ."

"Dates?" Elle supplied, eyes crinkled at the corners. "A little.

Nothing set in stone. We're kind of torn—December carries a lot of significance for us, but it's also a hectic month, and do we *really* want to organize a wedding around the holidays?" Elle shrugged. "I don't know. Ideally, I'd like to avoid the month of January. Not that I have anything against the month, but Venus is retrograde from the first to the twenty-ninth, so . . ."

"Yeah, probably not a bad plan to avoid that if you can help it."

Luke took a seat on the empty cushion beside Olivia, close enough that their thighs touched. He snagged the bag of marshmallows off the patio deck and offered it to Olivia with a broad smile. "Marshmallow?"

"Thanks." Olivia beamed.

". . . *definitely* want to avoid the week of Christmas, you know?" Elle continued.

Margot nodded. "Mm-hmm."

Luke passed Olivia a roasting stick, holding her beer for her while she skewered her marshmallow and set it over the fire.

". . . not like Darcy or I have much family that would be flying in, but I do have my cousins over in New Jersey, and Mom would probably have a fit if I didn't at least invite them, you know? And flights are going to be more expensive around the holidays, so *that* won't work . . ."

Luke said something that made Olivia laugh, this time so hard she threw her head back, golden hair spilling over her shoulders and down her back, her beanie slipping and her eyes shutting. Luke bit his lip, staring unabashedly.

Margot narrowed her eyes. So far the guy had done very little to ingratiate himself to Margot.

Olivia, on the other hand, seemed to be eating it up.

Literally.

When a tendril of inky smoke curled from the crusted black shell of the marshmallow Olivia accidentally burned, Luke whistled. "Here." He handed Liv a preassembled smore, golden-brown marshmallow oozing out from between the graham crackers. "You can have mine."

"Oh." Olivia accepted it from him with a smile. "Thanks."

"Hold on, you've got a little something . . ."

Seriously? Luke reached out, thumbing away a smudge of chocolate at the edge of her bottom lip.

Olivia wasn't a toddler. She could wipe her own mouth.

Luke smiled affably and popped his thumb into his mouth with a wink.

Olivia ducked her chin, cheeks turning a rosy shade of pink. "Um, thanks."

"Happy to be of service."

Margot rolled her eyes. Could this guy possibly *be* more textbook?

"Earth to Margot." Elle snapped her fingers. She frowned. "Did you hear what I said?"

"Of course I was listening. You said the thing about the stuff, um . . ." *Shit.* Margot winced. "Sorry?"

Elle's brows pinched. "Are you okay?"

"Me?" Margot scoffed. "Why wouldn't I be?"

Elle dropped her eyes and twisted the stem of her wineglass between her fingers. "I don't know. You've been acting kind of . . . *off* lately."

"*Off*," she repeated.

"Off." Elle chewed on her thumbnail. "Look, I know weddings aren't really your *thing*, so if you don't want to be my Maid of Honor I can always ask—"

"Whoa, whoa, *whoa*." Margot held up her hands, cutting Elle off before she could finish that truly absurd statement. "You could always ask *who*?" There was a tightness in the back of her throat that made swallowing painful. The thought of being replaced, of some random cousin of Elle's taking her place and standing up there beside Elle on her special day, was so far outside the realm of acceptable that Margot's whole body rejected the idea, muscles stiffening. "You don't need to ask anyone else, Elle. I'm—I'm game. I'm *so* game."

She'd be the most enthusiastic Maid of Honor Elle had ever seen. Margot would be Pinterest-level enthusiastic, queen of DIY hacks and rustic elegance—whatever the fuck that meant—and Ball mason jars and inspirational quotes with unattributable sources. She'd tattoo *live, laugh, love* on her ass if it would make Elle happy.

"That's good, because I don't have anyone else to ask, and even if I did"—Elle's smile wobbled—"there's no one I'd rather have as my Maid of Honor than you."

Aw, *fuck*. Margot's vision swam, eyes flooding with tears. She ripped off her glasses and tossed them on the cushion, quickly pinching the bridge of her nose. "Shit, Elle. You're going to make me fuck up my eyeliner. Do you know how hard I worked to get these wings even?"

"Hey." Elle nudged Margot gently with her knee. "I haven't wanted to push, but . . . what's going on with you, Mar?"

She opened her mouth—

"And please don't say *nothing*, because there's obviously something."

Margot puffed out her cheeks. Well, there went *that* plan.

Elle leaned closer and dropped her voice to a whisper. "Does this have something to do with Olivia?"

Margot jerked back. "What?" In an attempt to cover the way her voice cracked, Margot laughed. "Why would this have anything to do with *Liv*?"

Elle stared at her, smile small and gaze knowing. The skin between Margot's shoulder blades itched, and she rolled her arms back.

"I don't know." Elle's lips tipped up in a wry smile. "Maybe because you keep looking at Luke like you're imagining eviscerating with him your eyes or brainstorming new and inventive ways you might torture him."

"There's no need to reinvent the wheel," Margot muttered under her breath. "Or rack."

Elle stared.

"Joking." Margot huffed. "One hundred percent not serious."

Elle's brows rose.

"*Fine.* Ninety-nine percent not serious, and that one percent only wishes he'd step on a Lego."

Elle sighed. "Margot."

"*Ugh.* Do we really have to do"—she gestured vaguely, tipping her beer bottle back and forth between them—"*this*? My feelings are—"

Margot's heart seized, panic gripping her as she stared across the fire at Luke and Olivia. Their legs were angled toward one another, knees touching, and Olivia spoke with her hands, animated when she answered his questions, her flushed face lighting up each time she laughed.

Margot drew her bottom lip between her teeth.

Fuck.

Her feelings.

Feelings.

Margot wasn't supposed to *have* any feelings, not of the *chest variety*. God, her chest *was* doing all sorts of ridiculous things right now, clenching and fluttering, her heart pounding against her sternum like a battering ram.

Damn it, it was supposed to be *sex*. Supposed to be casual. Feelings weren't on the menu. Feelings were strictly prohibited; that was the whole point. Friends with benefits, satisfaction guaranteed, all gain no pain, reward with none of the risk, have her cake and eat it, too.

It wasn't like the sex wasn't great. Sex with Olivia was . . . Words couldn't do it justice. Mind-blowing, toe-curling, *amazing*. But Margot wanted more.

She frowned sharply when Luke said something that made Olivia shove his arm playfully. She wanted *that*. To sit beside Olivia and let her hand linger on Olivia's thigh, to be the person offering Olivia marshmallows off her stick, to be the person making Olivia laugh. To be *the person*. Olivia's person.

Not Luke, not Brad, no one else. *Her.* She wanted it to be her by Olivia's side.

She could picture it perfectly.

Waking up beside Olivia every morning. Falling asleep beside her every night.

How easy it would be to let these feelings grow, let herself fall in love with Olivia, fall in love with her *again*.

Too get in too deep.

How awful it would be, telling Olivia she wanted more, baring her brittle heart, offering up all her many messy feelings, only for Olivia to turn her down gently. For everything between them to become strained, sharing a seven-hundred-square-foot apartment, their lives entangled in new ways. To ache each time Olivia stepped through the front door, to hold her breath each time Olivia left, wondering when the time would come that Olivia would leave and never come back, Margot's feelings too big, eating up all the oxygen in the room, making it so the two of them couldn't coexist inside the same space.

How hard it would be to put herself back together.

History repeating itself and her the fool for letting it happen, believing that Olivia would ever choose her, ever want Margot as much as Margot wanted her.

Margot swigged her beer, bottle shaking slightly in her hand as she lowered it back to her side. "I just don't . . . *vibe* with Luke, okay?"

Elle made a face, nose wrinkling. "You don't *vibe* with him?"

"Yeah." Margot crossed her arms and stared across the fire. "What do we really *know* about him? What if his real name isn't even Luke?"

Elle laughed. "Okay, Margot. I'm pretty sure if Brendon— his college roommate and *friend*—thinks his name is Luke, it's probably Luke."

"It could be short for something," Margot argued. "His

name might actually be—I don't know." Her brain blanked. What the hell was Luke short for? *"Luketh."*

Elle lost it, snorting so hard she dribbled wine on the deck. Darcy threw a napkin at her, lips twitching in fond exasperation.

Margot ached. She wanted that, someone to look at her with fond exasperation when she was being utterly ridiculous. Not someone. *Olivia.*

"You mean *Lucas*?" Elle pressed a hand to her stomach, trying and failing to rein in her laughter. Olivia's eyes flickered across the patio, her lips tipping up in a smile when she met Margot's eye.

Margot dropped her gaze to the deck, face burning in a way that had nothing to do with the heat from the fire pit. Her heart stuttered and her stomach swooped. How she hadn't seen this coming was anyone's guess. She hadn't *wanted* to see it coming. If she'd have spared a moment to really think about it, she'd have known that this? This was an inevitability. From the moment Olivia kissed her—hell, from the moment Margot invited her to move in—this was always going to happen.

Casual was nothing but a weak safeguard against the inexorable; like waves beating against rock, it was only a matter of time before her feelings wore her down, weakened her resolve, until leaks started to spring and her feelings spilled out where they didn't belong. She could plug the holes up, but a new one would always appear.

Margot didn't know how to be anything but *all in* when it came to Olivia.

Elle's brows rose. "Do I have to tell you you're being ridiculous, or do you already know it and you're just being difficult?"

She sniffed. The second one. "I'm just saying, Luke's this . . . this Hallmark actor look-alike with perfect teeth and perfect hair and a job that literally involves saving people's lives and—and his *shoulders*."

Elle blinked. "You're upset that he has shoulders?"

"*Broad* shoulders."

"Ah. An important clarification." Elle nibbled on her lip. "You know you can talk to me, right?"

Margot looked at her askance. "I am talking. My lips are moving; sounds are coming out of my mouth."

"But you're not really *saying* anything," Elle said.

With that, Margot couldn't argue. Elle had a point.

"Okay." Margot glanced quickly around the patio to make sure everyone was sufficiently occupied with their own conversations, that no one was listening. This confession was for Elle's ears only. "Olivia's and my friendship might be slightly more complicated than I previously led everyone to believe."

"No, really?" Elle deadpanned.

Margot shoved her. "Hush. I'll tell you more later, okay? I don't—this trip is supposed to be about Annie and Brendon and, *hello*, your engagement. That's huge. And here I am, making everything all about me and my feelings."

"You never make *anything* about you, Mar." Elle frowned. "I think I speak for all of us when I say—hey, Brendon."

"Hey." Brendon crouched down, resting his arms on the back of the sectional behind them. He jerked his chin toward

Luke and Olivia and grinned. "Looks like they're really hitting it off, huh?"

A pit formed in Margot's stomach. "I don't know."

He frowned. "What do you mean?"

Margot lifted one shoulder, giving Brendon a tight shrug. "I'm not sensing it."

"Hmm." His frown deepened. "Really?"

Elle nodded quickly. "Totally. I'm getting super-platonic vibes."

Across the patio, Luke leaned in, whispering in Olivia's ear. Her face turned pink.

Margot felt like she was going to be sick, her stomach queasy, a sour knot forming in her throat.

Brendon, completely unaware of her inner turmoil, smiled smugly and stood. "I don't know. Looks like some pretty stellar chemistry to me."

He rapped his knuckles against the back of the couch and returned to his seat next to Annie, who curled into his side as soon as he sat down.

Stellar chemistry? Margot's jaw ticked as she leaned forward, fishing her phone out of her pocket.

Maybe Luke had perfect hair and perfect teeth and a perfect job, all points in his favor, but he had questionable taste in beer, and Margot would be damned if she let some Ryan Gosling look-alike mess up what she *did* have with Olivia. It might not be everything Margot wanted, everything she craved, everything her greedy heart desired, but it was something.

And something with Olivia Grant would always be better than nothing.

Margot rested the mouth of her beer bottle against her bottom lip and swiped at her screen.

MARGOT (11:03 P.M.): What's my record, four?

Margot pressed her phone against her thigh, screen side down, and feigned interest in the conversation happening around her. Jian was telling a story about something that had happened at work, lightly roasting Brendon, who took it like a champ, laughing along with everyone else. Margot laughed when everyone else laughed, nodded when everyone nodded, not really paying attention, instead glancing at Olivia surreptitiously from the corner of her eye.

Olivia wiggled her phone free from her pocket and looked at the screen, eyes briefly flitting up, glancing Margot's way. Margot sipped her beer and pretended to be engrossed in the story. Her phone buzzed against her thigh.

OLIVIA (11:05 P.M.): Record for what?

Margot's lips twitched.

MARGOT (11:06 P.M.): Times I made you come in one night.

Across the deck, Olivia fumbled her phone, dropping it against the couch. Margot bit her lip, swallowing a laugh as

Luke reached for it, handing it to her without looking at the screen. Olivia's face had turned a violent shade of red, her flush spreading down her jaw. Margot typed quickly.

MARGOT (11:07 P.M.): God, you're pretty when you blush. The best part is how you turn the sweetest shade of pink all the way down to your pussy.

Olivia must've swallowed funny because she started to cough. "You should drink something, Liv," she said, biting the inside of her cheek when Olivia leveled her with a heated stare. Firelight caught on Olivia's blond lashes each time she blinked and turned the gold of her hazel eyes into a warm, cinnamon honey, only a thin ring of green hugging her blown pupils.

"I'm fine," Olivia gasped, waving Luke off when he tried to offer her his beer, barely even looking at him. A flicker of satisfaction flared inside Margot's chest.

A minute later Margot's phone vibrated.

OLIVIA (11:09 P.M.): Not fair.

MARGOT (11:10 P.M.): How am I not being fair?

MARGOT (11:11 P.M.): Am I turning you on or something? Making you think about last night?

MARGOT (11:11 P.M.): Because I'm thinking about it.

MARGOT (11:12 P.M.): You sound so sweet when you're begging me to let you come. When you're begging me to fuck you a little bit harder.

MARGOT (11:12 P.M.): I promise I'll be so fair, Liv.

Even across the patio, several feet away, it was obvious how Olivia's hands shook when she typed. How her throat jerked convulsively with each swallow. How her blush had yet to abate, how if anything, it had deepened into a scarlet flush. Olivia's tongue swept out against her full bottom lip, wetting it, and Margot had never wanted to bite something so badly in her life that she *ached*.

All the noise around her—the conversations, the laughter, the popping and cracking of the wood in the firepit—faded into the background when Olivia's eyes lifted and locked on Margot's face across the deck, expression intense and inscrutable, a precursor to the text that vibrated against Margot's thigh.

With great reluctance, Margot tore her eyes from Olivia's and looked at her screen.

OLIVIA (11:13 P.M.): Is it later yet?

Staring directly at Olivia, unwilling to even blink and miss one of the micro-expressions that flitted across her pretty, flushed face, Margot tipped her beer back and drained what remained in one swallow. Neck of the bottle dangling from her fingers, she stood and addressed the group at large. "I hate to be a party poop, but I'm going to call it a night."

Everyone wished her a good night's sleep, the conversation winding down as others expressed their desire to hit the hay and wake up bright and early to hit the slopes.

She made it to the patio door before her phone buzzed.

OLIVIA (11:16 P.M.): Don't lock your door.

Margot smiled.

Maybe she wasn't Olivia's perfect person, the one Olivia wanted with her whole heart and soul, the person Olivia ached for and dreamed about at night. But Margot could give her this.

Margot could be the *best* at this.

Chapter Fifteen

*O*livia begged off ten minutes after Margot left the patio.

She'd have left sooner, had it not been for Luke trying to convince her to stick around and have one more beer with him.

Nothing against Luke. He seemed like a nice guy, friendly, charming, accomplished. But Olivia didn't want *nice*.

All she wanted was Margot. Margot's hands on her body, her mouth on her skin. Margot making good on her promises. Margot, Margot, Margot.

Her brain was on a constant loop, her body burning before Margot even touched her. The mere suggestion was enough to make her flush from head to toe. To make her want with a fierceness that verged on need. Like if she didn't have Margot's hands on her in the next minutes she'd spontaneously combust, which sounded a little extreme, but she wasn't exactly thinking coherent thoughts at the moment.

Everything she felt for Margot verged on extreme, too much, too fast, and nothing she felt was very sensible, but here she was. The smartest thing she could've done was probably walk away before Margot caught on that what Olivia felt was so much *more* than what they'd agreed on, but she couldn't. How could she walk away from Margot when she had everything she'd ever wanted . . . except what she *couldn't* have? Except what was off-limits?

Olivia was a lot of things, but greedy wasn't one of them.

By the time she made it inside and to the door that separated her room from Margot's, she was already buzzing, practically vibrating with need, her underwear uncomfortably damp. She'd been forced to suffer since Margot had teased her with the promise of *later*, and her suggestive texts hadn't helped.

She was beyond ready for Margot to make good on her promise.

No sooner had she rapped her knuckles gently against the door to Margot's hotel room, did it open inward. Margot reached out, dragging Olivia inside with a hand fisted in front of Olivia's sweater. The door slammed shut, and Margot pressed her up against it, covering Olivia's mouth with hers, no greeting necessary.

The kiss was bruising. More teeth than anything else. Margot nipped hard at Olivia's bottom lip, soothing the sting with a flick of her tongue. Margot's hands skimmed the sides of Olivia's waist before going straight for the hem of her sweater, breaking the kiss only so that she could drag the Henley over Olivia's head. Margot flung it somewhere behind her and immediately dove back in, burying her face in the side of Olivia's neck. She ran her lips along the edge of Olivia's jaw, leaving a trail of kisses down Olivia's throat, then biting at the skin stretched taut over her collarbone.

Olivia panted into the quiet of the room and gripped Margot's waist, fingers biting into the strip of skin left bare where her cropped sweater rode up. Below, she was already down to her underwear. "*God*, Margot. What—what brought this on?"

Margot lifted her head. It was late, fully dark out save for the silvery glow of the almost-full moon and the scattershot of stars sprinkling the sky like glitter. There was just enough light streaming through the window to make out the plains of Margot's face, most of her in shadow save for the tip of her nose and the center of her forehead, the crest of one cheek, and the bright gleam of her equally dark eyes. Margot's hand slipped between Olivia's thighs and cupped Olivia over her leggings, pressing hard against Olivia's clit with the heel of her hand. Olivia hissed through her teeth and bit down on her bottom lip.

"Are you complaining?" Margot asked, pressing a little harder.

Lip still trapped between her teeth, Olivia shook her head.

"You sure?" Margot slid her hand higher, fingers teasing the elastic band of Olivia's leggings before slipping beneath, lower, before pausing, the very tips of her fingers framing Olivia's clit, not quite touching. Margot's lips twitched. "Because I can stop."

Olivia shook her head so fast she went dizzy.

"Good." Margot dragged her lips back up Olivia's throat and rewarded her with two fingers sliding along Olivia's slit before sinking inside her. A stuttered gasp escaped Olivia's mouth, and her head thunked against the door. "Because I'm just getting started."

Olivia clutched Margot closer, fingers biting into the soft skin of Margot's waist beneath her sweater. Another gasp spilled from her lips when Margot dragged her fingers against Olivia's G-spot.

"You're dripping, Liv." Margot buried her face in the crook of Olivia's shoulder and pressed her lips to the dip above Olivia's collarbone in a kiss that was achingly sweet compared to what she was doing with her fingers below Olivia's waist, in contrast to the words coming out of her mouth. "Were you thinking about this? Thinking about how good my fingers were going to feel buried inside you? Were you thinking about me fucking you while you were talking to our friends?" She raised her head and met Olivia's eyes from beneath her lashes. "While you were talking to Luke?"

Margot's fingers crooked forward, hard, tearing a moan from Olivia's throat.

"Is that a yes?" Margot asked.

Olivia gasped when Margot pinched her nipple through the lace of her bra. *"Yes."*

With one more kiss pressed to the hinge of Olivia's jaw, Margot removed her hand from Olivia's underwear, causing Olivia to whimper at the loss. Margot kept her fingers curled beneath the band of Olivia's leggings and used them to drag Olivia toward the bed, to the side of the room less bathed in shadows, turning and pressing her down against the sheets.

Margot grabbed the waist of Olivia's leggings and made quick work of stripping them down her thighs and over her feet, her underwear, too. There was an urgency to Margot's touch that wasn't always there. Eager, yes, but that was nothing new. This felt almost like Margot *needed* Olivia naked.

Like Margot needed *her.*

There was a sudden pressure in Olivia's chest that hadn't been there before, a pressure that crept up the back of her throat and made it hard to breathe until she had no choice but to drag a gasping breath in when Margot's fingers slid through her folds and back inside.

"Is this what you were thinking about?" Margot ghosted her lips over the skin along the inside of Olivia's thigh as her fingers sped.

Olivia's back bowed against the mattress, her fingers grasping for purchase against the sheets that she couldn't find, the bed still perfectly made, unrumpled until now.

"Fuck." She gasped, rocking down on Margot's fingers. *"Yes."*

Margot sucked on the tender crease of skin where Olivia's hip met her thigh. She looked up at Olivia with dark eyes and lips that were full, shiny and red, her arm moving steadily between Olivia's legs. "Fuck, Liv. If you could see yourself. How pretty you look, all swollen and soaked, fucking yourself on my fingers."

Olivia's face burned and she shut her eyes, biting down hard on her lip to stifle the string of sounds coming from her mouth. One hand still gripped the tightly tucked sheets and the other reached up, squeezing her breast, pinching herself through her bra the same way Margot had.

"That's it," Margot bit the crease of her thigh. "Take what you need."

Tension built low in Olivia's belly, the pleasure deeper and different than if Margot had been focused on her clit. Margot's fingers sped, curling harder against that spot inside her, causing Olivia's breath to catch and her thighs to shake uncontrollably.

Olivia slid her hand down her stomach to touch herself, but stopped just shy of her curls.

Margot hummed against her hip, sounding pleased at Olivia's show of restraint. "You want to come?"

Her hips rocked, back arching. "*So* bad. Fuck. Please."

Margot sucked another one of those bruising kisses into her thigh, this time on the opposite side. "Not yet, baby."

Olivia pressed the heels of her hands into her eyes and bit down hard on her tongue to keep from begging. A strangled groan slipped out, an echo of it ringing in her ears.

Margot's fingers sped, stringing Olivia tighter, tighter— Margot's thumb barely ghosted over Olivia's swollen, neglected clit and the tension building inside her snapped and she clenched and shattered under Margot's touch.

Olivia's thighs snapped together, trapping Margot's hand between them. Margot didn't let up, didn't even give Olivia a second to recover before she pried her thighs apart and pinned one leg down against the bed with her forearm, fucking Olivia through the aftershocks and straight into another orgasm that stole the air from her lungs and made her chest burn.

Too much. Eyes still shut, Olivia reached down and weakly pushed against Margot's shoulder. Margot took the hint, backing off.

A sweet kiss against the skin beside her belly button made Olivia crack open an eye sometime after her heart rate had slowed to something close to normal. Margot was staring up at her. A slow smirk tugged at the corner of her mouth that made Olivia's pulse flutter and caused her to clench around the fingers still buried inside her.

Margot bit down on the swell of her bottom lip, smiling, as she slipped her fingers free and prowled up the bed. Margot lifted her hand and brushed her damp fingers against Olivia's mouth, covering her lips in her own arousal. "Open up."

A ragged breath escaped her when she parted her lips and darted out her tongue, tasting herself on Margot's fingers, sharp and a little sweet. Margot matched her breathing, panting softly, eyes darkening. Her breath stuttered, catching loudly. She dropped her hand to the side of Olivia's neck, thumb brushing the hollow at the front of her throat as she leaned closer, covering Olivia's mouth with hers and grinding her hips down against Olivia's thigh.

Olivia slipped her hands under Margot's sweater, fingers skimming her sides, brushing the undersides of her breasts. She broke the kiss to help Margot yank the sweater over her head, then went back to touching Margot everywhere she could, unable to keep her hands still. She swept a path from the small of Margot's back up her sides, tugging down the left cup of Margot's bra and closing her lips around Margot's nipple.

Sweat broke out along Margot's skin, dotting the space between her breasts, the hollow of her throat, the small of her back, slick beneath Olivia's hands. She gripped Margot's hips, helping her grind down a little harder.

Broken sounds spilled from Margot's mouth as she rocked a little faster, chasing her own pleasure until her hips stuttered and she cried out against Olivia's shoulder, her whole body shaking as she came apart.

Once she caught her breath, Margot lifted her head and

looked at Olivia, lids heavy and smile sweet, and for a heart-stopping moment Olivia couldn't get her lungs to work because Margot was looking at her like she was something special. Like she was something Margot wanted to keep.

Slowly, Margot leaned in and brushed her lips against Olivia's in a gentle kiss that curled her toes and made her heart flutter wildly inside her veins. It had none of the urgency of their earlier kiss, when Margot had pressed her up against the door, but it was no less passionate, still managing to rob Olivia of her breath. This time there was no teeth, only the gentle pressure of lips on lips, the sweet friction of Margot's tongue sweeping against the seam of Olivia's mouth.

She must've made a noise, a gasp, because Margot's lips curled, smiling against Olivia's mouth. Margot drew back, pressing one chaste kiss to Olivia's bottom lip in parting. She smiled, dark eyes shining. "Hi."

Olivia reached out, tucking a strand of hair behind Margot's ear before it could fall in her face. Her fingers lingered against the side of Margot's neck, stroking the skin over where her pulse still thundered. "Hi, yourself."

Margot shivered and reached for the covers, tugging them up around them, forming a little cocoon of warmth. Sweat had begun to cool against Olivia's skin, and she gladly burrowed beneath the comforter.

Olivia drew her feet up, tucking her toes beneath the underside of Margot's calves. A laugh erupted from her lips when Margot hissed, face scrunching in a way that was oddly—*adorably*—reminiscent of Cat. "Sorry."

Margot's bottom lip jutted out in a pout and Olivia couldn't help herself. She reached out, tracing the outline of Margot's mouth, the bow of her lips, the divot beneath her nose.

"Cute," she whispered.

A furrow formed between Margot's brows and Olivia immediately reached up, smoothing it away. "And to think, I was striving for sexy."

Margot fluttered her lashes.

Olivia snorted. "You look like you have something in your eye."

Margot laughed and reached up, snagging Olivia's hand and lacing their fingers together. She brushed her lips against the inside of Olivia's wrist and grinned. "Is this when you tell me I'm sexier when I'm not trying?"

Olivia shut one eye. "Sure."

"Rude." Margot reached under the covers, pinching Olivia's side, making her squeal.

"Sorry, sorry." Olivia laughed. "You have to know by now I think you're *extremely* sexy." Her lips twitched. "Even when you pout and look a little like Cat. *Especially* when you look like you have something poking you in the eye."

Margot preened. "I guess I'll take it."

"So." Olivia burrowed deeper beneath the covers, rolling onto her side, facing Margot. "You never said what brought this on."

The texts. Margot's inability to keep her hands to herself. How she'd seemed determined to take Olivia apart, more determined than normal.

Margot stared at their hands, fingers still tangled together. "Am I supposed to have a reason? Isn't wanting you enough?"

Yes. No. Maybe? Olivia swallowed a sigh. She'd didn't know where her head was at, only that she'd hoped for Margot to have said something . . . *more*. More revealing? More vulnerable? Something closer to what Olivia felt, that maybe she wanted to talk about it. Her feelings. If she had them. What they were. How deep they ran.

One thing was for certain. Olivia didn't want *enough*. When it came to Margot, she wanted everything.

She sat up, reaching over the edge of the bed, searching for her sweater, not because she was cold but because she felt vulnerable enough without being totally naked.

"Where do you think you're going?" Margot wrapped her arm around Olivia's waist, drawing her back beneath the covers. "I'm not done with you yet."

Olivia's heart squeezed, the line between pain and pleasure whisper thin.

Yet could never come, and it would still be too soon.

Chapter Sixteen

$\mathcal{S}$omeone knocked on her bedroom door.

Margot burrowed deeper into her pillow. *Too early.* She was warm, almost too warm, the arm wrapped around her waist— *Hello.*

Margot's eyes shot open. This wasn't her bedroom. This was—

Last night came rushing back in one fell swoop. Arriving at the lodge. Hanging out on the patio. *Luke.* Texting Liv. Her thighs clenched. Everything that had come after, until the early hours of the morning.

Whoever was at the door knocked louder, causing Olivia to release the cutest little whimper before burrowing her face against the back of Margot's neck.

Pale gray light filtered through a gap in the curtains. It was too early for housekeeping.

"Hey, Mar? Everyone's already downstairs. Are you coming?"

Shit. Elle.

Eyes still adjusting to being open, Margot patted the nightstand, searching for her glasses. She slipped them on, then grabbed her phone to check the time. 7:06. Early, but not as early as she'd expected. She had two texts and a missed call, all from Elle.

ELLE (6:45 A.M.): we're all meeting for breakfast at 7
ELLE (6:57 A.M.): mar?

One missed call 7:00 a.m.

"Fuck," Margot muttered, earning another whine from Olivia, whose arm tightened around Margot's waist. She sighed and ran her fingers along the back of Olivia's forearm. "Liv, I've got to get up."

Carefully, Margot extricated herself from the bed, wincing at how cold the floor was under her feet. Picking up clothes as she went, Margot pulled yesterday's sweater on over her head, grateful that it hit midthigh. She cracked open the door and poked her head out, the bed within direct view of the doorway.

Elle's smile fell. "You aren't ready yet?"

"Um, no. I—I overslept." She winced. "Sorry."

"It's fine. Do you just want to meet us . . ." Elle's eyes widened comically. "Um. Sorry." She shut her eyes and shook her head, laughing under her breath. "Lost my train of thought. Do you just want to meet us downstairs?"

Margot nodded. "Sounds good. I'll be down in fifteen, okay?"

"No rush." Elle smiled brightly. "Take your time."

As soon as the door was shut, Margot dropped her head and groaned. All she wanted was to crawl back into bed beside Liv and revel in this little bubble they'd built, an oasis of soft sheets and softer skin, the fireplace churning out heat they didn't even need, not with the way she burned when Liv touched her, even in the most innocent places. The inside of her wrist or the back of her knee, the small of her back, a kiss against the top knob of her spine capable of undoing her completely.

"Is everything okay?"

Margot spun around. Olivia was sitting up, sheet wrapped around her, hair mussed and eyes sleepy, lips kiss-swollen and pink.

Margot jerked her thumb behind her at the door. "That was just Elle. We overslept, I guess."

Olivia's eyes widened. "Wait, what time is it?" She swiped her phone off the nightstand. "Shoot. I still need to check my email."

Olivia hopped out of the bed, stumbling and catching herself when the sheets tangled around her legs. She kicked them aside and bent down, snagging her clothes. She looked up, lips twitching. "You're wearing my sweater."

"Oh." Margot ducked her chin and laughed. No wonder it hit so low on her thighs. Olivia was taller, longer in the torso than she was by several inches. "I guess I am."

Olivia crossed the room on bare feet, bare *everything*, and rested her arms on Margot's shoulders. She leaned in, ghosting a quick kiss against Margot's mouth that made her shiver. "It looks good on you."

The tips of Margot's ears burned. "Thanks." She dragged her eyes up Olivia's body in a slow, exaggerated leer. "Maybe I'll have to steal your clothes more often."

Olivia bit her lip and blushed, color spreading down her chest. "I should probably go shower and get ready."

Margot's stomach chose that moment to give a vicious-sounding growl, rumbling loudly. She and Olivia both laughed. "Not a bad idea. We're supposed to meet everyone downstairs for breakfast."

Olivia stepped back, hands falling to her sides, and Margot immediately missed her warmth. "Okay, meet you back here?"

Margot nodded and headed for the bathroom, running through a record-fast shower. She didn't bother with makeup, just brushing her hair and throwing on her clothes, a simple black sweater and pair of jeans.

Five minutes later, Margot was in the middle of fighting with the zipper on her left boot when Olivia returned, looking the part of an adorable snow bunny in a pair of pink insulated cargo pants and a cream-colored fleece. In her arms was a pink jacket that matched her pants.

Olivia's brows knit. "Is that what you're wearing?"

Margot tugged on her sleeves. "Yes?"

Olivia fiddled with the zipper pull at the top of her fleece, lowering it an inch before drawing it back up to her neck, distracting Margot with that tantalizing sliver of skin. "Okay. You ready?"

Margot patted her pocket, double-checking that she had her room key and cell before locking up. "I heard back from the DJ, by the way," Olivia said as they stepped inside the elevator. "He has the set list, along with the song requests from the RSVP Google Form—that's a relief."

"I told you." Margot kicked Olivia's shin lightly. "You were worrying over nothing."

Olivia blew out her breath. "You're right. I'm just—nervous? Everything has to be perfect."

"It's not even your wedding, Liv." Margot laughed.

"I know that." Olivia tucked her hair behind her ear, worrying her bottom lip. Margot itched to reach out and draw that lip from between her teeth. Giving in to the urge, she skimmed her hand along Olivia's jaw, cupping the side of Olivia's face, and rubbed the pad of her thumb along Olivia's bottom lip, gasping when Olivia's tongue darted out against her skin. Olivia smiled impishly.

Margot dropped her hand with a shaky laugh. "Tease."

Olivia's smile wavered at the edges. "Brendon's been a loyal client of my boss's for years, and she's trusting me to make sure this wedding goes off without a hitch. You have no idea how I had to actually *beg* for Lori to let me have this." Olivia scratched her eyebrow with her thumbnail. "That's not even taking into account that I actually *like* Annie and Brendon. Even if my career weren't riding on this wedding being a success, I'd still want everything to be perfect because they deserve it."

The fact that Olivia cared about Margot's friends, about the people *she* cared about, the people she'd do anything for . . . that pushed buttons Margot didn't even know she had. She had to swallow twice before she could speak. "I know Annie and Brendon appreciate everything you've done. You've been . . . amazing."

Olivia ducked her chin. "It's nothing."

It wasn't nothing. Olivia's selflessness, her endless capacity to care, made her so fucking *special*.

Margot's heart made a new home inside her throat. "It's not. You have no idea how—"

The elevator dinged, the doors opening, saving Margot from word-vomiting her feelings all over Olivia.

Olivia made no move to leave the elevator, instead staring at Margot with wide eyes. Her lashes beat against her cheek with every blink, seeming to match the frantic fluttering of Margot's pulse at the base of her throat.

"I have no idea what?" Olivia whispered.

Margot gulped, the sound embarrassingly loud inside the small space, even with the elevator doors open. "How amazing you are." *Fuck.* Too much. "You know." Margot coughed. "At what you do."

Olivia's eyes darted over Margot's face. One corner of her mouth rose. "Thanks, Margot."

A throat cleared. A man stood outside the elevator, one hand braced against the elevator door, holding it open. He smiled tightly.

"Shit," Margot muttered. "Sorry."

She hurried out of the elevator, taking a second to get her bearings once she reached the lobby.

"I think the restaurant's this way." Olivia wrapped her fingers around Margot's elbow, gently tugging her toward the left. Around the corner was a hostess stand, empty, a chalkboard sign proclaiming that visitors could seat themselves. Margot stepped through the door and glanced around looking for—

"Margot!"

At the back of the restaurant, occupying a long table, were her friends. And Luke. Elle stood partway, hovering over her chair, one hand braced against the table, the other waving them over.

Two empty seats remained, both together, Elle to one side, Luke to the other. Making a split-second decision she was likely to regret, Margot slid into the seat beside Luke, leaving the chair beside Elle for Olivia.

"First one to bed and last one awake?" Brendon grinned.

"It, um, took me a while to fall asleep," Margot said, stealing a quick glance at Olivia from the corner of her eye. "I don't know. I kept tossing and turning."

Elle choked on her orange juice.

Margot frowned. "Are you okay?"

"Fine," Elle croaked, accepting a napkin from Darcy.

Luke leaned his forearms on the edge of the table, peering around Margot. "How about you, Liv? I, uh, knocked on your door this morning." He smiled at her, adorably lopsided, and Margot's chest clenched. *Liv?* Since when did anyone call Olivia *Liv,* but her? That was *Margot's* nickname. *Hers,* not his. "You must be a heavy sleeper."

Olivia blushed and nodded quickly. "I am."

Margot reached for her glass of water at the same time Olivia did, their fingers brushing above the table.

"Sorry." She slid Olivia's glass toward her, taking a quick sip from her own before setting it to the right side of her place setting.

How ridiculous was it that she'd had her hands and mouth

all over Olivia, had used her fingers to drive Olivia wild, and still the simplest touch made her jolt like she'd stuck her finger in a damn light socket?

Elle cleared her throat. "We all already ordered. Mar, I went ahead and ordered you your usual." By *usual*, Margot was willing to bet Elle meant pancakes and bacon, Margot's go-to no matter where she ate out. Elle flashed Olivia an apologetic smile. "I would've ordered something for you, but I had no idea what you wanted. I told our waitress to—oh, here she is."

Olivia swiped the menu off the table, eyes scanning it quickly. She turned to the waitress, "I'll have the wild-mushroom-and-pesto omelet." Olivia smiled and handed over her menu. "And can I get a cup of green tea? Thanks."

Margot snagged the carafe of coffee from the center of the table and filled her mug.

"You're not wearing that to the pass, are you?" Brendon asked.

"Wait, me?" Margot lowered her mug and frowned down at her outfit. What was with everyone asking about her choice of clothes? "What's wrong with what I'm wearing?"

Luke snorted out a laugh that immediately put Margot's back up. "Those jeans are going to soak through in an instant."

Margot recoiled, jaw dropping. "What the hell?"

They were at breakfast; that was gauche, even for her.

Brendon sputtered, laughing so hard tears welled in his eyes. "Oh, shit." He laughed harder. "No. *Margot.*"

Annie rested her hand on Brendon's shaking shoulder and smiled. "I think what Luke was trying to say is, denim isn't water- or wind-resistant. If you wipe out, you're going to freeze up on the mountain."

"Cotton kills." Luke nodded as if that was supposed to make sense to her.

Margot glanced around the table. Everyone, save for her, was wearing some version of what Olivia had on—insulated ski pants and plenty of layers. Margot frowned, her stomach beginning a slow descent toward her knees.

"I mean, we're not *all* skiing, right? There's a lodge at the summit where we can sip spiked cider and shoot the shit around a fire, yeah?"

Annie shrugged. "I think so? I honestly don't know. I haven't been skiing since I was in Courchevel with my cousins, so I've been really looking forward to hitting the slopes."

Margot bit her lip. "Elle? You don't ski."

Elle wrinkled her nose. "I don't *often*. But I went to Whistler with my family every winter when I was younger. It's been a while, but it could be fun?"

She turned to Olivia, who winced. "Brad and I used to go to Stevens Pass. I'm not *great* at skiing or anything—"

"I was a volunteer ski instructor in high school," Luke said, leaning across Margot. "If you need me to show you the ropes, I'd be more than happy to." His lips twitched. "Ropes on the slopes."

Olivia laughed.

Doctors Without Borders, volunteer ski instructor . . . "Where are you from?"

Pleasantville?

"North Lake Tahoe," Luke answered, smile broad and Chiclet white.

"Hmm." Margot sipped her coffee.

"You know, I think I'll be okay." When Olivia gestured to Margot, her stomach sank. No, no, no. "But maybe Margot might need a little instruction?"

"I'm fine." Margot tore the paper holder off her napkin. "Seriously."

"Nah, it's cool." Luke shrugged. "I'm used to teaching kids, so it's really not a problem."

Woo boy. Margot stole a deep breath in, nostrils flaring, and released it slowly.

The rational part of her brain realized that chances were, Luke was a decent guy. He'd have to be, in order to be Brendon's friend. Brendon, himself, was a golden retriever in human form, a six-foot-four-inch marshmallow encased in muscle. The chances of him associating with some smarmy asshole were slim. Luke was probably an awesome, all-around great dude.

But jealousy *wasn't* rational.

She was self-aware enough to *know* why she didn't vibe with Luke, that her feelings had less to do with *him* and more to do with her. Her and Olivia, specifically her feelings for Olivia, feelings she didn't know what to do with, feelings that were very much unresolved because she didn't know *how* to resolve them without saying something to Olivia, which, *ha*, right.

She didn't hate Luke. She hated what he represented. The reality of her situation. That Margot had no right to feel the way she did, because Olivia wasn't hers. That Luke or anyone else could come along and sweep Olivia off her feet and ride off into the sunset and—

Pain radiated up her jaw from clenching her back teeth too

hard. It didn't hold a candle to the sharp stab between her ribs that nearly stole her breath at the thought of losing Liv.

Insecurity *sucked*.

Knowing the root cause of her irritation didn't make her like him any more than she did, but hey, she wasn't in denial about it. Score one for enlightenment.

At least she could choose how to react. She could be cool. Completely relaxed. *Chill*. The last thing she needed was for her twisted-up, uglier emotions to get the best of her and put a damper on Annie and Brendon's wedding week.

She pasted on a smile. "Maybe I'll take you up on that, Luke."

Not. She'd be fine. If Elle—the least athletic person Margot knew—could ski, how hard could it be?

"We'll have to get you some proper ski gear, for starters," Luke said, eyeing her clothes with a frown. "Ski pants, ski jacket—you can rent the rest at the summit."

Elle perked up. "I think I saw some cute options in the gift shop. We can wander over after breakfast and take a peek?"

"Works for me."

The waitress appeared, trays laden with food. "Denver omelet?"

Brendon lifted his hand. "That's me."

As soon as everyone had their food, the conversation turned to the wedding.

"I heard back from the caterer on your question about the vegetarian option for the reception," Olivia said. "It *can* be made gluten-free, so your mom should be fine. I'll make sure to remind the kitchen on the day of the wedding."

Brendon nodded along with a grateful smile. "Thank you. Mom, uh, kind of blindsided us with this new, uh, diet she's following."

Darcy picked at her eggs and rolled her eyes. "I still have a feeling Mom's going to do something dramatic like wear white to the wedding."

"I don't know," Annie mused, tapping the tines of her fork against her lip. "My money's on black. Full funeral veil and everything."

Brendon cringed.

Olivia set her fork down, looking concerned. "Is that something I'm going to need to run interference on, because I don't exactly have any firsthand experience dealing with parental conflict during—"

"We're kidding," Darcy said, smirking. "Our mother is a little . . . difficult, but she shouldn't make a scene."

"Whew." Olivia pressed her palm to her chest. "I was a little worried there."

"Don't be," Margot said, leaning into Olivia and jostling her lightly. "Even if something were to go down, Brendon's already tasked me with running interference."

His smile verged on a grimace. "We're calling it *Plan G*."

At Olivia's frown, Darcy said, "Our mother's name is Gillian."

Brendon looked across the table, meeting Margot's eye. He gave his patented staggered blink, his inability to wink both charming and hilarious.

Margot buried her smirk in a bite of her pancakes.

Olivia nudged her before leaning close, breath ruffling

Margot's hair when she whispered, "Why do I get the feeling that's not what it's really named for?"

Margot finished chewing and said, "No, it is. It's just a little more complicated than it sounds, me running interference. Because Gillian's a bit of a loose cannon." Margot shivered at the memory of Brendon's mother trying to crawl on top of the bar at his and Annie's joint shower. "She's got a bunch of personal hang-ups, and none of us are entirely sure how she's going to react on the day of the wedding, so Brendon and I have discussed several different problems that might arise and how best to solve them before they, um, blow up? Perks of being Best Woman."

Olivia smiled. "With great power comes great responsibility?"

Margot snickered into her napkin. "Hmm, I like that. Makes me sound *way* more important than I am."

Olivia cocked her head, staring, studying Margot closely in a way that made her stomach flutter. "I think you're pretty damn important, Margot."

She had to stop saying things like that. Giving Margot hope that maybe this *thing* between them could be more. That Olivia wanted more. Wanted Margot and not just the parts of her that were easy and sexy and fun, but the hard parts, too. The edges and the sandpapery bluntness and the parts Margot didn't always like about herself, but that were part and parcel to the whole package. Everything that made Margot who she was.

Margot ducked her chin and laughed. "So what? You're suggesting all I need is a flashy suit to round out this new superhero persona I've got going?"

Olivia pursed her lips and hummed as if pretending to think about it. "I don't know. I've heard good things about the tux you picked out." Her smile turned sly. "I'm looking forward to seeing you in it."

Heat crept up the front of Margot's throat. "You sure you don't mean that you're looking forward to seeing me *out* of it?"

"Hmm." With a tiny shrug, Olivia reached for her tea. She cradled the mug between her hands, slender fingers laced together around the ceramic. "I don't know. I happen to like unwrapping my presents."

Margot bit back a whimper.

Olivia swiped a piece of bacon off Margot's plate with a wink and smile.

Devious. Margot swallowed hard and tuned back in to the conversation only—no one was talking.

Almost everyone was staring at her with varying degrees of shock splashed across their faces, eyes darting between Margot, her plate, and the bacon in Olivia's hand.

She frowned. "What?"

"You never share your food," Brendon said.

"What?" Margot laughed. "That's not true."

Brendon's face screwed up. "You went on an entire rant about growing up with brothers and—and you almost took my finger off when I tried to steal your Reese's, Margot."

Elle was watching her curiously, eyes narrowed and lip trapped between her teeth, like Margot was a puzzle and Elle was bound and determined to solve it. Her eyes darted to Olivia and back and—Margot's stomach somersaulted. Unless Elle had already solved it.

"It's just bacon," Margot said, rolling her eyes. She lifted her plate and shook it at Brendon. "You want some?"

He waved it off. "Nah, I'm stuffed."

Margot set her plate down and stretched across the table for the carafe to refill her coffee. She had her mug halfway to her mouth when, from the corner of her eye, she saw a hand sneak out from the right, heading directly for her bacon. Acting on instinct, an impulse to protect the food on her plate ingrained in her from years spent fending off her brothers . . . and okay, whatever, she wasn't Luke's number one fan. She snagged her plate and dragged it to the side, further out reach.

"Were you raised by *wolves*?" she demanded.

Luke lifted his hands up and laughed. "Geez, you *offered*."

Yeah, to Brendon. She sniffed. Her bacon, her rules; she was under no obligation to share.

Only . . . everyone was looking at her like she'd lost her mind, including Elle, including *Olivia*. She stared at Margot, hands still cradling her mug of tea, her lips parted in apparent shock, and—

Margot flung a strip of bacon at Luke's plate. "Enjoy."

She wiped her hands on her napkin and pushed away from the table. "I'm going to—"

Elle stood so fast her chair almost toppled over. "Come to the gift shop with me?"

She swallowed her sigh. No point in delaying the inevitable. "Sure."

They made it out of the restaurant and through the lobby without speaking. By the time they reached the gift shop, Elle appeared to be practically vibrating out of her skin with the restraint it was taking to hold her tongue. Her eyes were wide as she stared at Margot, her lips a thin, pale line as she pressed them together. Elle's eyes might actually fall out of her eye sockets if she stared any more meaningfully.

"Stop looking at me like that." Margot chuckled, slightly unnerved. "It's freaking me out."

Elle held up her hands. "I can't *look* at my best friend? My best friend who should know she can tell me *anything* and I'll listen. Eagerly, even."

Margot's eyes narrowed. "I'm on to you."

"What?" Elle feigned ignorance, her blue eyes flaring with faux innocence. "I didn't say anything."

"Elle."

Elle gave a tiny shrug. "Like I said, whenever you're ready to talk, I'll be ready to listen." She smiled guiltily. "So . . . are you ready to talk yet? Or do I need to dig deep for a little more patience?"

Heaven forbid.

"It hasn't even been twelve hours." Margot shook her head but wasn't able to churn up any true exasperation. *"Hours."*

Elle bit her lip, brows rising, expression eager. "That was before you smacked Luke's hand away from your *bacon*." Her brows wiggled.

"It's breakfast meat, Elle. It's not that deep."

Elle jutted out her lower lip.

Margot rolled her eyes, aiming for affectation and missing by a landslide when she swallowed, her throat suddenly parched to the point that her gulp was audible. Fuck. "I don't even know where to start."

"At the beginning?" Elle suggested, nodding in the direction of the ski apparel. There were several racks of options at the back of the shop, most in garishly bright colors that made Margot cringe at the thought of sliding down a mountain looking like a traffic cone.

"The beginning," Margot repeated, rifling through a rack of jackets. "Which beginning? The beginning eleven years ago? The beginning when Liv and I met in kindergarten? Or the beginning where we ran into each other last month?"

"Either? All?" Elle shuffled awkwardly on her feet. "*Or* I guess I could tell you what I already know?"

Margot froze, one hand wrapped around the hanger of an ostentatious coat in pea green. "What you already know . . . which is what, exactly?"

Elle bit her lip and winced. "Um, the walls of the hotel are thinner than you might think."

"What." Margot gripped the metal rack and stared.

"Um, was that a question?" Elle laughed through another sharp cringe. "I—yeah, so last night, Darcy and I sort of . . . heard some things. And this morning, when you answered the door, you were wearing the sweater Olivia had on last night. It was, uh . . . A lot of things suddenly made a lot of sense."

The rush of blood to her head left Margot dizzy. "Ah. I see. That would be, um . . ." Awkward laughter burst from her lips. "Illuminating."

"Oh my gosh. You're blushing, Margot." Elle giggled.

"Well, *yeah*. You just told me you heard . . ." She trailed off, making a vague gesture with her hand that didn't mean much of anything but communicated plenty.

"We lived together for ten years. It's not the first time one of us has heard the other"—Elle mimicked Margot's hand movement—"*you know*. I mean, for goodness' sake, my *mom* walked in on you freshman year."

And to this day, Mrs. Jones wouldn't look Margot in the eye. Margot maintained that if Mrs. Jones hadn't wanted to see Margot naked, astride the RA, she should've knocked before entering the dorm room she and Elle shared.

"Yeah, well, I guess I just didn't anticipate the cat being let out of the bag quite so . . . I don't know—"

"Pornographically?" Elle supplied. "I mean, from the sound of it, *good* porn. The kind you have to pay for and where you know they're actually treating the actors nice, you know? Quality stuff." Elle cringed. "Not that we were *listening*, ew, it was just difficult to tune out. But we tried. Really hard. We, um, turned the TV on *really* loud." Elle smiled sweetly. "But kudos, Mar. It sounded like you guys were having an A-plus time."

"Oh, Jesus Christ." Margot buried her face in her hands and groaned. "Kill me now."

Elle bumped her with her hip and laughed. "Lighten up. Don't worry, it's not like Darcy and I are going to say anything. Clearly, this isn't how you wanted anyone to find out about . . ."

Margot peeked through her fingers as Elle trailed off, brows lifting as she waited for Margot to fill in the blanks.

Margot lowered her hands from her face and sighed deeply, the sound coming from what felt like all the way down in her bones. "I don't know what I'm doing, Elle. But I'm in so far over my head, it's not even funny."

Elle's smile slipped. "Okay, not laughing anymore. Why don't you start from the beginning?"

Margot glared.

"The beginning that makes the most sense to you," Elle clarified.

Margot took a deep breath and just . . . let it all pour out.

"Like I said, Olivia and I were friends. We were *best* friends. Wherever she went, I was sure to follow. If you were looking for her, you'd find me." She bit her lip. "I mean, there was one summer where Liv practically moved in with us, my family. I had mono and she skipped cheer camp and gave up her spot on the varsity squad just so I wouldn't be alone."

Elle smiled, and if Margot wasn't mistaken, it was a touch sad. Grim. Expectant. Leave it to Elle to read between the lines, to hear what Margot wasn't saying. "Sounds like you two were really close."

Margot scratched her forehead. "Yeah, you could—you could say that." She swallowed, the lump in her throat growing. "It doesn't really take a genius to see where this is going. At some point—I don't know exactly when, because whoever knows exactly when these things begin—I fell for her. Hard. I was ridiculously, stupidly, ass-over-heels in love with her, and I didn't realize it until she started dating someone else. Brad. He was an ass." She rolled her eyes. "Not just because he was dating her and I wasn't."

Elle nodded and, to her credit, waited quietly for Margot to go on.

"It was fine. I—okay, no. That's a lie. It sucked. There were copious amounts of teenage angst, and lying in bed, staring up at the ceiling and listening to Ingrid Michaelson sing about fragile hearts, and journaling. So much journaling." She ducked her head and scoffed out a laugh. "I'm sure I filled *several* diaries up with entries about how painfully unfair my life was."

She'd yearned, pined, burned, perished. If it sounded painful and emotionally fraught, Margot had probably been there, done that.

Elle nibbled on her bottom lip. "Did you ever say anything?"

"Are you serious?" Margot snorted. "Of course not. Olivia was with Brad, and I didn't want to ruin our friendship, so I kept my mouth shut." Her lips twisted. "I managed to mess everything up without ever saying a thing."

Margot glared at that atrocious jacket the color of pea soup. "Spring break senior year. Brad and Olivia were in one of the many *off* phases of their on-again-off-again relationship. He'd broken up with her that time. I did what I always did and came over with junk food and old movies and was prepared to be the shoulder Liv needed to cry on. But it didn't happen like that." Her mouth had gone dry, tongue sticking to the roof of her mouth. She swallowed hard, trying to generate some moisture. "Liv's dad was away on some trip with his friends. We had the house to ourselves. Suddenly we were breaking out a bottle of bottom-shelf vodka, and next thing I knew"—her voice cracked—"she was kissing me."

Elle squeezed her arm.

"It was, um, everything I wanted right there, and I just . . . I rolled with it. I didn't ask questions. I mean, my best friend who I was stupidly in love with was kissing me, and I was

eighteen and perpetually horny; what was there to question?"
She laughed. To be that young and stupid. "One thing led to
another, and we had sex. A lot of sex. I stayed the whole week
at her house and we weren't—we weren't drunk the whole time.
After that first day, we didn't touch the vodka. But we didn't
really talk about it, either? I mean, we *talked*. It wasn't like a
constant sex marathon."

"I imagine there'd have been some serious chafing if it were."
Elle snorted, immediately looking apologetic. "Sorry."

Margot waved her off. "We talked, we just didn't define it.
And it was my bad, I guess, for assuming we were on the same
page."

"You weren't?"

An iron fist gripped Margot's heart. If it didn't suck so badly,
Margot would almost be amazed at how a decade-old wound
could still hurt so badly. "No. Brad came back from his trip
to Cancún." She rolled her eyes. "He and I had homeroom
together. Someone asked about the breakup and he shrugged it
off. Said he and Liv had talked the night before. That they were
working it out. Getting back together." She swallowed over the
knot swelling in her throat. "The first thing he did during passing period was head straight to Liv's locker, and he—he just
kissed her and . . . Liv let him." The burn at the back of her
eyes worsened with every blink, the ache in her chest growing
larger until she feared her next breath would escape her as a sob.
Fuck. Margot pinched her lips together, forcing air through
her nose, getting a grip. She sniffed hard. "I told the nurse I
wasn't feeling well and went home. Liv texted me that night.

Something along the lines of, *Brad wants to get back together. Can you believe it? What should I tell him?* I told her she didn't need to worry about me saying anything to anyone about what happened over spring break. Because what happened on spring break stayed on spring break. And I, um, I told her she should get back together with Brad."

Elle frowned. "Why would you do that?"

Margot laughed even though the last thing she felt was amused. "What was I supposed to do, Elle? She asked. She shouldn't have *had* to ask. I thought—I thought a lot of things, and none of them mattered. Things were awkward for the next few weeks, but there was still a tiny part of me that hoped maybe it would be different when we left for college. Brad didn't seem like the kind of guy who'd be down for long distance, you know?" She took a deep breath. "Right before graduation, Liv dropped a bombshell on me, telling me she was going to WSU instead of UW. She chose Brad over me, over all of her plans, all of *our* plans. *Again.*

"So Olivia left. She moved across the state to Pullman with Brad, and that was it. Eleven years pass, and I don't see or talk to Liv, and then one day I walk into a building in Queen Anne with my best friend to go meet up with my other friends and *bam*! She's the wedding planner, and she's . . ." Margot blinked hard and dropped her eyes to the floor, staring hard at her scuffed shoes. "She's just as beautiful as I remember, and she's standing right in front of me. And then she needed a place to stay and I gave it to her."

Without warning, Margot had an armful of Elle. Elle's

hands cradled the back of Margot's head, and—*ow*, that was Elle's foot standing on the tender top of Margot's instep. Margot winced but hugged Elle back; the inevitable bruises would be worth it for this momentary comfort.

Elle drew back and blinked. "Okay. That's a lot."

Leave it to Elle to manage to make Margot laugh at a moment like this. "I know."

"How did I know *none* of this?"

"Because I didn't want you to? No offense, but it's really not the sort of thing you want to tell your brand-new college roommate. *Hi, my name's Margot. Would you like to hear all about my teenage heartbreak?*"

"I'd have listened," Elle said, sounding indignant. "If not then, I can't believe you never mentioned this. *Eleven years.*"

"Honestly? Not to be a walking cliché, but this is really one of those *it's not you, it's me* things. I haven't wanted to talk about this with anyone. No one knows. Not my brothers or my parents, not anyone. I could've gone the rest of my life without telling a soul, but . . . I don't know what I'm doing," she admitted. "I thought I could do this, but I don't know, Elle. I really don't know."

"What's *this*?" Elle asked. "You're, um, clearly . . ."

Elle trailed off, expression earnest as she made another one of those vague gestures with her hands.

"Having really great sex? It's not a question of whether she wants me like that. It's everything else." Margot needed something to do with her hands, so she moved on to the next rack of jackets, these in far less offensive hues.

"Did you consider, I don't know, asking her how she feels?"

Margot snagged a charcoal-colored jacket off the rack that looked like it had promise and, bummer. Not her size. It was beginning to look like her only option was the awful green number. "Sure. I considered it."

And decided against it.

Elle stared, face twisted in disappointment. "Margot."

"Olivia is living down the hall from me, Elle. She's Brendon's wedding planner. Do you realize how messy it would be if things between us went south?"

"She's only Brendon's wedding planner for the next week. Not even a week."

"She's still going to be my roommate," Margot argued. The lump in her throat swelled. "She's still going to be my friend."

Elle frowned. "What are you actually worried about here?"

Margot drummed her fingers against her thighs. "I don't—I feel like I just got Liv back and . . . I don't want to lose her. I don't want the same thing that happened before to happen again. Me wanting Liv and Liv wanting . . . *not* me. I mean, do you realize how awkward it would be, sharing an apartment, after pouring out my feelings and having Liv tell me she doesn't want the same? That *this* is all she wants? There's no way we could live together."

She wasn't sure their friendship could withstand the same blow twice. Her heart definitely couldn't.

"You're making a lot of assumptions, Margot. Don't you think you should talk about it? About what happened then and what's happening now?"

That sounded like the worst idea, the exact opposite of what Margot wanted.

Communication was the cornerstone to any relationship—yeah, she *got* that. Margot had read enough books and fanfiction, watched enough movies to know the pitfalls of miscommunication, the frustration of watching two people flounder simply because they failed to speak their minds. If she had a dollar for every time she'd wanted to reach through the screen and throttle someone, to scream and say *just fucking talk about it* or *just tell her how you feel*, she'd be able to afford those ridiculous leather boots she'd been eyeing in the window display at Nordstrom, praying for them to go on sale.

Reality was different. Talking, *sharing*, like so many things, was easier said than done.

"Look, normally I am totally on team *talk about it*. But it's so much easier to tell someone to talk than to actually do it. The problem isn't opening my mouth and saying the words—that's the *easy* part. It's—it's what comes after. When the words are out there, and I can't take them back. Right now, I'm living out the Schrödinger's cat of relationship probability. I am half hope, half agony until proven otherwise."

"How is living in relationship limbo any better?" Sweet, *sweet* Elle stared, eyes wide and expression guileless.

Margot raked her fingers through her hair, tugging on the ends. "It's not." She sighed. "You're right. It's sucks. I'm just—"

"Scared?" Elle smiled gently.

She slipped her hands beneath her glasses and rubbed her eyes. "Terrified," she said, dropping her arms back to her sides.

Elle reached out and grabbed Margot's hand, squeezing hard. The pressure in Margot's chest lessened. "I promise that nothing that will happen will be as bad as the worst-case scenario you've imagined."

Margot huffed. "Hate to break it to you, Elle, but that's less reassuring than you think. You underestimate my ability to catastrophize."

"I'm not going to say your worries are unfounded. I'm not inside Olivia's head. I don't know how she feels, but I see the way she looks at you and . . . I think you should just tell her how you feel. Let her know what's going on inside *your* head, because I love you, Margot, but right now what you're doing isn't fair to either of you. You've got to tell her what you want."

Once again, Elle was spot-on. What Margot was doing *wasn't* fair, saying she wanted one thing but acting like she wanted another. Margot's breath caught, and it hurt like hell to swallow. Olivia deserved better than *this*, being unwittingly caught up in Margot's emotional whiplash.

Elle was right. Margot needed to tell Olivia how she felt. That she wanted more.

After the wedding.

Elle could tell her she was worrying for nothing until she turned blue in the face, but there was no way for Elle to know that for sure. To know that Olivia wanted Margot in all the ways Margot wanted her.

For all Margot knew, everything could go sideways. That wasn't a risk she could take with Brendon's wedding days away. He was counting on her, and Olivia's career hinged on the success of the wedding.

If part of her reason for putting it off was because she was scared . . . that was her prerogative. Sue her if she wanted a little more guaranteed time with Olivia before she introduced the possibility of—of losing her into the equation.

It wasn't like she was never going to say something. Margot had *years* of practice hiding her feelings from Olivia. What was a few more days?

She swallowed hard.

That was somehow both too long and not nearly long enough.

Chapter Seventeen

*O*kay, so you've got the wedge technique down. That's fantastic. The next technique you'll want to practice is the parallel turn, which is the complete opposite of the wedge. We call it the parallel turn because your skis are—"

"Parallel?" Margot arched a brow, the sharp shrewdness of her gaze tempered by the garish green puffy coat she had zipped all the way to her chin, making her look a little like giant pea. A cute pea. A cute pea Olivia very much wanted to kiss, but couldn't because they were in public and this was *casual.*

God, for a word that Olivia usually associated with so many of her favorite things—her most comfortable pair of jeans, her favorite threadbare T-shirt that she'd happened to have *borrowed* from Margot years ago and never returned, the restaurant down the street that had the best crab Rangoon she'd ever eaten in her life—*casual* was beginning to grate. She'd ban it from her vocabulary if she could, scrap it altogether.

Screw *casual.* She wanted the opposite of whatever that was. Complex? She'd take *complex* any day.

"Yeah, exactly." Luke nodded. "Parallel turns are kind of the bread and butter of skiing. It's the ideal position for edging."

Margot's brows rocketed to her hairline as she met Olivia's eyes over Luke's shoulder. "Sorry, come again?"

Olivia lifted a gloved hand to her mouth, muffling her small snicker. Margot's lips twitched, eyes sparkling with mischief as she met Olivia's stare.

"Edging," Luke repeated, and Margot turned, staring at Luke agog, the tip of her nose turning red and small flurries gathering on her dark lashes. "It's how you control your speed. By scraping the edge of skis against the snow, you can slow down. The harder you edge—"

Margot snorted loudly.

"Is something funny?" Luke frowned.

Margot's lips pressed together and a bubble of laughter built in Olivia's throat, Margot's laughter catching. A tiny giggle escaped Olivia before she bit down on the inside of her cheek.

"Nope," Margot bit out, barely managing that one word before her chin quivered and her shoulders started to shake.

"Okay." Luke looked less than convinced, but shrugged, moving on. "Like I was saying, the harder you edge, the more in control you'll—"

Margot bent at the waist and burst out laughing.

A smile tugged at the corners of Olivia's mouth, the sound of Margot's unadulterated joy filling her chest with more than enough warmth to combat the freezing temps.

"Is she okay?" Luke asked Olivia, dropping his voice and leaning a little closer than strictly necessary.

Olivia nodded and shuffled back to put a bit of distance between them, her legs hampered by the skis attached to her feet. It had been over a year since she'd been skiing and even then, she could count on one hand the number of times she'd been in total. *Rusty* was an understatement. "Margot's fine. She's just—"

"Sorry, sorry." Margot flapped her hands in front of her face and exhaled sharply. "I'm good. You were saying?"

Luke frowned, staring at Margot like she'd lost her marbles. "Why don't you head back up the magic carpet and try a parallel turn at the bottom of the bunny slope? Edge hard to stop, okay?"

The magic carpet was a conveyor-belt-style people mover that pulled passengers up a small hill so they could master the basics before moving on to more advanced terrain. The summit offered two such people movers—one that led up to a small bunny slope, and another that led to a slightly steeper hill for those looking for a more intermediary option. Still not advanced, by any means, but a longer descent perfect for practicing trickier turns.

The rest of the group had headed off to the ski lift, skilled enough to tackle the actual slopes. Luke had volunteered to hang back and help Olivia brush up on her skills and teach Margot the fundamentals. After two trips on the beginner magic carpet, Olivia felt pretty confident that she wasn't going to fall on her ass, or worse, faceplant into a snowbank.

Margot lifted her hand in a sassy two-finger salute before waddling over to the magic carpet, her skis spreading further apart with each step she took. Olivia cringed. "Shuffle, Mar. Don't lift. Push forward. Use your thighs."

"Got it." Margot waved a gloved hand.

"Liv and I are going to head up to the next hill, okay?" Luke said, resting one hand on the small of Olivia's back, guiding her toward the longer of the two magic carpets, the one that would take them slightly higher up on the mountain.

Margot's shuffled footsteps faltered, her eyes dropping to where Luke's hand rested on Olivia's waist. Her jaw slid forward and she nodded. "Sure. Meet you back down here."

Olivia bit back a cringe, at the touch, the use of her nickname, *and* Margot's reaction. It wasn't that she minded being called Liv, it was that Luke hadn't bothered to ask. It grated, reminding her of how Brad had glommed on to the nickname Dad called her. For over ten years she'd suffered in silence, because at first she hadn't wanted to be rude or abrasive, and later because it was too late. She'd let it go on too long to say anything after he'd been calling her Livvy for over a year.

Now, she didn't want to make a scene. What did it matter if Brendon's friend called her Liv? The chances of seeing him again after this weekend were slim.

He was a nice guy, but that was just it. Olivia didn't want *nice*. She wanted Margot.

Olivia smiled as Margot waddled over to the people mover, shuffling awkwardly, looking a little like she had a wedgie. Olivia wanted *that*. Margot with her sharp laugh and sly smiles and dirty jokes and huge heart. Her quiet confidence and how fiercely loyal she was. Even her inability to ski—though she seemed bound and determined to figure it out—and her tendency to act first and ask questions later. Everything, even Margot's flaws, was endearing to Olivia.

What Margot wanted, *that* remained a mystery. It was hard to say, with how she blew hot one minute and cold the next, acting like this *thing* between them was casual before looking at Olivia like she was something precious, looking at her in a way that no one else ever quite had, not even Brad. Keeping a solid three feet between them when they were around Brendon and the rest of her friends but kissing her sweetly in the privacy of the elevator. Wanting to keep whatever this was between them quiet, keep it from her friends for the week—or so she said—but glaring at Luke from across the deck.

It didn't feel like she was imagining a shift, an intensity in Margot's gaze and an urgency in the way she touched Olivia that hadn't been there before. But a terrible, anxious little voice in the back of Olivia's brain whispered that Margot was only acting this way, acting like she wanted something more with Olivia, because someone else wanted her, too.

Olivia wasn't sure how much more of this whiplash she could take.

"So would you want to?" Luke stared at her expectantly as they reached the top of the slope.

Olivia winced. "Sorry? I missed that. Would I want to what?"

Luke smiled patiently and repeated himself. "Would you want to hang out sometime? You said you were relatively new to the city, and I haven't lived here in a few years, but I've got a good grasp of the general lay of the land." The right corner of his mouth lifted a little higher than the left, his smile going crooked. It was a credit to how intensely *gone* for Margot she was that her heart didn't stutter at the sight of his dimple or his perfectly white teeth. Her heart didn't even speed up. "I could show you around. Take you to some of my old haunts. If you're interested."

Internally, Olivia cringed. "Um, yeah. You know, last night was so much fun. Wouldn't it be fun if we *all* got together again? As a group. I think *that* would be great."

Hint, hint.

"Here." Luke fished around in one of the many pockets of his cargo pants, pulling out his phone, pressing it into her palm. "Give me your number and I'll text you mine. We can set something up sometime."

"Sure." She added her number to his contacts and handed him his phone back.

She breathed a sigh of relief when he simply pocketed his phone with a smile and didn't push the issue, asking her to commit to a date. She adjusted her grip on her poles, leaning forward, bending her knees slightly in order to gain speed. As she approached the bottom of the slope, Olivia pointed her skis together, careful to keep the tips from crossing. Snow fluttered around her legs as she stopped fairly quickly, managing to keep herself steady, only wobbling slightly.

Luke sent a spray of snow up as he cut his skis hard to one side. "That's it. You look like you're getting the hang of it." He slipped his goggles over his head and grinned. "You think you're ready to head up to the lifts?"

"Um." She raised her goggles and glanced around the base of the slope looking for Margot. Her pea-green jacket and matching ski pants were hard to miss and yet *zilch*. Margot was nowhere. Olivia licked her slightly wind-chapped lips and shuffled her ski in a semicircle. "Have you seen Margot?"

"Huh." Luke lifted a hand to his forehead, blunting the glare from the sun, eyes squinting as he searched. "No. It's not like she could've gone far or—"

"Hey!"

Olivia's jaw dropped.

Wobbling slightly, knees too straight to balance properly, Margot careened down the hill Olivia and Luke had just skied, gaining speed. She lifted one of her poles and waved. "This isn't so hard!" Margot laughed, shrieking when she hit a bump that caused her to veer slightly to the right. "This isn't—*fuck*." A flicker of fear flashed across Margot's face, visible even from several yards away. Olivia's gut clenched, her chest tightening. "How do I slow down? How do I stop?"

"Wedge!" Luke shouted. "Skis together!"

Oh, *shit*. In her panic, Margot brought her skis closer together, but not only at the front, causing her to pick up even more speed.

Luke swore under his breath. "Pizza, not fries! Pizza, not fries!"

"What?" Margot shouted.

"Did I forget to mention that analogy?" Luke gripped the back of his neck. "Shit."

Shit was right. Margot was rapidly approaching the bottom of the slope, with no sign of slowing down.

Olivia cupped her hands around her mouth. "Wedge, Margot! Wedge!"

Margot bent her knees, the front of her skis coming together,

her speed slowing as she skidded to the bottom of the slope and kept on sliding, beyond where Luke and Olivia stood, heading straight for the neon-orange plastic mesh barrier.

Olivia's heart stuttered then seemed to stall out completely as Margot skied straight into the snow net, coming to an abrupt stop before toppling backward. Powdery snow flew up around her, raining down softly.

Luke started to shuffle forward on his skis, but Olivia wasn't willing to waste that much time. She crouched down and pressed on the heel levers at the backs of her bindings, stepping free from her skis. Leaving her poles and skis in the snow, Olivia sprinted across the clearing to where Margot lay, staring up at the sky with a dazed expression.

"Mar?" Olivia fell to her knees beside Margot, hands trembling as she patted Margot's snow-streaked face. "Are you okay? Say something."

Margot's face scrunched and a terrible whimper escaped her lips, the sound piercing Olivia's heart and putting a lump in her throat.

"Mar?" she repeated, this time softer, more desperate, her voice cracking as a flurry of the worst what-ifs flashed through her brain. She cradled Margot's face in her hands. "Please say something."

"Ow." Margot coughed, lashes fluttering as she cracked open first one eye, then both, blinking dazedly up at Olivia.

Olivia's throat seized. She had to swallow twice before she could get another word out. "What hurts? Your back? Is it your back? Don't move. I'm pretty sure you aren't supposed to move."

She'd read that somewhere. Heard it? You weren't supposed to disturb someone after a bad accident, falls and collisions and—Olivia gulped in a breath, needing air.

Margot groaned, then made the sweetest sound Olivia had ever heard in her entire life. She laughed, albeit slightly pained-sounding, her lips twisting in a grimace as she huffed softly. "My pride."

"Your *what*?" Olivia swept her thumbs along Margot's cheekbones, fingers trembling softly.

Margot shifted, lifting up onto her elbows with a slight wince. Olivia let her hands fall to Margot's shoulders.

"My pride," Margot repeated, face turning scarlet, and that was what Olivia had thought she said. Margot's lower lips jutted out. "And my ass." Her eyes swept down her body, lower lip jutting out in a pout as she stared at her feet. "And my pinky toe."

Driven by a soul-deep sense of relief, Olivia clutched at the collar of Margot's hideous green ski jacket and hauled her closer, sealing her mouth over Margot's, swallowing the tiny gasp of surprise Margot made.

One of Margot's hands rose, cradling the back of Olivia's head, fingers threading through her hair. Her hand trembled, or maybe it was Olivia that was trembling. It was hard to tell, pressed so close, Olivia's knuckles aching from the ferocity with which she clutched at Margot's jacket, keeping her from going far. Keeping her from going anywhere.

A throat cleared from somewhere behind her, and with great reluctance, Olivia loosened her stranglehold on Margot's coat. She lifted her head and froze.

Luke smiled, albeit awkwardly. "Looks like you fell pretty hard there."

Olivia's heart stuttered over one beat then sped, crashing against the wall of her chest as she met Margot's eyes.

Yeah. She had.

Chapter Eighteen

Margot glared at the purple bruise mottling the side of her left foot. Her pinky toe was swollen, double the size it was supposed to be. It throbbed in time with her pulse, an annoyance more than anything, though when she put pressure on it, pain licked at the top of her foot, radiating all the way to her ankle.

A knock sounded against the door. Not the one that led out into the hotel hall, but the door adjoining her room to Olivia's.

Margot tried to swallow, her mouth suddenly dry. She stole a stuttered breath in, air whistling between her lips. "Come in."

Olivia poked her head into the room. In the time since they'd returned to the hotel, she'd changed into a pair of leggings and an oversized hoodie. The arms were too long, slipping past her wrists and over the back of her hands, hiding all but the tips of her fingers. She shoved her sleeves up to her elbows and shut the door, leaning against it, leaving the entire room between them. The space felt larger than it really was. "Hey. How are you doing?"

Awful. Better now that Olivia was here.

Margot sniffed and shrugged, dropping her gaze to the em-broidered coverlet folded at the foot of the bed. "You know. Been better."

"Your foot?" Olivia shoved away from the door, approaching the bed where Margot lay, three pillows behind her back keeping her propped up, another stack keeping her foot elevated. "How's it doing?"

Margot pressed her lips together, offering a wry smile. "Hurts like hell. Looks even worse." She sat up, adjusting the pillows, wincing at the sharp twinge that traveled along the side of her foot from her pinky to her ankle. "Gnarly, right? I took two extra-strength Advil and am hoping they kick in sometime this century." She snagged a spare pillow from beside her and hugged it. "But I think Luke's assessment was right. It's not broken. I can move it, it just hurts like a bitch when I do. I guess it's only badly bruised." She bared her teeth in a grimace. "Same as my pride, apparently."

Talk about feeling like a complete idiot. Not only had she wiped out, but she'd done it publicly, in full view of a dozen skiers. Olivia and Luke had had a front-row seat, and granted, she'd been more focused on the pain that anything else in the moment, but she had a vague recollection of several small children pointing at her. Yikes.

Olivia nibbled on her bottom lip. An hour after their kiss and Margot would swear she could still taste the buttery sweetness of Olivia's vanilla-flavored ChapStick.

"Why would you do that, Margot?" Olivia asked. She shook her head slowly. "I mean, no offense, but you are *terrible* at skiing."

"I—"

"The *worst*."

Margot pursed her lips. It was on the tip of her tongue. *Not everyone can be perfect at everything like Luke*, but that would've taken bratty to a whole new level, even for her. Jealousy and insecurity had gotten her into this mess in the first place, leaving her with a swollen foot, bruised pride, and a tender heart.

Maybe it was time to try something new. Take Elle's advice. Be honest.

"There isn't a chance we could put a pin in this conversation and circle back around in, say . . . a few days?" she joked.

Olivia didn't laugh. Her teeth sank into her bottom lip, no longer nibbling, but biting down on it outright. Her lashes fluttered with every rapid blink, the skin around her eyes turning pink. "Do you realize how scared I was?" Her voice broke and Margot's chest splintered open. "Watching you hit that barrier? Not knowing if you were okay or hurt or—"

"I was fine, Liv." She gestured to her propped-up foot. "A little bruised, and I'm going to have to limp down the aisle on Saturday—no heels for me, un-fucking-fortunately—but I'm fine."

Olivia sniffed hard and scrubbed the side of her hand under her eyes. "I didn't know that. How was I supposed to know you were fine? I saw you careen down a hill, collide with a barrier, and *collapse*. My mind went to the worst places, but can you blame me?"

Margot hugged the pillow tighter, chest panging with remorse, a sharp stab between her ribs that stole her breath for a split second. She hadn't meant to make Olivia worry, to give her any cause for concern. Hurting Olivia was the last thing she wanted, right up there with losing her.

Collapse might've been a bit of an overstatement, but what had Margot told Elle this morning in the gift shop? Not to underestimate Margot's ability to catastrophize? Margot could definitely relate, imagining the worst possible scenarios, watching them play out inside her head.

Contradictory to the ache in her chest, her stomach fluttered. The timing was completely terrible, but the proof that Olivia cared about her enough to get choked up made Margot hope that maybe all of *her* worst-case scenarios were as farfetched as Elle had guaranteed they'd be. The way Olivia had kissed her at the base of the slope, trembling hands cradling her face, was the first sign. This was the second. Now all Margot needed was confirmation.

"I'm sorry, Liv. I didn't anticipate crashing. Who would? You can't see something like that coming." She swallowed hard, the analogy hitting a little close to home, making her pulse flutter wildly inside her veins, nerves turning her stomach queasy. "You and Luke made it look so easy, and I was doing great on the bunny slope." When Olivia's brows rose, her expression calling *bullshit*, Margot amended, "I was doing *okay* on the bunny slope. I figured I knew how to stop at least." But it was different, stopping after gaining that much speed. "I just . . ."

Saw Luke with his hands all over Olivia, watched her put her number in his phone at the top of the taller slope, saw red, didn't think. Naturally, Margot was a competitive person. At the time, it had made perfect sense to push herself a little harder, put the skills—she was being generous, in hindsight—

she'd acquired to the test. Prove that she could be every bit as athletic as Luke, as *desirable* as Luke. She wasn't proud of it, but that's where her brain had been at, what had driven her to ride that people mover to the taller slope before she was ready.

Olivia crossed her arms, shifting her weight from one foot to the other. Aside from that small show of impatience, Olivia seemed content to wait Margot out.

Here went nothing.

"I was jealous, okay?" Margot clutched the pillow tighter. "I was jealous, and it's stupid. I'm not proud of it. The opposite. I mean . . . *hell*, Liv. You think I like feeling this way? Because I don't. I hate it." She swallowed before her voice could crack. "Luke keeps flirting with you, and I thought I could handle it, but then I saw you give him your number—I mean, I *think* that's what you were doing?—and I just . . . I didn't think."

She'd acted on impulse.

"So what?" Olivia crossed her arms, teeth scraping her lip, abusing it further. "You're upset because someone else wants me?"

"No." Her heart stuttered, her stomach dropping. "That's not it at all. I'm halfway convinced the whole world wants you, Liv. You have no idea, the—the appeal you have. I don't want you because Luke wants you. I want you because I . . ." Fuck. Margot took a deep breath in, air shuddering between her lips. "I've always wanted you. I have feelings for you, okay? I care about you. I've never felt this way about anyone. No one gets me the way you get me. I've never felt like I'd die if I didn't touch someone. *You* make me feel that way." Margot's jaw clenched and slid forward in a bid to keep her tears at bay. "This isn't *new*. This isn't because of Luke. It just—it just is. It's how I feel."

Olivia crossed her arms and scoffed. "You're ridiculous. Do you realize that?"

Fuck. She'd known this would happen. Knowing didn't dull the ache in her chest. Her pulse pounded painfully in her throat, the ache worsening when she swallowed. "I'm sorry, okay? I can't help the way I feel about you. If you think I'm so ridiculous—"

"Shut up." Olivia laughed and pressed the heels of her hands against her eyes. "You are the most infuriating person I've ever known, Margot."

Margot hunched over her pillow, breath coming too fast. She sniffed hard, eyes burning and vision blurring. *Fuck.* "Got to admit, not the superlative I was aiming for. *Best at delivering a witty repartee* or *greatest at giving head*, but most infuriating. *Whew.*"

God, she'd fucked up. Stepped in it. Crossed a line. Gone too far. All she'd wanted was to keep Olivia, but in trying, she'd pushed her away. How fucked up was that? Jealousy was never an attractive trait in a partner, and they weren't even that. They were friends—and Margot would be lucky if Olivia even wanted to remain that after her atrocious behavior. She steeled herself for rejection.

Olivia dropped her hands, letting them hang limply at her sides. "Luke is a really nice guy."

Shit. Here it was. Tension knotted in the pit of her stomach, her insides churning. She didn't need to hear the rest. "You don't need to—"

"Oh my God, Margot, please, for the love of all that's holy, be quiet." Olivia huffed, and her hair, gathered in a high ponytail, skimmed her shoulders as she shook her head.

Margot bit her tongue, all the words she wanted to say clogging her throat.

"Luke is a nice guy," Olivia repeated, twisting the knife a little deeper. Her shoulders rose, and her spine straightened as if she was fortifying herself to deliver the final blow. Her gaze locked on Margot, and the look in her eyes—steely and determined, a flicker of something Margot couldn't name flashing through them—snatched the air straight out of Margot's lungs. "But I don't want Luke." Her throat jerked and a small smile tugged at her lips. "I want you."

Margot's heart rose into her throat like a helium-filled balloon.

Olivia wanted her.

Her heart stuttered.

Olivia wanted her *how*?

She clutched her pillow like a lifeline.

"I don't think I can do *casual*, Liv," Margot confessed, laying her cards and heart completely on the table. "I'm, uh, apparently not capable of keeping things casual. Not when it comes to you." She laughed and scrubbed a hand over her face. "I'm really terrible at it. Almost as bad at it as I am at skiing."

Olivia laughed, and the sound loosened the knots inside Margot.

"I don't know how to be anything but *all in* when it comes to you, Liv," she confessed.

Olivia took a slow, hesitant-looking step toward the bed, and then another, this one a little surer, faster. Every step caused Margot's nerves to ratchet. Olivia sat on the edge of the bed and wiped her palms against her thighs. "All in, huh?"

"All in," Margot confirmed, voice shaking. She tossed the pillow aside and shifted, facing Olivia as best she could with her foot propped up, elevated above her heart. *Doctor's orders.* "Any time you want to, I don't know, say something reassuring, feel free."

She reached out and grabbed Margot's hand, lacing their fingers together. That gesture, in and of itself, gave Margot hope. People didn't often hold hands with someone they were planning on letting down gently. "*I* kissed *you*, remember?"

"How could I forget?" Margot teased.

"I don't . . ." Olivia blushed. "I've only ever been with you and—and Brad. I've never *done* casual." She smiled. "I guess, suffice it to say, it was never casual for me, either." Olivia squeezed her fingers and laughed. "We could've avoided this by talking about it. I'm going to blame your dirty mouth for distracting me."

Margot's ears burned, and a laugh bubbled up past her lips. "My bad?"

"If it wasn't what you wanted, how come you acted like it was?"

"I didn't know what *you* wanted, and I worried that if I told you what *I* wanted and we weren't on the same page, you'd . . . I don't know . . . feel weird about it and it would mess up Brendon's wedding. Or you'd feel uncomfortable and want to move out of the apartment. And I didn't want that. I *don't* want that. So I thought I'd play it safe. I thought I could keep feelings out of it." Her lips twisted in a wry smile. "Considering . . . you know, I really should've known better."

Hand still gripping Margot's, Olivia frowned. "Considering what?"

Margot dropped her eyes to her lap and huffed out a laugh. "I don't really want to rehash the past, Liv."

"Not to be pedantic here, but I think we'd have to have *hashed* it before we could *rehash* it."

Margot shut her eyes, cringing inside. "We slept together. Brad wanted you back. You got back together. End of story."

Olivia dropped Margot's hand, her face cycling through a flurry of expressions before she shook her head, jaw hanging open. "I'm sorry. *What?*"

"You were there. You know what happened." *Please* don't make her spell it out.

Olivia scoffed softly. "The way I remember it, I texted you, told you Brad wanted to get back together, asked you what—"

"You shouldn't have *had* to ask," she blurted, cringing almost immediately. God, she couldn't believe they were really doing this. "We spent the week together. We—I thought it meant something. I thought—" *Fuck.* Margot exhaled harshly and met Olivia's eyes. "You were my first, you know? And it's not like I ever planned to put a lot of stock in that sort of thing." She licked her lips. "Or, I didn't, until it was you. So yeah, it meant something to me. And I thought you knew that. Then you text me telling me your ex wants to get back together and you ask me what I think you should do? I'd have hoped the answer would've been obvious, but the fact that you asked, that you asked *me* . . . fuck, Liv. How do you think that made me feel? How do you think it made me feel when a few weeks later when I found out—secondhand—that you weren't going to UW like we'd talked about, like we'd planned? That, instead, you'd thrown all our plans away to go to WSU instead. To be with Brad. How do you think I felt?"

As if Olivia choosing Brad hadn't been bad enough, Margot had felt like her best friend, the girl she loved, the person she believed would always be there . . . suddenly wasn't. Like Olivia was abandoning not just their plans, but Margot, too. Like maybe Margot hadn't meant as much to Olivia as Olivia had to her. Not if she was so easy to move on from. So easy to forget.

Olivia guppied, mouth opening and shutting before she blurted, "That's not what happened *at all*."

Margot crossed her arms. "I was there, Liv. I'm pretty sure I know what happened."

Olivia pressed a hand to her forehead and sighed. "Okay, first, I didn't follow Brad to WSU. The scholarship I applied for? I got rejected." Her lips twisted and she dropped her eyes. "Even with the scholarship, UW was going to be more expensive than WSU. Without it?" She shook her head. "If I had told Dad I had my heart set on UW, he'd have tried to figure something out, but I couldn't ask him to do that. I couldn't ask him to burden himself financially when I'd gotten into another perfectly good school that *was* offering me a scholarship." Olivia scratched the tip of her nose. "Did it help that Brad was going there, too? That we were back together and that—at the time—he wanted me? That I *knew* he wanted me? I won't lie and say that wasn't a perk, a point in WSU's favor. But it wasn't the reason, Margot."

Margot swallowed over the lump in her throat. "Oh."

She bit back the next words that almost came out of her mouth. *Why didn't you tell me that?* But she already knew the answer. They were barely talking back then, mostly because post-hookup, Margot had avoided Olivia, preferring to lick her wounds in private. To suffer in silence. Look how well that had served her.

"As for why I asked what you thought I should do, it's because I wanted you to *tell* me that. I wanted you to tell me you wanted me. That's *why* I asked. We hadn't talked about it. What it meant. How we felt. I'd hoped you'd tell me . . ." Olivia's teeth sank into her bottom lip. "All I wanted was for you to want me the way I wanted you."

She had. *God*, had she ever. "I did. I . . ." She shook her head. "That was eleven years ago, Liv. We were eighteen and—"

"We shouldn't waste time on what-ifs." Olivia's lips quirked, smile small and subdued. "You're right. Who's to say what would've happened? There's a million ways it could've gone right and a million more ways it could've blown up in our faces."

Margot nodded. As much as she'd wanted Olivia back then, she hadn't been ready for a serious relationship at eighteen. Clearly, her communication skills had needed some work—in all likelihood they still did, but she was a work in progress and she was trying and wasn't that half the battle, really?—and all that teenage angst had been a recipe for disaster. "But now?"

Olivia leaned in, lips brushing the corner of Margot's mouth in a kiss that was far too brief. She drew back and met Margot's eyes. "Now."

Chapter Nineteen

*O*livia stretched an arm out toward the nightstand, rolling onto her side when her fingers skimmed nothing but smooth wood, her phone too far to reach.

"Mm, where do you think you're going?"

One of Margot's arms wrapped around Olivia's waist, dragging her further into the bed, snuggling up close behind her.

"I was trying to check the time. We don't want to be late to dinner."

Margot burrowed even closer, like merely *close* wasn't close enough, like any amount of space between them was unacceptable. Olivia could relate.

This was all so new.

Not just lying here, wrapped up in Margot's arms, but actually having what she wanted.

For so long, everything she'd wanted had been unattainable, either by some huge, insurmountable margin, pie-in-the-sky dreams, or by a smaller gap, fingertips skimming, just shy of grasping. *Almost* was always worse, the hope it stirred leading to a harder letdown when it, inevitably, didn't pan out. A scholarship to the school of her dreams. A relationship with Margot. All the little desires she'd given up here and there, incidents explained away as coincidences until the pattern became clear, irrefutable evidence stacking up against the small measure of hope to which she'd held fast. Sacrifices she'd made thinking they were worth her happily ever after with Brad, bargains she'd made in the name of love that became lies she told herself because the truth was too grim. Only to discover that happily ever after, in and of itself, was a sham.

After a certain point, *wanting* became pointless when *having* remained hopeless. Why bother? Why continue to put herself through constant disappointment? Maybe some people just weren't meant to have what they wanted, to be happy. So she'd settled on the next best thing, little crumbs of contentment where she could find them. Never wholly satisfying, but enough to get by on, to subsist.

But now . . .

All in. Warmth flooded her chest. Margot wanted her.

Maybe disappointment wasn't an inevitability. Maybe everything in her life so far had happened for a reason, the way it was supposed to. All those little disappointments not the dead ends she'd thought, but turns she had to make, all leading her to something bigger, something better, something lasting, something real. *Hers.* A perfect convergence of being in the right place at the right time.

Margot pressed one chilly foot to the back of Olivia's calf, her other foot still elevated, the pillows beneath it slightly askew, one hanging off the edge of the bed, in danger of falling.

"I don't want to get up," Margot complained. One hand swept the hair away from the back of Olivia's neck, icy fingers sending shivers down her spine. Warm lips brushed against her nape, featherlight, and her skin prickled all over, Margot's touch giving her goose bumps. "I'm cold and you're warm and this bed is too comfortable."

It *was*, but she had a feeling she could've been lying on a cinder block and she'd have been equally as reluctant to move, her desire to stay in bed having less to do with the comfort of the mattress and warmth of the duvet and everything to do with having Margot wrapped around her.

"We skipped lunch."

Margot's mouth curved against her skin. "Debatable," her voice lilted, sounding coy. "I ate."

Laughter burst from between her lips. *"Margot."*

"What?" Margot shifted, rising up onto an elbow, peering down at Olivia with wide eyes, a placid little smile on her lips, the picture of innocence, if Olivia didn't know better. The left corner of her mouth twitched, eyes creasing in amusement, cracks appearing in her composure. "I *did*."

"You're ridiculous." Olivia bit her lip, shaking her head slowly.

Margot smiled impishly and rested a hand on Olivia's waist. "Don't act like you don't like it."

Before she could answer, Margot leaned in, capturing her mouth in a kiss that curled her toes and sent a flood of warmth through her. Her eyes fluttered shut, and she sank into the kiss, surrendering to the feeling of Margot's tongue tracing the seam of her mouth, her lips still tender from Margot's teeth.

"Reservations," she gasped out. "We can't—"

Lips trailing kisses from her mouth to her chin and down along her jaw, Margot shushed her. "Brendon said reservations aren't until seven thirty. We have time."

The hand resting on her waist slid down her belly, cupping her between her thighs, Margot's thumb strumming her still-tender clit. Her breath caught in her throat, her pulse jumping as her hips jerked softly, thighs falling open.

"That's it," Margot murmured against Olivia's skin, forehead pressed to her cheek, staring down her body as she ran her fingers along Olivia's slit.

Two fingers sank inside her, crooking upward, giving her something to clench down on, and—*God,* this was going to be over impossibly fast.

Margot pressed an achingly sweet kiss to the hinge of Olivia's jaw.

"Close, aren't you?" Margot nuzzled the side of her face, lips brushing the space beneath Olivia's ear, teeth nipping at her earlobe. That subtle sting sent a bolt of pleasure straight to her core and made her clench. Margot smiled against her skin, fingers crooking harder. "Come on, Liv. Come for me."

Her breath hitched and her chest burned as she tipped over the edge, thighs quaking and hips jerking as Margot's fingers curled, drawing out the pleasure. When it became too much, Olivia shoved weakly at Margot's hand, knees closing. Margot pressed another one of those sweet kisses to Olivia's cheek and slipped her fingers free. Olivia bit down hard on her lip, swallowing a whine at how empty she felt.

Margot flopped back against the bed with a contented sigh. "Still think I'm ridiculous?"

Olivia snorted. "The fact that you're still thinking about that proves how utterly ridiculous you are."

"Utterly?" Margot laughed, bright and sharp and the sound did something funny to Olivia's heart, not quite a clench, closer to a flutter. Like there were butterflies trapped inside her chest. "I'm been upgraded to *utterly* ridiculous as opposed to regular ridiculous?"

She pressed her lips together so they wouldn't twitch or curve. *"Upgrade?"*

With a scoff, Margot rolled over, fingers digging into the soft side of Olivia's stomach. She thrashed, squirming, feet tangling in the sheets as she tried to escape.

"Stop, no!" Olivia laughed, shoving at Margot's arm.

Margot quit, fingers falling still, palm resting high on Olivia's waist, just beneath her breasts.

"You're in luck." Olivia rolled over, careful to avoid Margot's injured foot as she crawled between her thighs. "I happen to like ridiculous."

Margot beamed at her and reached up, tangling a hand in the back of Olivia's hair. Margot dragged her down, her neck arching to meet Olivia's mouth halfway. Her knees fell open, allowing Olivia to settle between her thighs. Olivia's lips skimmed over the black lace encasing Margot's breasts, then lower, over the flat plain of her stomach, her tongue darting out against her belly button just to see what would happen. Margot made a high-pitched keening sound, her hands scrambling against the sheet and her hips rocking upward as she bit down on the swell of her bottom lip.

Olivia brushed her mouth against the skin between Margot's hip bones, the waist of her bikini-cut panties riding low, lower still when Olivia tucked her fingers beneath the elastic and tugged.

Fingers stroked the side of Olivia's face, skimming the bottom of her jaw. She lifted her head, resting her chin lightly on Margot's lower abdomen, careful not to dig in. Margot stared down at her from beneath low lids and pressed the pad of her thumb to the center of Olivia's bottom lip. "You look unbelievably hot like this."

Her face heated, warmth blooming in her chest at the compliment, as she licked the crease of Margot's hip where the black lace of her underwear scalloped in. She sucked a kiss into Margot's skin, drawing back when Margot hissed and her hips rocked upward. The skin faded from red to pink. If Olivia wanted to leave a mark, which she most definitely did, she'd have to try harder.

Atop the nightstand, something buzzed, rattling against the lamp. Either her phone or Margot's.

Margot huffed. "Ignore it."

Good plan. Olivia hooked her fingers around the band of Margot's underwear. The phone quit buzzing as she dragged Margot's underwear down her thighs and—

The buzzing started up again and Margot punched the bed in frustration, whining softly. "Damn it. I swear to God, if this is Brendon calling, I'm going to lose it. There's no way it's even after six." She huffed loudly and sat up, twisting at the waist to reach the nightstand. She frowned. "It's not me." Margot stretched further, fingers wiggling in a bid to reach Olivia's phone on the far end of the nightstand, and she managed to drag it close enough so that she could read the screen.

Margot's brows drew together, a quick flicker of irritation sharpening her gaze before her expression smoothed, too neutral, too blank to be natural. A muscle in her jaw just beneath her ear jumped, as if she'd clenched her back teeth together and Olivia's stomach twisted into a knot.

"Here." Margot swiped the phone off the nightstand and held it out. She cleared her throat softly, eyes darting around the room, looking everywhere but at Olivia. "It's Brad."

Olivia traced the back of her teeth with her tongue, staring hard at Brad's name on the screen until the letters blurred together and the backs of her eyes burned, forcing her to blink. A reverse image of his name floated behind her lids, white on black. She'd answer and take care of it, whatever *it* was this time, tell Brad what he needed to hear, and—then what? She'd do it all over again the next time he called? The next? How long was this supposed to go on for?

In those minutes, no matter how brief, it was like she'd never left, still *giving* even from miles away. She dreaded seeing his name appear on the caller ID, hated knowing there was a ninety-nine percent chance he was calling for something innocuous, using her. But there was that one percent chance, that small part of her, that little voice in the back of her mind that couldn't help but wonder, couldn't help but worry, *what if?* What if this time he was calling for something actually important? What if the one time she sent him to voicemail Dad needed her and—

Margot's eyes dropped to the phone still vibrating in the palm of her hand. "Are you going to answer it?"

Maybe it was because she asked, giving Olivia the chance to make the decision rather than telling Olivia what she *should* do, that her heart swelled.

She took the phone from Margot, their fingers brushing. Margot averted her eyes and scratched her neck, fingers lingering in the hollow of her throat.

Olivia swallowed hard and swiped at the screen, sending Brad to voicemail. "If he has something important to say, he can leave me a message."

Sending Brad to voicemail wasn't merely satisfying, the absence of his name on her screen a relief. It was *necessary*, something she should've done a long time ago. She was doing it now, not to wipe the subtle frown from Margot's face, but for herself. Because Margot was right. This pattern of being at Brad's beck and call wasn't healthy and it wasn't fair.

Olivia deserved better.

Margot surged forward, pressing her mouth to Olivia's. Her lips curved, and maybe Olivia hadn't sent Brad to voicemail for Margot or because of her, but the way she smiled was an added benefit.

Margot drew back, fingers sliding against the shell of Olivia's ear after she tucked a strand of hair behind it. "Okay?"

"Yeah, I'm—" Olivia's phone vibrated, still in her hand. One brief buzz, a text. Olivia shut her eyes. "Damn it," she muttered.

She swiped against her screen, entering her passcode with her thumb, tapping on the text notification at the top of her screen.

BRAD (6:03 P.M.): hey i called u

Enough was enough. The time for point-blank was now.

OLIVIA (6:05 P.M.): I'm busy, Brad. Unless it's an emergency, you need to stop calling me like this. It's not okay. I'm not your mother.

She stared at the message, chewing on the inside of her lip, reading and rereading until she had the whole thing memorized. She held her thumb down on the backspace key, deleting the last line before pressing *send*. Margot's hands rested lightly on her shoulders, her touch reassuring. Her thumbs swept gently against Olivia's collarbones in a soothing circuit. When Olivia lifted her head, one side of Margot's mouth tipped up. "Okay?"

"I told him to stop calling unless it's an emergency." She lifted her brows and offered up a wry smile. "I'm not holding my breath."

Her phone vibrated with another incoming text.

BRAD (6:07 P.M.): u don't need to be a bitch about it livvy

Right. Because asking for a boundary made her a bitch. She rolled her eyes and flipped her phone around to show Margot the text. Margot squinted and brought the screen closer, tongue poking against the inside of her cheek.

"What a fucking ass goblin," Margot muttered, sneering at the screen.

"A *what*?" Olivia snickered.

Her phone buzzed, sending another spike of irritation through her. Before she could turn her screen around, Margot leaned in, reading what he wrote.

"I don't even . . . I think he sent you a link." Margot wrinkled her nose. "I wouldn't open it."

As Olivia turned her phone back around, it buzzed with another incoming text. *God*, was he persistent.

BRAD (6:09 P.M.): <link>

BRAD (6:09 P.M.): u didn't tell me your dad was moving

What did he mean Dad was moving? Moving *what*? The URL had been shortened, a Bitly link that provided zero contextual clues, no help. Without clicking, she wouldn't know what he'd sent her or what it had to do with moving.

Fingers crossed that Brad hadn't sent her porn—she wouldn't put it past him—she tapped the link. A new browser opened, the site loading, loading, slow as molasses. The bar at the top of the page inched along, her screen white until suddenly it wasn't.

Zillow? Brad had sent her a link to a Zillow real estate listing. A Zillow listing for Dad's house.

Dad's house, which was on the market, not only listed for sale, but had been on the market for *two weeks*.

A lump formed in her throat, making it nearly impossible to swallow. She pressed a hand to her stomach, able to feel her pulse against her palm. Her heart was beating too fast, and—she sat back, bouncing against the bed, drawing her knees to her chest, suddenly dizzy.

"Liv?" Margot rested her hands on Olivia's knees. "What's wrong?"

Without speaking, she passed Margot the phone. Margot frowned and shifted back, swiping her glasses off the nightstand. She scrolled back up to the top of the page, brows rising as she scanned the screen. "Brad sent you this?"

She nodded.

Margot pursed her lips. "Are you sure this is legit? Are you sure Brad didn't send you a doctored web page or something?"

"I don't think fabricating a real estate listing is really in Brad's wheelhouse. Why would he even do that?"

"I don't know." Margot shrugged. "It's Brad we're talking about. Why would he bother sending you this? What's in it for him?"

Olivia pressed her thumb beneath the ridge of her brow bone. A subtle throbbing had started behind her eyes. "I asked him to let me know if he heard anything about Dad, remember? I guess this is him letting me know? Either that, or . . . I don't know, Margot. Maybe he's being nosy? I don't know."

She knew nothing.

Margot glanced back at the screen. "It's been on the market for two weeks?"

Apparently. In that time, Dad hadn't mentioned anything about selling the house. Not once, not even a passing mention, or that he was considering putting it up for sale. Nothing.

Olivia reached for her phone. "I need to call my dad. I don't—I don't understand why he wouldn't tell me if he was moving."

It didn't make sense.

Margot passed her the phone without a word, only a grim smile.

Olivia navigated to her recent calls, bypassed Brad's number, and tapped on the icon beside *Dad—Cell*. It rang once, and Olivia sucked in a stuttered breath. Twice. She exhaled harshly. *Pick up*. Three times. She held her breath.

Hey, you've reached Gary Grant. Sorry, I'm not available to take your call at the moment. Leave your name and number and I'll return your call as soon as I can. Thanks!

"No answer?" Margot asked when Olivia lowered her phone, ending the call before the line could start recording.

She shook her head and stared at Dad's contact page. "I'm going to call one more time."

Margot leaned over the edge of the bed and plucked her shirt off the floor. She slipped it on, flipping the ends of her hair over her shoulders, and leaned back against the headboard. She snagged her phone off the nightstand, fingers swiping against the screen.

Olivia hit *call* and held her breath.

One ring.

Two rings.

Her stomach sank.

Three rings.

Hey, you've . . .

She shut her eyes and huffed. Damn it, Dad. Of all times for him not to answer, when she needed to talk to him.

She waited for Dad's voicemail message to finish and stayed

on the line this time, waiting to leave a message. Even though she was expecting it, the shrill beep made her pulse leap. "Hey, Dad. Call me when you get this." She wet her lips, weighing out whether to give her reason for calling. "Just—call me. Please. Love you."

Margot's hand wrapped around Olivia's thigh, thumb sweeping against the inside of her knee. When Olivia opened her eyes, Margot offered a smile that didn't reach the corners of her eyes. "I'm sure he'll call you back when he has the chance."

Maybe he would, but . . . "I still don't understand why he's selling the house. And why he didn't tell me. He loves that house. I grew up in that house. He and Mom—" She swallowed hard over the lump in her throat that wouldn't go away, if anything swelling further. "He and Mom bought that house when they first got married. I don't—I don't understand. He's never mentioned selling the house before."

Dad loved his house. He—God, even the parts of it he didn't love, like the yellow toile wallpaper in the downstairs half bath, he'd kept unchanged because Mom had picked it out. It didn't make sense.

"I bet there's a logical explanation for this, okay?"

"The house has been on the market for two weeks. Do you know how many times we've spoken, how many chances he had to mention it? We just spoke yesterday."

"Hey." Margot reached out, cradling the side of Olivia's face gently. Olivia closed her eyes and leaned into Margot's palm, pressing her lips to the inside of her wrist. "Why is this freaking you out so badly?"

She opened her eyes and sucked in a rasping breath, throat raw. "What *else* hasn't he told me?"

How many times had he told her he was fine? That his blood work was good, that his doctors were happy with his progress, that he was taking care of himself, eating better, and working less? Was any of that true or was he placating her, brushing her concerns aside so she wouldn't worry?

"He'll call you back," Margot repeated herself, thumb sweeping against Olivia's cheek.

When? "He's going out of town tomorrow, remember?"

Even if he did call, who was to say he wouldn't do what he always did, blow off her concerns and tell her not to worry before changing the subject?

She wouldn't be able to sleep until she figured out what was going on. If Dad was truly okay or if . . . if . . .

What if Dad was selling the house because he was sick? What if he wasn't answering the phone because he *couldn't*? What if there was no fishing trip—what if he was back in the hospital and he didn't want her to know?

Even if she didn't have his health to worry about, this still would've struck her as odd. Unsettling. They talked, often.

But she did have his health to worry about.

God, what she wouldn't give to press rewind, go back to ten minutes ago when she and Margot had been tangled together in the sheets, the only fluttering in her gut from butterflies, a pleasant sort of squirminess. Not this awful anxious churning, her mind suddenly flitting to all sorts of worst-case scenarios.

Until she got to the bottom of this, her brain would try to

fill in the blank that came after *if* with one terrible option after another. Not only would she not be able to sleep, but tomorrow was Annie and Brendon's rehearsal. Their wedding was the next day. She couldn't afford to be distracted, wondering, worrying.

Chapter Twenty

Olivia's tongue darted out, sweeping against the lip she'd chewed red. She crawled off the bed, swiping her sweater off the floor. "What's if he's not okay? What if he's—"

"Whoa, whoa." Margot slipped out of bed, wincing when a twinge of pain shot up the side of her foot from putting too much weight on it. Walking was going to be a real bitch. "You need to take a deep breath, okay? Breathe in with me."

Panicking wouldn't solve anything.

Sweater clutched in front of her, Olivia pinched her lips together and mimicked Margot as she inhaled through her nose. Margot held it, lifting a hand to make sure Olivia would do the same. She exhaled slowly, lowering her hand. Olivia's exhale was ragged, her shoulders sagging and curling forward. She scrunched her eyes shut, looking upset but no longer on the verge of hyperventilating.

"What if he isn't fine?" Olivia repeated, voice breaking.

Margot's heart clenched at the sound, at the way Olivia scrunched her eyes shut.

"He promised to tell you if he wasn't. I was there, remember? I heard your entire phone call. He told you he didn't want you to worry."

Olivia turned her sweater right side out and slipped it on over her head. Static caused strands of her hair to stick straight up in multiple directions. "Exactly. He doesn't want me to worry. All the more reason for him to keep me in the dark."

"Don't you think"—Margot winced, already anticipating Olivia's reaction to what she was about to say—"if your dad says he's fine, you should trust him?"

She swept her fingers through her hair, wincing when they snagged on a tangle. "I told you. He drove himself to the hospital when he had a heart attack, Mar. He only let the nurse call me when he had to stay overnight."

Margot blew out her breath. "Okay, I can see where something like that might not engender a whole lot of trust. That's— that's shitty. I completely agree, and I—I can understand that your brain is probably going to the worst possible place right now." Anxiety and fear weren't always rational. Fuck, most of the time they were the complete opposite. Brains were assholes sometimes. "But, offering an outside perspective, I don't think the fact that he's selling the house necessarily means there's something wrong with his health." She cracked a smile. "Who knows? Maybe he's selling because he plans to retire and wants to move down to one of those all-inclusive retirement villas in Florida. You know they have a huge nudist community right outside of Tampa? I watched this whole show on HGTV on it. Everyone carries a little personal towel around so when they visit they can sit on that instead of directly on the furniture.

And they specifically cater to retirees. Maybe your dad wants to broaden his horizons."

She wiggled her brows, managing to get Olivia to crack a smile.

"Dad hates Florida." Olivia gathered her hair off her neck and swept it up into a bun, securing it with the scrunchie on her wrist. Several wisps of hair fell loose, framing her face. "We have cousins in Kissimmee. Last time we visited, all he did was complain about how hot and humid it was." She sighed, shoulders slumping. "I just wish I knew why he didn't tell me. I grew up in that house. I still have boxes in my old bedroom, clothes in the closet I didn't bring with me—all my yearbooks are still on a bookshelf in the hall. I don't get it."

Margot hobbled around the bed until she could grab Olivia's hand. She tangled their fingers together and squeezed, drawing her closer so she could wrap an arm around her waist. Olivia ducked her chin, smiling down at their hands softly, expression subdued but no longer looking like she was on the verge of making herself sick with worry. Progress. "Until you talk to him, I think you're just spinning your wheels, Liv. You need the whole story."

She pressed her lips together, throat jerking when she swallowed, nodding slowly. "You're right. I—I need to talk to Dad." She huffed through her nose, a little agitated noise punctuated by an eye roll. "He's the only one who can answer my questions. Until then, it's all hypothetical and—"

"So you'll talk to him." Margot swept her thumb against the back of Olivia's knuckles, trying to soothe her the best she could. She lifted their joined hands, raising them high enough that she could brush her lips against the side of Olivia's thumb in a quick kiss. Her chest clenched when Olivia smiled and— God, why had she been fighting this? Caring about Olivia came as easy as breathing. Margot should've known resistance was futile, that she'd always wind up here. "You'll talk to him and he'll explain and it'll all make sense."

Olivia sucked in a shuddering breath. "Or he'll just tell me not to worry. You heard him on the phone. He's really good at brushing things under the rug and sounding okay when he's not."

Words of reassurance failed her. There were only so many times Margot could say that everything would be all right before the words lost their value. "Just wait and see what he has to say, okay? Take it from there."

Olivia's lower lip wobbled before she trapped it between her teeth, blinking fast. "Am I a terrible daughter?" she whispered.

"What the hell, Liv? Why would you think that?" That was absurd. "You're not. Jesus. If you're a terrible daughter, I don't even want to know what that makes me."

Olivia lifted a shoulder in a half-hearted shrug. "I don't understand why he wouldn't tell me something like this."

Maybe because he knew it would make her worry? "He probably doesn't want to worry you. That's the vibe I got from the call in the car."

Olivia's teeth scraped her bottom lip. She was going to bleed if she wasn't careful. "If he doesn't want me to worry, that means there's something worth worrying over."

Margot's back teeth clacked together. That was *not* the direction she'd meant to send Liv's thoughts. That was the *opposite* of what she wanted, to rekindle Olivia's concerns. "Just wait until you talk to him, okay?"

Olivia sniffled. "I think—I think I need to talk to him in person. See that he's actually okay and—it's harder for him to fib to my face, you know?"

That made sense. Seeing was believing and all that. "Sure."

"You think?"

Margot nodded. "Totally. You know, I haven't seen my parents since . . . God, since Christmas. If you want, we can drive down together on Monday. Or Sunday, I guess, if we're not too tired or hungover."

Olivia's fingers slackened around Margot's, and she stepped back. "I was thinking more along the lines of, I need to talk to him in person *now*."

"Now? Liv, that's . . ." She swallowed hard, the next words out of her mouth about to be *ridiculous*, and that would've been a shitty thing to say even though a part of her *did* think it was ridiculous. "I think you need to take a deep breath and relax, and we can head down to dinner—"

"There's no way I can relax until I talk to my dad. I'll be no fun to be around. I'll just be worrying, and Annie and Brendon shouldn't have to put up with—"

"Hey, hey." Margot settled her hands on Olivia's waist. "No one's putting up with anything, Liv. I know Annie and Brendon. Trust me, they would hate the idea that you're more worried about their reaction to you stressing than what's *actually* stressing you. I promise."

Olivia took a step back, then one more, too far away for Margot to reach. Margot's hands fell to her sides.

"There's no way I'm going to be able to sleep tonight," Olivia said.

"It's early. Your dad could still call you."

"But—"

"You want to talk to him in person, I know." Margot sighed and slipped her fingers under her lenses, rubbing her eyes. "But you can't just pick up and go to Enumclaw right now."

"It's not even an hour away. If I leave now, I could make it there before eight. I can talk to Dad and figure out what the hell is going on and why the house is for sale."

If I leave now. Leave. A pit formed in Margot's stomach, the word tripping a trigger in her brain. Olivia wanted to leave. Leave and come back . . . right?

"Look, I know you're concerned, but . . . the rehearsal is tomorrow. The wedding is on Saturday."

Olivia was already moving across the room, gathering up a sock from the foot of the bed and her leggings from the floor. She plopped down on the edge of the bed and slipped a foot into her pants. "Trust me, Mar, I am *well* aware of when the wedding is. I'm the wedding planner, remember?" She shot Margot a tight smile. "It'll be fine. I'll drive down tonight, talk to Dad, spend the night, and leave tomorrow morning. The rehearsal isn't until one, the rehearsal dinner not until later that evening. Setup starts at three. I'll make it back in time. Heck, there's a decent chance I'll beat you all back to town, depending on what time I hit the road."

Margot worried the inside of her cheek, weighing out a gentler way to say what needed to be said that wouldn't piss Olivia off. "Liv, don't you think you should maybe . . . sit on this for a second? Think it through. Call your dad again, text him. See if he calls you tonight, talk it out on the phone, and if you're still worried, we can drive down on Sunday. Together."

"And if he doesn't call?" Olivia smoothed the stretchy spandex leggings up over her knees, standing to tug them the rest of the way on. She set her hands on her hips and frowned. "He's heading up to Forks tomorrow. He said he might not have coverage, and he's not always going to have his phone on him. Plus, like you said, the rehearsal is tomorrow, and me driving down tonight isn't going to be a problem. I'm going to make it back in time."

"It's not a question of whether you'll make it back or not, although anything can happen. It's more a matter of you dropping everything to go check on your dad when just yesterday he told you he was fine and promised he'd tell you otherwise. He told you not to worry. He told you to have a good time and he made *me* promise to make sure you do."

Olivia stared out the window, lips pursed. "He also conveniently left out the part about the house being on the market. I can't exactly hang much on that conversation, can I?"

Margot buried her face in her hands and groaned. "You're overreacting, Liv."

Shit. As soon as the words were out of her mouth she wished she could take them back. Press rewind or hoover them up, make them disappear. She peeked between her spread fingers.

Olivia turned her head slowly, eyes widening and lips parting. "Gee, thanks, Margot. Are you going to tell me I'm acting crazy next?"

"No, I'm just—*God*, you're always thinking about what

everyone else needs, but what about what *you* need?" Margot dropped her hands, letting them hang limp at her sides. "I know you love your dad, but it's his job to take care of you, not the other way around." Olivia opened her mouth, but Margot wasn't finished. "I know you care about him, but there's a difference between caring about someone and taking care of them, and right now you're mixing them up."

Olivia crossed her arms. Everything from the set of her jaw to the way she was standing perfectly still, her back ramrod straight, screamed *defensive*. "Really? Tell me—how, in your *expert* opinion, am I confusing the two? Because the last time I checked, you aren't in my head, Margot."

"I never claimed to be an expert. I'm speaking as someone who cares about *you*." She couldn't believe she was having this conversation in her underwear. "In an ideal situation, would your dad have told you before he listed the house? Totally. But he didn't, and that's his prerogative. Maybe he had a good reason for not telling you. Maybe, Liv . . . maybe he doesn't think it's your business. Is it something you need to talk about? Okay, sure. But is it something you need to talk about *right now*? Maybe you make it to Enumclaw tonight and back in time for the rehearsal tomorrow, but where does it stop? Where do you draw a line? If Brad calls and he needs help finding a garage door opener, are you going to hop in your car and drive to Enumclaw to help him find it?"

Olivia scoffed and stepped back. "This has *nothing* to do with Brad."

Didn't it? Maybe not directly, but . . . "It's about you putting everyone's needs above your own."

How she'd been doing it for years. For so long that half the time, Margot was pretty sure Olivia didn't even realize she was doing it. It had become that ingrained in her.

"I don't understand why you would bring Brad up. I didn't answer his call, did I? I texted him and told him to stop calling me. I showed it to you. What more do you want from me, Margot? You want me to block Brad? You want me to act like he was never a part of my life? What can I do to show you that I don't *want* Brad? I want *you*."

Margot bit the tip of her tongue and counted to three so she wouldn't say something she'd regret, because she was *this* close to pulling her hair out because Liv might've heard everything Margot had said but she wasn't *listening*. "You're right. You did. And like I said, I think that's great. You setting a boundary. I just hope you did it for yourself and not because I was sitting there. Because it shouldn't be about me or what I want. None of this is about me, and I'm not asking you to block Brad or forget he ever existed." Though Margot sure as hell wouldn't mind putting Brad out of her mind for good. "I'm not asking you to do anything except what's right for you. It should be about *you*. That's what I'm trying to say, and *you* saying what you just did is proving my point. You left Brad and you moved to the city, saying you were tired of making sacrifices for Brad, and—all I'm saying is, it's a slippery slope and it's easy to go from being selfless to being self-sacrificing. Self-*sabotaging*."

Olivia had a history of that, and if Margot was being completely honest, she'd benefited from Olivia's selfless nature a time or two or *twelve*. In the moment, she'd never stopped to consider it beyond thinking that Olivia was a great friend, but maybe she should've. Maybe she'd taken Olivia's selflessness for granted just like everyone else. Maybe she had, but she wasn't going to keep doing it. Olivia was always going to bat for everyone else; she deserved the same in return. Even if it wasn't fun in the moment. Olivia deserved that.

"I'm not self-sabotaging because I want to check on my dad," Olivia argued. "And I didn't send Brad to voicemail because of you, I did it for me."

Margot crossed the room toward Olivia, footsteps uneven as she avoided putting too much weight on her left foot. "I'm not trying to pick a fight with you, okay? Fighting with you is just about the *last* thing I want to do right now. Ever." When Olivia ducked her chin, Margot took a leap of faith and reached for her hand. She swallowed a sigh of relief when Olivia let her lace their fingers together. "I care about you, Olivia. I wouldn't be wasting my breath saying any of this if I didn't care. I'd throw you your car keys, kiss you on the cheek, and tell you I'd see you sometime tomorrow. And then I'd go downstairs and hang out with my friends and I definitely wouldn't spend the night worrying about you making it to Enumclaw safely or how your conversation is going to go with your dad. I wouldn't—" She sniffed at the unexpected burn in her sinuses, the blur at the corners of her eyes. "I think about you all the time, Liv." She laughed. "I think about you even when I'm not supposed to, when I *wasn't* supposed to, when I convinced myself I wasn't. I care about you, and I love—" Her throat narrowed. "I love that you have such a big heart and that you care about everyone else, but it can't be at the expense of yourself."

If Olivia kept it up, she'd give everything away until she

had nothing left. Burn herself out trying to keep everyone else warm.

A pretty pink flush colored Olivia's cheeks. "It's not."

Margot nibbled on the corner of her lip. "Do you remember what you said when Brendon asked why you wanted to be an event planner?"

A tiny wrinkle appeared between Olivia's tawny brows.

"You told him you wanted to make other people's dreams come true."

Olivia frowned. "There's nothing wrong with that."

"There's not." Margot traced circles against the back of Olivia's hand with her thumb. "I'm only saying, it's okay to want things for yourself. You deserve nice things."

The corner of Olivia's mouth rose. "I kissed you, didn't I?"

Margot chuckled. "Are you calling me a nice thing?"

"The nicest," Olivia said, swaying close, knees bumping Margot's.

Margot bit the inside of her lip, trying not to smile. "I'm not very nice."

"No," Olivia agreed. Her smile softened, subdued, but no less sweet. "But I like you anyway. I like you a lot. I—*like* sounds trivial for the way I feel about you."

Margot's heart squeezed. "Ditto. Which is why I'm saying all of this." Still holding Olivia's hand, she sucked in a deep breath. "Forget I brought up Brad. Let's say you get home and your dad wants you to move back to Enumclaw. What would you do?"

Olivia jerked her head back and frowned. "What kind of question is that?"

Margot's teeth scraped against the inside of her cheek. "Just answer the question."

"Dad would never ask me to move back." Olivia argued, continuing to frown. "He's the one who practically pushed me out the door, remember?"

Margot stared, loosening her grip when Olivia winced. Without meaning to, she'd strangled Olivia's fingers. "And you seriously don't see how that's an issue you need to address? You don't need anyone's permission to follow your dreams. You don't need anyone's permission to be happy."

"Issue." Olivia scoffed softly and tugged her hand free. "Gee, I didn't realize you were my therapist now."

Margot's jaw worked from side to side. A hot flush of frustration wound its way up her throat, making her dizzy. "I'm not trying to be your therapist, and that wasn't an indictment. Maybe this is novel for you, having someone who cares about *you* for once, but this is what it looks like. Maybe it's not always pretty or fun, but it's . . ." Real. "It's what it is. So just answer the question. Forget about your dad asking you; if you go home and you find out your dad isn't okay, what's your plan? What are you going to do?"

Olivia crossed her arms, frown deepening into a scowl. "I would . . ." Her lips folded together, shoulders rising in a helpless looking shrug. "I don't know, okay? The truth is, I don't know what I'd do. I can't just answer on the spot like this. I'd have to think about it. But I don't have time for this right now. I need to go."

"You can't." Margot blurted, immediately cringing at her volume. "You can't just leave."

Olivia froze, expression shuttering, the look in her eyes frosty. "I *can't*? No offense, but you don't get to tell me what I can or can't do, Margot. I got enough of that from Brad to last a lifetime, and I don't need it from you, too." Her nostrils flared. "Are you going to tell me what kind of books I can read next? The sort of company I can keep? What sort of job I can have?"

Margot pulse sped, white noise filling her ears. "Don't compare me to him."

"Don't act like him, and I won't," Olivia bit out.

"I'm not telling you what you can or can't do. I'm not saying you shouldn't go see your dad if that's what you feel like you need to do. Do I think it makes more sense to wait until he calls or to drive down on Sunday? Yes. But I'm not trying to stop you. I'm just trying to figure out where your line is in the sand. What happens the next time you think someone needs you? What if next time, it's not the night before the rehearsal but the night before the wedding? Or the day of? At what point do you drop something big, give up on something that matters to you because you think what someone else needs is more important? At what point do you leave and not come back?"

Olivia pressed the heels of her hands against her forehead and groaned. "I'm not moving back to Enumclaw, Margot. I'm not going anywhere."

Maybe not now, but could Margot count on Olivia to come back the next time? Could she count on Olivia *always* coming back or had she been right? Was it always only ever a matter of time before she lost her?

She bit down on the inside of her cheek, hoping that brief flash of pain would banish the burning at the back of her eyes, the sting inside her nose. She sucked in a rasping breath. "I just got you back, and I don't want to always be worried about whether I'm going to lose you. Whether you're going to leave."

Olivia's frown had softened leaving only a furrow between her brows. "You need to trust that when I say I'm coming back, I will. And if you can't"—her throat jerked—"maybe that's an issue *you* need to address."

She pinched her lips, her eyes, too because—*fuck*.

"Not so fun to hear, huh?" Olivia whispered.

Margot clenched her jaw. "And there you go again, making the situation about someone else. Deflecting away from yourself."

Typical.

Olivia scoffed and stepped back. "Whatever, Margot. I should go pull my bag together."

She hugged her arms around herself and dipped her chin. "You should probably do that."

Rather than watch Olivia leave the room, she stared at the floor, tracing the whirls and knots in the wood with the tip of her toe, biting down hard on her tongue when her vision blurred and everything went soft and out of focus.

As soon as Olivia was out of the room, Margot stumbled back a step, the side of her foot throbbing from standing for too long. She lowered herself to the bed, fingers twisting in the sheets she and Olivia had been tangled up in not even half an hour earlier.

It couldn't have been five minutes before Olivia returned, duffel bag bouncing against her hip with every step she took. She stopped a foot in front of Margot.

"You're okay getting a ride back to town with someone else, right?" Olivia said, fidgeting with the strap of her bag.

"I'll figure it out." She'd ask Elle if she could catch a ride back with her and Darcy.

Margot blinked hard and fast. This was only a disagreement. Not the end of the world, even if it felt a little like it was.

The corners of Olivia's mouth pinched, her lips flattening into a thin slash. Her throat jerked, and she adjusted the strap of her bag, hiking it higher on her shoulder. "Bye, Margot."

Any iteration of *goodbye* felt too final, so Margot kept her mouth shut.

The floor creaked and the door shut with a soft *snick* and then—

Silence.

Margot was alone.

Chapter Twenty-One

Olivia gripped the steering wheel until the leather groaned, a pull in the cover's stitching biting into the side of her thumb. The *for sale* sign posted in the thatch of grass beside the mailbox wasn't a surprise, but actually seeing it with her own two eyes put an unexpected lump in the back of her throat as she pulled into the driveway beside Dad's Volkswagen and cut the engine.

It was real. Not that she'd honestly believed Brad had the ability or inclination to fabricate a real estate listing—not only did he lack the skills, but he was too lazy to go to such lengths just to . . . what? Prank her? Piss her off? Brad couldn't even bother to hunt down a garage door opener by himself—but there'd been a tiny part of her that hadn't wanted to believe it. That had *refused* to believe it on principle. Dad had always been a man of few words, never the most forthcoming, not even about the small things. But this? This wasn't small. This was big, and—why hadn't he told her?

Time to find out.

Olivia hopped out of the car, the door rattling when she slammed it with a touch too much force. Instead of heading immediately up the drive, she walked over to the *for sale* sign and flipped the lid on the attached plastic box full of flyers. There was only one left, and it was a little damp, the edges of the paper rippled from all the moisture. The ink was blurry, making the copy read as if the house had eight bedrooms instead of three. Paper clutched tightly in her fist, Olivia made a beeline for the front door, pulse ratcheting as she took the porch steps two at a time. Little flecks of black paint stuck to her skin when she rapped her knuckles against the door.

The gauzy curtain beside the front window fluttered, Dad probably curious to see who was banging on his door.

"Livvy." Dad's smile fell at the look on her face. "What are you doing here? Aren't you supposed to be—"

Olivia shook the flyer in his face. "The better question is why I had to find out you were selling the house from Brad."

"Brad?" Dad's head snapped back, eyes widening. "Why are you talking to Brad?"

A flush crept up the front of her throat. To make up for it, she stood a little straighter, lifting her chin. "That is entirely beside the point. Were you ever planning to tell me you were selling the house or was I just going to be in a for a rude awakening the next time I came to visit?"

Dad heaved a sigh and gripped the back of his neck, ducking his head. "Don't be ridiculous, Liv. You usually call before you visit . . ."

Her back teeth clacked together. She was getting really tired of being told she was being ridiculous or that she was overreacting when all she wanted was a straight answer.

"I called. I called twice. I left you a voicemail," she said. "You didn't pick up."

Dad grimaced. "Ah, damn. I think I left my phone in the car."

He still hadn't answered her question, the big, overarching one, the one that had brought her here. "And the house?"

Dad scraped his hand over his jaw and gave another weary-sounding sigh before stepping back from the door, gesturing for her to come inside. "You want something to drink? I think I still have a box of that tea you like floating around in the cabinet somewhere."

She wanted answers, not tea. But if she was going to drink anything, it needed to be a whole heck of a lot stronger than chamomile.

"You know what?" She set her hands on her hips. "I think I'd like one of the beers you keep in the fridge in the garage you think I don't know about. Thanks."

Dad headed down the hall without a word, returning a minute later with an uncapped bottle in each hand. At least it was light beer, better for him than the regular kind.

She took her bottle with a tight smile. "Thanks."

Dad nodded to the sofa before taking a seat in his recliner, the one that was older than she was. He took a long pull of his beer and she did the same, wrinkling her nose at the taste. She'd never been much of a beer drinker, but over the last few weeks, she'd gotten used to the flavor of the dark, bitter brews Margot favored. This tasted like water by comparison.

Dad must've seen her make a face because he snorted. "Weak, huh?"

"But doctor approved." She settled back against the couch and tossed the flyer on the coffee table.

"Okay." Dad heaved another one of those great big sighs and set his beer on a coaster before leaning forward, bracing his forearms on his knees. "I didn't want you to find out like this. I was going to tell you, I swear, but—"

"Never once did you even *hint* that selling had crossed your mind, let alone that you were already in the process. I just . . ." Her eyes had started to sting, but if she blinked she was terrified she'd cry. "Why didn't you tell me?"

"Honest to God, I was planning on it." Dad scrubbed a hand over his face. "Look, Livvy, my insurance covered most of the hospital bills from last year, but there are still some out-of-pocket charges I've been paying off because of some rigamarole between the hospital and insurance company."

Her stomach sank. This was the first she'd heard of Dad having to pay anything out of pocket. "Okay. But not a lot . . . right?"

Dad waffled his head from side to side. "My savings—"

"You had to dip into your *savings*?" She strangled her beer bottle so tightly the seam where the glass had been molded bit into the palm of her hand.

"Only a little," he promised, holding a palm up as if to placate her. *A little* was still shitty when his savings were slim to start. "And I only had to do that because they've got me working fewer hours. Remember? I told you I scaled back."

She nodded.

"I've got more money going out and less coming in and . . ." Dad swept a hand out. "Too much house for one person. I don't need this much space and, to be honest, things have been getting a little tight at the end of the month. Much more of this and something was going to have to give, and I've got too much equity in the house to lose it in a short sale."

A little tight and *short sale* didn't go together. "If money was tight, how come you didn't say something? If you'd have told me, I could've—"

Her grip went slack and she nearly dropped her bottle, catching it around the neck. A dribble of beer ran down the back of her hand and she stared at it blankly.

She could've *what*? Offered Dad money she didn't have? Volunteered to move back home and help with the bills? She winced. Maybe there was more truth to what Margot had said than Olivia had first been able—or willing—to acknowledge. Where *was* her line? Did she even have one? Something told her the fact that she didn't know was a problem. An *issue* she needed to address.

"I've got it under control, okay?" Dad said. "This is the best solution all around. Your mom and I refinanced when you were a kid, which set the clock back on the mortgage, but the property values have really skyrocketed in the past five years. I can sell, get the equity out of the house, and downsize into something smaller, with a more manageable monthly payment. Or, hell, I might even be able to buy something with cash."

Olivia nibbled on her lip and glanced around the living room. Pencil marks that had never been scrubbed away marred the trim of the kitchen entry, each tiny tick capturing her height over the years. If she craned her neck, she'd be able to see into the bathroom, with its god-awful toile wallpaper that Mom had picked out. "But you love this house."

Dad's eyes swept the room, lingering on the photos hung on the wall, family portraits and her old school pictures. "I do love this house." He smiled softly and met her gaze steadily. "But, at the end of the day, it's just a house. What I loved about it most were all the things that made it feel like home." For a brief moment, the corners of his mouth tightened. He sucked in a deep breath and released it noisily, laughing while he did, scrubbing his hand over his face. "Your mom and you made it home, Livvy. It's too much house for one person."

Her eyelids felt hot and itchy, and there was a burn in the back of her throat that no amount of swallowing could relieve. This was the house she'd grown up in, the first home she'd known. But Dad was right; it was only a house, and it had been a long time since she'd considered it her home. If he wanted to sell, if it was the best solution—which it sounded like—she supported his decision. She just wished he'd kept in her in loop.

"Besides—I've been thinking of cutting my hours back even further." At her frown, Dad chuckled. "Retiring."

She laughed. "As long as you don't plan on retiring to a clothing-optional community in Florida."

Dad's brows rocketed to his hairline. "You know I hate Florida."

"And yet you have nothing to say about the clothing-optional community?" She narrowed her eyes, snickering when Dad merely looked confused. "I'm kidding. It's just something Margot said."

"Margot, hmm?" Dad leaned back in his recliner, crossing his ankle over his knee. He studied her for a minute, eyes narrowed and head cocked slightly to one side. "Must be nice, reconnecting with her after all these years. From what I heard on the phone yesterday, it sounds like you two managed to pick up right where you left off."

She dropped her eyes to her lap and picked at her thumbnail. He had no idea. "You could say that." When Dad said nothing, she bit back a sigh. "We kind of had a fight, actually. Right before I came here."

"You want to talk about it?"

She swallowed around the sudden ache in her throat. "Not really."

Dad hummed. "Would you feel *better* if you talked about it?"

She dropped her face into her hands and huffed. Damn his Dad logic. "Maybe? I don't know. We—we both said some things and . . ." She took a deep breath and started over from the beginning. "Brad called me. He—"

"Why is *Brad* calling you?" Dad's face wrinkled.

She pressed her fingers to the space between her brows. "Are you going to let me finish?"

Dad grumbled something under his breath, words she couldn't quite make out, and waved for her continue.

"I—okay, he calls me sometimes. About silly little things. I answer because . . . I asked him to keep an ear out." She cringed, dreading Dad's reaction. "If he heard anything. You know. About you."

Dad frowned. "Why would you do that?"

"Because." She wiped her palms against her legs and stood,

needing to move. She stepped around the coffee table and stood in front of the fireplace, wringing her hands in the sleeves of her hoodie, which were too long. "You tell me you're fine, but what does that *mean*? I worry, okay? And, I mean, clearly for good reason, since you decided to put the house up for sale without ever mentioning it to me."

"I didn't tell you because I didn't *want* you to worry." Dad huffed. "And I had every intention of telling you, but then you mentioned this big wedding you were working on and I—I decided to wait until after."

"We could've avoided this if you'd just *talked* to me. I worry because you leave things out and because you say things like *I'm fine*."

Dad threw his hands up. "Because I *am* fine, Livvy. I am and—okay, I can admit, keeping you in the dark about the house was a mistake." His brows rose, lips twisting in a wry smile. "Clearly. But when I say I'm fine, I wished you'd believe me. I have it all under control, okay?"

She knotted the excess fabric of her sleeves between her fingers and nibbled on the inside of her lip. "That's what Margot said."

Dad bobbed his head. "And I'm guessing you didn't like hearing that."

No, she'd hated it. Hated it even more now, because Margot's points had been decent. But that still didn't excuse the fact that Margot had told Olivia she was overreacting.

"Not particularly. Brad texted me the link to the property listing after I'd sent him to voicemail, and when I called you and you didn't answer, I kind of freaked out a little. Margot thought I should wait for you to call me back or wait until after the wedding to drive down, but I was worried, okay? And she accused me of overreacting and told me I needed to stop putting everyone's needs before mine, and *I* accused her of"—she cringed—"having a fear of abandonment, which was a pretty awful thing to blurt out, I'll admit, but also may be true?"

Dad frowned. "Obviously I wasn't there, so I don't have all the specifics, but it sounds to me like you both said some pretty hard things you felt like the other needed to hear?"

That was a . . . fair assessment of the situation. "I guess."

"Can't say I disagree with her, Liv. You've spent enough time taking care of other people. And, just to offer some perspective, saying what she did probably wasn't the easiest. Think about it. She probably knew you might react poorly, but she said it anyway because she thought you needed to hear it." Dad stroked his chin, looking thoughtful. "It sounds to me like Margot cares about you."

"That's what she said. That she said what she did because she cares."

"It's not always the easiest to let someone care about you, is it?" Dad's brows rose pointedly.

God. Her chin wobbled, and she bit down on her lip to keep it from quivering. It really *wasn't.* Despite being something she desperately wanted, it was hard to let it happen. To let herself have it and—*shit.* Margot really was right. Olivia didn't need anyone's permission to be happy.

Only her own.

Her teeth scraped her bottom lip. "She's not the only one. I mean, I care about her, too."

"That doesn't surprise me in the least, kid."

She rolled her eyes. "Why? Because I care about everyone?"

Dad chuckled. "Because it's Margot. I might be your dad, and I might not always know the right thing to say or how to say it, but I've got two eyes, and it was obvious to anyone who looked at you two that you weren't just friends."

Her face burned at the insinuation that Dad knew more about their past—or at least her feelings—than he'd ever let on. She rolled her lips together, weighing out how much she wanted to share. "She was my *best* friend."

Dad's brows rose.

"She *was*. But fine. I had a crush on her, okay? And for a while I thought . . ." When Dad's lips twitched, she set her hands on her hips, huffing softly. "You didn't snoop through my diary, did you?"

Oh, Jesus. She pressed a hand to her cheek, skin on fire. Talk about mortifying. She'd never be able to look Dad in the eye again if he'd read even *half* of what she'd written.

"Your diary?" Dad guffawed, the recliner rocking with the ferocity of his laughter. "Jesus, no. I probably would've had a heart attack a decade before I did, if I had done that."

Her jaw dropped. "*Dad!* That's not funny."

"Eh." He seesawed his hand from side to side, nose wrinkling. "Come on. It's a little funny. If I can't laugh at myself, what the hell am I supposed to laugh about?"

Her lips twitched. "Nudist retirement villas, obviously."

"Jesus." He dragged his hand down his face. "And you said *Margot* put that idea in your head?" He tsked, shaking his head. "Consider me doubly glad I never read your diary."

Her chest loosened when she laughed. "Me too, Dad. Me too."

The corners of his eyes crinkled. "It's good seeing you laugh, Liv. You haven't done nearly enough of that in the last few years. It seems to me like moving to the city's been good for you. And maybe . . . Margot's been a part of it, too?"

A flicker of warmth flared to life inside her chest, catching, growing, spreading outward until her fingertips tingled. She pressed her fingers to her lips and nodded, sniffling. "I'm really happy, Dad," she whispered.

Dad heaved himself out of the chair and wrapped his arms around her, enveloping her in a hug. Olivia buried her nose in his chest, breathing in the smell of his laundry detergent, the one he'd been purchasing for years because it was the one Mom had used. "I'm happy you're happy, Livvy."

When he finally released her and took a step back, his face was red and his eyes were suspiciously damp, or maybe they only seemed that way because her vision was downright blurry. She bit her bottom lip and sniffled. Dad rested one of his large hands on her shoulders, the heavy weight pleasant, grounding. "Are these happy tears, or . . . ?"

Using the sleeve of her sweater, she mopped beneath her eyes. "I'm just worried I messed up. What I said wasn't great. I don't know."

Like Margot, everything Olivia had said had come from a place of care only . . . her words had been reactionary, in response to Margot pushing her out of her comfort zone. She didn't regret *what* she'd said as much as she regretted the way she'd said it, lashing out. Not fighting fair. Margot had made it clear she cared about Olivia, but had she?

"This isn't your first rodeo, kid. You know not every argument means it's over."

No, but sometimes all it took was one argument. And this was their first, their first *real* one, not a mere difference of opinion. It could be make-or-break. Besides . . . "Look how my first *rodeo*, as you call it, turned out. That's a shit—*crappy* example."

Dad snorted. "Fair point. But Margot's not Brad."

"Thank God," she muttered, making Dad laugh.

"What is it you said that you're so worried about? Something about Margot having a fear of abandonment?"

She nodded. "It's—not just me. It's with her friends, too, and . . . I stand by what I said. Just not *how* I said it."

Dad puffed out his cheeks. "And she wanted you to stay? To wait until after the wedding to drive here?"

She nodded.

"And you left anyway?"

"I had a reason," she defended. "And I'm coming back tomorrow."

Dad squeezed her shoulder. "Sometimes the things that trigger our fears don't make the most sense. Sometimes they aren't the most logical."

She winced. The same could be argued for her own actions. "True."

Except maybe Margot's fear *was* rooted in something logical. Not the truth, but Margot's version of it, her version of the past that she'd believed to be true up until only today. Believing that eleven years ago Olivia had chosen Brad over her. That Olivia had thrown their plans out the window in favor of following Brad across the state.

"You want to know how you make it right?"

She lifted her head and blew out a breath, ruffling the strands of hair that never quite made it into her sloppy bun in the first place, others having escaped confinement since. "I am *all* ears."

Dad chuckled and patted her arm. "You show up tomorrow and you keep showing up."

Olivia nodded. Show up and keep showing up. She could absolutely do that. Prove to Margot that she was in this, *all in*. "Thanks, Dad."

"Anytime." He stepped back and tucked his thumbs in the front pockets of his jeans. "You eat dinner yet?"

She shook her head and pressed a hand to her stomach. "No, I was too nervous to eat."

Dad's mouth twisted briefly before he jerked his thumb over his shoulder in the direction of the kitchen. "I made chili. With ground turkey, don't worry. I'm sticking to the heart-healthy diet."

Her stomach growled. "Sounds good. Is it okay if I spend the night here?" She bit her lip, shrugging softly. "Maybe we could find a movie or something?"

As long as she hit the road no later than ten, she should make it downtown with time to spare.

"Sure thing, kid. You should know you're always welcome wherever I live."

She smirked. "I'll withhold judgment on visiting you wherever you move, in case that whole clothing-optional community idea grows on you."

"I don't know. I'm starting to think Margot's *not* the best influence." Dad shook his head, lips twitching like he was fighting a smile. "I'll go heat you a bowl. You want to find something on TV?"

"Sure thing." She smiled. "Thank you, Dad."

He winked and disappeared around the corner into the kitchen.

She collapsed onto the couch and yawned. The stress of the day—skiing, Margot getting hurt, her panic, their argument, the drive down here, all of it—plus the lack of sleep from the night before, seemed to be catching up with her.

Before reaching for the remote, she fished inside her pocket for her phone, swiping and pulling up her text thread with Margot. She'd promised to text, and she was going to keep her promise.

OLIVIA (9:08 P.M.): Hey. Made it to Dad's safely. He's okay. We had a good talk, cleared the air.

She stared at her screen. It was probably silly to wait for Margot to text back. It was the last night of Annie and Brendon's bachelor-bachelorette trip. Margot should be spending it with her friends, not—her phone vibrated in her hand.

MARGOT (9:10 P.M.): I'm glad he's okay.
MARGOT (9:10 P.M.): Are you still staying the night, or do you think you're going to drive back?

Olivia winced. Getting back in her car and driving the forty-five minutes from Enumclaw to the lodge on little sleep, only to have to make a similar, if not slightly longer because of traffic, drive in the morning sounded unappealing. Even if she got right in her car, she wouldn't make it to Salish until after ten.

OLIVIA (9:12 P.M.): I'm going to crash here and head out in the morning. I'll see you tomorrow and we can talk more then. Okay?

Three little dots danced across her screen, starting and stopping, starting and stopping, almost hypnotic if not for how they caused her heart to race.

MARGOT (9:15 P.M.): Okay.

Her stomach sank. That was it? *Okay?*
Her phone buzzed.

MARGOT (9:16 P.M.): I'll see you tomorrow.
MARGOT (9:16 P.M.): ❤️

How silly was it that a simple heart emoji had the power to loosen the knots inside her stomach? She pressed her fingers to her smiling lips and typed back with one hand.

OLIVIA (9:17 P.M.): 🖤🖤

"Hey, Livvy?"

God, no. There was no way it was time for her to wake up. Hadn't she *just* fallen asleep?

"*Whattimeisit?*" she slurred, burrowing deeper into her pillow. She cracked one eye open. Through the gauzy curtains covering the window of her childhood bedroom, it was still pitch-black out.

Dad chuckled. "Early. I just wanted to let you know I was heading out. Fishing, remember?"

Fishing. Right. She nodded. "Uh-huh. Okay."

"You're okay with locking up?"

She nodded. "Mm-hmm."

Dad laughed again and leaned in, buffing his lips against her temple. "I'll call you. You drive safe, okay? And good luck tomorrow with the wedding. I'm sure it'll be great."

She smiled. "Thanks, Dad."

"You go back to sleep."

She did. Or something close to it. The blaring of her phone's alarm jarred her awake at eight thirty, and she dragged herself out of bed and down the stairs, in desperate need of a cup of coffee.

And the pot was empty. She shut her eyes. Figures that Dad would've filled a thermos for the road, but he couldn't have left her even one cup? She sighed and reached for a new filter to make a pot, checking the clock above the stove. She had time to brew a pot and slug down a cup before running through a quick shower and hitting the road.

While the coffee maker sputtered and hissed, the pot filling, she opened the refrigerator, surveying her breakfast options. Eggs, *bacon*. Dad had no business eating—oh, turkey bacon. That was better. Maybe he was taking his diet seriously after all. The produce bin was stocked, and there was a tub of Greek yogurt tucked behind a jar of applesauce. Kudos to Dad. The next time he said he was doing fine, she'd take his word for it.

After filling a bowl with yogurt and topping it with fresh raspberries and a handful of granola, Olivia perched a hip against the counter, spoon in one hand, phone in the other, studying her checklist for the next two days while she ate. The coffeepot beeped just as she set her empty breakfast bowl in the dishwasher.

Mug in one hand and phone in the other, Olivia padded back up the stairs, setting her favorite Spotify playlist to shuffle and running through a speedy shower. Her ancient blow-dryer—the one she had from high school that smelled more and more like burning metal with each use—conked out halfway through drying her hair, so she let the air do the rest while she rifled through her toiletry case in search of her mascara, which, in all likelihood, was probably buried at the bottom of the bag. Concealer, no. Lipstick, lipstick, lipstick—how many tubes did she *have*? More than she needed—but no mascara. Screw it. Olivia upended her bag, shaking the contents out atop the counter and—

No.

At the very edge of the counter, her phone teetered before taking a tumble and bouncing not against the tile floor but the open rim of the toilet seat.

Plop.

Oh, *fuck.*

Her stomach made a slow descent, sinking all the way to her knees, *further.* She palmed her face and groaned. *Gross.* Reaching inside the water, she snatched her phone up and grabbed a spare towel from the hook beside the sink. She dried it off, crossed her fingers that by some miracle the screen would still come on, and—*oh, thank God.*

The screen lit up and she pressed to enter her passcode and—everything went black.

Fuck.

Rice. She needed rice. That's what you were supposed to do when your phone wound up waterlogged, right? You were supposed to shove it in a bag of rice and it would soak up all the moisture over the course of a few . . . hours? *Days?* She didn't have that long.

She'd have to get a new phone later, once she made it back to town. She'd head to the apartment, meet up with Margot, go to the rehearsal, and pop into the Verizon store before the rehearsal dinner this evening. Solid plan. She was past due for a phone upgrade, anyway.

After tossing her phone inside a Ziploc bag and tossing that inside her purse, she snagged a thermos from the top shelf of the cabinet above the stove and filled it with coffee, shutting off the pot so the hot plate wouldn't stay on. Duffel over her shoulder, purse in one hand and coffee in the other, Olivia slipped into her flats and left through the front door. She dropped everything off in the car before heading back to lock the front door with the spare key Dad kept beneath the flower pot at the far end of the porch.

House secured, Olivia hopped in the driver's seat, fastened her seat belt, and stuck the key in the ignition, and—

It cranked, but didn't start. She swallowed hard and took a deep breath before twisting the key again. The starter clicked, clicked . . . and failed to stay engaged.

Sweat broke out along her hairline, dampening the small of her back, too.

One more time. Her car had to start. It *had* to. Swallowing past the sour knot inside her throat, she wrapped a trembling hand around the key. *Please start.* She scrunched her eyes shut and twisted the key.

It clicked, and the engine grumbled to life.

Thank God. Olivia let her head fall back against the headrest and sighed. She had no idea what she would've done if the car had failed to start. That would've been a complete and total nightmare today of all—

A rapid knocking sound came from the front of the engine before it died altogether.

Olivia jabbed the heels of her hands into her eyes.

Fuck.

Chapter Twenty-Two

$\mathcal{S}$ilence greeted Margot when she stepped inside the apartment. "Liv?"

She dropped her bag in the entry and briefly poked her head inside the kitchen before limping deeper into the apartment. She frowned. No answer. Except for the gentle hum of the refrigerator, it was quiet.

"Liv? Are you home?" she called out again, hobbling toward the hall. Her foot didn't throb quite as badly as it had yesterday, and most of the swelling had gone down overnight. Luke's advice about rest, ice, compression, and elevation had been spot-on, and the extra-strength Advil hadn't hurt, either. "Liv?"

The door to Olivia's room was left ajar, as always. Margot pressed her fingers to the door, pushing it open the rest of the way, poking her head inside to—

A shadowy blur shot past, darting down the hall. Margot gripped her chest, heart clawing its way up into her throat. A high-pitched yowl came from the living room and Margot sagged against the door frame. *Cat.* Phew. She chuckled and—

She stopped laughing because she was the *only* one laughing. Olivia wasn't here. Margot reached inside her pocket for her phone. *10:58 a.m.* She shot off a quick text.

MARGOT (10:58 A.M.): Hey, where are you? I just got back to the apartment and you aren't here.

She tucked her phone into her pocket so she wouldn't be tempted to stare at it, waiting for a response, and ducked into her bedroom to change out of the yoga pants and sweatshirt she'd worn in the car.

The plan for the day was straightforward; the wedding party would meet up at the venue at one o'clock to run through the ceremony proceedings with the officiant to make sure everyone knew where they needed to be and when they needed to be there. From there, Annie and Brendon would head to the airport to pick up her parents. Setup for the pre–rehearsal dinner cocktail hour was scheduled to start at three, the cocktail hour itself was at five, and the dinner was scheduled for six thirty.

Bringing her phone with her, Margot wandered back out into the living room. Cat was curled up on the couch in a tight little ball that made it difficult to see where she started and ended. Two green eyes peeked out at Margot when she carefully—*cautiously*—sat. Her eyes shut, and she started up a low purr that made Margot smile.

11:12 a.m. She had over an hour to kill before she needed to leave, let alone before the rehearsal started. An hour to kill. That felt like an absurd amount of time to wait around, twiddling her thumbs, and yet . . . Olivia was cutting it close. *Awfully* close. Margot sighed, earning a serious side-eye from Cat. She reached for the remote.

The channel was still set to Turner Classic from the last time she and Olivia had curled up on the couch. Currently, the hosts of the cocktail hour–style intermission were sipping on flutes of champagne while discussing—Margot pressed the *volume up* button—*Breakfast at Tiffany's*, the film du jour.

Olivia's favorite.

The intermission ended, the movie picking up at the scene where Holly Golightly and Paul Varjak spend the day together. Margot glanced at the Kit-Cat Clock hanging on the wall, perpetually crooked no matter how many times she straightened it. *11:20.*

Leaving the movie on in the background, Margot opened up her Chrome browser and selected one of the many open tabs at random. One hundred and thirteen thousand words of angsty fanfic tagged *slow burn*, *hurt/comfort*, and *hate sex*, sure to eat up the hour and twenty minutes before she had to leave.

Except she couldn't get into the story no matter how hard she tried, couldn't lose herself in the distraction the way she needed to. Her eyes kept flitting to the corner of her screen, desperate to see how much time had passed. She navigated over to her texts and reread the last message she'd sent to Olivia before hitting *call*.

Each ring ratcheted her nerves tighter, her heart rate higher, until she reached Olivia's voicemail.

Hey, this is Olivia! I can't come to the phone right now, but if you leave your name, number, and a brief message I'll get back to you as soon as I can. Thanks!

The line beeped, but when Margot opened her mouth, nothing came out.

What was she supposed to say? *Where are you?* She'd already texted. Leaving a voicemail saying the same thing she'd already typed out was overkill. *Needy.* She ended the call, praying she hadn't breathed too heavily during the brief three or four seconds before she'd hung up.

11:31. A pitiful little whimper escaped her lips as she let her head flop back against the couch. She couldn't do this. Another hour of sitting around and doing nothing, waiting and worrying, was going to drive her up the wall.

She needed to do *something.* Go *somewhere.* She hit the *power* button on the remote and stood. Cat cracked open one eye.

"I'll be back later, okay? Be good."

Cat blinked at her and—she definitely needed to get out of here.

Hobbling down the hall, Margot snagged her purse off the bed and checked that she had her wallet and phone while she made her way to the door. She snagged her keys off the entry table and backtracked to the kitchen, stopping in front of the whiteboard on the fridge. Olivia had left a smiley face on the board days ago and Margot hadn't erased it. She *still* couldn't erase because—she didn't even want to think that maybe this could be the last little message that Olivia left for her.

Rather than erase, she wrote beside it.

Went to Elle's. Meet you at The Ruins at 1.

She clutched the dry-erase marker in her hand and added a heart beside her message. She cocked her head. It was a little lopsided, her hands unsteady, but it would do.

Seventeen minutes later, Margot knocked on Elle's door. A shadow passed on the other side of the peephole right before the lock flipped and Elle opened the door. One eye was lined and the other wasn't and she was wearing the polka-dotted silk robe Margot had given her for Christmas four years back.

"Hey, I thought we were meeting at . . ." Elle's face fell. She reached out, dragging Margot inside. "What's wrong?"

Nothing. Everything. Margot flicked her bangs out of her eyes. "I can't get ahold of Liv. I called and texted and—nothing." She cringed. "Sorry. I should've called before just showing up here and—"

Elle's grip tightened around Margot's wrist, cutting off her apology and her circulation. *Damn.*

"Don't even, Mar. It's fine." Elle tugged her over to the couch. "Olivia's probably just driving. Or maybe her phone died and she doesn't have her charger?"

Olivia had Bluetooth in her car, and she was far too organized to lose her charger. Even as rattled as she was yesterday, there was no way she'd have left it behind. Besides, Margot had done a quick sweep of Olivia's room this morning before checkout, just to make sure nothing got left behind. "Maybe."

Margot's chin wobbled and Elle frowned.

"Hey, no." Elle reached out and grabbed her hand. "You're not okay. What is it?"

Margot dragged in a breath, air stuttering between her lips. She held it until her lungs burned, then let it out slowly. "Liv and I, we had a fight last night. Before she left. Before I came down to dinner. It was . . ." She scoffed out a laugh, brows rising and falling. "Not fun."

Elle squeezed her fingers and offered up a small, crooked smile. "Fighting with you never is. You always make good points, and it sucks when you're right. And outside of the fight itself, the not-talking part is awful and—"

Margot threw herself across the cushion and flung her arms around Elle, burying her face against Elle's shoulder, scrunching her eyes shut. Elle's hair tickled her nose, adding to the burn inside her sinuses. She sniffed hard and tried to lean back, but Elle wouldn't let her, only squeezing harder.

"How come you didn't say anything?" Elle asked, leaning but not letting go, fingers wrapped around Margot's upper arms. "Last night or this morning in the car? You just told us all Olivia had to leave. You didn't say anything about a fight."

She scratched the tip of her nose and shrugged. "I didn't want to put a damper on the trip. Today. The weekend. I didn't *want* to talk about it."

Elle rubbed her arm. "Would it help to talk about it?"

Hell if she knew. She'd rather there not be something to talk about in the first place, something she felt like she needed to get off her chest, this weight, this—this *fist* wrapped around her heart.

"Come on," Elle cajoled. "Talk to me."

Margot took a deep breath. "Olivia, she's generous, you know? She's always putting everyone else first and—and I love that about her. But there has to be a point where she puts herself first, otherwise she's going to give and give until she's got nothing left. I basically told her that. Only, I also said she was overreacting. As soon as I said it, I realized it was a shitty thing to say, and now I'm worried that might've overshadowed my point. I don't know. I just didn't understand why she had to leave *then*, and she told me I have a fear of abandonment, which—"

"Why would she say that?"

Margot gave an awkward laugh. "Because I kind of do?"

Elle continued to look confused, the furrow between her brows deepening. "*You?* Afraid of something? I'm sorry. I'm just . . . having a little difficulty processing that. You're the bravest person I know. In my experience, nothing scares you. You're the one who charges in headfirst." Elle smiled, lopsided. "You always killed the spiders when I was too chicken."

Spiders weren't shit compared to opening up, making herself vulnerable.

Margot laughed. "Things scare me. I just don't love talking about them, especially not this. And I haven't exactly had a reason or a need to talk about it. But I guess a lot of old feelings and fears I didn't realize I was still holding on to have sort of . . . floated to the surface. Fears about how I spent the last eleven years believing Olivia chose Brad over me and abandoned all of our plans when, apparently, there was more to it I didn't know about." Margot ducked her head and sniffled. "It's just . . . everything is changing. Brendon and Annie are getting married tomorrow and you and Darcy are engaged and everyone is going to couples' yoga and—I'm so happy for you guys. You have no idea how happy. But there's a part of me that's worried you all have each other and you won't need me." Like how Olivia hadn't needed her because she'd had Brad. "That, slowly, you're going to forget about me and move on with your lives because I'm just me and—"

"What did you tell me once? *Just Elle* is pretty great?" Elle gathered both of Margot's hands in hers. "Well, *just Margot* is amazing. You're my favorite person."

Margot bit down on the tip of her tongue so she wouldn't cry. "*Darcy's* your favorite person. She's your *person*. Your perfect person."

"You also told me we can have lots of perfect people. You told me I was one of your perfect people and you're one of mine, Mar. I mean, look." Elle scooted closer until their knees bumped. "You care about me and you care about Olivia, and I'd never ask you who you care about more because you care about us differently and I believe love is one of those things that doesn't run out."

One of her favorite things about Olivia was her endless capacity to care.

"I'm not going anywhere, Margot. None of us are, okay? Change is inevitable, you know that, but that isn't necessarily a bad thing. Okay, so we might not see each other every day, but I feel confident speaking for everyone when I say we wouldn't know what to do without you. You're *Margot*. You could never be a fifth wheel. If you're worried we're going to stop wanting to spend time with you, don't. We don't need you to change who you are or be sunshine and roses for us. You are the glue."

Margot sputtered out a weak laugh. "Glue?"

"*Gorilla* Glue." Elle pinched her lips together, the very picture of sincerity save for the twinkle in her eyes. "And don't forget it."

Being called *glue* wasn't something she'd soon forget, and neither was the sentiment behind it. The next time she worked herself up with irrational worries about her friends ditching her as they entered a new chapter in their lives, she'd remind herself that they were just that—irrational. She was Margot Cooper, damn it, one of a kind. The *glue*. "Thanks, Elle."

She nudged Margot with a knee. "You're still worried about Olivia, aren't you?"

Margot sucked in a shuddering breath and dipped her chin. "What if what I said went too far? I said what I did because I care and because I didn't want to lose her and—what if I pushed her away?"

"If she said she's going to be here, I think you have to trust her. Do you think you can do that?"

What other choice did she have?

Chapter Twenty-Three

It could be your mass air flow sensor."

Olivia wrung her hands together and stared over Mr. Miller's shoulder as he poked around under the open hood of her car. Mr. Miller, Dad's next-door neighbor, was a recently retired HVAC repairman, not a mechanic, but his brother apparently owned a garage and—Olivia hadn't known who else to ask for help. "Is that bad?"

Mr. Miller huffed. "Well, it's not good."

Her stomach sank. "Oh."

"But there could also be a problem with your fuel pump. A leak."

She stepped closer. Beyond knowing where to check the oil and where the battery was located on the off chance she needed a jump, the guts of her car were a mystery. Everything under the hood looked confusing, coils and wires and metal all covered in a sheen of grease. Mr. Miller could've told her that her *thingamabob* needed a new *thingamajig*, and it would have made as much sense as *mass air flow sensor* and *fuel pump*. "Is *that* bad?"

Mr. Miller grunted and craned his neck, staring at her over his shoulder with a grimace that knotted her stomach. "That's even worse."

"Fuck." She clapped a hand over her mouth. "Sorry, Mr. Miller. I just—whatever it is, can you fix it?"

Or did she need to call someone who could?

"In my experience"—Mr. Miller ducked back under the hood, did *something* she couldn't see, and a low groan came from the belly of her car, making her wince harder—"you can fix just about anything."

Olivia gulped. There was probably a worthwhile metaphor buried in there somewhere, a lesson to take away about the power of positive thinking or hard work or endurance or *something*, but she *really* just wanted her car to start so she could fix her *actual* problems.

"Do you know what time it is?"

Mr. Miller pointed across the driveway to where his chest of tools lay open. His phone rested atop a grease-covered rag. Olivia felt a little weird touching someone's phone, but hey, he'd offered. She pressed the *home* button. *11:08.* A little under two hours before she had to be at the venue. The drive was forty-five minutes, an hour to be safe.

Olivia stepped back over to the car and leaned her hip against the front bumper, nibbling on her thumbnail. "I have a wedding rehearsal I have to be at in Seattle by one." Mr. Miller said he could fix anything, but could he do it in under an hour? "Do you think you can have it running by noon?"

He gripped the inside frame of the car and gave a heavy sigh. He lifted his head and pinned her with a stare, one of his bushy white brows rising high on his forehead. "Olivia, I won't be able to fix a damn thing with you hovering."

Shit. He was right. She was absolutely hovering and in the worst way possible, standing right over his shoulder, doing nothing more than leaking anxiety all over the place. Literally. Her armpits were beginning to sweat and—it was March, for crying out loud. March in Washington. How in the world was she sweating *this* much?

"Sorry." She offered him a contrite smile and stepped away from the vehicle. "I'll just . . ." She jerked her head toward the opposite end of the driveway. "Go stand over there and let you work in peace."

Hopefully quickly, because time was of the essence, but she had a sneaking suspicion that if she reminded Mr. Miller of her time crunch one more time, he'd toss in his grease-covered towel and tell her to find someone else to fix her car, and Olivia—

Had no one.

Her phone was a waterlogged hunk of plastic, *worthless*. Why she was still clutching it in her fist, holding it as if she had a shot in hell of resuscitating it was beyond her. Dad was long gone, probably halfway to Forks by now, and—could she even get an Uber to drive her from Enumclaw all the way to Seattle?

Olivia paced the end of the driveway, careful not to twist an ankle where the pavement cracked and dropped off abruptly, a pothole Dad had never bothered to fix because it was on the opposite side as the mailbox. That was the *last* thing she needed, an injury on top of everything else.

But that would be just her luck, wouldn't? Never had she

wanted anything in her life as badly as she wanted her damn car to start so she could get to Seattle, to the rehearsal, to *Margot*.

Olivia shut her eyes.

"I figured out your problem."

Olivia rushed over to the car, stopping behind Mr. Miller, close enough to hear him explain, but not so close as to crowd him. "I am all ears."

He reached for the towel tucked inside the front pocket of his jeans and wiped his hands. "Your spark plugs aren't just corroded, they've started to erode." He pointed at the top of the engine. "See that green cast to the metal? You've got some severe oxidation going on, too. Your spark plugs are burned out. Probably causing a timing issue with the ignition. Have you noticed the car runs rough when you idle?"

"I—maybe? To be honest, I haven't driven it much in the past few months. I walk most places. It sits in a parking garage most of the time."

Mr. Miller grunted, acknowledging he'd heard her.

Olivia wet her lips. "So . . . corroded—sorry, *eroded* spark plugs . . . is *that* bad?"

Mr. Miller frowned. "Mm-hmm."

"But you can fix it."

She held her breath, crossing everything she could possibly cross. Fingers, toes, everything save for her eyes.

"I can."

Her breath escaped her all at once, and with it, a laugh of relief as she bent over, bracing her hands on her knees. Oh, thank God.

"As soon as I can get a replacement."

Her stomach fell away completely, and her heart stuttered, reminiscent of her stupid engine. "I'm guessing you don't have any of those lying around in your garage, do you?"

His lips twisted.

Swallowing required effort. It took two tries before she could force words up past the lump in her throat. "I'm going to go out on a limb and guess it's going to take a little while?"

Mr. Miller grimaced and dipped his chin. "I can call Auto-Zone, see if they have them in stock, but . . ."

It was a fifteen-minute drive from Dad's to the other side of town, where the store was located—thirty minutes roundtrip. Accounting for the time it would take to actually pick the parts up and install them . . . she was looking at over an hour just to fix the car, easy.

She pressed her lips together and forced a smile. "It's fine. Thanks for, uh, trying. I appreciate it." The lump in her throat swelled, the backs of her eyes burning, because what was she supposed to do now?

"Sorry, Olivia," Mr. Miller said, sounding genuinely apologetic. "I wish it would've been an easy fix."

So did she. She scrubbed a hand over her face and exhaled harshly. She couldn't believe she was about to ask this, but . . . "You wouldn't possibly be able to give me a ride into Seattle, would you? I'd be happy to pay for—"

Mr. Miller lifted a hand, cutting her off. "I would, gladly, no money necessary, if it weren't for the fact that Mae and I are down to one car." He jerked his thumb over his shoulder. It had drizzled overnight, and a dry patch of concrete the size of a car stood out against the dark, rain-soaked drive.

"Right." She swallowed hard and pasted on a flimsy smile. "Thanks, anyway."

Mr. Miller lowered the hood and bent down to gather his tools. "You need me to call someone? Triple A? Your dad?"

She shook her head. There was no need to interrupt Dad's trip. It would take him longer than an hour to make it back. Pointless to bother him over something he could do nothing to fix.

Unless replacement spark plugs magically fell from the sky, there was nothing she or anyone could do to fix this. It was unfixable. Her phone was dead, her car was dead, and—

Margot was right.

If Olivia had just *waited*, she wouldn't be in this mess. But she hadn't listened, and now she was stuck an hour outside of town with no way to get back. Not only was she going to miss the rehearsal, a critical faux pas as the *wedding planner*, but what would Margot think? Olivia couldn't call her, couldn't let her know. *God*, she knew Margot's old number by heart, but her new number? There'd been no reason to memorize it with it programmed in her contacts.

Just show up.

Olivia had had *one* job, one means of proving to Margot that she was in, that she was *all in*, and she'd blown it. Sure, she could apologize, but would Margot even care to listen?

"Do you happen to have the Coopers' number? If not, I can give it to you."

Maybe she could ask Margot's dad for her new number.

Mr. Miller scrolled through his contacts and nodded. "Here you go."

Olivia took the proffered phone and hit *call*, raising the phone to her ear. It rang four times before going to voicemail. She handed the phone back to Mr. Miller and shook her head. "No answer."

"I, uh, could call the Taylor kid." His lips twisted. "Brad?"

Brad. God, no, Brad was the absolute last person on Earth she wanted to . . . *well*.

Asking a favor from her ex was just about the least appealing thing she could fathom, but not as terrible as missing the rehearsal. Not showing up. Letting Margot down.

If she was going to do this, she didn't have time to stand around debating it. If she was going to go, she needed to go *now*.

"It's okay, Mr. Miller." She hurried around the car, popping the door, and grabbing her duffel from the back seat. "But thanks, anyway."

Mr. Miller frowned. "Are you sure?"

She nodded, already moving down the drive. She waved. "I'm sure. I've really got to go. Tell Mrs. Miller I said hi!"

Brad's house, *her* old house, was two streets over, a ten-minute walk at a brisk pace. Olivia booked it, moving as fast as she could in a pencil skirt that kept her from being able to fully spread her legs. Her underwear were beginning to ride up, the lace chafing against the insides of her thighs while the outsides of her thighs and calves burned from this hybrid speed-walk/jog combo. Even though it was only in the midfifties, sweat dampened her hairline and the space between her boobs, leaving her sticky and gross. By the time she made it to Brad's, she was breathless, and her hair was stuck to her neck and forehead, but she made it.

Hustling past the god-awful bass-shaped mailbox, which was *definitely* new, she made a beeline to the front door and pounded the side of her fist against it. *"Brad."*

Her heart pounded, chest heaving with every rapid breath that burned the back of her throat. She waited less than thirty seconds and rapped her knuckles against the door, following it with a long, hard press of her thumb against the doorbell.

For a moment, she could've sworn she heard the sound of footsteps approaching, thundering down the stairs to the front door, but that was just blood thrumming inside her head.

Olivia whimpered and let her forehead fall forward against the front door. How *stupid*. It was Friday, midday. Of course Brad wasn't answering the door. He was at *work*. She scrunched her eyes shut. Just like she needed to be in an *hour*.

For a second there, she'd honestly believed she could have everything she wanted. As if wanting badly enough could translate into having.

Olivia dragged a hand across her eyes, ruining her makeup. Not that it mattered. No one was going to see it because she wasn't going to make it to Seattle, not on time. Showing up late was better than not showing up at all, but what would Brendon and Annie think? *Lori?* God, goodbye promotion, goodbye raise. And Margot?

Her heart clenched.

Olivia didn't want to say goodbye.

She had *promised*. One simple thing: show up. She couldn't even do that. With the way she'd left, how she'd left things between them, Margot might think Olivia didn't *want* to show up, when that wasn't it at all.

How ironic that the moment she decided to get out of her own way, life had to toss umpteen obstacles in her path. How the hell was that *fair*?

Olivia backed away from the door. Sunlight glinted off metal out of the corner of her eye. She sniffled and turned toward the side yard and—almost fell over.

The red Ford F-650 six-door pickup that she had failed to convince Brad he didn't need—he'd had a perfectly good Ford F-150 he planned to keep—was parked in the grass beside the house. Nine feet tall and with wheel wells higher than her hips, the truck had intimidated the hell out of her to the point where she'd never even *dreamed* of getting behind the wheel. Why would she when she had her efficient, reasonable, *reliable* Subaru that could get her everywhere she needed to go?

She pinched her lips together and threw one last glance over her shoulder at the front door before crossing the yard. Her flats sank into the grass, wet blades tickling her ankles. She stopped beside the truck and held her breath as she reached *up* for the handle on the driver's-side door. All she wanted was to see whether it was unlocked and—

The door cracked open, and her heart climbed inside her throat.

Holy shit.

She wet her lips and checked over both shoulders. The street was quiet, no busybody neighbors puttering around their yards wondering what Olivia was doing, breaking into her ex-husband's truck. It wasn't *technically* breaking into if he left it unlocked, right? Brad had never bothered to lock his car at home, something he could get away with in a town like Enum-claw.

He also a had a terrible habit of leaving the keys to his truck under the visor because—who would be bold enough to steal a truck like *this*?

Her pulse pounded in her throat as she threw her duffel to the ground. She gripped the door with one hand and rested the other on the leather seat. One foot braced on the footrail, Olivia levered herself up into the cab. The air was different up here. She snorted and with a shaking hand flipped the visor open.

Brad's keys clattered against the dash, gleaming in the sunlight streaming through the windshield. She snatched them up and hopped down, landing in the grass with a soft squish, mud squelching under her feet and running up the sides of her flats. The metal was cold against her skin, sharp, too, as she ran the pad of her thumb idly over the teeth. Breaking into his truck was one thing; taking it was something else altogether.

You don't need anyone's permission to be happy.

All those years spent *compromising*, storing books under her bed, giving, giving, giving, answering his calls even after their divorce, so much time wasted trying in vain to please Brad at the expense of her own happiness.

How did that saying go? Better to ask for forgiveness than permission?

She reached inside her purse for a pen and a piece of paper.

Brad owed her one.

Chapter Twenty-Four

12:49 p.m.

Hey, this is Olivia! I can't come to the phone right—

Margot ended the call.

Elle winced. "No answer?"

Margot shook her head. No answer, just like the last five times she'd called. Four rings followed by voicemail and each time the pressure inside Margot's chest swelled a little further, squeezing her heart until it hurt to breathe.

"There's still time," Elle said.

Right. Eleven—*no*, ten minutes until the rehearsal started.

Elle was right. Olivia was cutting it close, but she could still make it.

Unless Olivia wasn't coming.

Margot lifted a shaking hand, resting her fingers against the notch at the base of her throat. Her pulse fluttered wildly under her skin, her heart going haywire. She couldn't think that way. She couldn't *let* herself think that way. Olivia would be here. She *had* to be here. There was too much riding on this wedding, it mattered too much to Olivia for her to simply blow it off.

Unless . . . unless Margot was wrong. Unless Olivia had changed her mind. Made it home and talked to her dad and decided to do what Margot had feared she would, set what she wanted aside to take care of whatever was going on in Enumclaw that she hadn't even let Margot know about.

Margot had never felt so utterly in the dark in her life, desperately wanting to believe that Olivia would show up, but not knowing. Not knowing where Olivia was, what had happened last night with her dad and his house and his health, if Olivia was on her way. A million terrible scenarios flashed through her head. That Olivia's dad wasn't actually okay. That maybe Olivia was there in Enumclaw, needing Margot and afraid to say so after their fight. That the reason she wasn't picking up her phone might not have been because it was dead like Elle had suggested but because she didn't *want* to pick up. Or worse, maybe she couldn't.

The pressure in her chest ballooned further, each breath she sucked in shallower than the last.

Or, there was always the possibility that she'd made it to her dad's and thought about everything Margot had said and had taken it all to heart, but instead of deciding that putting herself first for once meant getting in the car and coming back to Seattle, she'd realized that this—the city, this career, this life—wasn't what she wanted. That *Margot* wasn't what she wanted.

Margot set her jaw.

No, absolutely not. Olivia cared too much to simply blow off the wedding. She would, at the very least, show up to make this weekend happen, and then—

Only time and talking to Olivia would tell what would come after. What their future would hold.

Eight minutes.

"She'll be here," Margot said, sounding a whole hell of a lot more confident than she felt.

Elle smiled and reached out, squeezing Margot's hand, a brief show of support that made a tiny bit of the pressure in Margot's chest release.

"It's starting to rain," Elle murmured, and Margot turned her face up.

A light sprinkle, heavier than a mist but lighter than a driz-zle, had started to come down. Margot hadn't even noticed. She shrugged and reached behind her neck, flipping her hood up over her head.

"Hey, you guys?" Darcy poked her head out of the door of the venue and frowned. "You can wait inside, you know?"

"Darcy's right," Elle said. "We can wait right inside by the window. You can see the street and stay dry. So when Olivia shows up you won't look like a drowned rat." Her lips quirked. "Though I'm sure you'd make an adorable drowned rat, Mar."

Margot snorted. "Nah. You go on. I'm going to wait out here."

Something about going inside the venue, even to wait by the window, carried a note of finality she wasn't ready for. Like if she walked through that door without Olivia by her side, she'd be accepting that Olivia wasn't going to show. That this thing between them was over. Over before they'd barely gotten the chance to begin.

Maybe it was silly and symbolic, but Margot was going to wait right here, on this sidewalk. Where she was standing gave her a perfectly unencumbered view down the street in each direction. Even if the clouds overhead opened up and unleashed a torrential downpour, Margot's feet were glued to the pavement. Nothing short of Olivia showing up would make Margot come inside before she absolutely had to. Until she had no choice.

"Meet you inside?" Elle gave Margot's hand one last squeeze before letting go.

Margot nodded. "I'll be there in a few minutes."

Elle slipped away, and a moment later, the heavy door behind Margot shut with a *boom* that made Margot lurch, nerves shot from lack of sleep and spending most of the day on edge.

Despite being midday on a Friday, the street was quiet. This part of town was far enough away from the downtown market to attract fewer tourists, but there was usually a little more action. Several cars zoomed down the road, and across the street a group of friends laughed before ducking into a coffee shop.

The door opened a minute later, and Margot shut her eyes. "I said I'll be there shortly, Elle."

A throat cleared and Margot craned her neck, looking over her shoulder. With one hand braced against the door, Brendon poked his head out from under the awning and frowned up at the sky for a second before lowering his gaze to stare at Margot. His lips turned down at the corners and—her stomach dropped. She knew that look. What it meant.

Her raked his fingers through his hair. "It's, uh, one o'clock.

The officiant's already here and the facility manager has"—he winced—"*kindly* reminded us that we need to be out of here no later than two so they can start setup for the event they have here tonight."

Right. The, uh, *show must go on*. Margot clenched her back teeth together and pasted on a smile. "I'll be right in."

Brendon stared at her for a moment before shaking his head and throwing the door open the rest of the way. He stepped out onto the street, rain be damned, apparently, and wrapped her up in a hug so tight that something in her chest cracked and her toes actually skimmed the ground. She buried her nose in his shirt, breathing in the smell of his aftershave and the faint smell of Annie's perfume that clung to his collar.

She pressed on his shoulders and ducked her chin, sniffling hard at the sidewalk. "Just give me a minute, Bren. Just—one minute, please?"

One of his fingers lifted her chin. When she raised her eyes, he offered her a crooked smile. "I'll stall for you, okay? I can ask a bunch of questions about . . . I don't know . . . the timing of the dove release or something."

She smacked him on the arm. "You *didn't*."

He snickered and shook his head. "No. No doves. But I bet if I ask, I can buy you *at least* a couple minutes. Sound good?"

She scratched the tip of her nose and nodded. "Thanks, Brendon."

"What are best friends for?" He squeezed her shoulder before backing up toward the door. "You just take your time."

As soon as Brendon was inside, Margot hugged her arms around herself. Take her time? There *wasn't* time.

But Margot had to trust that Olivia would show up. And if she didn't, she had to believe she had a reason.

She relaxed her death grip on her phone and stared at the screen.

1:01 p.m.

Four more minutes. Margot would give her four minutes before she sucked it up and accepted that Olivia wasn't coming.

Each second inched by. A horn blared from several blocks over, and across the street, that group of friends who'd ducked inside the coffee shop hurried back out onto the street, zipping up their jackets and hiding under their hoods, the rain falling heavier than before.

1:04 p.m.

One arm still wrapped around her stomach, Margot jammed the heel of her other hand against her breastbone—it was time to accept that, for whatever reason, Olivia wasn't—

An engine roared a split second before a bright red monster truck took the corner, tires—all six of them—squealing. Margot stared, dumbstruck. In Seattle, she saw Priuses and Subarus and Hyundais, small cars ideal for squeezing into tight spaces, street parking the norm. Even the parking spaces in garages were narrow, all but encouraging drivers to pick smaller, more fuel-efficient vehicles than the gas-guzzler burning rubber as it ate up the pavement, coming toward her up the hill.

Holy shit. Margot leaped back as the right front tire of the truck hopped the curb, brakes screeching obnoxiously, drawing the attention of every pedestrian in a two-block radius.

Who the fuck was this asshole, and where in God's name did they get their license?

Heart racing for an entirely different reason than before, Margot inched a little closer to the door to the venue, focus still firmly on the truck. She covered her ears when the driver's-side door opened, hinges screeching like nails on a chalkboard. The door slammed, and Margot froze.

One hand braced against the headlight, chest heaving, her dark blond hair a halo of frizz around her face, stood Olivia.

Mud streaked the sides of her calves, caking her feet, and there was a tear in the side of her skirt along the seam, too ragged to be a slit. Even filthy, totally disheveled, and standing beside a monster truck, Olivia had never looked more breathtaking because she was *here*.

Margot opened her mouth and gestured weakly to the monster truck parked partially on the curb. "Truck?" She huffed and tried again. "Since when do you drive a truck?"

Was this thing even street legal? Fuck it. Margot couldn't care less, because Olivia was here, and she was looking at Margot like she'd never been happier to see someone in her life. She was *here*.

Olivia stepped closer on wobbling legs, and when she laughed there was a frantic edge to it that made Margot's heart clench. She stumbled over the curb, and Margot rushed toward her, catching her with both hands around her waist, steadying her. Olivia melted against Margot, her whole body shaking as if there were a current running through her, clearly adrenaline and who knew what else. "I stole it."

Margot jerked back and her jaw fell open. "You stole a truck? *Olivia*."

She wasn't sure whether to be scandalized or proud or a little turned on or terrified or some dizzying combination of all of the above.

Olivia sputtered out another laugh and dipped her chin. "I stole a truck."

That was—Margot didn't have words. Or, she had words, but she wanted to hear what Olivia had to say. Needed to hear it. "Start from the beginning. Please."

Olivia's tongue darted out, sweeping against her bottom lip. "My dad is fine. You were right. You were absolutely right. He's selling the house, but he's okay and we cleared it all up. We're fine. This morning I dropped my phone in the toilet while I was getting ready and now it's a waterlogged hunk of junk and then my car wouldn't start because of my plug sparks or *something* and I couldn't call you because I don't have your new number memorized and my neighbor was trying to work on the car but he couldn't fix it and my dad had already left for his fishing trip and—and—"

"Hey." Margot reached up, tucking a strand of hair behind Olivia's ear. "Breathe."

Olivia nodded and sucked in a rasping breath. "My car wouldn't start. I didn't know what to do. I was going to go to Brad and ask to borrow his car, which I didn't exactly relish the idea of"—her lips twisted in a wry smile—"but I figured he owed me one."

He owed Olivia several, but Margot held her tongue.

"He wasn't home." Her throat her jerked. "I had no idea how to get here, and I couldn't contact anyone, but then I saw his truck in the yard and he left the keys inside and I—I thought about what you said. About not needing to ask anyone's permission to be happy, so . . . I didn't. I just took the truck."

The pressure in Margot's chest didn't so much disappear as it was replaced with laughter that built until she couldn't contain it. It burst from her lips. "You stole Brad's truck."

Olivia laughed. "I stole Brad's truck!"

A throat cleared from behind them. Standing in the doorway, Brendon smiled crookedly. "Look, I'm really happy for you guys, but maybe you should talk about your grand theft auto at a *slightly* lower volume."

"I'm so sorry I'm late," Olivia said, cringing sharply.

Brendon waved her off. "No worries. We've got a little cushion."

"We'll be in in a minute," Margot promised.

He winked, both eyes shutting instead of just the one, and ducked inside.

Margot's cheeks ached from smiling. "That's kind of hot, you know."

"Me stealing a truck?" Olivia's eyes crinkled at the corners.

"You stealing *Brad's* truck," she clarified.

Olivia brushed her fingers against Margot's wrist and goose bumps erupted on her arms. Her lower lip wobbled gently. "I should've listened to you. Instead I almost didn't make it and—I don't know." She ducked her chin. "I was standing there on Brad's porch and it just hit me, how badly I want *all of this*. To be here. My whole life is here, and I love it here, I love what I do, and I—I've worked too hard this last year to just give up on it all. To throw it all away. When I was standing there and I realized I might not make it on time, I realized how badly I wanted everything I've worked for and how far I was willing to go to have it." She tangled their fingers together and squeezed. "How far I was willing to go to keep it."

Keep it. Margot's heart soared. "Keep it, huh?"

Olivia laughed, free hand skimming Margot's waist and wrapped around her, palm settling against the small of Margot's back. Her smile fell, and her eyes went serious. "I am so sorry, Margot. For what I said. I—you were coming from a good place and I reacted poorly. When you said I was overreacting, it felt like you were belittling my feelings, and I lashed out. It was no excuse."

Margot swallowed hard and brushed her thumb along the curve of Olivia's cheek. There was a mysterious smudge that might've been grease, maybe mud, but Margot didn't care. "I'm sorry, too. What I said about you overreacting was shitty, but everything else? Please tell me you understand that everything I said, I said because I care about you. You know that, right?"

Olivia sniffled softly and nodded. "It's not the easiest, letting someone care about me."

"Well, you'll have lots of time to practice," Margot joked, stepping closer until their knees bumped. "Because I'm not going to stop caring about you any time soon. Definitely not after one fight. I'm a lot harder to get rid of than that."

Olivia's laugh was watery, her smile bright. The hand resting on the small of Margot's back traveled higher, tangling in the back of her hair. "So am I. I'm not going anywhere."

Heat crept up Margot's jaw, and the inside corners of her eyes prickled. "I know."

"What were you doing standing out here?" Olivia asked.

"Everyone else went inside." Margot lifted her free hand and rested it on the side of Olivia's neck, her thumb brushing the hinge of Olivia's jaw. "But I was waiting for you."

Olivia smiled, and the hand in Margot's hair tightened, drawing her close. Olivia dipped her chin and her nose slid against Margot's, her breath warm against Margot's mouth. Olivia's lips brushed hers, a whispered tease of a kiss. Her hair smelled like shampoo and rain and her breath like toothpaste, and Margot *wanted*. She smiled and chased Olivia's lips, gripping the front of Olivia's blouse, dragging her in, and sealing their mouths together.

"I'm pretty sure a part of me has been waiting for you for eleven years. Just like I'm pretty sure, no matter what happens, I'm always going to be at least little bit in love with you, Liv. Waiting a few extra minutes wasn't going to kill me." A drop landed on the tip of Margot's nose. A little rain wouldn't kill her, either.

Olivia's lips parted, hazel eyes widening. "Really?" she whispered.

Margot's heart raced from the confession, from Olivia's closeness, the warmth of her hand against the back of Margot's neck. The thumb of Olivia's other hand swept gentle circles over the inside of Margot's wrist, where she could probably feel Margot's pulse flutter wildly. "Really."

"Always?" Olivia whispered against Margot's mouth, seemingly as reluctant to drag herself from the kiss as Margot was.

"Always."

Epilogue

About Two Years Later

*M*argot. You can say it. *Margot.*"

"*Buh!*" Caroline Lowell smacked her lips together. A bubble of spit dribbled from the corner of her mouth as she burbled incoherently, staring up at Margot with wide brown eyes.

Margot jostled the baby on her lap and snorted. "My name isn't *buh*, but I have the utmost faith in you, Care Bear. It's simple. *Mar-go.* Margot."

Caroline Lowell clapped her chubby little hands together and giggled. "*Buh!*"

"I'm going to cut you some slack because you're not even a year old. Or"—she rolled her eyes—"sorry, twelve months. Why does everyone do that? I don't go around telling everyone I'm . . ." She did the math. "Three hundred seventy-two months, do I? No, because that would be ridiculous."

Caroline laughed and kicked her legs, bouncing atop Margot's thighs. Beneath her dress—a sparkling silver number with a full crinoline skirt dotted with multicolored glitter—she sported dark blue leggings. Atop her head, her crown of evergreen sprigs and eucalyptus sat askew. One tiny tuft of hair had been scraped into the world's saddest ponytail atop the center of her mostly bald head. The silver bow meant to hold it in place kept sliding, her strawberry blond hair too fine, too sparse.

"You are great for my self-esteem, kid. I hope you still laugh at all my jokes once you can understand them."

"Buh!" Caroline pointed at Margot's half-empty bottle of beer. Not just any beer, but the recently released Aries brew from Bell and Blanchard Brewing Company in partnership with Oh My Stars. It was a hazy IPA with a slightly peppery bite that paired perfectly with the fruitiness of the Galaxy and Simcoe hops. Profitable *and* delicious. As far as Margot was concerned, it was the best business partnership she and Elle had made yet.

She glanced at the dance floor. *Second*-best business partnership.

"Yes, that's beer," Margot said, turning back to Caroline. "But you can't have that for another . . ." She wrinkled her nose. "We'll talk about it when you're a little older, yeah?"

Caroline gurgled and lurched forward, smacking Margot's cheek with damp fingers. *Why* Caroline had such sticky fingers was a touch unsettling. *"Buh buh BUH!"*

Margot nodded. "If you say so."

Caroline dimpled and pressed her other hand to Margot's cheek and—that hand wasn't merely a little moist, it was covered in something. Something she smeared all over Margot's cheek with undisguised glee, babbling excitedly, her fingers creeping closer to the edge of Margot's mouth.

"What the fu—fudge is on my face?" she muttered, equally as horrified to find out what it was as she was to simply leave it there, ignorant. "This had better not be from your diaper."

Reluctantly, she reached for her napkin and dabbed at her cheek. Caroline blew spit bubbles and watched with wide brown eyes. Margot sniffed and sighed in relief.

Frosting. It was the lemon buttercream from the wedding cake. Margot didn't exactly want it on her face, but it could've been worse. It could've been *far* worse.

"How'd you get your hands on cake, Care Bear?"

Caroline gummed at her fist. More frosting seeped out from between her tiny dimpled knuckles.

"Okay." Margot tossed her napkin on the table and stood, cradling Caroline to her chest, careful to keep her fingers from coming anywhere near her face. "Time to take you back to your parents, I think."

The best part of being an honorary aunt? At the end of the day, Margot got to give Caroline back.

"Here." Brendon was staring off into space, lids heavy like he was about to conk out at any moment, so she nudged him. He blinked blearily up at her, then smiled at Caroline. "I don't know how, but she got into some frosting."

He hummed softly and snagged the baby under the arms. "Curious Care Bear."

"*Sticky* Care Bear," Margot corrected.

Caroline cooed and Brendon cringed, one hand on her bottom.

"*Wet* Care Bear."

Caroline pressed her face against his chest, wiping her spit on his shirt. *"Buh."*

At first, Brendon looked disgusted, then resigned, before his face settled on a look of pure adoration as he pressed his lips to the top of Caroline's mostly bald head. She had him wrapped around her pinky finger. To steal Brendon's favorite word, he looked utterly smitten. *"Buh*'s right, baby. Let's get you changed."

"Have fun." Margot snickered.

She left Brendon to it, making a pit stop at her table to polish off her beer and retrieve her clutch.

"There you are."

Margot turned, heart fluttering as Olivia approached, one hand outstretched, reaching for her. She looked stunning in a pale green dress that brought out the flecks of gold in her eyes.

"Here I am." Margot met her halfway, tangling their fingers together. "I was just about to find you. You left me all alone."

It was an exaggeration. Olivia had only stepped away for a few minutes to make sure the airport car service was on the way.

"I'm all yours for the rest of the night." Olivia's lips twitched like she was trying not to laugh. "You have frosting on your nose."

"Caroline," she said, thumbing it away, not really caring. The party was winding down, the DJ playing slower songs. Half the guests—not that there were many—had retreated to their tables, chatting idly.

Olivia nodded and propped her hip against the table, eyes scanning the room. Margot could practically see her running down her mental checklist, making sure—even at the end of the evening—that everything was going according to plan.

After Brendon and Annie's wedding, Olivia's career had taken off, her boss at Emerald City Events promoting Olivia as promised. Word of mouth had spread, thanks to the article in the Vows section of the *Seattle Times* and because Brendon had listed Olivia, specifically, on the preferred vendors page of OTP's website, referring her to all the happy couples who matched via the app.

Each wedding she planned got the time and attention it deserved, but Olivia had really poured her heart and soul into making this one special.

In the center of the dance floor, looking for all the world like they were the only people in the room, Elle and Darcy swayed slightly offbeat, like they were dancing to a song only they could hear. They were beautiful—Elle wore a strapless silver A-line dress that matched Caroline's down to the glitter, and Darcy rocked the hell out of a winter-white fit-and-flare dress—and they looked over the moon, happier than Margot had ever seen them.

Olivia smiled and cocked her head, resting it against Margot's. "Last dance."

As soon as the words were out of her mouth, the song ended to scattered applause, and Elle and Darcy parted reluctantly, hands still entwined as they made their way off the dance floor. Annie trailed after them, holding both their bouquets. Elle's had tiny sprigs of cilantro tucked in amongst the eucalyptus and baby's breath, a subtle nod to an inside joke between her and Darcy.

The DJ said something about seeing the brides off, and most of the guests stood, following Elle and Darcy out of the ballroom and down the hall, shuffling out onto the sidewalk where the black town car taking them to the airport waited, the back door already open. Darcy whispered something in Elle's ear, and she froze, sputtering out a sharp laugh before looking up at the sky. Several snow flurries fell around them. Darcy's hatred for snow was no secret, but she didn't seem to mind it at the moment.

Elle chuckled and wrapped her fingers around Darcy's wrist, tugging her inside the car. She met Margot's eyes, flashing her a smile and an excited wave before the driver shut the door.

Margot's vision blurred softly at the edges as she gripped Olivia's hand, leaning up against her as the car took off down the road, taillights disappearing around the corner.

If this was what change looked like, maybe it wasn't so terrible after all.

"Hey. Are you *crying*?"

"I'm just really happy for them." Margot sniffed hard.

Olivia reached out, tucking Margot's hair behind her ears. Her fingers were warm against Margot's skin. "Sap."

Maybe she was. "You love me anyway."

"I do." Olivia smiled. "I really do."

I do. Margot's heart skipped a beat as she leaned into Olivia. "You really outdid yourself this time."

Elle and Darcy had gotten the happy ending they deserved. That's what Brendon kept calling it. A happy ending. Margot was pretty sure it was only the beginning for all of them.

Olivia beamed. "It was a beautiful wedding, wasn't it?"

Margot swept her thumb along the back of Olivia's knuck-les, lingering over the understated pavé engagement ring on her fourth finger. She dropped her voice to a conspiratorial whis-per, "Ours will be even better."

Olivia leaned forward and brushed her lips against Margot's, smiling into the kiss. "I think so, too."

Acknowledgments

To my rockstar agent, Sarah Younger, thank you for everything you do. You're the best and I am *so* beyond lucky to have you in my corner.

To my fabulous editor, Nicole Fischer, thank you, thank you, thank you! I cherish your insight, support, and for helping to shape this book into what it is.

Thank you to the entire team at Avon/HarperCollins. The work you do behind the scenes to bring these books to life and get them into the hands of readers is nothing short of magic. I want to give a special shoutout the design team, Ashley Caswell and Elizaveta Rusalskaya, for creating such stunning covers.

As much as my books are obviously about romantic love and relationships, they're also about the importance of found family and friendships. Rompire—Anna, Amy, Em, Julia, Lana, Lisa, and Megan—I cannot thank you enough for your support, your cheerleading, and your friendship. Hugs! To S., R., A., C., M., G., A., and J.—some of you entered into my life for a season, a reason, or a lifetime, but you all taught me what friendship means and helped me learn a little (some of you, a lot) about myself. I will cherish you and those lessons for the rest of my life.

Mom, thank you. Unlike several of the characters in this series, I feel so very fortunate to have an amazing and supportive mom. I could write a whole book about how much I appreciate you and everything you do and it still wouldn't be long enough. Love you!

To my fur baby, Samantha, I've been so blessed to have you in my life for the last twenty years. You can be a little monster, but I wouldn't have you any other way.

To the reviewers, book bloggers, bookstagrammers, booktokkers, and booksellers, thank you for the tireless, and too often thankless, work you do for this community. Romance would not be the same without you.

Last but not least, I want to thank my readers. Words can't do justice to how much I appreciate each and every one of you. Your comments, messages, and emails mean the world to me. Thank you for choosing to read my books and spend your time with my words and characters. It's an honor.

About the Author

Alexandria Bellefleur is a nationally bestselling author of swoony contemporary romance often featuring lovable grumps and the sunshine characters who bring them to their knees. A Pacific Northwesterner at heart, Alexandria has a weakness for good coffee, Pike IPA, and Voodoo Doughnuts. Her special skills include finding the best pad thai in every city she visits, remembering faces but not names, falling asleep in movie theaters, and keeping cool while reading smutty books in public. She was a 2018 Romance Writers of America Golden Heart finalist. You can find her at alexandriabellefleur.com or on Twitter @ambellefleur.

More from
Alexandria Bellefleur

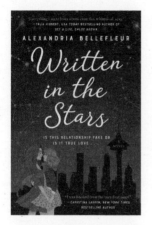

WRITTEN IN THE STARS

"I was hooked from the very first page!"
—Christina Lauren, *New York Times* bestselling author of *In a Holidaze*

A National Bestseller and winner of the Lambda Literary Award for Best Lesbian Romance!

With nods to *Bridget Jones* and *Pride & Prejudice*, this debut is a delightful queer rom-com about a free-spirited social media astrologer who agrees to fake a relationship with an uptight actuary until New Year's Eve—with results not even the stars could predict!

HANG THE MOON

"Smart, sexy, and sweet. Readers will be over the moon for this rom-com."
—*Kirkus Reviews* (starred review)

In a delightful follow-up to *Written in the Stars*, Alexandria Bellefleur delivers another queer rom-com about a hopeless romantic who vows to show his childhood crush that romance isn't dead by recreating iconic dates from his favorite films...